ARION

Tales of Melvin The Magnificent

By

Dave Burkey

DEDICATION

I would like to dedicate this novel to my five daughters, who the princesses and Empress are based on. And to my son, who is also the basis of Elvin King.

About the Author

Dave Burkey wrote his first novella in 1996 as a very long term paper in college. He has been writing for over 25 years. This particular novel has taken over 15 years to complete. Dave now resides in Washington State with his wife and three of his six children. He is also LDS and likes to incorporate his beliefs in his novels.

MAP OF ARION

Pyne
Mengard
Navan
Retlik's Castle
Penelope's Cave
Nõrden
Stüdenhiem
Undarhaven
Lilenhamür
Melvins Toun
Zoltans Castle
Vültaran Plāns
Hamneth-Dor
Wazervīl
Bilby's Palace
Sēsid
Winkleton
Lāncaster
Jigabuji
Westiun
Eldõria
Grāslund
Estun
Estport
Riverbend
Ēsten Plāns
Thrall
Boglunds
Helaeth Mountains
Sōden Port
Sōden Desert
Sōden Bā
Sōden Bā Lithous

PROLOGUE

I am called The Teller. I collect stories from across the vast Universe and tell them to the beings of the Milky Way Galaxy. Some are written and some are verbal. This story is meant for the people on the planet known as Earth. For such a story as this, they can relate to.

There lived a man on an unknown planet, except to the people living on it, in a small galaxy that "doesn't exist". This galaxy was located on the fringes of this vast universe, overlooked by the enlightened and highly technological beings of the universe. This planet, although large, was not even on any of the star maps in the great library of Ethos, which contains every star chart and all the knowledge and art of the Universe. He was not an ordinary man, but a wizard. Not an ordinary wizard, but one so rare that the ancient seers of the Universe hadn't known about him. But it is *he* who will change the course for the future. Well, at least for this planet anyway.

Table of Contents

Chapter 1
A Strange Rock

"Well? What do you think it is?" Reicuas asked excitedly. Reicuas's voice echoed through the cavern, bouncing off the jagged stone walls. His golden aura pulsed faintly in the dim light. "Well? Tell me—what do you see."

Standing in the back of a very large yet dim cavern stood a boy, skinny, bucked teeth, thick glasses perched on his nose. He scratched his head, uncertain. By Estrian standards, he was unremarkable. Yet here he stood, beside the great Reicuas, expected to prove himself. He looked like, as Earthlings would call him, a nerd. He was a wizard in training, and not a very good one at that, if the people around him realized he had talents at all. Reicuas, the Master Wizard under which the boy was apprenticing, stood next to him, waiting patiently for his pupil to figure out this enigma.

Now, if you Earthlings were to imagine a Master Wizard, what would come to your mind? A tall, skinny man, very aged in annums with a long white beard, long white hair, flowing gown, and a cone hat, with stars and moons adorning it, right? An Earthling's typical image of a wizard. Forget all that, Reicuas was nothing like that. He wore simple clothes: a tunic and pants that allowed him to move with ease. He especially hated the typical wizarding attire that most others around him wore. His tall, strong build set him apart from the robed mystics. His tall, strong, and athletic build made him stand out in contrast to his apprentice standing beside him.

A cold draft whispered through the immense cavern, carrying the scent of damp stone and something metallic. Reicuas's short light brown hair shifted slightly, as did his beard of the same color. His golden aura cast faint flickers of light against the cave walls. Reicuas was considered rather young —about three hundred and fifty annums old, which for him, and the people of that planet, wasn't all that old at all.

The boy answered with a stutter. He spoke rather slowlytrying to calm himself, because of his stutter. However, the more excited he got, the more he tended to stutter. "I-I-I-I-I don't know,

Master. L-l-l-l-looks to be gold, a big round l-l-l-l-lump of-of gold. But what would a l-l-l-l-lump of gold be doing, sit-sit-sitting out here in a cave? I-i-i-i-it would be worth a fortune. I could l-l-l-live like a king."

"It's not gold, it's just gold in color." The not-so-old wizard said tenderly.

"Well, if i-i-i-it's not gold, then it-it-it-it must be a rock of some sort that looks l-l-l-like gold. Sure is a strange rock. There are no st-st-st-streams here, how is i-i-i-it rounded like that? People would think it was gold, though."

"Look closer, you can touch it, you know, pick it up." He encouraged and knew that the boy would eventually figure it out.

The boy tentatively put out his hand and touched the rock with the tip of his small pointer finger. It was warm to the touch. He looked back at his Master, and once reassured and boosted with confidence, he picked it up. It was lighter than it appeared to be. "What a strange rock this i-i-is. I-i-i-it's warm and l-l-l-lighter than a normal rock." He put it down gently. "I-i-i-i don't think that this is a rock."

"You are right, my boy, you are right. Well then, if it's not a rock and it's not gold, what do you suppose it is?" asked the Master wizard in a quizative tone.

"Well, i-i-it might be an egg of some sort," the boy replied.

"Very good. What type of egg do you think it is?" He said, getting excited, the apprentice was finally catching on.

"P-p-possibly from a b-blasmoth." The boy quiried.

"No, not from a blasmoth. Those are much smaller," Reicuas told the youngster. "What else would have an egg this large and of this color?"

The boy thought he might know what this was, but he had never seen one before in his life; they were very rare. So, he asked hesitantly, "I-i-i-i-i-is it a D-d-d-d-dragon egg?"

"Yes, my boy, yes, it is!" Reicuas exclaimed excitedly, smiling at his apprentice. He was very pleased that the boy figured out what it was.

The boy swallowed hard. His voice dropped to a whisper, "A d-dragon egg!" the boy mirrored in wonder, "I-I-I-I have never seen a dragon egg, M-m-master."

Reicuas grinned. "Neither have a lot of people. Reicuas grinned. "And not just any dragon. A Gold Dragon. The first in three hundred annums." At least that I know of. This is a historical moment in the making!" The Wizard said excitedly, then his voice turned sober. "They say when a dragon is hatched, with it, brings new magic to the world. And depending on the type of dragon, the amount of magic that comes to the world."

"W-w-w-wow, that's how m-m-m-magic comes i-i-i-into the world? I-i-i-is that the only way magic comes into the w-w-world?" The boy asked excitedly. He noticed his stuttering got worse. So, he tried to calm himself down.

"Oh, other creatures are born with magic as well, such as Elves, Gnomes, Leprechauns, Borlogs, Fairies, Sprites, Unicorns, and the like. But, they only bring a small amount of magic. However, Dragons bring an enormous amount of magic into the world, since they are such enormous creatures. That helps Wizards, because that way, there is more magic for us to use."

"W-w-why hasn't there been a dragon hatched i-i-i-in such a l-l-l-long time, then?" The boy tilted his head with childlike innocence.

"I don't exactly know. As you can see, there are quite a lot of dragons in the world, but most of them are very old. There are very few young dragons in the world, younger than one thousand annums old. Dragons live a very, very long time."

"I-I-I-I thought *we* l-l-l-lived a very long life, M-m-master. Is-is-isn't a thousand annums a long t-t-t- time?"

"Yes, it is my boy. Yes, it is. But dragons can live up to one hundred thousand annums, and depending on the type of dragons, some can live up to two hundred thousand annums."

"Th-that's a very l-l-l-long time, I-I-I can't i-i-i-imagine l-l-living that l-l-long. Even one thousand annums i-i-is a l-l-long time to me." The boy said.

"Well, my boy, when you get to my age, you will think that it slipped by very quickly. You have a while yet to be a child. Then, when you become an adult, your childhood will seem like it was such a long time ago. You are only a child for two hundred annums or so, then you are an adult for the rest of your life, which is a very long time." Reicuas thought it was time to get going, so he motioned to his apprentice and said. "Come, we must go, I have things to tend to, and you have your studies."

"Y-y-yes, Master." The boy said, still in awe, that he saw a dragon egg.

As they walked back to town, the boy wondered if the egg would be okay all alone. He decided to speak up. "M-m-master, won't someone try to steal the egg?" he asked. "S-s-s-since there hasn't been a dragon egg seen in such a long time, I was thinking someone might think it would be a nice prize, especially since i-i-it l-l-looks like gold."

"You are probably right, my boy. However, a mother dragon never strays far from her egg. She has been keeping an eye on it the whole time. She can feel it through her magic. If it were ever in danger..."

The boy shuddered. "She'd know?"

Reicuas nodded. "And she would unleash a fury unlike anything you've ever seen." The master Wizard reassured as they headed out of the cavern.

"Oh, that's good. I-i-i-i-i wouldn't want it to be stolen or anything, the Mother dragon would be very angry," the boy said, trying to keep up with his master. He wasn't as tall as his master, and his stride was shorter, so he had to quicken his pace to keep up.

"Yes, I'm sure Percilla would be very angry indeed, if her egg was stolen." The master wizard said as he put his hand on the boy's shoulder to steady him as he slipped on a rock he was trying to kick.

"Percilla?" The boy asked. Trying to concentrate on where he was going.

"The name of the mother dragon," Reicuas replied.

"How do you know h-h-h-her name is Percilla?" The boy asked. He thought it was an odd name for a dragon to have. It didn't seem very dragon-y. He thought her name should be more like Dragon Firebreath or something like that.

"I know many things, my boy, many things it would take a lifetime to teach you. Also, I named her." The Master Wizard smiled at the memory of the baby dragon he saw hatch many annums ago and how she had grown up so well in these few annums. She was still considered a young dragon, however, she had grown enough to have a baby of her own. When a dragon gets to a certain age, as with many other animals and other people, they are meant to live life on their own. So the young dragon must leave and find their place to live.

"You named her? How?" The boy wondered how it was that his Master was able to name a dragon, and of all the great dragon names he could have chosen, why Percilla? It sounded like a stuck-up up rich snob name to him.

"It's a very long story, but I will tell part of it to you. Since this is a long walk home, we have the time." Reicuas loved to tell stories, he was a natural at it. He loved it about as much as he loved being a wizard, and whenever he had a chance to tell a story, he took it. Most of the time, he would embellish it, but this time, he kept it plain and concise. He began weaving the tale for his apprentice as they walked down the foothills.

"When I was about your age, I, too, was an apprentice Wizard. And just like you, I had a Master Wizard that I looked up to. One rev, he took me to see a dragon egg, just as I took you to see this one. But what he didn't know was that I kept returning to the spot every couple of revs to see if it had hatched. Dragon eggs take a very long time to hatch, almost an annum, so after a while, when I couldn't go every few revs, I cut it down to once a week. Still, no sign of hatching, then it went to once a moon. One rev, I was in the woods gathering herbs for potions I was studying, and decided to go check on the egg. When I peered through the bushes, I saw the egg starting to hatch, and the mother was right there; she knew I was there and had me come closer to watch. It was spectacular. Lights of every color flashed from inside the egg. Then the head emerged, shining like the head of a golden statue, golden light radiated from it, and I could feel the release of new magic coming into the world. Only wizards and other magical creatures can feel the magic from a dragon hatching."

"Why d-d-d-did the Mother Dragon l-l-l-let you c-c-c-come so c-c-c-close?"

"She knew me. She knew I was a Wizard and meant no harm. She was there most of the time I came to see if the egg had hatched. My Master knew her, so she didn't mind me coming around. Unbeknownst to me at the time, this was all planned by my Master Wizard and the mother dragon. Back to the story. As the shell fell away, a bright golden pulse of light emanated from the newborn dragon, releasing an immense amount of magic into the world. Since I was right there when it happened, some of the magic stayed with me, and I could feel the magic coursing within me."

"I-i-is that why n-n-not many dragon eggs are hatched?" the boy asked.

"There are a few reasons why not many people see a dragon hatch. First, there are not many dragons around to have an egg, near where humans can witness such an event." He replied. "But, what most people do not know is. That, when the magic comes from the dragon hatching, the person watching the egg hatch absorbs some of that magic for themselves. So, a normal person will be able to use some of the magic absorbed, and it might even increase their talents a bit. But," he lowered his voice to nearly a whisper "a magical creature or a wizard, or wizardess, will become even more powerful. The more powerful the wizard, the more he or she absorbs, and the more powerful he or she grows.

Reicuas stopped walking to explain firther "Since I was just an apprentice like you, I couldn't absorb that much of the magic, so my powers didn't grow that much, but enough to become a full wizard 50 annums early.

"Reason number two, and this is more important than the first. Any human or magical creature, especially wizards or elves, who sees a dragon hatch, gains control of that dragon. Usually, dragons will fly to remote places like the mountains, the middle of the desert, caves, and even to Dragonia, to have their eggs hatch. That's the main reason almost no one has seen a dragon hatch in about one thousand annums."

"What a-a-about you, M-m-m-master? You s-s-saw one, so it has been l-l-l-less than o-o-o-one thousand annums." The boy replied.

"That is true. However, I never told anyone I saw the egg hatch." He said.

"S-s-s-so you have c-c-c-control of the dragon?" the boy asked.

"No, I gave control to the mother, whose rightful job it is to control their offspring. What did I need a baby dragon for? Imagine what my mother would have said if I came home with a baby Golden Dragon. I'm sure she would have been handy for starting fires, and show and tell rev at school, but that's about it. My Mother would have sent sparks and lightning everywhere." The master wizard chuckled. "I didn't want to have to dodge lightning strikes for an annum, so I gave control to the mother, and in return, she let me name the baby dragon. So I named the beautiful creature, Percilla."

"W-w-w-why, Percilla?" The boy asked, then became more intrigued.

"It was my Grandmother's name, we were very close, till she went into the next life." Reicuas smiled, remembering his grandmother.

"Oh, that was n-n-n-nice of you." The boy said in response.

"I suppose it was an honor for both of them to be named after a loved one, and having a Golden Dragon named after you, Golden Dragons are a rare breed these revs. A very rare breed."

"So will you l-l-l-let me see the dragon egg hatch?" He asked eagerly.

"That's why I took you to go see it," Reicuas replied in a chipper tone. "Percilla has permitted me to let you share in the occasion. However, there are a few rules we have to abide by."

"Percilla told you I-I-I-I could see the dragon egg hatch? You can talk to dragons, that must be s-s-s-so awesome." He could only imagine seeing a baby dragon hatch. Reicuas was the only one he knew of who had been able to do that. It is a grand honor for a dragon to let a human see a dragon egg hatch.

Reicuas stopped in the middle of the road where they were. The suns were shining brightly on this warm afternoon. Birds were chirping. The light breeze rustled the orange and purple leaves of the trees that dotted the lane. He took in a deep breath. He could smell the wheat in the fields and wild flowers growing alongside the road. It brought a scent of freshness to the air. He looked up at the violet sky and thought about what to tell his young apprentice. This should be a teaching moment, he thought. Then he answered the boy.

"Well, yes, I suppose it is. But I don't really talk to her as we are doing now, dragons are more telepathic. They show you pictures in your mind, and you think of the picture you want to convey, and they can read it. You can talk, but the dragon doesn't really understand human words unless they learn how to speak human. As you talk, you must form the information into your mind, so the dragon can *see* what you are saying. It takes some practice, but as with everything, the more you practice, the better you get. Though it may be possible to teach a dragon to communicate with words, it is a very slow way to communicate, and the dragon would have to be willing to learn. I can communicate with Percilla with a few words, most of them have no picture to show, like love and music, you can't see either one. However, sometimes you can communicate the meaning through feeling or a thought. I can think of the tune of a song or feel the love for someone, and Percilla will understand."

"That i-i-i-is amazing, no words." Being able to talk without words would mean he wouldn't stutter.

"You can communicate very fast like that, and you wouldn't have the stuttering problem you have when you talk out loud. Instead of describing a thing such as your white house, you just think of it in your mind, and the dragon will know exactly what you are telling them."

The boy thought about it for a while, it would be great if people could communicate that way. But he really wanted to see the egg hatch, not for the power or the magic, just because he thought it would be neat, and no one has been able to do that, except his master. He went back to the topic they had discussed before. "So, when can we go back to see the egg?"

"It isn't supposed to hatch for a long, long time, could be annums, or perhaps   more, but I suggest we go check on it about once a moon or so, and until it does, you and Percilla can get to know each other." He said as he patted the boy on the back.

"S-s-s-sounds good to me." The boy said, with a smile on his face.

By this time, they had almost made the trek back to town, so their conversation changed to other topics, such as Wizard studies. Neither of them wanted anyone to find out about the egg. The next new moon, they went to see the egg, and as Reicuas saw the young wizard practice "talking" to Percilla, he was amazed at how well his apprentice had learned to communicate with her. Though he couldn't hear what the conversation was between his apprentice and Percilla, she told him that he was learning very well. This must be one of his many talents.

CHAPTER 2

THE FOUR PRINCESSES

On the northeastern coast of Arion, a small kingdom thrived, cradled between the Lascar Mountains and the endless sea. Its palace, standing proudly on an island, was flanked by Twin Rivers that branched from a mighty current before merging again on their journey to the ocean. The waters formed a natural moat, both a blessing and a defense, encircling the heart of the realm.

In the heart of the palace resided its most treasured jewels—not gold or gemstones, but four princesses whose very names inspired the people: Aria, Adara, Amira, and Anna. More fiercely guarded than any hoarded treasure, they were beloved beyond measure, each a symbol of beauty, intelligence, and destiny.

Daughters of the Great Bilby, the king of the Land of Bilby. The princesses were rivaled with none when it came to beauty as well as intelligence, and each had a distinctive talent to them, which made them stand out individually to anyone who came across them.

Aria, the eldest, was a vision of grace and strength. With yellow hair, yellow eyes, and an aura that shimmered like sunslight, she embodied music and dance, bringing beauty to the land. But she was more than an artist—she was a warrior, her skill in archery and swordplay unmatched. As the leader of the Special Forces, her blade sang as fiercely as her melodies.

Adara, the second eldest, was fire incarnate. Her crimson hair blazed like the suns, her aura pulsing with untamed energy. Though kind at heart, her temper was legendary enough to send even a Borlog fleeing in terror. In battle, her fury ignited, her hair blazed like a living torch, and flames erupted from her hands.

She also loved all kinds of animals, from slimy worms and tiny insects to the noble Lions of the plains, the Unicorns of the Highland Plains, and the mighty Dragons of the mountains and the Land of Dragonia. She had a talent for knowing what they were thinking, some say she could talk to animals, although she never admitted to it.

Amira came next, with her unquenchable thirst for knowledge. If you asked her a question, she would know the answer or find the answer. Though most of the time, she did all the asking. Purple was the color of knowledge. Her hair, eyes, and, of course, her aura, were all purple. She was also always willing to help. Princess or not, if something needed to be done, she would do it. Nothing was too big or too small a job. If some grand ball needed to be organized, she did it. If someone needed a roof thatched or clothes mended, she would help. She was not afraid to get her hands, or the rest of herself for that matter, dirty to get a job done. The messier the job, the better for her. Everyone loved her for the service she was always giving, rich or poor, it didn't matter. You could tell by her purple aura that she was helpful and giving. She had another special talent that you will find out about later.

The youngest Anna was the most beautiful of them all. She was world-famous for her beauty. She had pink hair, eyes, and, of course, a pink sparkly aura. Her infectious smile brightened everyone's rev, her gorgeous pink eyes inspired awe in all those who saw them. She had an aura about her that emanated love to all those who were near her. You couldn't see it, but you could feel it and knew it was there. Her touch was like being touched by an angel. People would come from far and wide just to get a glimpse of her. That was her gift, and sometimes her curse.

These princesses were the "Jewels of the Kingdom" because everyone loved them, and in return, they loved the people. King Bilby had always taught them that "The more influence you had over those around you, the more responsibility you had to them, too. And it was then your obligation to help those in need." They should use their talents to help others in the kingdom to be happy, to inspire them, and to bring a smile to their faces. And without fail, the four princesses took what their father said to heart.

CHAPTER 3

TO THE PALACE

Before we look ahead, let's step back to where it all began. This was when Adara was still in her umpteen annums, her talents raw and untamed. She had yet to master the gifts that would one rev define her. Meanwhile, Melvin—just a boy then—was also discovering his abilities, shaping the path that would lead him to his destiny.

"Focus, Melvin," Reicuas instructed, his voice firm yet patient. "You can get this."

"I-I-I'm trying M-M-Master." Melvin stammered. "S-s-s-seems l-l-l-like the harder I-I-I try, the worse I-I-I-I stutter."

"Yes, my boy, I know," Reicuas said thoughtfully, putting his hand to his bearded chin as he always did when he thought. "Incantations must be precise, and stuttering does not help. We must think about what we can do to help you with this problem. In the meantime, I suppose we should work on something else, like potions, that doesn't require you to speak."

Frustrated, Melvin lowered his head, his gaze landing on a small stone. He clenched his fists, anger boiling inside him. Suddenly, the stone erupted into flames. Startled, he instinctively willed the fire to vanish—and just like that, ice spread across the pebble's surface. Without thinking, he imagined it buried, and the earth swallowed it whole. A heartbeat later, a bud pushed through, unfolding into a delicate flower. As if answering his command, mist curled around the petals, droplets of dew forming at its core.

Despite his stammer making it difficult for him to chant the spells out loud a moment ago, this came naturally to him, and all he had to do was think of the action that he wanted to happen for it to take place. Melvin truly hoped that his Master did not see him do all that, since this was not what he had been instructed to do. Melvin did not like to go against his Master's directions, as they were mostly given with his betterment in mind. However, he knew he could do things that his master did not know about.

"Melvin," Reicuas said in a tender voice. "What exactly did you just do?"

Unaware that he had been watched, Melvin hesitated. His master's eyes gleamed—not with disapproval, but with something else. Curiosity? Amusement? A quiet knowing? Whatever it was, it sent a shiver down Melvin's spine. "I-I-I-I don't know, master, i-i-i-it just sort of happened," Melvin said humbly, expecting his master to give him a lecture.

"How did you do that, my boy?" he asked tenderly.

"I-I-I-I just thought about what I-I-I-I wanted to do, a-a-and it happened."

"Just thought about it, did you?" Reicuas said, smirking. "Do you know what you just did?"

"I-I-I-I'm sorry," Melvin said sadly, then lowered his head, guessing that he was in trouble for not doing what his Master instructed.

"Sorry?" Reicuas said excitedly with a big smile on his face. The world just became a little bit brighter. "Why be sorry? That is one of the best examples of wizardry I have ever seen. It hasn't been done in over four thousand annums." He was truly amazed. This had not been done that he knew of. He knew wizards with several talents, but not as many as Melvin had. He also did not know of any that could do magic by mere thought. Although Reicuas lived in a small town in a small kingdom, it did not mean he did not know other wizards. You would be amazed at what he has done during his relatively short lifetime thus far. But that is for another story.

"R-r-r-really, Master, W-w-w-why is that?" Melvin asked in wonder, lifting his head because he now knew he wasn't in trouble anymore.

"Yes, Melvin." He said. "I have known of no other wizards who can do what you just did. Which brings us to another topic, which has to do with your abilities. We haven't gotten to this part of your training, but I guess we'd best jump ahead. You will know why we are talking about this when we reach the palace. What do you know about auras, Melvin?"

"Well, j-j-just what everyone knows." Melvin stammered. "D-d-different wizards have d-d-different colors of auras for the type of magic they can do, l-l-l-like yours is Golden, I-I-I-I can see that, working with l-l-light is your s-s-s-specialty."

"Very good, my young apprentice. Do you know what colors go with what specialties?" Reicuas asked Melvin."

"Blue i-i-is for water, Red-fire, Brown-earth, the g-g-ground can open up and s-s-swallow you or make a hill r-r-rise, etc. Green i-i-i-is nature, such as plants and trees and stuff, Gray-weather storms, l-l-l-lightning and such. Gold i-i-is for light, suns rays, and concentrated light, and such like you have. White- well, I-I-I-I don't r-r-r- remember w-w-what that one is."

"Ice. However, there is more to it than that. There is also a black aura. But usually only dark and evil Wizards, Sorcerers, or Warlocks have those. Hopefully, you will never see one. So, who all has auras?"

"A-a-a-as far as I-I-I-I know, just Wizards. I haven't seen anyone else with auras." He answered.

"In that assumption, my boy, you are misinformed. It so happens that many people, not just Wizards, have auras and the ability to use magic. Though most of the time it is just a simple thing they can do, like make a garden grow, or sing well, or make an object hit a target every time, or be very athletic. They may or may not realize that their particular talent is magic. Most of the time, they do, though. However, their auras aren't strong enough for the normal person to really notice; a lot of times, they don't notice a wizard's aura. But you and I, being wizards, will be able to see them. You will have training in this. There is one maiden in particular I would like you to see. In fact, we have a meeting with her later this rev. And this will be your first lesson in auras."

"R-r-r-really? Who is it?" Melvin asked as his blue eyes lit up in excitement. Literally. "Princess Adara," Reicuas said with a smile.

"R-r-r-really? W-w-w-we a-a-are going to s-s-s-see p-p-p-princess A-A-A-Adara?" Melvin could hardly contain his excitement. He had always wanted to go to the palace and meet the princesses. He had heard how beautiful they all were. He had never gotten the chance to meet any of them in person, but now was his chance. His mother was their teacher and went to the palace all the time. But she had never taken Melvin to the palace. Melvin always wondered why they didn't live closer.

"Calm down, my boy, you know your stuttering gets worse when you get excited," Reicuas said, amused.

"Y-y-y-yes, I-I-I-I know." He said, a little embarrassed, "I-I-I-I just never met a p-p-p-princess before."

"Well, you will now. And probably many times in the future. You did not know this, but I am also an advisor to King Bilby and am training Princess Adara. As well as her sisters. And your mother is their teacher."

"That much I did know," Melvin said softly, managing without stuttering. "I-i-i-is the p-p-princess a Wizardess?" Melvin asked, looking up at his master.

"No," Reicuas said with a chuckle, "She is a little girl, approximately the same age as you, give or take a few decannums."

"W-w-w-when do w-w-w-we go?" Melvin asked excitedly.

"Our appointment is in a couple of hours, so we shall start heading there shortly," Reicuas answered.

They walked south on the road from their small village towards the city.

The Lascar Mountains rose to their right, while farmland stretched out to their left. Beyond the fields was the beach, and then the wide open ocean. As they made their way through the woods, where the trees grew as tall as any warble could fly, they passed through farmland with rows of purple grain swaying in the breeze. All kinds of crops grew there, enough to feed both the city and the nearby villages.

Along the way, they crossed several bridges—some with wide rivers rushing underneath, flowing fast toward the sea. In the distance, they could see waterfalls spilling down the mountainsides. The Lascar Mountains were especially beautiful this time of Annum.

On one bridge, Reicuas came to a stop. To one side, not too far away, was the ocean. The twin suns lit the water in shimmering colors, casting a rainbow across the waves. Far-off sailing ships looked so small, they might've been toys. On the other side of the bridge, where Reicuas was looking, stood a great mountain—and from its side poured a tall, majestic waterfall that seemed to fall forever.

"Look at that, my boy," Reicuas said in wonder. "Look at Deos' creations. Look at the beauty of this." Deo is their word for God, if you haven't guessed that by now.

Melvin looked and noticed what Reicuas was talking about. Not only the waterfall and the water flowing under the bridge, but also the beautiful trees with their orange and purple leaves. He noticed mandras, an animal resembling a bear, playing in the water and trying to catch fish. Reicuas was telling another story, but Melvin wasn't really listening. He was in awe of the beauty surrounding him. This would instill a love of nature in him that would last his whole life.

After a while, they continued their walk. Melvin noticed the many different types of animals, both wild and domestic. He pondered the mysteries of the universe, as well as he could, being a young boy. He pondered the meaning of life and why they were on this planet. Were there other beings more advanced than them that lived on any of the other planets they could see in the night sky? How was this planet formed? How was it that Deo created Estry and everything on it? He had many questions like this, about science, religion, nature, how things worked, and so much more. And as he was pondering on such things, his attention was grabbed by the color of the sky, looking at it for a moment, and without turning to his Master, he voiced out the question that ran in his head.

"Master," Melvin asked while he looked up at the violet afternoon sky. "W-w-w-why is the sky v-v-violet?"

"That is a very good question, my boy," he said, looking down at Melvin. "Do you see the dual suns?" he asked.

"Yes, Master," Melvin replied, looking up at the sky.

"What color are they?" Reicuas asked. Looking down at his apprentice.

"Arōs is r-r-red, and the s-s-s-smaller one, Helios, is yellow." He said, smiling. Melvin knew this answer because his mother taught him about such things.

"Right you are. What do you know about color mixing?" Reicuas asked.

"Color mixing?" Melvin asked, wondering what Reicuas was referring to.

"I guessed as much," Reicuas said softly, rubbing his fingers down his short beard. He looked at Melvin to explain. "You see, just as different ingredients can be mixed together for making food or potions, different colors can be mixed to make different colors. For example. Blue and yellow make green, red and yellow make orange, and…"

"R-r-red and b-b-blue make Purple." Melvin said, "Yes, my mother taught me that. B-b-but why is the s-s-sky purple?"

"You see, as far as we know, it is due to color mixing. There is a lot of water on Estry. The blue waves of light from Helios are reflected off the water and then go back into the atmosphere, which would make the sky blue. But since Arōs is red, there is more red color coming through the atmosphere, which is not absorbed by the water, and since red and blue make purple, this sky is purple. Or violet."

Melvin was excited to learn this. He was sure he would have figured that out on his own, but Master Reicuas was a very wise man and could tell him pretty much anything he wanted to know. However, at the same time, his mother was a very gifted teacher, and she knew everything there was to know about anything. So when he had questions, he would usually ask her, and she would know the answer. However, there was one question she did not answer. And that was about his father. Who was he, and where did he go? All she would say is that he had an accident shortly after Melvin was born, and is gone now. And that's all she got from her on that subject.

They continued their walk down the road towards the city. As they neared the city, Melvin saw small houses and shops scattered about. As they walked closer to the city gates, the shops and houses were closer together. There were vendors of all sorts selling their wares to the people traveling to the city, hoping to catch them before they spent their money in the city. Melvin looked at the wall of the city. It stretched as far as the eye could see in either direction. It must be at least three spans high. In front of them was a huge iron gate that was lifted open with soldiers in front of it. They passed over a wooden draw bridge with a river flowing about three spans below it, which ran the entire length of the wall. There were also soldiers on top of the wall and in the towers along the wall.

As some people entered the city, they were stopped by the soldiers and asked their business going into the city, and some who traveled there all the time for business were let right through. Melvin wondered if they would be stopped. They walked over the drawbridge and through the massive two-span high gate, and the guards just nodded as they walked through. Melvin was relieved that they weren't stopped.

"I-I-I-I-I have n-n-never s-s-seen s-s-so many s-s-s-soldiers before. I-I-I-I thought we would be s-s- stopped." Melvin said to his master in a sheepish tone.

"Well, my boy, I travel here at least once a week, sometimes twice, as a personal guest of the King himself, so the guards know me well."

"Th-th-that's good t-t-to know," Melvin said. As he looked towards the magnificent palace.

Inside the city walls, the houses and shops stood closer together, and most of them were taller than the ones outside. They walked down a wide cobblestone street with buildings on both sides, and carts of all shapes and sizes filled the road. Some stores had tables out front, showing off everything they had for sale. Melvin caught the sweet smell of fresh baked bread in the air. Mixed in were the rich scents of meats, herbs, flowers, and all kinds of food being cooked or sold. As they walked, he could see the different items being sold. Almost anything and everything you could ever want. He was amazed by all the people he saw rushing around. Restaurants had tables outside, where Melvin saw people eating and enjoying their meals. This was something that he had never seen before, as all they had in their small town was a small inn, where everyone went if they wanted to eat somewhere besides their homes, or if people were traveling.

The closer they got to the palace, the larger and more elaborately decorated the houses and shops appeared to be. Melvin could see the majestic palace off in the distance on an island between two rivers. The two rivers joined in front of the palace. With the way the light of the suns was hitting the palace, and also reflecting off the water of the rivers, it looked like the palace was sparkling gold. Melvin had never seen anything so beautiful in his life. Well, up till then anyway.

The master wizard and his apprentice eventually arrived at the large town square in front of the palace. There were purple banners and other decorations hung up all around, with shops of things that Melvin didn't even recognize. But what caught Melvin's eye in an instant was the Golden Dragon in the center of each banner that adorned the hangings.

The square was crowded with people conducting their business or children playing. In the middle of the square was a large fountain and a statue of the King, his beautiful queen, and their daughters, the four princesses. Although it was made of bronze, he could tell that the princesses were very beautiful themselves, and he was going to be able to meet one this rev. He got very excited.

As they continued their journey through the city, he noticed the houses closest to the castle were very large indeed, with large, finely kept grounds. He thought that some of these houses and grounds were larger than the whole village that he and Reicuas lived in. He didn't think it was right that one family lived in a large house like that, and people like him and his mother lived in a small house, and his whole village could fit in the large lots. He was determined to do something about it at some point.

As they walked, they came closer to the palace. Melvin noticed that there was a river running along the cobblestone road that they were walking on. Small boats were sailing along the river, filled with goods or passengers. He looked off into the distance towards the sea and saw docks where large sailing ships sat in the water, loading and unloading to take goods and people to other parts of Arion and the world. He was amazed at all this. He thought it would be an adventure to sail on one of those ships, but right now, he was about to meet one of the princesses. And to him, that was even more exciting.

Finally, they reached the palace proper. The drawbridge over one of the two rivers was down, but the gate was closed. Reicuas went up to the guard standing at the gate and whispered something to him, who immediately bowed and opened a small side gate to let them through. Melvin wondered what Reicuas had said to the guard. As they walked up the road leading to the palace, Reicuas told him that he was there for an appointment with the princess and that she was expecting him. The guard knew him, just as the ones they had previously come across did. Melvin was starting to think that there was more to his master than he let on. That maybe he was more important than he appeared to be.

As they walked through the palace grounds, Melvin was amazed at the size of the palace. He had never seen a building so large in his life before. The palace stood about ten spans tall, with floor after floor stacked on top of each other. Tall towers reached into the sky, and some even had smaller towers growing out of them. Big rooms lined with windows let the afternoon sunslight pour in. He spotted one room that was bigger than his whole house back in his small town. The whole place looked like it had been painted gold. He couldn't imagine what it would be like to live in something that huge. He would probably get lost trying to find his way around the place. He saw other things he had never seen before. They walked near a maze made of hedges. They passed statues, fountains, and walked over small foot bridges with streams flowing underneath. Palace guards were everywhere, which was interesting to him because this was a peaceful land, they hadn't seen war in thousands of annums, so why should they need all these soldiers? Melvin mentioned this to Reicuas and was met with a gentle explanation that, although they were in peaceful times, they had to be ready in case they were ever attacked. This never occurred to Melvin that there were other people out there who might want to hurt them.

"S-s-so, why are we going to s-s-see the princess?" Melvin asked. As they were now walking behind the palace.

"I am guiding her on how to use her talent, just as I teach you to use yours. You will see once we get there." He told Melvin in the way of a teacher and with a flick of his hand, like it was common knowledge that the only reason he did anything was to teach someone something.

CHAPTER 4
ADARA

As they rounded the final row of bushes and statues, a building loomed ahead, no more than four spans away. Unlike the wooden and plaster structures scattered throughout the kingdom, this one was carved entirely from stone, as if it had been hewn from a single colossal rock. The area around the door was blackened, not by paint, but by something more ominous, as though the stone had been scorched by fire and stained with the lingering traces of soot and smoke.

They went through the door, and inside, Melvin noticed the whole place was covered in this same black soot. Inside the stone chamber stood a girl, her red jumper marked with burn holes, her skin covered with soot. For a fleeting moment, Melvin mistook her for a servant, a girl tasked with cleaning the charred room. But then he saw her hair—flames danced along the strands, flickering like embers in the dim light. It wasn't a trick of the eye. Her hair wasn't just red—*it was fire*. But upon closer look, Melvin got the feeling that she was not just any ordinary girl; she had hair a fiery burning red, and the longer Melvin looked, the better he could tell that it wasn't just a trick of the light, but her hair was actually on fire. Her eyes glowed the color of burning embers. A gasp escaped his lips as he internally panicked. His first reaction was to use his ability to put the flames out with his water magic, but he was stopped when Reicuas put a light hand on his shoulder.

"Melvin, she is in no danger," he said calmly, looking down at him. "In fact, this is how I expected her to be, It means she has been practicing. You see, her talent is the use of fire. Princess Adara," he called to the young girl, "Would you mind giving my apprentice here a demonstration?" He asked her with amusement written all over his face as he winked at her and nodded his head in a show of approval. For what that was all about, Melvin had no idea.

"Y-y-you mean, this i-i-is the p-p-princess?" Melvin asked. She didn't look like a princess to him. He thought princesses always wore nice dresses and tiaras.

"Yes, Melvin. This is Princess Adara." He said quietly. Nodding in her direction. "And she is doing exactly what I expect her to be doing. Practicing her talent with fire."

Melvin was amazed. This was not at all what he was expecting Princess Adara to look like.

"Certainly," she replied with a giggle. She curtsied, then turned around and shot a fireball from her fist at a dummy, some five spans away. She missed by a couple of hands, and it hit the back wall. She turned to Melvin, "That's why I need Master Reicuas's help. My aim is horrible, and half the time I can't even manage to make a proper fireball." She made a little pouty face, and then smiled.

"Yes, my dear. That you do. Indeed, you need help with your aim. But I also have a lesson for Melvin here. Can you be a good girl and extinguish your hair? I want him to see how you look normally."

Adara let the flames go out and stood there. She turned around, looking so innocent, her red hair flowing down to her waist. Besides the flowing red hair, she had big, bright purple eyes. In them, he could see strength and determination, long eyelashes that she batted, unnerving him further, and a dimpled smile that radiated warmth, though in the future, he would see the fierceness of the other side of her. A light splattering of freckles adorned her face, as though kissed by the suns. She was about the same height as Melvin, and as of yet, had not grown into her young womanhood.

"Now, Melvin," Reicuas said. "What do you see?" he asked, wondering what a young boy who had just met one of the princesses would say. Reicuas knew Melvin wouldn't understand the point of this lesson right off.

"I-I-I-I, umm, I-I-I" he said, stammering. Just looking at Princess Adara lit his own heart on fire.

"Come on now, boy, don't just stand there with your jaw hanging open, let me know what you see," Reicuas said, amused as he figured that this would happen.

Adara just stood there giggling, like this was the funniest thing she had seen in a while. A boy standing there   stammering. However it happened all the time. Especially for her sisters.

"I-I-I-I s-s-s-see, umm, p-p-princess Ad-Ad-Ad-Adara," he said, blushing. He had never seen a prettier girl in his whole life.

"What about Adara?" Reicuas asked, amused as he witnessed this scene. This was pretty much as he imagined it would go.

"U-u-umm, pretty p-p-p-purple e-e-eyes, f-f-freckles, pretty smile, u-u-umm…" Melvin couldn't help himself. He couldn't believe his eyes; here he was in the presence of one of the four princesses. Their famed beauty didn't even compare to what he saw in real life. She was definitely one of the most beautiful girls he had ever seen in his whole life. Except for his mother, but she was older, and his mom, so she didn't count. He thought he was in love.

"What else about her, don't look *at* her, look *around* her" Reicuas explained gently, trying to get Melvin to focus on what he wanted him to see. However he was not surprised that Melvin seemed to be enamored with the young princess. For she was very beautiful, even if her clothes were singed and covered in soot as well as her hands and face.

Melvin tried to concentrate, but he couldn't stop looking at this gorgeous young lady in front of him. So, Melvin tried harder to see what his master was talking about. Then he noticed it. She had a red glow around her. She had a red aura, and this was no faint aura; this was very prominent. She had a fire aura, which only made sense because she could control fire. "I-I-I can see her a-a-a-aura." He said excitedly.

Reicuas started again. "Adara here can see auras too, yours is a bit faint still to the untrained eye, but she should be able to see it." Then he looked towards the princess, "Princess Adara", he said directing his attention now to the ginger haired girl, "Can you see Melvin's aura?"

She squinted for a bit and made a face like she was concentrating, then said with a giggle, "He's all sparkly.

It's like a rainbow dancing around him."

"Yes, yes, he is," Reicuas said. "Melvin, can you do what you did this morning with the pebble and such?" thinking that was the neatest thing he had ever seen. Great wizards can do great magic, but usually with only one or two talents. Melvin could use multiple talents at once with ease.

"I-I-I-I don't know M-m-master. I-I-I can t-t-try." So, they went outside into the warm afternoon sunshine, and Melvin found a small rock near the doorway. He thought about it bursting into flames, and it did, then he thought about putting out the fire, so it turned cold as frost covered it. Then, he thought of burying it in the ground and it did, then he thought that a flower should grow there instead, and a rosebush grew in the same place with a beautiful red rose blooming in the bush, water collected as dew around the leaves, and then this time, he added light, because he knew flowers needed light to grow. The red, perfectly shaped rose grew tall, so he picked it and handed it to Adara.

"I-I-I-I th-th-th-thought y-y-you w-w-would l-l-like th-th-th-this," Melvin said with a very bad stutter, and very enamored.

Adara just stood there with her eyes wide open and her jaw dropped in surprise. She finally composed herself and asked, "Did he just really do all that?" and then she hugged Melvin and said, "Thank you for the flower. Red roses are my favorite, and it doesn't even have thorns." At that moment, she felt a wave of peace, comfort, and love for this young man she had just met. She couldn't explain it, but she knew then and there they were meant to be together. And she thought he was also kind of cute.

Then and there, something happened for Melvin as well. Something he had never experienced before, but something he would experience many, many more times throughout his life. When Adara hugged him, it was like a wave of energy went through him, like a wave of light, of love, and other sensations, spread through him from his heart to his fingers and toes to his head. He knew then and there that he and Adara were meant to be together. He didn't know how he knew, he just knew.

This time he managed to speak mostly without stuttering "I-I-I-I don't think roses need thorns." Melvin was definitely in love. She said his aura was all sparkly, Melvin felt all sparkly, or maybe more like warm and fuzzy.

They returned inside the rock building, and Reicuas helped them both practice with fire. He helped Adara practice controlling and aiming her fireballs, and Melvin with starting and putting out fires. Melvin enjoyed his time with Adara and hoped to be able to spend more time with her.

Alas, it was time for them to go. It was getting late in the afternoon, and evening was coming soon. They had a long walk back to the village. Melvin did not want to go. He wanted to stay with his newfound friend, Princess Adara. He hoped that he would be able to visit again. They said their goodbyes, and Reicuas and Melvin headed back through the city and back towards their small village. The rosebush remained at the entrance of the rock edifice. And remained there many milleannums thereafter.

As the suns dipped below the horizon, casting a warm glow over the countryside, light time was waning, and Melvin's mind wandered to Adara and her red aura shining like a beacon of hope. The young lady, who stole his heart like a thief in the night. Then those eyes, those amazing bright purple eyes. He could not get them out of his mind. He could get lost in those wounderous eyes and never find his way back.

Beside him, Reicuas walked with the grace of someone who had witnessed countless sunssets and whispered with the wind. Melvin admired his master's wisdom, the way he seemed attuned to the very pulse of existence. Surely, Reicuas held answers to questions that danced like fireflies in Melvin's mind.

Summoning courage, Melvin cleared his throat. "Master?" He began, his voice a hesitant breeze. "What is it, Melvin?" Reicuas replied, his eyes crinkling at the corners.

"I-I-I-I w-w-w-was wondering about s-s-s-something," Melvin stammered. "What is that?" Reicuas asked, his gaze unwavering.

"Eyes," Melvin said thoughtfully. "W-w-w-why do people have d-d-d-different colored eyes? S-s-s-some people have them a-a-all the time, and s-s-s-some people have them only s-s-some of the time."

"What do you mean?" Reicuas asked softly.

"I-I-I-I w-w-w-was noticing that A-A-Adara had glowing r-r-r-red, e-e-ember colored eyes when she used her m-m-m-magic, but then p-p-purple eyes w-w-w-when she d-d-didn't, and y-y-y-you have g-g-gold eyes, and my m-m-m-mother has o-o-o-orange eyes, w-w-well s-s-s-sometimes, and s-s-s-sometimes they are b-b-blue like mine, but my blue eyes s-s-s-sometimes glow bright. And hair as well. Yours is l-l-light. Light Brown normally, but golden light when y-y-you use your m-m-magic. A-A-Adara's turned into flames, my mom, well, it's always o-o-orange."

"That is your answer," Reicuas murmured gently. "W-w-what do you mean?" inquired Melvin. Still wondering about this conundrum.

"Our eyes are the portal to our souls. They reflect the magic within us." Reicuas explained, "I use light magic, thus my eyes and my irises reflect that. Adara used to have bright blue eyes, just as you do; however, since she has been practicing her talent, they have changed. Adara has so much magic within her that it combines with the blue and turns them purple. When she uses her magic, they change to an ember color as her magic takes over. That happens to everyone who has a very strong talent and very strong magic and uses that talent. Your mother stores vast amounts of knowledge; she, as you know, has the talent for teaching. She knows the way people learn and has the ability to teach them in the way they are able to learn best. Hair is similar to eye color, it matches your talent. It matches your eyes and your aura. It all reflects the type of talent you have a home before it grows dark."

As the dusk waned, Melvin's footsteps echoed through the quietude. The world seemed to hold its breath, as if awaiting the unfolding of a secret.

Adara, the princess with purple eyes and hair of flames, once again occupied his thoughts. How beautiful she was, not merely in the way sunlight kissed her freckled face or how her hair flowed like a river of copper. No, it was the life within her, the determination that danced in her gaze. She was a fireball, a promise etched into the fabric of existence.

The road wound past farms, their rustic barns standing as sentinels against the dusk. Over bridges they ventured, where dusk surrendered to twilight, and the air held the scent of earth, scented trees, flowers, and possibility. Melvin's heartbeat in rhythm with the crickets' song, a melody of longing and hope.

Now, sitting on his porch, Melvin looked up into the sky as the first of the stars blinked into existence in the darkening sky. Melvin, still thinking about the events of the rev, and the amazing girl he had met, as he looked up into the sky. Then, under the watchful eyes of Deo, he made a vow that transcended mere words, a covenant etched into the marrow of his bones. He used his magic, whispered an incantation as clearly as he could muster. It was easier to speak clearly when he was alone, and he whispered. Adara would be his, not as a possession, but as a kindred spirit, as a companion, as an equal to him. Together, they would unravel mysteries, ignite galaxies, and dance upon the edge of magic.

And so, as the night embraced them, Melvin looked up into the multitude of stars that were winking into existance, and whispered his promise to Adara, to Deo, and to himself: "Adara," he vowed, "I will be your flame keeper, your protector, and your companion. We'll write our story across the canvas of time, and our love will be the brightest constellation in the sky."

And Deo, perhaps amused by his mortal audacity, answered back, a thousand celestial eyes witnessing the birth of a love that would span eternity. A night sky full of innumerable stars, vast galaxies, lit up the nights sky as a witness to that vow.

On the other side of the small town, Reicuas was deep in thought as he pondered on the afternoon's events. Initially, he had brought Melvin to the castle solely for a lesson for his two young pupils. However, something unexpected happened. Reicuas was wise beyond his age. He sensed an unspoken connection between the two. When these two met, he felt something between them, he knew that their destinies were intertwined and that they both had a great accomplishment to complete together. He did not know what exactly it was, but they needed to be together. Then and there, he made up his mind that he would take Melvin with him every time he taught Princess Adara. He would train them together. And he would do what he could to ensure this happened. But still, it was up to these two young ones to make that happen.

That night, sitting alone in her room, Adara thought about the boy whom she had met that rev. She had heard stories about him from Reicuas and his mother, but had never met him before that rev. There was something about him. Something different, something special. When they hugged, she could feel a bond between them. As if Deo was telling her that she needed to be by his side. She made a vow then and there, looking at the myriad of stars through her window. "Melvin, I will be by your side, I will help you become the great man that I know you're destined to be, and the greatest wizard you can become. Weather as your friend or as more. I will be the flame that will show you the way. I will be the light in your darkness." She smiled and thought about Melvin until she drifted off to sleep.

CHAPTER 5

A PROPER WIZARD

Several decannums had passed since Melvin had met Adara. He was better at his magic, but still had a long way to go.

"It is time, Melvin," Reicuas said excitedly after a while of staring up at the sky. He had been working with Melvin on his incantations, and trying to say them without stuttering with much effort he was able to say most of the incantation, but not all of it.

"T-t-time f-f-for what?" Melvin asked, looking up at his master.

"Time for the egg to hatch. My boy, it's time for you to meet your dragon." Reicuas said as he held out his hand to help lift the boy up. Melvin had been sitting on the ground, practicing his magic, trying to get a frog to hop backwards. Reicuas felt there was no harm in having a frog hop backwards for an hour or two. Melvin was getting very close.

Melvin, in all actuality, was not much of a boy anymore. He was growing more into a man, and was about 160 annums old now. It had been nearly thirty-five annums since he first saw the egg in that cave. By your Melvin had met Adara. But remember, their time and lifespans are much different.

During this time, Melvin had grown into a tall, strong, and handsome young man. He had worked hard on his magical and physical abilities. He and Adara became very, very close friends. They practiced their magic together under the tutelage of Master Reicuas. Melvin was devoted to Adara, helping her become the best wizardess she could become. He loved her with all his heart, but did not know if she felt the same way about him, so he kept his feelings to himself.

Meanwhile, Adara grew into a beautiful young woman. She was fit and trim, strong in strength, power, and will. She was always at Melvin's side. Helping him, encouraging him, and loving him. Though she never showed that love through outward appearances, other than friendship, because she did not know how Melvin felt about her. Nor did she ask. For the moment, she was content with how things were. But each time they touched, those feelings she first felt were renewed.

Melvin never forgot about the egg. He often wondered when it would hatch. But now, finally, the time had come for Melvin to become a proper wizard.

"H-H-How d-d-do you know i-i-it's time?" Melvin asked.

"Percilla told me. -Remember, dragons can speak through thoughts and pictures.- She showed me the egg, starting to get ready to hatch. So we must journey to the cave." Reicuas told him.

As they walked to the cave, where he first saw the egg so many annums ago, they discussed dragons and the history of the dragons, and why they were so important to the world. Reicuas found that this walk was a perfect time to delve into one of his many adventures. But Melvin wasn't really listening; he was instead thinking about finally being able to watch a baby dragon being hatched, just to be one of the very few humans who would be able to have this opportunity, which made his excitement grow.

As they slowly climbed the mountain path, passing the tall trees, Melvin, in time, started to hum to himself, then he made up words to the music he was humming. Soon, he softly started to sing a song. As he sang, his voice took on a magical tone, and he noticed that his stutter disappeared. His voice was clear with no signs of hesitation. He saw a deer in the woods, a little ways off, and sang the incantation that he was trying to use on the frog earlier. But this time, he adjusted it to work on a deer. And as intended, the deer, very startled, started to walk backwards.

This whole time, Reicuas looked on quietly, marveling at what he was witnessing. Even if it wasn't that common, he had known some hag witches to sing their spells, but he never took any stock into the singing having anything to do with the actual spell casting Well, whether or not it actually did, he still didn't know, but he did know this much: that at least it did work for Melvin, and that was all that mattered. It stopped him from stuttering, so he could recite the words of the spell properly. He also noticed that when he did sing, his voice and spell seemed more powerful. Reicuas also noticed that he had a very good singing voice. That was probably one of his many talents that his aura sparkled with.

Melvin often thought that when he went off and did something on his own that Master Reicuas would get upset with him for not listening, or for not paying attention. But to Reicuas, this was a trick that he used to get Melvin to do something that he had never done before. Reicuas often told his boring stories to subtly encourage Melvin into doing this more often, as every time he was bored, he would try something entirely different than his usual routine, and end up discovering something new altogether. And this time it had worked, as it had on many other occasions. Melvin had finally unlocked the secret to using part of his power. He could now be a proper wizard, for he could say, or rather sing, the spells or incantations needed, without facing the trouble of stuttering through the incantations. Reicuas also observed that singing the incantations for the spells made Melvin's magic more powerful, as he was able to focus without any distractions.

"Melvin, do you know what you have just done?" Reicuas asked excitedly, smiling at Melvin while they were walking.

"I-I-I s-s-sang a s-s-song." Melvin said, fearing that Master Reicuas would be displeased, even though he rarely was.

"What else did you do?" Trying to get Melvin to realize what he saw him do.

"I-I-I d-d-did make the d-d-deer walk backwards." He said, realizing that he actually did it.

"And, how did you do it?" Reicuas asked, trying to get the boy to notice what he did.

"I-I-I s-s-sang" he said. Then he thought a bit and realized what Master Reicuas must be getting at. Then, in a low voice, he sang *"I sang the incantation, and I didn't stutter."*

"That's right, you sang. You didn't stutter. You can recite the spells and incantations now, my boy, you can do it. You can finally become a proper wizard." And at this, Reicuas smiled a very big and wide smile and gave Melvin a big hug. "I am so proud of you. You have worked so hard to learn everything I have taught you. I have always encouraged you to discover things on your own, and you have excelled at that every time. You deserve to see the dragon egg hatch. You will be a great wizard, Melvin, you will even surpass my abilities. There is one more thing I would like to verify, if my hunch is correct."

"Okay," is all Melvin said, still happy from that huge compliment Reicuas just gave him.

"I want you to make three trees grow," Reicuas said as he picked up a pine cone from the ground, plucking out three seeds, and handing them to Melvin. "Tell the tree to grow, just use the word grow. I know you have done this many times, so I know you can say the word without stuttering. The first one, I want you to just think three times, the second one, I want you to say three times. And the third one, I want you to sing three times. I want to see if there is any difference between thinking, saying the word, and singing it. I know you have to think it all three times, but I want to compare all of them."

"Okay," Melvin said. Putting the first seed in the ground. He thought for it to grow in his mind three times, and it did. It grew from a seed to a hand-high tree. He then put the second seed in the ground and told it to grow by saying "grow" three times. This time, the seed grew into a three-hand-high tree. But the other tree also grew higher, though he wasn't focusing the spell on the first tree. He put the last seed in the ground and tried to direct the spell only on that seed, then sang the word "grow" three times, This tree grew a span high, but despite Melvin's attempt to direct his spell only on the third seed, the others grew as well, though not as much as the third tree did. Reicuas was awestruck, he could not believe it. In all these annums, he didn't realize the importance of songs in spell casting. Singing the enchantments made them more powerful somehow. But he didn't have time to research it now. He would have to do that some other time. Now, there were more important things to do, like getting Melvin to his dragon egg in time for hatching.

CHAPTER 6
THE HATCHING

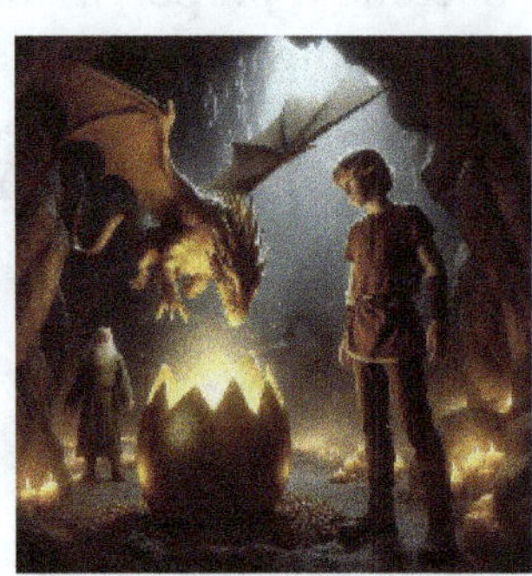

As they walked along to the cave, Melvin practiced singing his spells to do a variety of things. He made some animals bigger, or faster, but not by much; he didn't want to unbalance nature too much, or make plants grow, or use water from the air to do tricks too much. He was having fun with this, singing to the cave. Reicuas just let him enjoy his reverie as long as he did not harm anything.

After about another hour of hiking up the mountain, they finally approached the cave. As they entered the cavern, Percilla was waiting for them anxiously. She was curled up next to the golden egg.

Reicuas gave Melvin some last-minute instructions. "Melvin. I have not taught you how to absorb magic. I do not know how exactly to explain it. It will naturally flow into you, but with your talents, you could absorb more. Just open yourself up to it. Let it flow into you. Set your mind to receive it. Maybe you can sing an incantation to receive it. I know you will figure it out, like you always do."

"We are barely in time" Reicuas continued, "It is about to hatch. You go stand next to the egg and watch it hatch, I will be over here near Percilla. I will also absorb some magic, but you will absorb the most, since you are closer." With this, Percilla and Reicuas moved over to the other side of the cavern.

Melvin stood near the large golden egg, about the size of a small Blasmoth. It shimmered with a golden glow that it produced itself.

They waited, breath held in anticipation, as the golden egg stirred. Cracks webbed across its surface, revealing glimpses of the radiant light within. Melvin's heart raced; he could sense the magic awakening, a force beyond comprehension.

Sparkling golden light spilled forth, illuminating the immense cavern. It danced across the walls, painting patterns of wonder. As it touched Melvin, he gasped — the power surged through him like a river of energy. His skin tingled, and he sang — a soft melody, "Flow, flow into me."

The egg's top shattered, and there it was — the baby dragon. Its head emerged, eyes wide and intense. Wave after wave of brilliant light pulsed through the cavern, bathing them all— the mother dragon, Reicuas, and Melvin — in a brilliant lumous glow, in the magic that was being released into the world.

Melvin stood closest to the egg and the baby dragon. His song, a conduit, drew the magic like a moth to flame. It flooded him, a tremendous torrent, filling every cell. He felt invincible, as if he could shape reality itself. No longer awkward or weak, he stood tall, shoulders squared, the very essence of a wizard reborn.

And then it happened — his eyes changed. The blue irises shifted, swirling with newfound hues. His eyes were no longer blue, but a mesh of all the colors of the talents he possessed. Melvin blinked, and the world seemed sharper, more vivid. He was no longer a mere observer; he was a participant. His hair also changed to reflect the new magic flowing into him. No longer light brown, but a facet of multi colored strands. Reflecting the types of magic he could use. Like his eyes, every color from every type of magic was represented.

The baby dragon regarded him, her eyes knowing. She had shared her magic, her birthright. Melvin's purpose crystallized — he would protect this world, wield the golden light, and sing songs of wonder.

As the last remnants of the shell crumbled, a baby golden dragon emerged — a celestial marvel, her scales shimmering like molten suns. Melvin's breath caught; he had witnessed a birth beyond time, a convergence of magic and destiny.

Tentatively, he extended his hand, fingers trembling. The dragon regarded him with eyes that held galaxies — the wisdom of ages, the promise of eternity. But then, a whisper echoed in Melvin's mind: *Don't touch.*

He hesitated. The dragon's magic pulsed, a golden current that beckoned. It was a choice - a crossroads. To touch would be to absorb more of its power, to become something more than human. But at what cost?

Melvin withdrew his hand, the air crackling with energy. The dragon's approval resonated a silent acknowledgment. She understood. Melvin had absorbed enough for now.

And so, in the quiet of that cavern, Melvin stood — a bridge between worlds, a vessel of magic. His eyes, transformed by the dragon's gift, held the promise of a destiny yet unwritten.

In the sacred silence of the cavern, where golden light still pulsed like a heartbeat, Percilla, the mother dragon, spoke to Melvin. But her voice was not one of words; it was a tapestry of images woven into his mind.

"Because I have allowed you to witness the birth of this golden dragon," her message unfurled, *"and because you have received its power, you must wield it only for good. Your purpose: to help others, to vanquish evil, and to weave threads of peace across the world."*

Melvin's consciousness absorbed the images — the egg cracking, the streaming light, the emergence of the baby dragon. The magic flowed through him, a torrent of ancient energy, and he understood. His mind, once awkward and uncertain, now danced with clarity. He knew what he must do.

"I will do as you say," Melvin projected back to Percilla. His thoughts formed images of him standing against malevolent creatures, healing wounds, helping people, and kindling hope. *"Only for good."*

As the cavern echoed with their collective heartbeat, Melvin could feel the magic flowing through him. He felt stronger, more sure of himself. He felt like he could take on any challenge. Then Melvin made another vow, not unlike the one he made those many annums ago the night he met his beloved. "I am no longer awkward. I am a proper wizard. I have the power to protect the ones I love. I will learn to use the full potential of my power. I will protect Adara and my family from harm. I will be her guiding light, the protector of her flame. I will help her be the most powerful wizardess she can be. I will use my talents and abilities to do good. I will use my power to help those who can not help themselves. And vanwuish the world of evil, if it comes to that."

Percilla's approval resonated, a ripple of pleasure. She painted another scene: Melvin naming the baby dragon. The name Penelope surfaced to Melvin, a tribute to his mother, an honor shared between them. Percilla's approval deepened; it was a name that echoed through time.

"Penelope," he whispered, and the mother dragon's approval blazed like a comet. And then, Melvin's mind swirled with a daring thought: *What if Penelope could be free?* He envisioned releasing control, allowing her to grow, to explore the world on her own terms. A dragon unbound.

It was an agreement — an oath. Penelope would be her own master, yet bound by friendship. When Melvin needed her, she would come — a golden guardian, a winged ally. But not bound by loyalty, but bound by friendship, bound by love.

And so, in the quiet of that cavern, Melvin forged a pact with magic itself. His eyes, hair, and heart now transformed, held the promise of a new era — an era where a young man named Melvin and a dragon named Penelope would shape destiny together.

Reicuas's heart swelled with joy as Percilla carried him and Melvin on her mighty back. The wind tousled Melvin's hair, and the suns warmed his face. Reicuas glanced at Melvin, who wore an expression of pure wonder. Flying on a dragon was unlike anything he'd ever experienced.

"Will Penelope be able to fly like this?" Melvin asked, his eyes wide with anticipation. Percilla nodded, projecting an image of Penelope's future wingspan. "When she's big enough, she'll soar alongside us," she replied. Melvin's smile widened, and Percilla's heart swirled with affection for this young man who had become her friend.

The gold dragon descended, landing gracefully in a secluded meadow. Reicuas dismounted, gently placing Melvin beside him. They were far enough from town to remain hidden, yet close enough to visit.

"Penelope needs friends," Percilla said, her thoughts echoing in Melvin's mind. *"You can visit anytime."* Melvin's gratitude radiated, and he asked about bringing Adara along. Percilla sensed Adara's kind heart and granted permission. *"Penelope will adore Adara,"* Percilla assured him.

As the suns dipped behind the majestic mountains, Percilla spread her wings. *"Until next time,"* she communicated, launching into the sky. The wind carried her upward, and she glanced back at Melvin and Reicuas. They waved goodbye. She soared toward her hidden cave, where Penelope awaited her mother's return.

CHAPTER 7
MASTER WIZARD

Several decannums had passed since the rev that Melvin saw Penelope hatch.

Melvin still lived with his mother, as was the custom to live with your parents until such a time as you were married or had to set off to schooling or a vocation. However, he was in training to become a wizard. He could have gone to the wizard school in Wazervĭl; however, Reicuas, knowing his special circumstances, felt it better to personally train this particular young wizard himself, and was correct in doing so. His mother was not only the town school teacher, but also taught the princesses at the palace. She taught Melvin all the school learning he needed. Math, science, reading, writing, etc. She also taught him about Deo and to search the writings of the prophets, to pray, and to seek His guidance. However, she left the magic lessons up to Reicuas.

Melvin and Adara practiced their magic and became very powerful wizards. Melvin also became very knowledgeable in trades and other things as well, since he had aspects of all talents with in him, he decided to learn as much as he could about everything he could. He liked to help people with their tasks. Gardening, thatching roofs, building all sorts of structures, and anything imaginable that he would help with. This gave him the chance and opportunity to learn new ways to use magic, while also helping others.

One rev, Adara was talking to her sisters about this, and Amira, as competitive as she was, declared that she wouldn't be outdone by anyone, even though it was Melvin, whom they had known for many annums now. So, she decided then and there that whenever Melvin, often joined by Adara, was helping someone around the town, she would be right there alongside him, helping them. This way, she would get just as many opportunities to grow and be better as he would. So not only did the village have one princess visiting all the time, but now two. Everyone loved Melvin and the Princesses coming to the village. Before long, other towns and villages, even Bilby City, had people requesting Melvin and the Princesses to help them. Sometimes, they even got paid, well, mostly with food, even though all Melvin really wanted was to learn and hone his skills and talents. But being fed was a bonus. People were always willing to feed a growing young wizard and their beloved princesses.

During this time, Melvin and Adara spent as much time together as they possibly could. They practiced their magic together, learned together, served together (along with Amira), served together, more often than not with Amira, took flights on Penelope together, and did all sorts of other activities together. She mostly rode to the village on her qilin to visit him. Now, you may not know what a qilin is. It's similar to the mythical creature known on Earth as a quilin. They can be in various forms, but for the most part, they look like reindeer. However, they can also be scalier and look more like a dragon without wings. Melvin and Adara rode them regularly, as one would ride a horse. He went to the palace when Reicuas went to teach Adara or the other princesses, but usually just to the stone edifice, where Adara practiced controlling her fire. A few times, he had been in other parts of the castle, usually the kitchen, because they both liked to eat, and the servants made the best food. They both loved to ride on the beach and in the countryside.

As she grew older, Adara became very good at controlling fire and other forms of combat, such as swordplay. Axes, pikes, spears, and many others, as did her sister, Aria. However, there was always more to learn. Although she was very proficient with many weapons, naturally, she preferred using fire.

Usually, it would have been the eldest male of the family who led the armies, but seeing as King Bilby had no sons, it fell to his daughters, and they did a more than adequate job. Adara became the leader of the military for the Kingdom, and Aria, although she was the eldest, became the head of the special ops division, despite her passion for the arts, including singing and dancing. Aria, though very skilled in all sorts of combat, didn't want the responsibility of leading the whole army. Instead, she preferred to lead a smaller, more specialized team. They trained for special secret missions that needed stealth and precision. When and if the occasion ever arose, which they hoped it wouldn't, they would be ready.

Adara had come to Melvin's small town to practice magic with him and see some new ability he had discovered. Melvin was in front of Reicuas's house practicing his magic. His mother was there as well. She always liked watching Melvin discover and practice new things. He had learned to control the air, to manipulate it, to concentrate it underneath himself to propel himself upward and forward. In essence, he could float, but as a new discovery, he wasn't that good at it yet; he could only lift himself a few digits off the ground and a few spans forward, but it was a start.

Although Melvin, in appearance, looked to be of age now, he was still considered to be very young. He was no longer the small, skinny, awkward boy that we first met in the cave, looking at the dragon egg. He had grown tall and handsome. About a span high. From his physical work, he grew large muscles that caused all the ladies to go weak at the knees and fawn over him.

Meanwhile, Adara had fully blossomed into her womanhood, no longer the shy, freckle-faced girl Melvin had met in the stone building all those years ago. The timid child was gone, replaced by a striking young woman whose waist-length red hair flowed like liquid fire in the light. Strength had been etched into her frame through years of relentless combat training, each toned muscle a testament to her dedication. Yet, despite the warrior she had become, her smooth, unblemished skin retained a youthful softness, a contrast that made her appear both untouchable and impossibly young—a paradox of grace and power. In Earth years, one could say that they were in their early twenties.

Reicuas was busy in his house and called Melvin in, while Melvin's mother and Adara waited outside. "I must go on a journey, Melvin, and I don't know how long I will be. But, you must continue with your studies." Reicuas said tenderly as he stuffed bottled potions and other supplies from shelves and tables into a pack. Reicuas wandered around the small house, mumbling things to himself that he needed to take with him on his trip. The small house was cluttered with potions, scrolls, books, and other magical items.

"W-w-w-where are y-y-you going?" Melvin asked, surprised by the sudden news as he sat on a small stool near the cluttered table. He was surprised that there was no smell of cooking stew that was usually in the pot in the hearth.

"I am going to the Helaeth Mountains to get some rare herbs for a potion I am working on." He said, still organizing the things he needed for the trip.

"C-c-c-can't I-I-I go with you, Master?" asked Melvin with pleading eyes. Melvin loved going on adventures with Reicuas. As they had been on many.

The Master wizard stopped for a moment and looked at Melvin with his sunslit eyes, "I am sorry, my boy, but this journey is very perilous. I must cross the lands of the foulest creatures near the dark woods. It is far too dangerous for you. You are getting quite good in your studies, you are getting to be a proper wizard, but this is still beyond your ability." Said Reicuas as he rubbed the boy's head.

Melvin was not a boy anymore; he was two hundred and twenty-one annums old. He would be considered a man, but still very young in their reckoning. As they lived for about a thousand annums. Some wizards lived much longer with the help of magic.

What Reicuas wasn't telling him is that he wasn't going to pick herbs, he was actually going on a secret mission to stop a powerful sorcerer that was trying to invade the peaceful lands of the Jīgabuji and other surrounding areas.

There was news of a powerful sorcerer going through out the land on the west side of Arion, past the Helaeth Mountain range, conquering towns and villages with his magic and with his army of the vilest of creatures in the land. Ogres, goblins, witches, leprechauns, and even humans were terrorizing the land around the dark forest to the west. But fortunately till now, no dragons.

The Empress asked Reicuas to go to the wizard city of Wazervīl and gather other wizards to defeat this sorcerer. So he would go, because that's what was expected of him as a Master Wizard. Reicuas felt confident enough that Melvin was along enough in his studies that he needed no further instruction from him. Anything he needed to know, he would find out for himself or find out the answer somehow. Reicuas knew Melvin was far more advanced at this age than he was at the same age. Melvin was ready to become a full-fledged Master Wizard, no longer an apprentice. He knew he would eventually become the greatest wizard in the history of their world.

Right before he left, Reicuas put his arm around Melvin's shoulder, as a father would do. He felt he was like a father to Melvin for all the time they spent together, and Melvin had no father of his own, because he died in an accident when Melvin was a young child. Or so Melvin was told.

"My boy," Reicuas said tenderly, "You have learned everything I can teach you, you have found many things out on your own that I did not even know. You are very bright and intelligent. Your command of magic is very impressive. When you saw Penelope hatch, I saw the power flow into you, the confidence you gained, and you have only excelled from that point, and your eyes, hair, and aura reflect that."

Melvin didn't know what to think, he had never heard Reicuas praise him like this before. Master Reicuas had complemented him before on occasion on a job well done, but never like this. All he could think to say was "Thank you." And he didn't even stutter.

"Melvin, I have a surprise for you," then he opened the door, and they walked out to the front of the house where there was a small court yard, and his mother and Princess Adara stood chatting while they waited. There were also a lot of the townsfolk there as well.

Melvin didn't know what to think. He had never seen so many people in front of Reicuas's house. It wasn't his anniversary of his birth, it wasn't Reicuas's, or Adara's, or his mother's. Was it a festive? He didn't think so. Maybe it was for the townsfolk to say goodbye to Reicuas before his long journey. That must be it.

"I'm sorry it couldn't be more of a celebration, because I must leave as soon as possible," Reicuas turned to look at Melvin in his bright multicolored eyes, and handed him a piece of parchment. While doing this, he motioned to the crowd to pay attention. He lifted his head up high in an official manner and said aloud so everyone could hear "I Reicuas, Master Wizard, High Wizard to the Empress of Arion, and personal wizard to King Bilby, member of the order of Wazer, and with the authority of my status, do now promote you Melvin of Bilbylund on this rev, to the status of full Master Wizard. With all rights, powers, and authorities of this position. I want the fame of you to go far and wide so every person in every nation of this world will know the name of Melvin the Magnificent!! And thus, I officially give you the title of: ***Melvin, the Magnificent, Master of the Wizard.*** May you use it well, to be a help and to serve the good people of Bilbylund, the Arion Empire, and the world." Melvin smiled widely as it sunk in to him that he was now a full-fledged Master Wizard. He looked over at his mother and Adara and saw the wide, beautiful smiles on their faces.

Reicuas continued, "I also would like to give you this gift," he said, handing him a staff that looked more like a shiny, gnarled tree branch, about the same height as Melvin. "This is *the Rod of Arendale*, which I had the elves make for you for this occasion. It will enhance your abilities, it also has other attributes instilled within it that you will discover on your own, when you need them." Then Reicuas hugged him and told him how proud he was of him. "I also give you the permission to live in this house till I return. I do not know how long this journey may take, probably a long while. So, it is yours to use till I return. As you know, it is filled with many magical books and scrolls, other items, and potions for you to use to study and enhance your abilities. If you happen to get married before I return," he said as he looked towards Adara and winked, "You have my blessing to have your family live here." Although he knew, if the two did get married, they would most likely live in the castle, this was another push for him to go that direction.

Melvin knew Reicuas too well. He knew something was going on that Reicuas wasn't telling him. He was sure Reicuas was being sent on a quest of some sort, and it was very dangerous; otherwise, he wouldn't be letting him use the house.

His mother and Princess Adara, in turn, gave him hugs and said how proud they were of him. There weren't any other master wizards in this part of the country. Most of them lived and trained in the wizard city of Wazervīl to the west. So this was a big deal for them. Melvin was one of the very few wizards that did not attend the academy.

Percilla and Penelope didn't need to be there because they could see what was happening through their link with Reicuas and Melvin. Ordinarily, they wouldn't see through their eyes, but this was a special occasion for them all.

When the Empress, through King Bilby, asked Reicuas to go on this journey, and Reicuas told the King that Melvin was ready to be on his own, the King knew that Melvin would take Reicuas' place as the wizard of the land. Adara, being the commander of the military, also knew of this quest and knew she had to be there when Melvin became a Master Wizard. She knew she would have to use his help if there ever was a need, and she was sure she would, because this long peace they had had would not last forever.

You may be wondering why Adara didn't go on this quest as well, being the leader of the king's army. Well, to tell the truth, she didn't need to. Her kingdom was pretty small and insignificant compared to others in Arion. But being as Reicuas was a High Master Wizard and a personal friend of the Empress, he was specifically called for this mission. The Empress and other kingdoms would be providing the armies and other wizards for this mission. Also, they needed her to make sure Melvin continued practicing his magic.

"Melvin," Adara said tenderly. "I have a surprise for you as well." She said with a smile. She wrapped her arms around him in an embrace and kissed him on the cheek. This was a special rev for him, so she felt she could be a bit more affectionate. Besides, she was tired of waiting for them to become an official couple. She was being aggressive in letting him know how she felt. If he didn't catch on by the end of the rev, she was going to take matters into her own hands. Fireworks literally lit up the sky, and all the people in the town wondered what was happening, but since it was right above the Master Wizard's house, they weren't all that surprised, especially with one of the four princesses in the small village. Adara continued softly. "I'm sorry that Reicuas couldn't give you a better send off, or congratulations on your accomplishment. Would you mind coming to the palace with me? I would like to throw you a small party for your huge accomplishment." She said with a mysterious smile and a wink.

"B-b-but I-I-I have nothing t-t-to wear," he stammered. Even though he would agree to go anywhere with her.

 "You silly boy," Adara said with a chuckle, putting her finger to his lip to quiet him. "It's the palace, and you are my guest. We have clothes there you could wear."

"Yes, thank you." he said without stuttering, for he had been practicing talking without stuttering, small things he could say without stuttering, but longer sentences and when he got nervous, he still stuttered. "Adara," he said holding her hand "I-I-I would g-g-go a-a-anywhere w-w-with you."

"I know." She said back softly, rubbing the top of the back of his hand with her thumb. Then she led him and his mother out to the carriage.

"One minute," Melvin said softly "I-I-I-I want to t-t-talk to Reicuas again b-b-before we go."

"Alright," Adara whispered, her soft soothing voice barely audible. "Go ahead. We'll wait here." Her gaze lingered on his eyes — those mesmerizing, multicolored eyes that revealed his magic. Ever since he'd witnessed Penelope's hatching, he had transformed. His aura pulsed with newfound power, and his posture exuded confidence. But it was his eyes that captivated her — the once brilliant blue, now a kaleidoscope of colors. She could lose herself in their depths, tracing the threads of enchantment woven within. Time seemed to stretch as she drank in their beauty, and Adara wondered if she'd ever tire of gazing into those magical eyes.

Melvin went back inside the house, "Reicuas, I-I-I-I know there i-i-i-s s-s-something your n-n-not t-t-telling me." He insisted.

"You are right, my boy, you are right," Reicuas said in a low voice, as he hung his head. This was not how Reicuas usually was, so Melvin knew something more was going on. "The Empress has asked me to go on a quest. A dark sorcerer is taking over villages and lands in the west."

"Yes, I know, I heard about that." Melvin decided to sing slightly so he wouldn't stutter. "And I am guessing that the Empress asked you to go stop this dark sorcerer, am I correct?"

"Yes, you are, my boy. Yes, you are. So, there it is. It is a long journey, and as you see, very perilous. I didn't want to scare you. I didn't want to ruin your special rev by telling you this news." Reicuas told him.

"It's okay. I know you will do well, you are a master wizard, with powers and abilities that I may never have." Melvin sang softly. "I hope, in time, to be as good a wizard as you are."

"Melvin," Reicuas said sternly as he looked into Melvin's bright, multicolored eyes. "I don't want you to be '*as good a wizard as I am.*'" He emphasized each word. "I want you to be a *better* wizard than I am. I want you to exceed me in every way. I want you to be the best, most powerful wizard this world has ever known." He paused to let this sink in.

He continued, "The parchment I gave you is an official parchment from the wizard order of Wazzer with its official seal. It will show to anyone who asks that you are a Master Wizard with that title inscribed upon it. Show this to the king at the party, and he will officially declare it unto all those that are there. Whatever town or city you go into, present this parchment to the King or Magistrate, or his representative of that city or town, and they will treat you with the respect of this title. When you become a High Wizard, like myself, and I know you will, or even a 1st Wizard, which there are very few of. The parchment will magically change to bear the new title. Don't worry about losing it, it will always be there when you need it."

"Now, Melvin," he said in a more festive tone, "Don't worry about me. This is a special rev for you, go to your party, have fun, enjoy yourself. And for heaven's sake, ask Adara to be your girlfriend, or bride. She has been wanting you to ask her for a long, long time. She may not have told you. I am surprised, with how you can figure things out, you did not figure this out. Blind you are to the ways of women. She loves you, Melvin. Probably more than anyone else in this world, well maybe except her family, and I know how much you love her. You two are meant to be together. Love her, Melvin. Cherish her, as she does you. Your lives are meant to be intertwined. Deo has put you together." With that, Reicuas patted him on the back, gave him another hug, and brought him out to his mother and Adara.

Reicuas and Melvin said their goodbyes and after Reicuas loaded his supplies, climbed on his qilin and rode off into the distance. Melvin felt that a part of himself was gone.

Penelope told Melvin that he would not be alone, because she was always with him. She would always be there if he needed her. She put in the images of the visits he had with her throughout the decannums. All the flights they had taken together in the Lascar Mountains. So, he did not feel as alone as he did a moment before. She also told him that he had Adara, and she would always be by his side. And same as Reicuas had said, ask Adara for her Hand. Penelope knew this was one of her greatest desires. Unbeknownst to Melvin, Adara had talked to Penelope on many occasions. And even if she didn't, it was only very obvious. Well, to everyone but Melvin.

Adara gave him a big hug and said "Everything will turn out fine. And remember, you always have me." She put her hand in his and with this, Melvin smiled and they all got into the purple and gold carriage and they were on their way to the castle.

They had touched before—at the practice rock, during sparring matches, or in moments of quiet comfort when one needed the other's solace. Those touches had always brought him a quiet, grounding warmth, waves of peace and love washed over him. But this time, as her hand met his, it was different. This time, it wasn't just warmth—it was fire. Sparks raced through him, igniting something he had never felt from her before, something both exhilarating and terrifying.

As he got into the carriage and rode to the castle, Melvin thought about this. He pondered, he prayed. This news. How could he not have known, not figured it out? This beautiful woman was there by his side at every possible moment. He was sure that she left hints of her affection, but for some reason, he was oblivious to it. How could he not see how she felt? With all of his talents, with all of his magical abilities, this was one he did not have. To know the thoughts and feelings of females. Even the woman he was closest to on the planet. But this time it was different. Holding her hand felt different, felt more… Just more.

He could feel the love emanating from her, he could feel her warmth. He smiled. He said a silent prayer, if all this was true, if she was the one he was meant to be with, if their lives were intertwined. And there in the silence of his mind, solely focused on Deo, and the one he loved sitting next to him holding his hand, came an answer. A small voice, a still voice, but one so powerful that he could not deny it. *YES.* Then a powerful feeling came over him, more powerful than any he had felt before. A feeling of peace and love. Not only from Deo, but also for the beautiful young woman in the carriage next to him. He knew he loved her more than life itself. He would do anything for her. But that feeling expanded a thousandfold. Melvin was definitely going to make this official this evening.

Adara's mind was made up. This was the last straw. If he didn't know by now how she felt about him, then he would certainly know by the end of the night. She had left hint after hint. For annums, she had been by his side, loving him, encouraging him, and training with him. She even got physical, brushed him with her hands, batted her eyes, flirted, played with his hair, and looked longingly and lovingly into those beautiful multicolored eyes. If he didn't get it by now, she was going to take things into her own hands and ask him to be her boyfriend. She had waited long enough.

As she sat there thinking about this, a thought came to her mind. *He knows Adara. He knows. Everything will be alright.*

CHAPTER 8
A TIME TO CELEBRATE

The suns were high in the sky as they traveled to the castle. Melvin had never been in one of the royal carriages before. Sometimes, when he and Master Reicuas would visit the palace, they would ride in a carriage, but never one this nice. It was white on the outside, with purple trim and on the inside it had dark purple padded seats and backs. They even had snacks to eat on the way. He thought it would be nice to be royalty. Funny thing was, Melvin didn't remember Princess Adara coming in a carriage this nice, for that matter, he didn't remember her coming in a carriage at all.

As they passed houses, farms, fields, and businesses the people waved at them and they waved back. Everyone in the kingdom loved the Princesses and the wizards. As they continued through the tall city gates, the guards bowed as the carriage passed. He liked riding with princess Adara, not only because he got to sit near her, but because everyone waved and bowed and such, that they don't do ordinarily. He seriously thought about doing what Reicuas asked.

As they rolled up to the castle drawbridge, the special guards stood at salute to the princess, and she returned the salute in kind. They stopped in front of the castle, and the servants came rushing to help them out of the carriage. Two female servants were showing Adara some fine clothes, and she was talking to them softly, pointing to some and nodding. Others came to Melvin and his mother and whisked them away into the castle into separate rooms. These rooms were lavishly decorated with cushioned chairs and sitting stools, gold and purple drapes and carpeting with the symbol of a Gold dragon on them. The servant girls quickly undressed him to his underwear and took him to a bathroom, where there was a tub of hot water waiting for him. Though they tried to hide it, they were extremely thrilled to be helping Melvin. Not only was he now a Master wizard, but he was also tall, very muscular and very handsome. They took their precious time as they washed his hair, his back, legs, arms, and chest and other parts of him.

This was the best rev of his life, having three beautiful girls his same age bathing him. They they took their precious time scrubbed every inch of him clean, sometimes twice, as they said that some parts were very dirty. But he thought that was just an excuse for them to keep doing what they were doing. They seemed to be very much enjoying their job at the moment. Then they told him that there was a towel hanging near the tub he put the towel around his waist and the girls finished drying him off. Again, taking their time in doing so. When he was dried and he put undergarments on, they finished dressing him.

He really didn't need them dressing him, he was perfectly capable of doing it himself, but this was probably a once in a life time experience, so he would let them do as instructed. He liked being pampered for once. But he didn't think that he would want to do this all the time. The servants put on a simple but nice blue silk shirt, and some dark blue silk pants and socks and shiny black shoes. All fit him perfectly. He had never worn anything so elegant in his life. He felt rather uncomfortable and awkward in these clothes. When he was dressed, they escorted him out into the broad hallway, where Adara was waiting for him.

Melvin stood there, transfixed by the vision before him. The girl he'd known for cenannums, the one who he spent most of his time with, now stood transformed. Her red silk dress, adorned with delicate rose embroidery, flowed gracefully to the floor. Red — the color of fire, was her signature, and tonight it enveloped her like a warm embrace.

The flame necklace around her neck flickered, casting a soft glow on her skin. Rubies, like drops of blood, nestled in its curves, a reflection of her intensity, her power. And atop her head, a ruby tiara sparkled, its gems catching the light. She was no ordinary girl; she was now a queen, ruling over his heart. He gazed upon her and passion for her welled up inside.

Her red hair, usually tamed in a practical ponytail, now cascaded in loose curls down her back. Each strand seemed to dance, celebrating this moment of metamorphosis. And her face, oh, her face! Perfect makeup accentuated her delicate features, turning her into a masterpiece. Her shining purple eyes, framed by dark lashes, held love within them.

Melvin's breath caught. He'd never seen her like this — stunning, mesmerizing. She was no longer just his best friend; she was a revelation. And as he looked into her purple eyes, he wondered if perhaps this was destiny. In that hallway, surrounded by whispers and music, Melvin realized that love wore many faces. And tonight, it wore the guise of a girl in a red dress, a girl who had always been there, waiting for him to see her anew.

Then his mother came out into the hall escorted by one of the palace guards, who looked exceedingly happy to be doing his job at the moment. She was wearing a light blue floor length dress that sparkled in the sunlight coming through the windows. Her orange hair was put up and she even had on a small tiara. She told him she truly felt like a princess, or a queen at her age. However, she wasn't even all that old, quite young by their standards. She was the same age as Reicuas, 370 annums old. Melvin never really realized, how very pretty his mother was. She had never been done up like this. He knew she was pretty, but looking like this she was very, very beautiful. He wondered why she had never married.

Adara took Melvin's strong hand and gently escorted him to a grand round ballroom. Melvin had never been to this part of the castle before. The many times that he had been there, he went through the back door, and usually just to the kitchen to eat with Reicuas and Adara. This ballroom, it seemed, was larger than Penelope's cavern, which was very large, considering that they were very large dragons.

All around the ballroom were windows letting in the early afternoon sunlight. The same purple and gold drapes, with a gold dragon symbol on them that were in the other room, hung like banners on the walls. There were servants and tables of food everywhere, food he had never seen before was laid before him. He wondered if this was how parties were for royalty all the time. There were guests standing about talking one with another, all finely dressed. There was a band playing sweet music with flutes, violins and other wind and brass instruments. Tables with cushioned chairs sat around a large open dance floor. King Bilby and Queen Aurora sat in their thrones on top a dais, with three of their daughters Aria, Amira, and Anna.

"You said this was a small party." Melvin whispered singing to Adara so he wouldn't stutter. "I thought this was a small impromptu party, not a huge event. I was wondering why we were getting all dressed up. I could tell you were up to something. And not impromptu at all."

She just smiled and winked. "If I had told you it was a BALL in *your* honor, you would have never come." She said with a knowing smile. She took the piece of magical parchment that Reicuas had given him, and let go of Melvin's hand and gave the parchment to her father, then took her place on the stand.

Melvin stood there in amazement. She was right again. He wouldn't have come, if he had known it was all planned. Oh, how he loved her.

When she was seated, King Bilby stood and addressed the people in the room. "My friends," In a booming but gentle voice he started, with his large muscular arms wide to encompass them all. He wore a red silk shirt, black pants and a purple cape hung from his broad shoulders. Melvin thought he saw his mom go week at the knees when she saw him stand. He was a very handsome man, and the queen was very beautiful, sitting in her gold silk dress, also with a purple cape flowing from her shoulders. The princesses all wore the same style dress as Adara. However, they were different colors and different flowers embroidered on them.

The King continued. "We are here to celebrate a great accomplishment. Wizard Melvin has finished his training under the tutelage of High Master Wizard Reicuas, who has been my personal wizard for many annums. And also Princess Adara's and her sisters magic teacher. Melvin has advanced to Master Wizard status just this morning by Reicuas himself. Reicuas was called on a long and important journey and had to leave promptly so he could not be here for the festivities. Everyone in the room cheered for the accomplishment of Melvin. But at the same time were saddened that Reicuas had to go away on a journey.

"My daughter, Amira set up this little "party" he winked as he said it, "for her friend who has accomplished something that has not been accomplished in this land in nearly two thousand annums, the passing of an apprentice wizard to Master wizard status. Reicuas has also bestowed upon this young man a title, by the wizard order of Wazer, he is to be known by the title of *Melvin the Magnificent*. This rev we honor *Melvin the Magnificent* in this great achievement. We also recognize his mother the beautiful Penelope in attendance as well who is the personal tutor of the Princesses and the teacher of many of yours. Let us all show them both all the courtesy that would be shown to myself, the Queen, or any of the Princesses." Then with a loud official voice he declared "Let the party begin."

Cheers and applause rose up from the crowd for Melvin as the music started playing once again. Party goers, including dignitaries, Lords, and other important people throughout the kingdom all came to congratulate him on his accomplishment.

They all had a great time at the celebration. The princesses even showed off their talents. Aria sang, Amira danced, and Anna did a gymnastics routine. Melvin had never seen so much delicious food in one place in his life. He and his mother ate till they could eat no more.

All of the young ladies there, couldn't get enough time with him. For one he was a wizard, a rare thing in this part of the world, and second he had grown into a very handsome strong young man.

When he was younger, as was mentioned, he looked like what you would call a nerd. He was on the smaller side, weak, skinny, and awkward. He wore thick glasses, and his teeth weren't in the best shape. He had a squeaky nasally voice. He was the kind of kid, other kids would put in a locker at school. You get the picture. Over the annums he had conditioned himself to be well fit and muscular. Just as his master had. He also got his teeth straightened and his eyes fixed from a healer. Melvin remembered one of the things that Reicuas taught him, when he was young. One of his favorite things to learn is anatomy. He loved to look inside the body and see how everything worked. Not that a wizard needs to be muscular, but Melvin found manual labor invigorating. He didn't want to have to use his magic for things he could do himself. Over the annums, in his free time, he had learned to do other trades as well as being a wizard, using his talents helps him with these other tasks. He had learned leatherworking, blacksmithing, gardening, cooking, thatching roofs, repairing various items, construction, wood working and the list goes on. His magic does help him with these, but he prefers only to use it when necessary.

"Melvin, my boy," Reicuas told him when he was young. "You will learn how to use your magic to do many things. But remember, nothing is more important than a strong and healthy body. If you are weak, or sickly, or out of shape, that will affect your ability to think and concentrate, and that will affect how well your magic works. So be active, build your body up, and don't do or eat things that will harm your body." Reicuas continued "The reason I prefer to walk everywhere is that it gives me exercise. Keeps me healthy. I could ride everywhere on a qilin or ride in a carriage if I wanted to, however, I choose not to. Stay healthy, eat good foods, keep alert, then you will be able to do marvelous things."

Although Adara had many friends there, and a lot of people to talk to, she found herself wanting to be alone with Melvin. She made it a point to be at his side and introduce him to as many people as possible. She may have slipped the word "boyfriend" in once or twice trying to give Melvin a hint.

They danced, and danced. Melvin danced with all the princesses and all the other female guests, old and young, but couldn't wait to get back to Adara. This had to be the best rev ever for him in his life. He and Adara finally got to dance together again. Adara made sure the band played a slow ballad. She pressed her body close to his, and wrapped her arms around him as lovingly as possible. The feeling was exhilarating. She laid her head on his chest. Hopefully, this would give Melvin her intentions.

Melvin was in heaven. This beautiful girl that he has loved for decannums was pressing her perfect, soft body close. He could feel her warmth, he could feel her heart beat in time with his. Warmth flowed through his body, and not from her talent, but something else. Something more. It was love. Pure love pouring from her soul to his. Why did it take so long for him to understand this? While they were dancing there intimately, Melvin whispered in her ear mostly without stuttering. "Would you go out to the balcony with me?

"Of course. Always." She whispered back tenderly.

After the dance was over, he kept hold of her hand and he walked her out to the balcony. Making sure they were alone, he caught his nerves and sang her a song.

I am not good with words. Since I stutter I should sing I would like to be with you

Please take this ring.

One rev, I would like us to marry

But that will come in time

But until then I would be very happy,

if you would be mine.

On that warm Líten evening, the sea glimmered beneath the breathtaking sunsset, its waves bathed in hues of amber and violet. Adara turned to him, her bright purple eyes glistening like the waves of the sea, as tears slid down her cheeks. In reply to his song, she gave him a special smile—a smile so radiant it could have outshone the suns themselves. Without a word, she stepped closer, slipping her arms around his neck. And then, she kissed him—not a fleeting touch, nor a hesitant gesture, but a deep, lingering kiss. A kiss that was was filled with all the love and longing that had grown between them these many annums, a kiss that spoke of passion, devotion, and an unspoken promise that had been waiting for this very moment to be set free.

Once again, literal fireworks burst in the air. The party goers and those in the city thought it was for the celebration, but Melvin and Adara knew exactly what they were for. But just the same, they fit both occasions. Then Melvin sent his consciousness into the ground, into the nearby mountains and found a deposit of gold. He pulled some out then with his magic there in front of Adara shaped it into a ring. He added a firey hue to it and slipped it onto her finger. Not an engagement ring, mind you, but a promise ring, as was a custom for boyfriend/girlfriends to give one another at their coupling, while they were dating.

Adara was amazed. She did not know he could do this. She was amazed even more and more from all the things that Melvin could do. "How did you do that?" she asked. Staring at the ring on her finger tears running down her face.

"I don't know how to explain it exactly," He said not knowing what the big deal was, "I can just see into things, I just focus, I can search underground, look into bodies, look under water, etc. then I can cause something to come up out of the water or ground. I just told the gold to form into a ring and formed the image in my mind, like how we talk to Penelope and it just forms that way."

"You are amazing, Melvin, truly amazing. You don't know how long I have been waiting for this rev," she said softly, letting her excitement burst out. "I was beginning to wonder if you would ever figure it out. I have loved you ever since that first rev, we met at my practice rock.

Honestly tonight, if you didn't ask me to be your girlfriend, I would have asked you. I just could not wait any longer. I love you, Melvin, and I have for a very long time. And you amaze me more and more every rev." Without hesitation, she threw her arms around him, drawing him close once more. Her lips met his in a kiss that was even more fervent than the first—deeper, more unrestrained. Passion surged between them, mingling with an overwhelming tide of love that seemed to bind their very souls together. In that moment, the world around them faded into insignificance; there was only the two of them, lost in the exquisite euphoria of their shared embrace.

When they were finished, with love woven into the very essence of her being, she fashioned a ring for him— A ring of fire encircled his finger, mirroring the necklace she wore—a bond forged in flame, yet gentle as her touch. It neither burned nor felt hot, but its presence was undeniable, a constant reminder of her and the love they shared. The fire was eternal, unyielding, and harmless, yet alive with the glow of smoldering embers, like burning coals that carried the essence of her spirit. It wasn't just a ring; it was a promise, a connection that would never fade.

They held each other for a long while, then Melvin got the courage to speak. "Adara, I am an idiot."

"Don't say that, Melvin, You are one of the most intelligent people I know." She said softly. "Melvin, there has been something I have not told you. Something I should have told you a long time ago, but just didn't know how or when, the timing just wasn't right, but now I feel I must tell you."

"What is it?" He asked, not stuttering because he was more relaxed. "You know you can tell me anything."

"I know, Melvin, I know." She took a deep breath. Thought swirling through her mind and feelings through her heart like a fiery inferno. *Here goes nothing*, she thought to herself. "Remember that rev we first met? When Reicuas brought you to the palace, when I was practicing my fireballs? I was so terrible back then."

"Yes, I remember that, rev like it was last rev," he said back softly.

"That rev, when you gave me that rose, and I hugged you. Something happened that moment that would change my life forever, it would change me forever. I felt something. A surge of energy, a tingling, and my heart just opened up to you. I can't explain it. That moment I knew I loved you. And I have loved you more and more ever since that moment. That night, I preserved that rose you gave me. It still sits on my bedside table. A constant reminder of you, my love for you."

"I did not know that Adara, I wish I had." He said lovingly, looking into her purple eyes.

"That's not all." She continued softly "That night I made a promise to Deo. A promise to love you, a promise to be by your side, to help you learn your magic and be the best, most powerful wizard that you could become. And I stand by that, even more so now."

Melvin caressed her face and smiled. "I-I-I wish I had known" Melvin said softly. He sang the rest so he wouldn't stutter, "I had the same type of experience that rev myself. That rev when you hugged me, and every time since when we touched, a feeling comes over me. A wave of emotion, love, warmth, and the fuzzies. Also that night I could not get you out of my head. I made a vow to Deo that I would protect you, and I would be your companion. I will always be there for you. But I never really knew how you felt about me until this rev. I wish I had known sooner, then we could have been together a long time ago. I love you so much. I am so thankful for you. You have always been there for me, supported me in everything I do. You have encouraged me, you are the person above all others I can count on. I can trust you with anything. I want to be the same for you."

She kissed him gently on the lips and replied softly looking into his multicolored sparkling eyes, "It doesn't matter that it took so long, we were always together, we were by each others side pretty much every rev, we practiced together, worked together, played together, though we were only friends, we did keep our vows. And I vow to continue that, but more intimately." She smiled again and kissed him again on the lips. "We better get back inside, before they start wondering what we are doing out here."

"I-I-I don't think they are wondering." He said with a chuckle "But you are right. W-w-w-we should get back inside."

They walked back in to the party holding hands, and gave the news to the King, who in turn announced it to the rest of the party. Everyone knew what was happening out there, when they saw the rings. Everyone let up a cheer as they were excited for the new couple, well, most of them anyway, most of the single young ladies were jealous, but they knew it was only befitting a princess to get a handsome Master Wizard. The kingdom knew this was going to happen eventually even though they didn't know when, but this seemed like a fitting time.

Everyone enjoyed the rest of the night. When it was all over, he bid his new girlfriend goodbye, they kissed, and Melvin and his mother went home in the same carriage that brought them there, to his new home, the happiest he had ever been.

CHAPTER 9

REICUAS'S JOURNEY

Reicuas rode to Wazervĭl, the Wizard City. He was excited to meet with old friends. Normally, he would have walked, but this was a long journey and would take him weeks to walk there even speed walking as he could do, instead of revs, as it would be on a qilin. Also, this was important that he get there as soon as possible so he could gather forces, if possible, and stop the Dark wizard Zôltan. He put an enchantment on the qilin to give him extra stamina, so he could run faster and longer to hasten the pace, so he could get there as fast as possible. Still, it would give him a few revs to think.

He hoped he had done the right thing by making Melvin a Master Wizard. He knew he had the capabilities, but wondered if Melvin knew he could do it. Reicuas knew that he would eventually figure it out as he always did, and he had Adara there to help him. He also hoped they would finally get together.

Each evening, when he stopped at an inn, he put on the fancy clothes that Master Wizards of the area usually wore, though he found these to be unnecessary and uncomfortable. He gave the innkeeper an official parchment that stated his status as a Master Wizard and that he was on an errand for the Empress. With this, he was offered the best room and the best food the inn had to offer. Though Reicuas didn't necessarily want the best, he figured once in a while it would be nice to be pampered.

He rode into Wazervĭl, the wizarding capital of the Empire. As he rode down the main street, it looked much different than it had two hundred and fifty annums ago, when he was there last. He looked up and down the streets, and the buildings were much fancier than he remembered. Down the main road, off in the distance, he saw very tall spires of tall buildings and churches glistening in the morning suns. Carts and buggies filled the streets. Shopkeepers showed off their wares, fruit stands were on every corner. Sometimes, he missed this place. Back in the Kingdom of Bilby, they had shops and fruit stands, of course, but not of this size and quantity. His eyes were drawn to the center of the city. There, perched on top of a hill, with grand gardens spreading all around. Tall towers reaching into the heavens several hundred spans into the sky were his Alma Mater. Even though he remembered how the city had looked several annums ago, it had been so long that he could not remember the last time actually was that he had roamed this place. Most of his friends from school had stayed in Wazervïl. Not so much of a small town anymore, though. And some of those friends had become instructors at the school.

As he rode up to the school, it looked like a palace. Well, that's because it used to be one many millennia ago. This city used to be ruled by a king. But since then has become a Democracy, with magistrates and judges to judge the people. Though they were still in an Empire, ultimately ruled by the Empress, she allowed each Kingdom or area to be ruled as they wished. There were many such large cities in the empire.

The tall spires of the school glistened in the sunslight, the well manicured grounds wowed the eye. Students were playing in the grass or sitting on benches. Some were holding hands on an ornate wooden bridge that crossed a brook running through the grounds. He himself had stood on that bridge with a young lady on occasion.

He walked through the tall, elaborately carved doors of the school. They had pictures depicting wizards of the different styles of Wizardry. Light, as he was, Fire, Earth, Nature, Weather, Water, and many others were depicted on the doors. He walked into the grand hall. He remembered the first rev, he stepped foot into this great hall. It looked much bigger compared to now. Almost as large as Percilla's cave. Banners flew in the rafters, and windows on either side of the great hall let in the morning suns. He was greeted by the head master of the School, Ed. Yes, just plain Ed. Well, not actually just Ed, but his actual name was so hard to pronounce, as he came from a faraway land, that everyone just called him Ed. Reicuas and Ed hugged, since Ed was his professor when he was in school, and they became very good friends since both of them were light wizards. Reicuas gave Ed the parchment from the Empress and solicited their help in defeating this evil Sorcerer Zôltan. Ed, of course, beforehand knew of the quest and the circumstances surrounding it, and had prepared some of them to help in this quest.

As Reicuas gathered his supplies and other wizards, he thought about how he could defeat the Dark Sorcerer, Zôltan. Zôltan was once one of their colleagues and a student at the school. He was very bright and did well in magic. His specialty was controlling weather, in particular lightning. He was very ambitious and hungry for power. He liked to study the dark magic of the land. After his schooling was finished, he would visit the leprechauns and other evil creatures and learn their ways and magic. Secretly, he hoped to control them and everyone else. He was right now gathering followers and taking over peaceful lands to increase his control and dominion over them. This was why he must be stopped; if he were not, he would try to take over the world.

Now I bet you are wondering if the Wizards knew of the Evil Sorcerer Zôltan, and why it was Reicuas who was sent to stop him. Reicuas was at the top of his class. When he attended school there, he achieved the status of Master Wizard at only 257 annums old, whereas for most others it takes 350-400 annums. Though he lived in a small village, he was still one of the most powerful wizards in the Empire. Also, Zôltan was one of his closest friends in school, actually his best friend. Possibly, Reicuas could reason with him; if not, he certainly could defeat him.

The school was the perfect place to prepare. It had books he hadn't known existed, which would help him in this quest. He recruited dozens of wizards and wizardesses, who were also masters in the art and wanted to join this quest. They knew it would be dangerous, for the Dark Sorcerer had many magic users besides himself on his side. The First Wizard gave Reicuas the *Staff of Morab,* made by the high elf Madrila herself, which would help him defeat the dark sorcerer.

After the preparations were made and other wizards joined the quest, they set out for the land of the Jĭgabuji.

They set out west to the plains. The Jĭgabuji were to the southwest, on the other side of the continent. They must travel through large forests, plains, and a very large mountain range stood between them and the Jĭgabuji. Unless you could fly, which Reicuas could do with Percilla, if he wanted to. However, he couldn't take a large number of people on the back of a Dragon. So they were forced to go the long way west, through the large forests, plains, and the mountain pass. Each city or town they passed, they showed the official parchment from The Empress and asked for volunteers. Eventually, they came to the capital city of Lilenhamür. There, Reicuas took an audience with Empress Kayla.

CHAPTER 10

THE EMPRESS

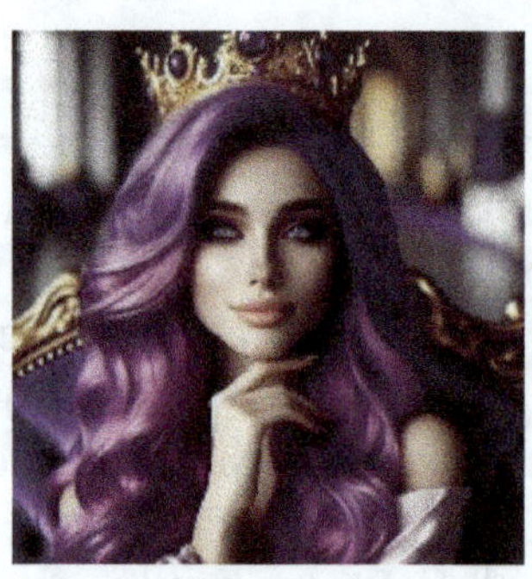

Empress Kayla was a strikingly beautiful young woman. Her bright blue eyes sparkled like sapphires under the dual suns, radiating a captivating brilliance. Her face was a flawless masterpiece, with full, crimson lips framing perfect teeth, and her dazzling smile had the power to warm even the coldest of hearts. Her slender, toned physique was complemented by cascading purple ringlets that flowed gracefully down to the middle of her back, exuding an air of elegance. It was easy to believe she appeared to be 180 annums old.

Beneath her gentle and kind demeanor, however, lay a resolute strength. Kayla was not one to tolerate nonsense, and her wisdom far exceeded her youthful looks, often leading people to assume she was much younger than she truly was. Even the revered sages would seek her guidance and enlightenment when in need. Yet, beyond her remarkable beauty and intellect, she possessed a rare and extraordinary talent—one seldom found among humans in her world.

Reicuas and a few of his most trusted wizards were permitted an audience with the Empress. As they walked into the throne room, which appeared to be the size and look of a very large cathedral, Reicuas looked around and noticed the immense marble statues of past emperors and empresses. Columns, which appeared to be made of gold, lined the red carpet leading up to the dais, where Empress Kayla sat on her throne. Now, you would think that it would be made of gold, or precious wood, or gems, but there you would be mistaken. Given the extended periods of time she spent attending to subjects, she wisely sought out a more comfortable seating option. Opting for practicality, she chose an overstuffed dark purple lounge chair. Its plush cushions enveloped her, providing a cozy retreat from the demands of her role. The rich hue of the chair added a touch of regal elegance to the room, inviting her guests to relax and engage in conversation. As she settled into its embrace, she found solace in its softness, allowing her to focus on her duties with renewed energy and comfort.

"Your Majesty," Reicuas said, arms flourishing, bowing his lowest. "We humbly seek your counsel."

"Reicuas," she said sternly. Her strong, commanding yet childlike voice rang through the air like trumpets playing a fanfare on a joyous occasion. Immediately, everyone in the room was at attention, eyes trained on the Empress.

"Come here!!" pointing to the spot right in front of her.

Reicuas immediately obeyed. And hastened to the spot that she indicated like a scorned child. Then the Empress's voice softened. "Why has it been so long since you have come to see me?" she asked, more like a daughter questioning her father.

"Kayla," he started… Now, this was a very honored thing to be able to do. Not just anyone was able to call the Empress by her given name, most didn't even know what it was. However, Reicuas was no ordinary wizard. He continued, "Sorry, Kayla," he said with a low voice, "I have been training a new apprentice to take over for me when I am gone. I just gave him the level of Master Wizard before I left on this journey."

"So, I have heard." The Empress replied with her eyebrows raised. "I have heard you have been teaching a new apprentice, not only that, but Princess Adara as well." Then she did something very uncommon in meetings like this. She smiled her very beautiful smile, stood up, and gave Reicuas a big hug. "Oh, I've missed you. Come walk with me," she said, and took Reicuas' hand and started walking to the side door that went outside. "The rest of you can make yourselves at home. Guards, escort them and their troops to the banquet room. Tell the kitchen staff to bring them something to eat and drink. They have had a long journey and still have a long way to go and a fierce battle ahead."

They walked to a large wooden side door that was elaborately carved with many animals and dragons, and went outside. As the door closed to the throne room, the Empress motioned for the guards to keep their distance from them, as if they were about to have a private conversation. They walked in a beautiful well well-tended garden. Rose bushes and other flowers grew along marble paths. Fountains dotted the garden area.

"Reicuas", she said sadly, "I have missed you. It has been so long since you taught me how to better use my power. Why haven't you accepted my invitation to be the official Wizard for the Empire? I have had to settle for Wizard Brennen Bailey. Don't get me wrong, he is a very good wizard, the best Wazervïl had to offer, but in my opinion, you were always the best."

"I understand, Kayla. And I am honored." Reicuas said sadly. "I would have loved to come and be the Wizard of the Empire. However, this apprentice needed my guidance more than the Empire needed my parlor tricks. And you know my history, so I'm sure you understand."

"Yes, I do, but it still saddens me that you were away from me for so long. You are like the only family I have left. You have a dragon, you can ride her here for visits a lot quicker than a qilin."

"I am sorry, Kayla, but as I said, I have been training a new wizard. But, there is more to it than that, though."

"I know," she said sheepishly back, "That's why I never pressed you about the position. I knew you had more important matters to attend to."

"Thank you for understanding," He said. Then he took a graver tone.

"I have spoken to no other about this, but this is of utmost importance." He said. Empress Kayla could tell the gravity of his words as he spoke. "There is great darkness upon the land. Zôltan is a very powerful Dark Sorcerer, as I'm sure you know. But there is someone else even more powerful than he who will seek to destroy all we know, and plunge the world we know into darkness for tens of thousands of annums."

"Are you certain? How did you come by this knowledge?" Kayla asked in surprise. "I have had no such impressions, and you know my talent, Reicuas."

"Some of my friends are seers; they have shown me the signs. I do not know who this wizard is, but there are prophesies that tell of him," He said in almost a whisper. "I have seen the books and scrolls in the secret room in the tower in Wazervĭl."

"Then you must stay with me and be the Wizard for the Empire. Protect the citizens from what is to come." She said desperately. "I have not seen this, this is hidden from me. This must be very powerful magic if this is hidden from me. I have not sensed anyone with the power to do so. Yes, Zôltan is a very powerful sorcerer, but I have not sensed anyone more powerful than he. And he can be stopped."

"I don't know if he's alive yet, or if something happens that makes him become this way. Maybe that's why you do not sense him. Not many know this, but I have not spoken of it to anyone. Except for one person. However, you probably know. I was in school with the Dark Sorcerer, Zôltan, in fact, we were best friends. But something happened, and he turned to using Dark Magic. I tried to convince him not to, but he persisted. Maybe this same type of thing will happen to someone else, even more powerful than Zôltan. I am sorry, but I cannot stay. I must go and stop The Dark Sorcerer Zôltan so these prophesies do not come to pass." Then Reicuas stopped and looked Kayla in the eyes. His own eyes shining like the suns, literally. He continued.

"Melvin, whom I took under my wing, is the answer. I have seen him do things no other wizard in thousands of annums could do. His aura has every color of the rainbow. He has discovered his power. He will be more powerful than I can ever be. However, he must be taught how to use it properly."

Kayla was intrigued, but had many questions. But the only one that she could say was, "How is that?" which pretty much summed up all of her questions together.

Reicuas responded, a bit livelier, "I told you about his Aura. He has a talent for just about anything. He can use light, wind, water, earth, ice, fire, he can make things grow, and he can sing. His songs make his magic more powerful, three hundred times more powerful. At least. And…" he let the last word trail off as a cliffhanger. Kayla stood hungering for more information.

"And what?" she demanded softly, her eyes wide open, hungering for more information. "And he has watched the hatching of a Golden Dragon." He said with a smile.

"He what??" she asked, her mouth wide open like a teenage girl hungry for gossip. "A dragon egg? How is that possible?"

Reicuas continued, "I know the mother. That's all you need to know. You know that those who see a dragon egg hatch absorb some of its power. I watched it hatch as well, and gained a bit more power, however, Melvin was right next to the egg. He sang an incantation as the egg was hatching and absorbed an extremely large amount of the dragon's power. Melvin doesn't realize how much power he actually has. Or what he is capable of. Since he knowingly has this ability to absorb magical energy, which is of itself very rare, only the greatest of wizards can do it, he needs to absorb as much as he can to become the greatest wizard possible. Both of his parents are wizards. Although you know who the mother is, no one, including him, knows who the father is. Except for me and his mother. And no, it's not me."

Kayla sat down on a bench. "That I do know." She said. She used her power to look for Melvin and look into his heart. She found everything that Reicuas said to be true. There was a lot more to him that Reicuas didn't tell her. But maybe he didn't know. "I would like to meet him." The Empress said.

"I would like you to meet him as well; however, I think if he were to come here it would overwhelm him. Remember, he is from a small village, and all this grandeur would probably scare him."

"What if I were to go there?" she asked thoughtfully.

"I think that might also scare him. Although he is, and will be, a great wizard, he has only just become a Master. He doesn't know his own potential. He still has a lot of learning to do. However…" Reicuas said stroking his chin with his hand "there still may be a way to meet him and not scare him. As long as you don't reveal what I just told you." He said with a determined look.

"I know more secrets than pretty much everyone in the Empire combined. You know I will keep it to myself." She smiled "How would that be?" She asked still intrigued.

"Melvin is practically engaged to Princess Adara from Bilbylund. But come to think of it, that is hardly a secret at all." He said as if deep in thought. "They are always together. If you set up a visit with King Bilby and invite the whole family, Adara would be in attendance and would most likely bring Melvin and his mother with her. They have become very close. Who in this Empire would not want to meet the beautiful Empress Kayla? During the visit, you could say that you would like to see Reicuas's replacement. He would not be as intimidated, and all should work out just fine."

Reicuas took a more serious tone as he continued. "I would love to stay and visit with you longer, it has been too long and this time has been too short, but we must be on our way to see if we can stop Zôltan before he wreaks any more havoc on the poor plains people."

"I understand Reicuas. I am glad you came to visit. When this war is over, you must come and stay longer, perhaps take me up on my offer. But for now, I will do what I can for you. I will pledge 100,000 soldiers and as many magic users as I can send. Hopefully this will help win this war and have it be over with.

"Thank you, Kayla. That is greatly appreciated. I will seriously consider your offer, though King Bilby will be sad if I leave. I have served him for so many annums, he is like family to me. As are you."

Empress Kayla smiled. Then said, "Reicuas, you have a long journey and a terrible fight ahead. Why don't you and your company stay the night? Dine with me. This will give me enough time to get your forces ready for you. I see a lot of those you have come here with aren't trained military, and could use a bit of merriment before you head off. Most of them won't be returning to their homes. So, a little music, dancing, food, and drink may just help them get their courage up. And you can go in the morning. And, this will give you and I some more time to visit." With this, they hugged and walked back inside.

That night they all ate, drank, and made merry, but also kept in mind that they had an important rev ahead of them and they had to be ready to head out. In the morning the company said their farewells and headed off to the west through the mountain pass.

After the dinner, the Empress went to her chambers and used her talent. With her mind, she again searched for Melvin in the small village where Reicuas was living. She found Melvin practicing magic with the princess. She was shooting fireballs at metal targets, and Melvin was using his power to shoot water to put the fire out. The Empress looked into his mind and heart. She saw someone very kind, gentle, and humble. She was amazed at the amount of magic within him. In all her life, she had never seen so much magical power within a human person. More power than a lot of magical creatures. Truly, he would become an amazing wizard. He would indeed be the one to save them from this terrible darkness. If he could just learn how to harness and use that great power.

Then she decided to look into Adara. She saw the same type of thing inside her. Loving, kind, humble, and a talent for communicating with animals. But more than that, she saw a big fireball within her. Kayla wouldn't want to be around her when she got mad. But also, she saw that she did not know how to fully use her power. She also noticed the love the two shared. These two would definitely be a force to reckon with. She was determined to meet with these two. So, she made plans to do just that.

Chapter 11
Through the Pass

It would take more than a moon to get through the mountain pass, for this was a very large mountain range that cut through the middle of Arion. Fortunately for the travelers, it was late in Líten. The mountain passes were clear of its deep snow, which made traveling through them much easier. However, there were still dangers in the pass.

Zôltan was no fool. In the annums that they have been in school together at Wazervĭl, Zôltan had always been in the top five of his class. He was smart and cunning and had sent multiple spies throughout the land to stay informed of the happenings. So, it wasn't so out of the ordinary that he knew Reicuas' next moves and his meticulous planning, and hence, sent his forces to ambush them in the pass. Just as Reicuas had wizards and wardresses, Zôltan had witches and sorcerers.

With the hundred thousand men the Empress had given him, the best foot soldiers, pike men, archers, mace men, and all sorts of warriors, as well as the magic users, and those he was able to recruit for himself, Reicuas set forth through the mountain pass following the Zigon River.

Though it was late in Líten, traveling through the pass was not easy. It was still warm out, however, the journey was still long and difficult. The road through the pass followed the curvature of the mountains and the Zigon River. There were long switchbacks, and many times they had to cross the Zigon River. Though it was difficult, the views in these mountains were spectacular. They traveled under Cascading waterfalls, as the road rounded the bend in the river. They slept in caves underneath the waterfalls. They camped in meadows and under towering trees. Although they had supply wagons, they also liked fresh fish and meat. They fished in the river for fresh fish, which were plentiful this time of annum. Some nights, soldiers went out in search of wild game. Some animals were large enough to feed an army.

As they continued their journey through the pass, they stopped for the night beside a peaceful lake. In the distance, a waterfall poured into the water, and a quiet river flowed out the other side. Tall trees stood like watchful guardians all around the shoreline, their reflections dancing in the gentle ripples.

That evening, the sunssset was truly breathtaking. Shades of red and pink from the low sunsss painted the sky, while the mountains stood like dark shadows on the horizon. Beams of sunslight broke through the mist forming along the mountain tops, casting golden streaks across the valley. The lake caught every bit of that light, shimmering like it held the sky itself. It was a sight none of them would ever forget. This was one of the most beautiful scenes that Reicuas had seen in a long, long time. He asked the troops if any of them were able to paint this scene, or at least draw it. For it truly was a sight to behold. There was a reply that one of them was indeed a painter, and he painted the scene of that majestic sunsset.

As Reicuas sat and thought about this, a cry rang up from one of the guards. The enemy was attacking. Creatures and men from Zôltan's army had come into their camp. A battle had broken out. The men fought valiantly. Fortunately, there weren't too many of the enemy, so the battle was over pretty quickly.

In the end, the Empress's army won. However, they had lost quite a few men. They would be on their guard, because you never know when they will attack again. There were many casualties on both sides. But most of Zôltan's army was wiped out. Reicuas wondered how Zôltan's men knew where they were. And even though Reicuas knew Zôltan well in the past, he could not have predicted his moves as Zôltan could his. Though for now, all they could do was find a secure place to camp and stay on their guard

CHAPTER 12
ONWARD TO BATTLE

One rev, Percilla told Reicuas of a large valley where they could make camp for the night, maybe even build a base camp. However, getting to it would be difficult. They would have to walk through a system of caves to find the valley. It was surrounded by cliffs all the way around. Percilla told Reicuas that is was a dormant volcano. Reicuas talked with the generals of the troops and agreed that it would be a perfect place to set up their base camp. They sent the scout with the talent for directions to mark the way through the maze of caverns to show them the way. This talent allowed him to always know where he was, which direction he came from, and where he was going. He was the only one who would be able to navigate the cavern without getting hopelessly lost. He marked the right path through the maze so Reicuas and the other troops could get through the maze.

Once the army got through the caverns, Reicuas looked around the valley. The scout was right. It was ringed by mountains. This reminded him of Dragonia, when he went there many annums ago with Percilla.

The valley was huge— from what he could tell, it was about 20 Megaspans wide. Wildflowers of every color dotted the meadows like paint splashed across a giant canvas. Groves of trees stood in quiet patches, and black lava rocks lay scattered all across the valley. A river flowed from the north, cutting through the valley until it reached a wide, still lake at the center. Then the river continued south, further than the eyes could see.

There were only two ways in or out. One was the winding cave system they'd just come through—narrow passages that looked like they were carved by giant claws or maybe even old tools. The other way was over the mountains that loomed high around the valley. But those peaks were far too steep and jagged to climb. You'd need dragons—or something just as powerful—to fly over them.

Reicuas dispatched scouts to determine if the valley was inhabited. Four scouts rode qilins in different directions. Upon their return, one scout reported an ancient settlement on the far side of the valley, possibly hundreds of thousands of annums old. Intrigued, Reicuas set out with a few captains to investigate.

This valley looked like a perfect place for a base camp. It was easily defendable and had the materials to build buildings. The rest were tasked with building a base camp.

They set up a base in the mountain valley. They built crude huts and cabins for the men out of the trees and lava rocks that were scattered around the valley. The other men set up cooking stations and armories. Nature wizards caused more trees to grow for wood. They found seeds from berry bushes and planted them and caused them to grow as well. There were also wild animals roaming the meadow, they sparingly used some for food. They fished in the lake for food as well.

Reicuas and his chosen companions rode with the scout across the valley toward the distant settlement. As they traveled, the valley stretched wider and wider—far larger than it had first seemed. But nothing could've prepared them for what they saw next.

Nestled in the middle of the vast crater was a small town. The buildings were like nothing they'd seen before—made of metal, aged with time but still standing strong. They looked ancient, like they'd been there for hundreds of milleannums, yet somehow untouched by decay. Smooth panels, strange shapes, and silent streets gave the place an eerie, forgotten feel—like a piece of the past frozen in time.

They dismounted their qilins and looked around. Reicuas communicated with Percilla and asked her if she knew anything about these strange buildings. She said they might have been the ruins of a civilization that lived on this world many hundreds of thousands of annums before. These people were much more advanced than they were. Reicuas asked what happened to them. Percilla told him that she was not sure, but she believed they went back to the stars, where they came from. She was sure the Elves would know and suggested he ask them when he returned from this war.

As they explored this little settlement, they were in awe at the things they saw. It looked like they left in a hurry because although everything was overgrown with grass, trees, and vines, it looked like what appeared to be stores that were still stocked with round metal containers, and what appeared to be an inn or a restaurant, still had ceramic dishes on metal tables. Multi-level homes still had furniture, though the outside appeared very weathered and decayed, the inside looked as if they left not long ago. It looked as if they didn't even try to take it with them. They walked down what looked like it used to be a metal street. On either side were poles with what looked like used to have some sort of lights in them, and what appeared to be ropes running from one to the other. They looked like they were well preserved for being that old. As they walked down the street, it rose to a hill. They noticed something peculiar. On the hill, there stood a building that was not like the others. It was not decayed, however, it did have white vines growing on it. It was made out of large, precisely cut, shining stones that glistened when the suns hit them just the right way. It appeared like it was glowing. As they walked up to the building, they stopped in sheer awe. A feeling came over them. A feeling of peace, a feeling of calm, a feeling of reverence. As they looked above the high doorway, there were letters engraved in the stone. They could not read them, but somehow the translation came to them. And not from Percilla.

The engraving said, **"HOLINESS TO THE LORD. THE HOUSE OF THE LORD."**

Reicuas could feel that this was a holy place — a sacred place — and thus, must be left alone. He told his captains to tell their troops that this place was off-limits. Actually, one better. Being a religious man and believing in Deo, Reicuas weaved a spell that concealed this place to anyone whom Deo did not want to find it. Thus, only those deemed worthy in the Deo's eyes would be able to find it. They continued exploring the small settlement. When they had explored the whole settlement, they went back to the camp.

At this camp, they would train the troops, plan, strategize, and prepare for the battles that were ahead. After a moon, the army and supply wagons continued onward to Jĭgabuji, who lived on the other side of the mountains. As they journeyed, Reicuas noticed the sheer awe and beauty of these enormous mountains. Many animals that he had never seen before lived in these mountains.

They passed through towns and villages filled with people who had unusual customs and spoke in strange tongues Melvin couldn't understand. The trees they saw along the way were the tallest he'd ever laid eyes on—towering high above, their tops hidden by clouds. They crossed over wide, rushing rivers that roared through the valleys, and saw waterfalls thundering down from cliffs hundreds of spans high, spraying mist into the air.

Their path through the mountains after that was quiet, with no more trouble along the way.

As they traveled on down the dirt road and out of the mountains, they passed a town at the edge of it. In the city of Ündarhaven dwelt the Gnomes. They tunneled under the mountains in search of jewels and gold. Under the mountain, there was a labyrinth of tunnels that, if you didn't know where you were going, you would get lost and never find your way out. There was a secret tunnel that only a few of the gnomes knew about that led through the mountains. However, like a maze, finding your way through to the other side was extremely hard and dangerous. For traps were set to protect their treasure. Reicuas discovered that the ancestors of these gnomes had tunneled the labyrinth that led to the valley where they made their base. Reicuas made sure that they were safe and set up a magical barrier around the town to protect them from Zôltan's forces. They also left some troops there to protect the gnomes.

Continuing on their way to the Jĭgabuji, the troops stopped at a magnificent city on the lake, called Hammoth-Dōr. Here, the dwarves, who inhabited the city, had many forges. They created magnificent weapons and armor, and other metal items. They had a relationship with the Gnomes at the base of the mountain. The gnomes would tunnel under the mountain and gather ore, then sell the ore that they retrieved to the Dwarves of Hammoth-Dōr. The dwarves would also quarry stone in the mountain. Besides being master blacksmiths, they were also master stonecutters and masons. This was their talent. They could feel the metal and the stone and could talk to it, cut it, and shape it precisely. They could create wonderful items from metal and stone. This city had many magnificent, beautiful stone buildings. They were called upon to build much of the architecture of Lilenhamür.

After resting and replenishing their supplies, they continued south to the land of Jĭgabuji

CHAPTER 13
THE JĬGABUJI

In the vast and sweeping plains of the land of Jĭgabuji, a peaceful people thrived, known for their close connection to the spirits of the earth and their harmonious and simple way of life. They lived in harmony with nature, celebrating the changing seasons and the abundant gifts of the land. But their idyllic existence was shattered one fateful rev, when dark storm clouds gathered on the horizon, heralding the arrival of the dreaded sorcerer Zôltan and his army of foul creatures.

As Zôltan's malevolent forces descended upon the plains people, spreading fear and chaos in their wake, the Jĭgabuji people stood bravely to defend their homes and loved ones. But the dark sorcerer's powers were strong, and soon the once peaceful Jĭgabuji were engulfed in flames and terror.

Just when all seemed lost, a glimmer of hope appeared on the horizon. In the distance, riding on majestic battle-ready armor-clad qilins, the army of the Arion Empire galloped to the aid of the Jĭgabuji. Their armor gleamed in the afternoon suns. Their banners were held high with the symbol of the Arion Empire. Thousands of men, their armor glistening, came to the plains people to rid the empire of this evil sorcerer. As they rode over a hill, the village came into view. The scene was a terrifying one. The huts and grass were burning, corpses of the brave plains people who fought valiantly against Zôltans minions lay spread across the burning village.

Before long, they rode onto the battlefield. Led by their fearless leader, General Aldric, the Arion Military charged fearlessly into the fray, cutting down Zôltan's minions with skill and determination. Arrows flew as the archers deftly dispatched many foul creatures. Earth Wizards caused the ground to open up and engulf the enemy. Other wizards, as well, easily dispatched their enemy. The few remaining Jĭgabuji, seeing that the tide had turned, fought more valiantly.

Zôltan caused dark clouds to come, and darkness hung over the plains. A flurry of lightning strikes lit up the sky and struck the opposing army. Lightning and metal armor do not mix. So, there were many crispy soldiers. To counteract, Reicuas let out an intense beam of light, dispersing the darkness. Light so brilliant that it blinded their foes.

The Jĩgabuji people watched in awe as the tide of battle turned, their hearts filled with gratitude for their unexpected saviors. With a mighty roar, General Aldric, Reicuas, and their wizards and warriors pushed back the dark forces, driving them out of the plains and restoring peace to the land once more. Zôltan's army retreated to their own lands, back to the castle.

As the suns set on the battlefield, the Jĩgabuji people gathered around their rescuers, offering heartfelt thanks and celebrating their newfound alliance. General Aldric smiled, his eyes reflecting the fires of battle, as he pledged to stand by the plains people in their time of need, forging a bond that would endure for generations to come.

After the battle, Reicuas's troops were dwindling, but they must push on. They left a few soldiers to keep watch over the Jĩgabuji and then continued after Zôltan and his army of miscreants.

CHAPTER 14

AT THE CASTLE

Reicuas and those who were left rode to Zôltan's castle. Lightning struck violently all around. Darkness eerily crept into every crevice.

"Zôltan," he called out, making his voice louder with magic than it otherwise could be. "I know you are in there. Why are you doing this? We can work this out."

"No," was the answer with a thunderous lightning strike next to Reicuas. "Now, leave."

"Zôltan, I can't let you continue this." Reicuas pleaded "We can work this out, I know this isn't you. You were my best friend, you still are!"

"I said leave!! We were friends, Reicuas. But not anymore. You can't stop me. I have become stronger than you could ever know." Zôltan replied.

"Why are you doing this? Is it because of what happened in school?" Reicuas asked.

"Are you that naive?" Zôltan asked. "Wizards should rule the world. We possess the magic and the strength needed. Among us, we need a leader who stands above all others. And, Reicuas, I am the mightiest wizard of all time. There should be no doubt why I should stand above everyone else. I should rule the land, even the world."

"You let this power go to your head, Zôltan. You know I am just as strong as you are." Reicuas shouted so he could be heard over the thunderous lightning.

"Then prove it!!" Zôltan said with another show of power. And just then, a fantastical display of lightning lit the skies. Bolts of lightning struck the ground with thunderous cracks that could shatter eardrums. The thunder boomed loudly, the ground shook the trees bent in the wind. It seemed all was in chaos. Then Reicuas parted the clouds, and sunslight shone forth, the sky was lit up like noon rev. There was no trace of the storm left. Reicuas stood there without saying a single word in response to Zôltan's provocation. Showing just the fragment of his power to warn his once best friend of just what he could bring to the table as a last resort to stop him in his evil and destructive ways.

There was quiet for a moment, the remnants of the bellowing thunder echoing around them. Then Zôltan spoke. "Reicuas, I don't want to hurt you. You were my best friend in school, but you cannot stop me now. Leave now, and I will spare you. Stay, and you will suffer the consequences." Zôltan commanded.

Reicuas didn't know what else to do. He summoned all his power and created a light brighter than the suns at mid-rev. The whole castle was illuminated in a flash of light. Heat, hot enough to turn sand to glass, enveloped the castle. Reicuas was sure no one could survive that.

And before he could do anything else, and make the first move. A crackling resounded in the air, making the air around them heavy and hard to breathe, charged. All of a sudden, Reicuas felt 10 thousand volts of electricity running through his body, He was paralyzed, unable to move. Pain shot through his body, starting from the top of his head through his chest, down his legs, then out to the ground under him. Leaving nothing but absolute blackness behind.

Reicuas was knocked unconscious.

CHAPTER 15
TRANSFERENCE

"What do you mean it isn't ready to hatch yet?" the Dark Sorcerer Zôltan scowled. "We have been waiting too long, we are nearly ready with the preparations it MUST hatch when we are ready." Lightning burst around the marble castle, it was nearly time for the great storm, the time during the annum, when the lightning burst in such intensity that you could feel the electricity in the air. Only a few with the talent could control it. This sorcerer was one, who could. Although he could create lightning, he could also direct real lightning when it struck and use it to horrify his subjects. There was a reason why his castle was high in Voltarian Plains. There were lightning storms very often. This one in particular was a very large storm.

"Yes, Lord. I will try to hasten the progress." A small thin wizard in dark robes answered.

"All the preparation and the time is nearly at hand. Do you two have everything you need to proceed?" he said in a dark menacing voice.

"Yes, my Lord, it is. We are ready." They answered in unison with shaky voices. "Is the sacrifice ready?" Zôltan asked cooly. His soft smooth voice demanding respect.

"Yes, my Lord, he is ready." He said with a shaky voice

"Then when the hatchling is ready, we will begin the transference." The lightning strikes came closer together.

"It is time." said the soft cool menacing voice beneath the black hooded cloak. "When I am ready, I will direct the lightning to the egg to break the shell and to kill the sacrifice. Make sure the sacrifice cannot see. You recite the chant directing all of the force, all of the magic to me."

"Yes, Lord Zôltan, as you command." they said bowing.

Then from the darkness, came flashes of lightning Zôltan directed one to hit the wizard lying on the table and the other to hit the dragon egg. The blind fold shifted and the wizard could see the egg. It was happening, the egg started to crack. Bits of smoky black colored shell broke off. Black smoke came from the egg and surrounded Zôltan, and the sacrifice. He could feel its dark power go into him. A small dragon head appeared out of the egg. Then the wizards that stood on the sacred platform chanted the incantation for transference of power. All of a sudden, the dragon came out of the shell, a stream of black smoke spewed from the shell into the air, they all could feel the magic come from the hatching dragon especially the sacrifice, since he was right next to the egg. As the lightning flashed, you could see the black smoky auras of the two wizards come from them and into Lord Zôltan.

When the lightning stopped, all was pitch black and silent. Then the horrifying screams of a man pierced the silence and could be heard many decaspans away. Three wizards lay on the ground, and one on a black marble alter, none of them moved. In the stillness and pitch black of the night, a smoky black baby dragon squealed for its mother.

The morning rays of sunsshine hit the tower of the castle. Through the slit opening sunslight shown on the wizard on the alter. He stirred, all of a sudden an immense pain shot through his body. He thought he needed to get in to the shadows, and then he dematerialized into a waif of smoke and floated to the shadows of the round tower. Once there, he rematerialized and looked around. The three other wizards were dead, shriveled and looked like they were burnt in an oven. A small black baby dragon was changing back and forth from solid to smoke, scared, alone, not knowing what to do.

Something had happened to his mind when he went through that experience. Most of his former memories were gone. Though he had fragmented memories of the magic from the baby dragon flowing into him changing him. Like sort of an amnesia he forgot who he was, forgot his former life, even his name, so he decided to make one for himself. He called himself Rellik, Lord of the Shadows. He surmised that when the dragon magic flowed into him with the addition of the lightning somehow, he got the abilities of that dragon, and could now only live in the shadows. He could no longer be in direct sunslight. That was deadly to him. He didn't know about other types of light though, but he had to remain in the dark, he was the dark. He was now shadow. Well more of a dark cloud of mist. He could appear and take physical form, but if it were in the light it caused him great pain.

As time went on, Rellik learned that he had new powers and abilities. The magic transferred to him from the other three wizards and the baby dragon made him more powerful than he ever was before. But as he gained this power he wanted even more power. He knew things he did not know before, he did not know if he got it from the other wizards, or if he knew it already, but one thing was clear. He had to get dragon eggs and watch them hatch. He remembered seeing that egg hatch and knew the power of that hatchling flowed into him, he also remembered that when you see a dragon hatch you gain control of that dragon. He wanted both, power and a dragon army, as well as other creatures and humans, then he would be able to rule the land, the world.

But there was something else. Something in the back of his mind. It felt like the presence of another being, another person was in this same body with him. He did not know how that had happened or who it was. Was it one of the three others that lay in that tower? He tried to communicate with this other being, to see if it would align himself with his desires. Alas, he would not, so, Rellik had to devise a way to subdue it, control it if he was going to rule the world.

Chapter 16
A Rev of Mourning

A few moons had passed since Reicuas had went to battle with Zôltan.

The light time was unusually dark. There were no clouds in the sky, but the light time just seemed not as bright as usual. Melvin was working on thatching the roof of the house when Adara rode up on her Qilin.

Adara dismounted and walked towards the house. She was as beautiful as ever. This rev she wore her official princess clothing instead of her normal riding gear. Which Melvin thought odd.

Melvin looked down from the roof. "Morning Honey" he called down. He could tell something was wrong. First, she was wearing her official clothing, Second, she did not have her usual bounce in her step. Her face was pained, her shoulders slumped. She kind of shuffled. Melvin expected her to come this rev, but now he was worried. He had never seen her like this. Did she have a hard rev of training the rev before?

Adara looked up, which she didn't feel like doing, and saw Melvin thatching the roof. He had his shirt off and his muscular body shined in the sunslight. He had a tan from all the time he spent outside working on the house. She could just stand there and watch him work for hours. Feelings of passion welled up inside her. However, this was not the time for passion. This was a sad rev, a somber rev. She hated having to come tell Melvin the news that she was tasked to deliver. The king could have sent a squire, or a messenger hawk, or some other communication. But this news, she thought, she must deliver herself.

"Melvin," she called quieter than she normally would. "Please come down, I have some news I need to share."

After he came down from the roof he asked, "What's wrong sweetheart?" wiping the sweat off his face then put his shirt back on. He put his hands on her shoulders. He could see her aura was somewhat diminished.

She continued. "We should probably talk to your mother as well." They hopped on their qilins and rode to his mother's home which was not that far away, about 500 spans.

Adara knocked on the door and Penelope answered. "Come in you two, you know you don't need to knock, remember this is your home too." She said motioning for them to come in. She was busy in the small kitchen fixing her mid-morning meal. "Sit down, have something to drink. H…"

Adara cut her off. "Penelope," she said quietly but in an official tone. "This is not a social call. You are the one that may want to sit down. We will all sit down." Adara did not sit casually, like she usually did when she visited with Penelope and Melvin, she sat like a princess on official palace duty. Once they all got settled she continued. "I have some unfortunate news I must tell you. We got news from the Empress this rev. Some of the soldiers that went with Reicuas to fight Zôltan returned." Adara took Penelope's hand gently with one hand and put her other hand on Melvin's leg. "Reicuas was not with them, they said, he was killed in battle. He was struck by a lightning bolt from Zôltan. He did not make it. As soon as Reicuas was dead, Zôltan told the rest of the troops that the battle was over, he would not fight them, to go home to their families. Some of them tried to storm the castle. Immediately, they, too, were struck by lightning. And lightning and metal armor do not go well together. You can imagine what happened to them. So, the rest fled."

They all started sobbing, for Reicuas was special to all of them. For Penelope, Reicuas was her best friend. They were friends from their youth, they went to school together. And spent a lot of time in each others company afterwards. For Adara, he was her teacher, her master wizard. Like a second father to her. For

Melvin, Reicuas not only his master wizard, and teacher, but he was like the father he never had. Melvin never knew his real father, but Reicuas was as close to one that he ever had. They sat there for a long while just dazed, mourning at their loss. However, they knew that the journey he was sent on, this might have been the outcome. Later that rev, Adara cried throughout the small town there was to be a gathering at the town square at eventide. All the townspeople came to the square and Adara announced her solemn message. Reicuas had died in battle. All at once the ladies of the town wailed and sobbed as was the custom. Not only because it was the custom, but also because he was truly loved by the towns people and would be sorely missed.

Adara spoke up again and finished the announcement. "Reicuas knew he might not return from this battle. So, instead of mourning he wanted us to throw a celebration of life for him, remember the good times, share stories of fond memories. For he went back to our Father who gave us life. He entered into his glory in the heavens above. So, let us celebrate."

They townspeople cheered. Instead of mourning, they had a celebration. Although Adara could have gone back to the palace, she opted to stay in town with the people. Melvin and his mother and the town's people were glad to have her there. Melvin also communicated with Penelope, his dragon, that Reicuas had died. She responded that she knew, and she was sorry for him, and his family, and her mother was Reicuas's dragon.

Melvin did not know what to do.

In the revs, moons, and annums that followed Melvin fell into a deep depression. He did not feel like doing anything. The man he considered a father was gone. He was his teacher, his master, his friend. It was hard for Melvin while Reicuas had been gone, but, at least, Melvin had the hope that he would be back. Now he would never come back.

Adara, and others tried to console him, to comfort him, but his mind was in such a haze that he mentally could not function. One rev Adara was at Melvin's house. They were sitting on the couch that Mclvin had built many annums ago. Adara was trying to console him when finally she had had enough.

"Melvin." She said lovingly.

"Yes, sweetheart, what is it?" Melvin replied in somewhat of a daze.

"You know I love you." She said tenderly. Looking into his amazing multicolored eyes. Her heart swelled for sadness for him. She knew what he was going through, she missed Reicuas as well as he did, She was very close to him as well. She grieved the loss of her teacher and mentor. Finally she had to get through it and get on with life. She was still hurting inside, but she had duties to attend to and so did Melvin. She knew it was not doing him or anyone else any good for him to continue in this state. Melvin had to get on with life.

"Yes, I know" he said softly. Not knowing what she was getting at.

"You know I am always here for you right?" she asked. Her hand in his.

"Yes, I know that too." He replied.

"Can I tell you something?" she asked tenderly .

"You know you can tell me anything Adara." He said rubbing her hand. "Snap out of it." She demanded.

"What?" he asked.

She paused between each word. "I- said-, Snap –out- of- it." Then her voice softened. She looked Melvin straight in his multicolored eyes and continued. "Reicuas is gone. And nothing will bring him back. We all miss him. I miss him, your mother was a wreck for a long time, but she has for the most part continued on. But you haven't."

"He was the closest thing I had to a father." Melvin responded slowly in a hushed tone "I never knew my real father, and now Reicuas is gone, too. Who will I look up to now? Who will teach me and guide me? "

Adara rubbed his arm and continued. "Who will lead you? And teach you? Who do you think?" She asked. Sharply. Then softened her tone again. "You will always have me, and you know you can always go to my dad for advise about anything. And your mother is the most knowlegable person I know. She knows everything about everything. But most of all, this should be a time you turn to Deo in prayer. He is the Creator of the universe,He is all knowing, All powerful. So, if *ANYONE* is able to teach you and guide you. It would be Him." Now her tone got a little more animated and a bit louder.

"Now, about Reicuas, What did he have us do when we got the news that he had died? Did he have us mourn?Did he have us wail and be sad? No. He wanted us to throw a party to celebrate his life. Reicuas would not want you to be all mopey for annums after his death. You are disgracing his memory. He would want you to be happy for him. He has graduated this life. Doesn't the gospel teach us that you return to that Deo who has created you, after this life, if you were righteous during this life? Reicuas was a righteous man. Reicuas is wrapped in the arms of our Creator. Now Melvin, Stop being selfish. Let go. People are counting on you, people need you. Didn't you make a promise that you would always be there for me, protect me and all that? Well you can't do that if you are moping around all the time. I know it will take time and effort, but I am here to help you through it. I will always be right by your side. Now get your butt up, go outside and do something. Then she took his hand and walked him outside to the bright sunsshine.

"You are right, Adara. You always seem to find a way to help me out of my slump." Then he kissed her. That rev, they rode their qilins on the beach, and just enjoyed eachothers company. It was the best rev Melvin had had in a long long time. Although, he still missed Reicuas tremendously, it didn't stop him from doing what must be done.

CHAPTER 17
THE EMPRESS COMES FOR A VISIT

Several Annums later.

A beautiful afternoon, the sky was bright and clear Melvin was outside of his house planting flowers. He could have just grown them with his magic, but he liked the feel of the dirt in his hands, although he did put a trickle of magic into the flowers and dirt so they would grow well, and all annum round. Even in darken. You wouldn't recognize the house from before Reicuas gave it to him.

He built a porch on two sides of the house, added a flower garden in front, put in some large windows in the front as well, because to Melvin, it didn't have enough natural sunslight. He rethatched the roof, painted it and planted some trees. On the inside, it was completely remodeled.

When Reicuas lived there, it was one large room, with a kitchen, hearth, living area, dining area, storage area, and a place for brewing potions. Books and scrolls were scattered everywhere and a separate bedroom that was also filled with potions, scrolls and other wizardy items. In the few short decades that Melvin had had it, it was completely redone. Melvin had cleaned all of Reicuas's things and stored most of it in a shed he built in the back yard. He kept the scrolls and the books, which he read and discovered a wealth of knowledge there in. He added a room where he could brew potions, though this was not one of his strong suits. He separated the living room from the kitchen and dining room, added shelves for the many books and scrolls Reicuas had left for him. Plus a separate larger bedroom for when he would finally take a wife, hoping that it would be Adara. He was sure it would be. Though it was close to town, the house had quite a large plot of land around it. In your reckoning, it would be about 5 acres. He started growing a garden in back, had a stable for the qilins, and a large workshop so he wouldn't have to build and tinker in the house. He also built a building for Adara to practice her fire magic in. Though she was much better with her fire magic, she still wanted a contained place to practice. At some point, he hoped, this would be her home too. He wondered why he hadn't asked her to marry him yet. Things were good how they were. He didn't know if he was ready for that step yet.

Just then, Adara came riding up on her qilin. They loved taking qilin rides together. Even more, they loved riding Penelope together. Penelope was more of a presence in Bilbylund, as was Percilla. Reicuas's Dragon. But now that he was gone, Adara sometimes rode her. Percilla was glad to have someone to be with. "Darling," Adara said with a wide beautiful smile. "I have some great news."

"What is that sweetheart?" Melvin asked curious looking up from the ground hands holding a glowing chrysanthemum plant.

Adara dismounted from her qilin and walked over to Melvin. Melvin saw her and his heart skipped a beat. She was so beautiful. She was wearing her riding clothes. Tan pants and a red blouse. She had her long red hair in a ponytail as usual and the suns reflected off her bright purple eyes. He smiled as she walked up to him. He loved the smell of her scent. It intoxicated him. She smelled like BBQ Brisket.

Adara saw the glowing plant and thought nothing of it, *this is Melvin here, he does stuff like that.* "The Empress is coming for a visit," she said with a huge smile. "Dad told me that she likes to visit all the rulers in the land every once in a while, so tomorrow she will be coming here. She would like to meet Reicuas's replacement. They are putting on a splendid ball for the Empress. You will go won't you?" she asked, more like made it a statement.

"Do you even need to ask? I mean it's the E-E-E Empress. I-I-I hear she's very beautiful, Kind, gracious and young. Who i-i-in their right minds wouldn't like to meet the Empress? Good thing I have a Princess for a g-g-girlfriend."

"Yes, the Empress is pretty incredible. And you could have any girl in this kingdom, a lot of them are a lot prettier than I am." she said with a pouty look "And Melvin, You," pointing her finger at him, and said matter- of-factly, "are a Master Wizard. You are the wizard for the Kingdom, You are just as important if not more important than I am. And also, Although your stuttering is getting much better, You still have to work on it. Especially when you are anxious or excited."

"I-I-I-I know I have t-t-to work on it. And, I-I-I wouldn't want any other girl in the kingdom, and YOU are the prettiest girl in the kingdom. I see how all the guys faun over the princesses, and out of you four, you are the best. Your fiery red hair, your amazing bright purple eyes and those cute freckles, so adorable. And your red full lips. So kissable." As he gave her a quick kiss on the lips "And who else can shoot fire out of their fingers? I mean WOW!" He said with a chuckle.

With this Adara smiled. "I know you can shoot fire out of your fingertips just as well." she said playfully. She was the lucky one. Who else in the kingdom could have a Master Wizard for a boyfriend? Not only that, but one that would become the most powerful wizard in the world. She could see his Aura it was big and bright and full of color and wonder. She knew maybe better than he did all the magic he could do. He had all the talents of any other wizard she ever knew of. Not only that, he was handsome, humble, kind, had a killer body, strong, and everything else a girl could want. She loved watching him do manual labor, though he didn't have to, he found it invigorating. She loved watching the sweat glisten on his muscles. The determination in his eyes to get the job done right. He could be rich if he wanted to, but that wasn't important to him. Helping people is what he liked to do, like her sister Amira. His only problem was his lack of confidence in himself. Something she was trying to help him with. She was afraid though, afraid that when the young Empress met him, she would instantly take him away to work for her. Adara wouldn't like that, but she knew the devotion and love that Melvin had for her, so she wasn't all that worried about them being separated. And she was determined to help him learn all that he could, so he would be the greatest wizard, that she knew he could be.

"I have ordered a royal carriage to pick you up in the morning, and servants in the palace to get you ready for the ball."

"Why can't I just take my qilin?" He asked. Melvin didn't like making a spectacle of himself. He didn't like dressing up, he liked just plain ol' clothes the best. Pair of trousers and a tunic, nothing fancy. Besides all those fancy clothes made him itchy and felt constrained.

"Melvin," Adara said sternly. She looked him right in his beautiful sparkling eyes. "This is the Empress.

You don't just wear any old thing to a ball with the Empress."

"You know I don't like getting all dressed up. Makes me feel uncomfortable, besides, I have nothing to wear that's nice like that."

"You're silly Melvin. Remember, it's the Palace. We have all kinds of clothes you could wear."
"I would just rather wear a tunic and trousers like I have on."

"I know you would Melvin," Adara said tenderly putting her hand on his muscled chest. "That's one of the things that I love about you. You are humble, You like simple things, But…" she said that part sternly. "You know that won't fly Melvin. If it were just a visit with my dad, or his officers, that would work. They know how you are, but this is the *EMPRESS*" she said getting frustrated. She loved Melvin. Loved him for his simplicity, his humility, but sometimes he just needed to get out of his comfort zone and dress up nice. Especially for the Empress. "I'll tell you what." She said softly in his ear, putting her arms around him. "We have some of Reicuas's old robes he used while meeting with dignitaries from other lands at the palace. Not too fancy, but fancy enough for this gathering." Then she smiled, batted her eyes, and put on a sexy look "Do this for me and I'll make it worth your while."

"Ok, ok," he sighed "if it will make you happy, I'll wear some of Reicuas's robes."

"Thank you," she said softly then gave him a long kiss on the lips. When they broke she asked "You need some help with those plants?"

"I don't think they need any fire." he said jokingly. She shot him a harsh look, "Ok, if you want to." he said sheepishly. Then they both laughed.

They spent the rest of the afternoon planting flowers in the garden in front of the house. She was hoping, that although she was a princess, one rev this would be her home too.

The next morning a purple and gold carriage rolled up in front of Melvin's house. Melvin walked outside to a gathering crowd, everyone wondered what a carriage was there for. Everyone in the kingdom knew that Melvin and Adara were a couple, so it was no surprise to see her there when she came. Which was often. But there was rarely a royal carriage there for him. Especially the Kings own personal carriage. The doorman came and opened the door for Melvin to get in. When he got in, he noticed Adara was in the carriage as well.

"What are you doing here?" he asked.

"I just thought I would ride along with you. Make sure you got in the carriage and behaved yourself." "Well, you have me pegged don't you? You know I hate riding in these things." He said as he climbed in

and sat next to his sweetheart.

"I know it makes you feel uncomfortable." She then slid over right next to him and held his hand, gave him a kiss on the cheek, then put her arm around him and snuggled in close. "Maybe this will make the trip go a little better and you may enjoy it a bit more."

"You win," He said with a sigh. He sat back and she played with his hair while the carriage took them to the palace. He enjoyed the ride.

Once inside the palace, they separated and he was led to a bathroom where some pretty servant girls proceeded to give him a bath, which he thoroughly enjoyed. He thought they were enjoying their task as well as they were taking their own sweet time bathing him, washing some parts more than once. They opted not to use wash rags and used their hands instead. They used the reason that this would clean him better. But he was sure of the real reason, and he guessed he couldn't blame them. He wondered why he didn't come here more often. After the bath the ladies dried him off, and again took their time with it. Melvin actually didn't mind. Then they got some of Reicuas old clothes and robes for him to choose. One of the robes was purple with a simple design of a gold dragon on the back, kind of looked like Penelope. He thought he could live with that one. So, he let the girls put the robes on him, as well as some dark purple suede shoes. He then headed out into the hallway where Adara was waiting for him. She wore the same red dress as she did when he became a master wizard, a few annums prior, and wore her ruby tiara on top of her head. Her hair flowed down her back in loose curls. She had on just enough makeup on to accentuate her beautiful face, but not over done. He thought she looked amazingly beautiful.

Adara saw him come out of the room. She couldn't believe her eyes, her wonderful boyfriend was all dressed up. She thought he looked very handsome, very wizard like, and noble. But she could tell he was a bit uncomfortable in this robe. "It will be alright" she said as he walked up to her. "Just one party, then you can take those robes off."

"Actually, these aren't too bad. Kinda comfy, and I have some of his pants and tunic on underneath though." He raised his arms and turned around. "Not too flashy."

"Well, I think you look handsome. A proper wizard." she nodded. She took his hand and they walked to the grand ballroom where the ball was to be held.

Once the Empress arrived, the party officially commenced. Adara and Melvin navigated through the crowd of people stopping to shake hands of the nobles and dignitaries and other important people from the kingdom and surrounding areas. They ate, and danced and ate some more. The Empress stood on the dais and greeted guests with a beautiful sincere smile. Adara was right, she was very beautiful, and young. She looked to be about one hundred and eighty annums. Which in their reckoning is very young. People on earth, would would consider her to be about 18 years old. She had the perfect figure. Her red full lips curved up into an infectious smile that lit up the room. Her bright blue eyes were sparkling in the afternoon light, her long loosely curled purple hair brushed her bare back. She had the face of an angel, soft and smooth. She wore a shimmering blue dress that hugged her body. All the men couldn't help but stare at her.

Once Melvin and Adara got to the Dais, the Empress got all giddy, and you thought Adara was giddy to be able to meet the Empress, for this was a special and rare honor.

"You must be Adara." Empress Kayla said with a huge smile. "And you must be Master Wizard Melvin, who Reicuas put in, in his stead."

"Yes, your excellency," they said in awe.

"Enough of this, Your Excellency stuff." She said with a smile, "Reicuas was my teacher and was my very dear friend. I am so sorry that he was lost in the war with Zôltan. He has told me about you when we met last. He came to see me on his way to confront Zôltan. He sends his love. I am excited to be able to meet both of you. Reicuas isn't the only one who spoke of you two. You are known throughout the Empire. You can call me by my name, Kayla." Then she paused a moment, then looked at Adara. "I hear, Adara, that you can command fire." Just then, Adara smiled and put up her pointer finger, and a flame emerged on top of it. "Impressive. But I also know that you can do more than that." Empress Kayla said with a wide, genuine smile. "And I hear you…" looking at Melvin, "are an extraordinary wizard," she said slowly, smiling, her bright blue eyes sparkling. She may have been the Empress, but she was still a woman and a very pretty one, and Melvin was a very handsome man. Looking at him made her heart flutter. She looked into his amazing multicolored eyes. Eyes that looked like a thousand stars dancing in the night sky. They just drew her in, she had to concentrate to focus on the conversation. She knew all the ladies at the ball were fawning over him, and now she knew why. She could demand that he come to Lilenhamür and be her personal wizard, but she also knew the love that Adara and Melvin shared, and both of their destinies, so she would not do that.

"Some people have said that," he said humbly, "I guess I have many magical talents, but I don't like to show off."

Adara interjected, "Don't be modest, Melvin. Everyone knows you are the best wizard anyone has seen in a long, long time. Master Reicuas is a great wizard, don't get me wrong, but you,

you can do things that no other wizard can do. See this ring?" she asked while showing Empress Kayla the ring Melvin had made for her. "Melvin somehow got this gold to come out of the ground *by itself.* Then, he fashioned this ring without any tools. Just sang to the metal and told it what to do, and it did it. Have you seen or heard of any other wizard being able to do that?"

"Very impressive. I have not heard of one wizard doing all that," the Empress said, eyes wide in wonder. "I see the ring on his hand, Adara, looks like flames that do not burn. Like a living tattoo. Did you do that?"

"Yes, I did," she said, smiling.

"That is very impressive as well. I have heard of no one who can work with fire like that. Sure, they can blow things up, which is pretty cool in itself, but nothing like that ring. I see that you two are a couple and love each other very much. Are you two married?" The Empress asked with a smile. She knew the answer, but asked anyway.

"No, Empress, we haven't gotten that far yet," Melvin said. "Engaged?" she asked expectantly.

"No, not that either, just promise rings. But we are considering." Adara said, "We wanted to wait a while till Melvin finished his studies. Although he is a master wizard, there is still much for him to learn."

Empress Kayla thought for a moment. "I have decided. I want you two to come visit me in Lilenhamür. You two are welcome any time, as well as the King and Queen, and your sisters, of course. And Melvin, your mother is welcome as well. Also, when you two do get married, and from what the whole kingdom thinks, as do I, hope it is soon, it will be at Lilenhamür. I know, Melvin, that you don't like grandeur and fancy things. You don't like the spotlight like many others do. Reicuas has taught you well, he did not either. But let me tell you, Melvin. It isn't always bad. Sometimes you just have to accept the fact that you are an incredible wizard with extraordinary powers, and there are going to be occasions when people are going to want to be in your company, do things for you, or ask you favors that no one else can do. People will want to invite you to parties and balls, give you free rooms at inns, and all kinds of things. You may not realize this, Melvin the Magnificent, even though you live in a small village, you are already famous in the Arion Empire. And as time passes, and your ability grows, you will become more famous. But I know you are not the type of person to take advantage of it. You are humble. Stay that way."

Adara nudged him and whispered in his ear, "See, I told you."

The Empress then stood up and waved off the others waiting to talk to her. "Come. Dance with me," she said with a smile as she held out her hand for Melvin to take. Then she spoke to those others waiting. "I will return to converse with the rest of you in a moment, but I must first have a dance with this handsome young wizard." Many thought this was an odd thing for her to say since she looked like she was younger than Melvin was.

This came as a shock to Melvin, not so much to Adara, since she knew the Empress thought he was handsome. As did all the other maidens in the kingdom, maybe even the Empire. But the real reason the Empress wanted to dance with him was to tell him something so no one else could hear. She could have summoned him outside, or had an official meeting in one of the palace rooms, but knowing how Melvin was, she knew that this was the best way to discuss what she needed to with him. Plus, she had other, more personal motives. She told the musicians to play a long, slow ballad. The longer the better.

Melvin was in awe. The beautiful Empress of the Arion Empire wanted to dance with him. Nothing against Adara, for she was very beautiful herself, but Empress Kayla was the most beautiful woman he had ever seen. As he put his arm around her waist, and felt her soft, smooth skin of her back. It sent tingling through his spine. He took her soft, dainty, delicate hand in his. He felt like he was going to break it just by touching her. She then pressed her body close to his, he could feel her warm body against his. He could feel her breasts pressing against him. Shivers again went up his spine. This was not the typical ball dance that was usually done, but an intimate dance. It was almost more than he could handle. This was an extremely rare privilege for anyone in the Empire, and no offence to his beautiful girlfriend, he was going to enjoy every moment of it.

Empress Kayla was not void of feeling, though she needed to act tough and professional almost all of the time, sometimes she had to let her guard down and enjoy herself. This was one of those times. Melvin was very handsome, very muscular, and very humble. She pressed her body as close to him as she could, one of the guilty pleasures of being the Empress. She could feel his tight muscles against her body, she felt the strong hand on her back, and in her hand. It sent shivers down her body. She could feel both of their heartbeats beating in unison. Emotions of longing welled up inside her. Tingling sensations were felt throughout her body. She started having thoughts unbefitting of an Empress towards this young handsome man. She very well could have him come to Lilenhamür. Now she knew how Princess Adara felt. She was a very lucky young woman. She was happy for Adara, who was able to hold Melvin any time she would like. She was sure he made her feel this way as well, but then again, their destinies are entwined. She had to get her head out of the clouds and deal with the task at hand.

As they danced close together, Kayla whispered softly in his ear. Her sweet, melodic, soothing voice made Melvin feel warm and comfortable. "I wanted to talk to you privately without anyone else hearing," she said. "I know I could have summoned you to my chambers, or gotten you alone some other way, but to tell you the truth, I prefer this method." She blushed. "Now, to what I came here for." She took a long breath and smiled. She was enjoying this as much as he was, maybe even more.

"Don't let your lack of self-confidence hinder you from your ability to reach your full potential. I see greatness in you if you just let it happen. Stop being afraid of your feelings and your abilities. You have more power in your little finger than all the wizards in Wazervïl combined. Remember that!! You just need to learn to use it."

She continued, "You have a very beautiful, wonderful, strong, powerful, faithful woman by your side. She will never leave you. Adara loves you more than you can imagine, even if you don't realize it, and even if she doesn't tell you how much she loves you. She has been waiting a long time for you to ask her to marry you. She will be there as you learn to hone your skills and your power. And as you have been doing, you will be able to help her develop hers as well. I am not sure if you can comprehend how much she loves you. And I know how much you love her. So, for heaven's sake, ask Adara to marry you. As soon as possible."

"H-h-h-how do you know a-a-a-all this? D-d-d-do people tell you all this stuff?" Melvin was getting much better with his stuttering, however, the Empress made him nervous, so he tended to stutter a bit more.

"No, Melvin, they don't." She spoke softly, shaking her head. "Do you know why I am Empress?" "I-I-I-I s-s-s-suppose you were next in l-l-line."

"No, Melvin. It's because of my talent. My family is not royalty. Barely nobility. But I can read people. I can see things in people that no others can. I can see potential, I can see what they are seeing, and feel what they are feeling. I know what's in their hearts. If anyone is plotting against anyone, I can tell. If someone loves someone, a person's true intentions, I know. I was put in this position for the safety of this Empire. I even sometimes have visions and dreams. Though I am no prophetess, they always come true. Deo has put me in this position for a reason. Deo has seen fit to give you these powers for a reason." she paused, thinking of how to tell Melvin the next part. This was something only her most trusted associates knew. "I am much older than anyone realizes. Except maybe the elves. I am over fifty thousand annums old."

"Y-y-y-your what??" he said in shock. "So I-I-I-I'm dancing with someone old enough to be my great, great, great grandmother? I'm dancing with an old lady?" he chuckled.

She giggled as well. "Yes. The elves put an anti-aging spell on me when I was about 180 annums old. In this time I have aged about 40 annums. They did this for the security of this land. I would be able to tell if anyone was going to attack this empire far in advance. If anyone was plotting anything against the empire. Any secret plans done in back alleys and questionable establishments. Believe me, because of my ability, I have been able to stop many plots against the empire before they have happened." She paused for a moment to let that sink in. Plus, she wanted to enjoy this intimate dance with Melvin.

"There is another reason I wanted to speak to you, this rev." She spoke in his ear, barely a whisper. Her warm breath in his ear sent shivers down his spine. "There is a great darkness that I see befalling this land in the future. Not immediately, but perhaps in about 40 to 50 Annums or so. I see that you and Adara are the only ones who will be able to stop this. You will have to travel great distances, even to the Land of the Dragons in Dragonia across the sea."

"B-b-b-but the d-d-d-dragons hate humans." He responded.

"Not all dragons, and not all humans." She responded "Remember, one of your best friends is a dragon. I know the bond that you two have. Penelope would do anything for you. And there's more than that."

"W-w-what do you m-m-mean?" he asked.

"Their queen, Lorainc, is a human. I know it sounds weird, but it's true. There are some humans they are peaceable with. I am one of them, I have known NöGard for a very long time, and I am sure you will be one as well," She said softly. "They moved to the island continent hundreds of milleannums ago because they didn't want to deal with the affairs of humans, elves, dwarves, and all of the creatures here. They wanted to be left alone. But that won't be possible in the future. Something will happen, I don't know exactly what yet, but something horrible, that if it isn't stopped, it will throw this world into darkness for many thousands of milleannums."

"How would I stop such darkness?" He asked.

"As I mentioned earlier, you are more powerful than you know. You also have Adara and Penelope there to help you. When you are ready, go to the Elves. Learn from them, they can teach you many things you would not be able to learn on your own. They can help you improve your magic. And I am sure you can teach them many things as well."

"There will be a time when I may have to call on you and Adara to come help defeat this darkness." She continued, "But until then, live life, use your talents to help and serve others as you have been doing, study and grow your magic, and for heaven's sake, marry Adara. And come visit me."

"I will." He said. She gave him a stern look, and he knew what she was inferring. "I will ask Adara to marry me, and we will come visit you."

Kayla smiled a beautiful smile and nodded just as the song was ending. "Very good." She replied. "Am I allowed to tell this to Adara?" Melvin asked.

"Yes, you may, but only her, as well as Penelope, your dragon. For Now. But then again, you can't keep any secrets from either of them. I know Adara will not mention it to anyone else. If you two are to wed, as I'm sure you will, then there must be no secrets between you. I know she is the leader of this kingdom's armies, so any information she can get on the coming war would be beneficial to her and the armies. You two have a bigger destiny than you may now realize. Don't think that since you are from a small kingdom, you have to or will stay small-minded. Now, Melvin, I must get back to greeting guests. I hope I shall see you two at my palace soon. Especially for a wedding. When you two do get married, I insist that you marry in Lilenhamür. I will take care of everything." She said, reaffirmed as she winked. They walked back to the dais, and she once again met with the guests.

CHAPTER 18
ENGAGEMENT

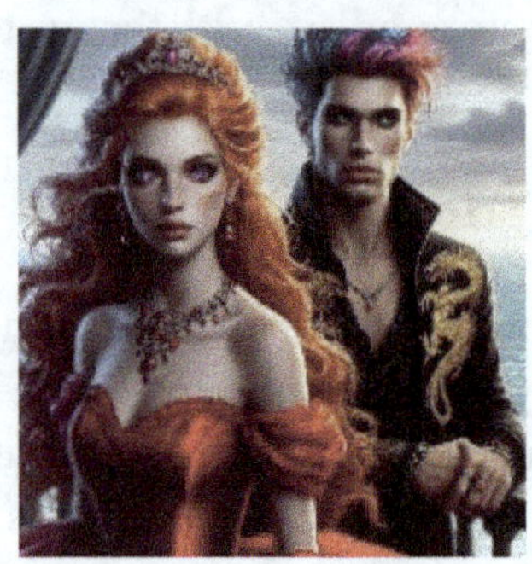

Adara walked briskly back to Melvin. Half in shock, half in wonder. "Wow," she said as she came up to him. "That never happens. Rarely does the Empress dance with anyone. And when she does, it's usually with kings and higher up nobility, and dignitaries of other countries, and not like that. But she danced with you, very close, very intimate. It must have been such an honor."

"Yes, it was. She is very beautiful, and dances very well, and I don't want to lie, I did enjoy it. But there was a reason why she wanted to dance with me."

"Why is that?" She asked.

"Let's go somewhere where we can be alone, and I will tell you what I can," Melvin responded. "Well, we can dance. Close like you two did." She said in a sexy voice, winking at him.

"Yes, we can, but I cannot tell you here what I need to tell you," he said softly. They held hands and walked to the dance floor. Melvin asked the band to play another slow ballad, and they did so. Melvin and Adara danced close together, pressing their bodies close to each other. As with the Empress, feelings welled up in Melvin that gave him warm fuzzies. He loved the feeling of her body and her breasts pressed against his chest. Adara also loved the feeling of Melvin's muscled body pressed against hers. She laid her head on his chest.

"I love you," she said lovingly, looking up into his amazing multicolored eyes. "I love you too, Adara," he said tenderly back to her. Then they kissed.

Adara did not want this dance to end. She was caught up in the feeling of the moment. The intense love they both shared. But unfortunately, the song ended. After the dance, they walked out to the balcony, the same balcony where they became a couple. He closed the glass door and put up a barrier around them so no sound could escape. He held her, looking up at the multitude of stars like he was trying to think of what to tell her and how.

The Heli night enveloped them in warmth. Silence hung in the air, broken only by the rhythmic crash of waves against the shore below. From the balcony, their gaze swept across the expanse of the sea. They could see the large moon rising on the horizon, its glow giving them a soft, white romantic glow. There, ships floated in the harbor and ventured out into the open waters. The tips of their white sails, illuminated by the moon's glow, resembled the spectral fins of ghostly sharks gliding through the depths.

"Adara, how much do you know about the Empress?" he asked her as he leaned on the railing, looking out to sea.

Adara thought awhile and replied, "About as much as anyone, I guess. She is young and beautiful and kind, stuff like that. Very intelligent and apparently knows everything about everyone."

"There was a reason why she wanted to dance with me." He said, then turned to face her, looking into her bright purple eyes, he continued. "She told me some things about me, about you, about herself, about the future. I don't know how much she wants me to tell people or what I must keep to myself. But she did say it would be ok if I shared it with you."

"Melvin, you can trust me, you know that." She said softly, "But if the Empress doesn't want me to know things, then I'm ok with that."

"She said I can tell you that I should tell you. Just like you, she knows my abilities, my talents, and my potential." He started.

"Go on," Adara whispered, her gaze fixed on Melvin's bright, multicolored eyes. Her fingers entwined with his, trying to give him solace and reassurance in their connection.

"So part of what the Empress told me." He paused to think of how exactly to tell her, "Remember how Reicuas went off to fight Zôltan?"

"How could I forget?" Adara responded sadly. "I can never forget the rev we heard the news he would not be coming back."

"She said that there is a darkness coming that is much worse than Zôltan and will last many thousands of millennia if I don't stop it." He paused for a second, then stressed the next sentence. "If *we* don't stop it."

"Oh, NO. How terrible," Adara said in shock. "When will this happen? Wait, we?" She asked in surprise. "She said it won't be for about 4-5 decaannums, so not to worry about it just now. But we must prepare.

But I don't want to dwell on that right now." Then he looked into her beautiful purple eyes. "She said something else as well, much happier. She knows we are in love, well, I guess everyone knows that. And, she says, just like I guess everyone else is thinking. She thinks we should get married, like right away."

"So, what are you saying?" her eyes starting to light up, literally.

"I-I-I-I guess, w-w-what I am saying i-i-i-s…" He gets down on one knee. Very nervously, he says, "Adara of B-B-Bilby. Would you give me the honor of being your husband?"

"Ummm.. Melvin, let me think about it," she responded, "I mean, being your girlfriend is great and all, but marriage? That's a big step. I mean, I would have to be around you like all the time."

"Y-y-y-you're already around me a-a-a-all of the time. B-b-b-but if that's how y-y-you feel, then I g-g-g-guess we can just stay b-b-b-boyfriend and g-g-girlfriend. W-w-we d-d-don't h-h-have to get m-m-m-m-married." Then he looked down and looked as if to cry. Though he really didn't. He knew what she was up to, but he played along.

"Melvin." She lifted his head up gently with her finger under his chin and looked him straight in those beautiful eyes. She smiled her most beautiful smile. And said softly, "Calm down. I was just messing around." Then she winked a sly, sexy wink. Then said slowly and very clearly, so Melvin was sure to understand. "I will absolutely, affirmatively, definitely, assuredly, certainly, indubitably, undeniably, unequivocally, unmistakably, unquestionably, gladly marry you." She replied with a huge smile. Her bright purple eyes brimming with love, tears streaming down her freckled face. "You have no idea how long I've been waiting for you to ask me that." And then, with a fervor, she kissed him more passionately than she had ever kissed him before. Which is saying something. Feelings of warmth and love, and intense fuzzies ran through both of them.

Once again, fireworks lit up the night sky. And this time, only the Empress knew the true reason why, and she smiled.

"Well, you know," Melvin said jokingly, "You could always have asked me." She jokingly punched him in the arm. "I-i-i am sorry, Adara, but I don't have an engagement ring for you."

"That's alright, Melvin, I am still happy you finally asked me. Besides, I still have this one," and she showed him the one he made for her when they became a couple.

Melvin thought for a second. "No, that won't do, it has to be new, has to be better, has to be fitting for a princess. For the future wife of a wizard."

"Melvin, I would be happy with any ring you gave me. Even if it is a string tied around my finger. Because it would be from you." She said, lovingly holding his hand.

"I-I-I-I think I have a solution. H-h-hold on tight." Melvin told Adara. They floated up. Adara was awestruck. She didn't know he could do this. "How are you doing this?" she asked.

"I have been practicing this for a while. I take the gravity and the magnetic flux of the planet and have them react with the metals in my body, and add some magic, and I can float. Also, I concentrate the air below me so I can stand on it." They floated to the ground.

"I didn't understand a word of that. However, that was incredible." Adara said. "Can you fly?" "Unfortunately, not yet," he said. "But I'm sure it will come eventually." That gave him an idea that he would mention to her later.

They floated to the grass. Below the terrace. He knelt on the ground and concentrated. He put streams of consciousness down into the ground and found the same gold deposit deep beneath the earth that he made her promise ring from. He then got some of the pure gold and brought it up he found a titanium deposit and brought some titanium up as well. With his magic, he sang and weaved a spell over the two metals and combined them on the molecular level to make a strong alloy and fashioned it into a ring. Because he made the promise ring for her, he knew her ring size. "What is your favorite stone?" He asked.

She knew he was concentrating, so she kept the answer to the point. "A fire ruby, of course."

"I should have known that," he said. He then searched for rubies. Deep underneath the ground, under the mountains, many many decaspans away, he found a small deposit of hollow rocks with red ruby crystals in them. He separated a crystal and brought it to the surface, floating in front of him. With his magic, he cut the ruby to fit in the ring. He looked within the ruby and designed a starburst pattern within it. "Give me your hand," he said. She did so gladly without questioning. He looked within her and found the core of her power. He knew exactly where it was because he had done this before. What he saw inside her was incredible. He saw a fiery inferno of the fiery power within her. He knew now how much power she had inside of her. Knowing this, he was determined to help her learn to use it to its fullest. He took a very small stream of that power and had it flow into the ruby. It glowed from the fire inside.

He fit all the pieces together and fashioned a ring like no other, made from both of their powers. The alloy he created, the fire ruby, and the fire within it, from her own power. He also used both their powers while he sang and put an enchantment on the ring.

Fire without, fire within

Create a barrier from the wearer's power.

Protect her from all harm,

Just like she is within my arms.

Create a shield from her fire within her heart

And from the gem that is a part

When any power tries to harm

Protect her with fire from now on.

Let her feel my love, and I hers

That we both share.

Then he took the ring and with his magic engraved "For my Love, Adara, Forever," and slipped it on her finger. "There, my love, here is your engagement ring."

She couldn't keep it in. Tears of joy streamed down her face. "This is the most beautiful ring I have ever seen in my life. Oh, thank you, Melvin." Then she gave him a big hug and a big kiss. More fireworks shot up into the night's sky.

"Adara," he said when they were done, while they were still holding each other, "There is more to it than that. I put an enchantment on the ring."

"Yes, I know Melvin," she said. "Remember, I was standing right here the whole time. A spell of protection.

I could feel you using some of my power and putting it into the ring."

"Yes, that's right. There's more, though. This enchantment will only work for you. If someone else tries to use the ring, the protection will not work. It uses your power inside you, and inside the ring, combined to protect you from *any* power trying to harm you. Whether it be physical, like a sword, or magic, from anyone or anything. As long as you wear this ring, nothing can harm you. And I hope you wear it forever. It doesn't mean you won't age or anything. I haven't figured that part out yet." He then produced a small knife and said, "Ok, let me see your hand." She held out her hand. He tried to put the tip of the knife into her pointer finger. When he did so, a red fire barrier surrounded her finger. He tried harder, once again the barrier came, but it was larger. "See, you are protected. No one will know the barrier you have comes from the ring. You would probably be able to do this yourself, but I figured since I was making it, I would do that for you. It will also let you know that I am alive. You will be able to feel that through our bond of love." They kissed again.

"I could stay out here all night with you," She whispered. "But I feel it prudent, since the Empress is here visiting, that we should get back inside."

"You're right. Hang on tight," He said as they rose into the air back up to the balcony. "Always." She smiled and clung to him as they rose.

They went inside the ball again and told her father the news. In turn, he announced it to the crowd. There was a large cheer from the crowd. King Bilby smiled widely and winked at the two of them. Even the Empress smiled and applauded. They kissed again, and real fireworks shot up into the sky for everyone to enjoy. Everyone was thinking it was about time.

Adara showed everyone, especially the Empress, her engagement ring and told her that Melvin had made the ring that very night while they were outside on the balcony.

Chapter 19
The Shadow Lord Rellik

West of the Helaeth Mountains. And west of the plains people, on the western coast of Arion, far from Bilbylund or even Lilenhamür, in the uppermost Northwest corner of Arion, was Nŏrden forest, a land of darkness. Also known later as *The Land of Shadows.* This was ruled over by a man who wanted to turn the world to darkness. The Shadow Lord Rellik. You would think it would be a desolate wasteland, but exactly the opposite was true. It was a lush rain forest due to the much rain and many thunderstorms. Trees and plants grew very tall and big to capture what small amount of light there was. Many levels of tall trees made an impenetrable canopy where the suns rarely broke through to the ground. It was always dark and cloudy. Dark, thick clouds and rain covered the area most of the time. At night, it was nearly pitch black underneath the thick canopy of leaves. Many types of trees, plants, and animals lived there, as well as many different types of people and creatures. Orcs and goblins dwelt in vast caverns under the dark forest. Shriekers, ogres, imps, and mischievous leprechauns lived in the woods. There were also humans, malcontents, evil thieves, and liars who lived in magnificent estates, and some even in castles. As well as sorcerers, evil witches, sorceresses, thugs, mostly the non-congenial sort. Some towns and cities were in this land also, however, mostly on the coast and on the river, and heavily fortified and guarded. No decent person would live in this forest.

The Shadow Lord Rellik wasn't exactly a man, but a creature made from a ritual gone wrong. The magic of the three most evil and most powerful sorcerers, Grubble, Wodahs, and Zôltan, and a powerful sacrificial wizard, and the magic of a baby shadow dragon hatchling, combined to make an extraordinary wizard into one of incredible strength and magic. The only problem is is they succeeded. Well, sort of. They intended to make their leader Zôltan the most powerful Sorcerer, but it backfired. They intended to create a sorcerer to be able to conquer all the lands and give them to the two other sorcerers to rule. But the transference backfired, and instead, all of the power went into the wizard sacrifice, and the other three sorcerers did not survive the transference. Not only did the power of the wizards go into the sacrifice's body, but this transference also gave the wizard, now calling himself Lord Rellik, tremendous power, but also altered his mind, and his state of being, and he became delusional and insane. The magical transformation had another effect besides giving him superior magical abilities, it also transformed his body. He was no longer completely solid, but his matter was loose and not completely defined. He was more like a smoky shadow, but a living smoky shadow, though he could appear in a solid form, he was not entirely like a ghost, but more solid. He cannot stand bright light, especially sunsshine. He has to stay in the shadows. He could not be in direct light. Sunlight caused him tremendous pain due to the shadow dragon's magic within him. He would form back into a solid state, and it reduced his powers to almost nothing.

Rellik had to wear a heavy, hooded cloak and be completely covered if he wanted to venture out into any light. He caused a magnificent castle to be built deep in the Nŏrden forest of Nŏrdenland. Though he was evil, twisted, and not at all sane, he did appreciate beauty. He had built a large, magnificent black obsidian castle. It had well-maintained grounds with sculpted gardens, many types of flowers, and small streams scattered around the castle grounds. Inside, there hung beautiful pieces of art in all the rooms and hallways. Lush carpets lay on the floors, tapestries hung on the walls with dragon battle scenes on them, also banners that depicted a wizard with lightning coming out of his hands. Beautiful hand-carved furniture was placed around the castle. He had beautiful servant girls to attend him, well, more like slaves. He had rooms full of treasures that his underlings brought him. All this was the spoils of the towns and cities he had conquered thus far. He had many rooms in this castle. However, the most interesting room was one in the center of the castle, surrounded by thick walls. This room was very large, so several adult dragons could fit inside. It was round with a domed ceiling. The ceiling was covered in polished brass that had a high luster, so it would reflect light like mirrors. However, that was not its purpose. This room was built to hatch and torture dragons. As has happened before, when you see a dragon hatch, you gain control of that dragon, and you can absorb that dragon's magic. If you are a wizard, you can absorb more of its magic, which Rellik planned to do. However, first, he caught young dragons and bent them to his will. He would chain them in the middle of the room with unbreakable, enchanted iron shackles. Then, he would shoot lightning from his hands towards the ceiling that would concentrate the lightning and then be shot from the domed ceiling onto a certain spot on the dragon, causing them tremendous pain. This he would do till the dragon pledged allegiance to him with an unbreakable vow. Others willingly followed him and did his bidding because they were evil and were promised riches and power.

The darkness of the shadow lands was perfect for a being that could not be in the light.

In the heart of a dark forest, where sunlight barely reached the forest floor, stood a towering castle made from massive blocks of black obsidian. The stones, smooth and sharp-edged, glimmered like glass in the faint light, reflecting the twisted shapes of the ancient trees that surrounded it. The castle's high towers rose like jagged fangs into the sky, cutting through the shadows like the teeth of some great beast. Heavy iron gates sealed the entrance, holding in the prisoners trapped inside.

This was no ordinary stronghold—it was Rellik's fortress. Built as much for beauty as for power, it was a place of fear, a prison for the creatures under his command. Deep beneath its foundations, Rellik had ordered enormous caverns to be dug—so vast and wide they could hold dragons. Not just one or two, but an entire army.

Here, below the castle, in the cold darkness, he locked away the beasts he had captured and broken—dragons, borlogs, and many others. He kept them hidden, waiting in the shadows until the rev he would call them forth to serve in his plans. He ravaged the Nŏrdenland, taking over towns and cities, kidnapping fair maidens to tend to his every need, and the rest he took as slaves to build his castle and dig the caverns beneath the castle. He also recruited fighters, thugs, warriors for hire, hag witches, sorcerers, pirates, imps, ogres, orcs, leprechauns, and any other vile creature he could find. And dragons. If he could not recruit the dragons, He would simply make them do his bidding. However, dragons were scarce in Arion.

Word spread of Rellik's conquering towns and spreading his empire, but as of yet, there was nothing the Empress or those east of the great mountains could do about it, except wait and watch and prepare for eventual war.

CHAPTER 20
ADARA GETS SICK

Adara arrived at Melvin's house for training, but something was off. Her steps were slower, and her posture slouched.

"I don't feel right," she admitted, rubbing her temple.

"Maybe I didn't eat enough this morning."

Melvin's brow furrowed as he studied her. She was pale—too pale. The usual fire in her eyes seemed dimmer, her energy subdued. Concerned, he quickly fetched her something to eat. "Here, try this," he said, watching for any sign of improvement.

Once outside, they chose swords—no fireballs this rev. Steel clashed as they moved, but something was wrong. Adara was slow, her movements sluggish. She missed blocks that she would normally catch with ease. She hesitated instead of striking when openings presented themselves.

Melvin's grip tightened on his sword. This wasn't just fatigue; he could tell something was very wrong.

"Adara, are you sure you're ok?" he asked, concerned. "You are not performing like you usually do." "I will be fine." She replied, "I just have to work through this. It has been happening quite a bit lately." "How didn't I notice?" Melvin asked while easily blocking her thrust.

Adara grunted, forcing a weak smile. "I guess I'm good at hiding it." She spun, aiming a kick—then suddenly, her legs buckled. A gasp escaped her lips as she crumpled to the ground.

Melvin's sword clattered as he lunged forward. His heart pounded. She had never fallen before.

"We need to get you to a healer. Something is wrong." Melvin said, concerned, holding his hand out to help her up.

"I can do it," Adara said, trying to lift herself. She struggled to stand and fell back to the ground, almost unconscious.

Melvin swept Adara into his arms, cradling her as he rushed to the qilin. He placed her on its back, but she slumped forward, her body limp against him. Panic clawed at his chest.

"Hold on, love," he whispered.

Mounting behind her, he wrapped an arm around her waist to keep her steady. With a whispered enchantment, the qilin surged forward, hooves pounding the earth as they raced toward the town healer.

Once there, the healer laid her in the bed and took out some potions and herbs. As he was doing that, Melvin explained what happened. He rubbed a poultice on her arms, legs, and head and did an enchantment. Bright green wisps of clouds circled her. The healer gazed into the mist. He knew that there was nothing broken and nothing external. He gave her some herbs and told Melvin to take her home.

The healer sighed, his face lined with sorrow. "I'm sorry, lad," he said quietly. "There is nothing I can do for her."

Melvin stiffened. "What do you mean?"

"My talents lie in mending bones and curing common illnesses," the healer admitted, voice heavy with regret. "But this… this is beyond me." He lowered his gaze. "She needs an expert healer from Wazervĭl—if she is to have any chance at all."Take her back to the castle and have the king get an Expert Healer from Wazervĭl." Then he hung his head, saddened by the fact that they may lose one of the beloved princesses to an unknown ailment.

Melvin picked up his sweetheart and carried her to his qilin. He cast an enchantment on it that he learned from Reicuas, so it would run a lot faster than it normally would. He would have called Penelope to pick them up, but it would have taken the same amount of time for her to get them and take them to the castle as it would to ride there. The qilin rode as swiftly as he could, carrying two people. Melvin did not know what was going on. He pleaded with Deo to save her life. Past farms, meadows, forests, and rivers, they went hurrying as fast as they could. They ran through Bilby City and across the bridge to the castle finally reached the castle gates. Onlookers crowded the streets, wondering what was happening.

"Hurry," Melvin said urgently to the guards. Something happened to the Princess, I have to get her to the castle as fast as I can. Call a healer." The guards opened the gate, and they rode as fast as possible to get her to the castle proper.

Melvin carried her inside and laid her on a couch. The palace healer was there waiting for them. Melvin rehearsed what the town healer had done and what he said: "Time is of the essence."

The Castle healer surveyed her and did an enchantment, none of which Melvin understood. He hadn't practiced the art of healing much yet, although he did study anatomy somewhat. The King and Queen shortly arrived to see what was going on, and Melvin explained it to them as well.

After the Healer was finished with the examination through the use of his talent, he spoke in a soft tone full of sadness. "You're Majesties, Master Wizard Melvin, I have grave news. The Princess has an infection within her body. For now, it is localized in her lungs, which makes it hard for her to breathe. I do not have the proper herbs that will cure her. We must call a Master Healer from Wazervïl if she has any hope of being saved. Fortunately, she still has time. But for now, she needs to rest."

"I'll c-c-carry her t-t-to her r-r-room." Melvin told them in a somber tone. "I-I-I will stay by her side." He gently picked her up and carried her up to her room. They all followed Melvin up to Adara's bedroom, where he gently placed her in her large four-poster bed. She looked so peaceful lying there asleep, but they did not know the extent of the turmoil that was raging within her body.

Melvin got a chair and sat right next to the bed. The king or queen could have ordered him to leave the room, and they knew he would have refused, but they knew that right now, he needed to be by her side, for both of them. Melvin's mother was in the castle teaching the other princesses, Amira and Anna, and the servant children, when she heard the news, and they all came to the room as well.

A few weeks passed, and Melvin was by her side the whole time. He did not eat or drink. All he did was pray that his sweetheart would be ok. His mind did not work. All he could think of was her. How did this happen? How couldn't he tell? He blamed himself for not noticing something was wrong. She was the one he spent the most time with. He knew her more intimately than anyone else. And yet he had no idea that this was happening to her. How many times had he held her close to him, talked for hours late into the night? He loved her more deeply than anyone on this planet. And here she was, in her bed, unconscious from an unknown disease. He was upset with himself that, with all of his power and ability, all the many talents he possessed, this was the one talent he hadn't learned yet. This was the one he needed the most. Well, he was going to change that.

Finally, a Master Healer from Wazervïl came to look at her. He took a long while examining her. He examined her skin, her eyes, her mouth, felt her stomach, and yes, even her breasts, which were off limits to everyone, except apparently him. He listened to her shallow breathing, then he cast an enchantment, just as the two healers did, yet this was different. He took a long time looking at her. Then, finally, he spoke.

"This is very grievous indeed", he said while looking at her. "The only way to relieve her of her malady is to extract it manually."

"What?" they all said in unison, surprised and not exactly understanding what he meant.

The healer sighed, "It means, it is very bad, and it has to be cut out of her. But I am afraid that it has grown bigger than it was initially. There is an herb from the canbas plant that I can use, but it will take a long time to take effect and cure her. Without the operation, she will die."

The King was in shock. His usual cheery demeanor was gone. With his head hung low, he asked quietly, "How did we not know she was sick? How long does she have to heal?"

"I am not sure," responded the healer. "Could be one moon, it could be less. All we can do is keep her comfortable. You know how stubborn the princess is. You know she would not tell you if she were sick. She has always been that way. The fire in her usually keeps her core body temperature above normal, so it kills anything that tries to attack it, like a bacteria or a virus. From what I have noticed of this. This IS her. It's a cancer that grew from her own body. That may be why her core temperature didn't kill it. Her breathing is very labored, and her heart is barely beating enough to keep her alive." He hung his head low and continued. "All we can do for now is keep her comfortable and wait till she wakes up. If she wakes up."

"I will continue to stay by her side," Melvin said. "Master Healer, may I talk to you in private?"

"Of course, young Melvin, any time," the Healer responded. Although they had not officially met, the Healer knew of Melvin and all his abilities. It was a shame he did not go to Wazzer academy, for he would have learned so much more and have been so much further along than he was, however, Reicuas had done a marvelous job with him. In a lot of areas, he surpassed the levels of the masters in Wazervĭl.

The two walked out of the room into the hallway. Melvin dismissed the guards. And asked, "What did you just do?

How did you know what was wrong with her? What was that enchantment you just cast on her?"

"All very good questions," he replied. "I would expect you would already know the answers, though, with all of your abilities."

Melvin sighed, "I have not yet delved into the healing arts much, so I don't yet know how this works. Please explain this to me so I may learn."

"Of course, young Melvin. The enchantment enables me to look into her body and see what's inside her. Her muscles, her organs, her heart, lungs, and stomach. And her power. Which is in enormous abundance within her. I could see this cancer, which did not belong in her. It was at first isolated to her lungs, but it has spread further, to her heart, her stomach, and other organs. Slowly taking over and will eventually shut them down. The only way I know to rid her of this is to physically cut it out of her. I know of no other magical way to heal her. As I mentioned, there is an herb that could be used that destroys this type of thing. If it were caught earlier, it may have been a solution, but it has spread so much that it would not heal her faster than this evil disease would spread."

"Can you use the Canbas anyway to at least slow the spread of this?" Melvin asked. "Well, at least it can do no harm," The healer said, stroking his long white beard.

"I will find a way to save her," Melvin said assuredly.

"If anyone could find a way to save her, it would be you." The Master healer said with a reassuring smile and nod. They both walked back into the room. Melvin sat back down in his chair and began to think.

A few weeks later, Adara woke up. The first thing she saw was Melvin praying and sobbing at her bedside. She heard him say *"Please don't let her die, Please don't let her die."* She smiled weekly. He looked tired, weak, and sad. His face was sunken more than usual. His face was stained with tears. "Hi Melvin," she said weekly. What did I miss?"

"Adara, you're awake," he said happily and kissed her gently. "You were asleep for about three weeks. The Healer said you have cancer." He told the servants who were standing by to go tell the king she was awake. Melvin took Adara's hand and held it and looked into her beautiful purple eyes, but her eyes were changed again; they were more of a blueish hue than a purple. Her complexion was unnervingly pale; her usually rosy red cheeks were now faded. Her hair was a duller red. Was her power beginning to fade?

"I know Melvin, my love. I could hear everything you were talking about. I just had no way to respond. When my parents get here, I wish to speak to you all."

The servant ran to the king's council room and knocked on the door. The guards told her that the king was in an important meeting and could not be disturbed.

"I have important news about Adara," she said quickly. The guards immediately let her in. She ran into the room and exclaimed. "King Bilby. Adara is awake and wishes to speak to you, and the queen and her sisters."

"I will come at once," he rejoiced. "Meeting is adjourned until further notice." Then he got up and went to Adara's room. The servant ran to fetch the others.

When they all arrived, Adara was able to sit up and was drinking a little broth. "You are probably wondering why I summoned you all here this rev." She said with a smile. Melvin thought, even when she is sick and dying, she still starts with a joke.

"I know what is wrong with me. I know I have cancer. I should have told you when I started not feeling well, but I did not want you to worry, so because of my pride, I have put myself and all of you in this position." She smiled a sweet but painful smile. "Do not be sad for me. I am not afraid to die. We know the words of the prophets. We know Deo's plan for us. There is a better place for me. I will return to live with Deo. We will be together again as a family. I will wait for you to come." Then she looked directly at Melvin. "I will wait for you on the other side." Then she smiled and closed her eyes, and her hand went limp.

However, she was not dead. She went back into her comatose state, slow heartbeat, slight breathing. Melvin could not sit there and let his sweetheart die. The one person he loved more than any other. He got up from the chair and walked out of the room with determination. "I will not let her die. Just keep her alive long enough for me to find a way." He directed the Healer.

Melvin walked numbly across the castle grounds, his feet dragging with each step. He pushed open the door to the old stone practice rock—the place where he had first met Adara. The air was thick with the scent of soot and ash, untouched by time.

Collapsing to his knees, he let the darkness swallow him. His shoulders shook as sobs racked his body.

"Why?" he choked. "Deo, why can I do everything else but not this?"

The silence offered no answer. How could this be? He felt like a failure. With all of his magical power, he could not do the one thing he most desperately wanted to be able to do. He could not save the one person who meant more to him than anything else in this world. Adara was the love of his life, she was his world. If she died, he didn't think he would be able to go on living. His soul was wracked with sorrow, confusion, and anger.

"Deo," He pleaded. "With all this power that I have, why can I not heal?"

A voice echoed through his mind—not a sound, but a presence, vast and undeniable, but at the same time a powerful voice. He knew exactly who it was from. It was short and to the point. Four simple words that were so simple, yet so profound that it shook him to his core.

"You have not asked."

Melvin's breath hitched. His pulse thundered in his ears.

"I-I'm asking now," he whispered, his voice raw with desperation. "I am begging. Please. Show me how to save her. I know with your guidance I will be able to do it."

Silence stretched, thick and heavy. Then—

"Yes, you will, my son."

A warmth flooded through him, like the first rays of sunslight piercing a storm.

The voice came once again to him, "I have given you the power to do many things, and you have used them well. I will give you the power to do all things if you use them to do My will and bless the lives of others, and not for your own gain. I know you want to save Adara, but is it because you want it for you, or her?" He asked.

"Can't it be for both?" Melvin pleaded. "Don't the prophets say that the man and the woman must be together, mustbecome one? I need her, and she needs me. She completes what I lack. We need each other. Plus, I made a vow. I made a vow to her, and to *YOU*, to protect her, to love her, to support her. And if she dies, then I fail. And if I can't protect the one I love the most in this world, then how am I supposed to protect anyone else?" Then he sobbed some more, completely putting his heart out to Deo.

"Melvin." The voice said. "I have given you the power to save her. You just need to learn how to do it. You are capable. Just go do it." The voice said. Then a powerful feeling came over him. Just as the time he watched Penelope hatch. He felt invincible.

Melvin got on his qilin and rode home for the first time in weeks. He went to the place where he kept his books and scrolls and looked through the books and scrolls for anything about healing.

Then he went to the town healer's house and asked him for any scrolls or healing books.

"I was wondering how long it would be before you came to look for these." The Healer said with a chuckle.

"Don't worry, I won't take your job. I have too many other things I have to do." Melvin said. They both chuckled. "But right now, I have to find out how to save Princess Adara."

"I expect no less from you. Go, Melvin, save the princess." The healer said reassuringly.

He then went to the castle's library and got every book on healing he could find. He took all these back to Adara's room, where she still lay unconscious. They put a straw in her mouth so they could pour broth and canbas juice into her mouth in hopes that that would keep her alive until Melvin had the opportunity to heal her. Melvin pored over the books and scrolls. However, nothing in any of those books told him how he could cure her. They were useless to him.

Then an impression came to him, just as it did in the stone building. *You know how to do this.* It said. Melvin knew who the impression came from.

"*How?*" he thought.

The same way you made Adara's engagement ring. You know how to look into her body; you have done it before.

Use that method.

Then he understood.

First, looking into his own body, then into hers. He used the same technique as he did to make Adara's engagement ring when he looked under the earth for the metal and the ruby. He had put an enchantment on the ring that, with her power, nothing could harm her. However, that was from external forces. But this was from within. Her own body was making her sick. She did not have a defense for that. He would remedy that problem.

Now he sent his consciousness into her body. After looking into his own body, he looked into Adara's. It was basically the same, except a few extra feminine parts were used in reproduction. He asked if he could use a female's body to look into, to compare it to Adara's body, so he would know what was cancer and what was not. Aria volunteered. Because they were closest in age, she would be a good comparison.

"This isn't going to be creepy, is it? I don't have to get naked, do I?" she asked looking at Melvin sternly.

"I am going to look inside you, not at you. Everything will be under the skin. You can stay fully clothed. Now, if you could lie down next to Adara, I will compare you."

Melvin sent his consciousness inside Aria and scanned her organs first, the heart, the lungs, the uterus, and all the areas inside the body. Next, he scanned Adara. He had done something like this before, but not to this extent. Before, he was looking for the source of her power in her heart. Now, he was looking for what was killing her. The disease. After looking into Aria and then Adara, he was able to tell the difference between what was supposed to be there and what wasn't. He found it had spread throughout Adara's body. To all her organs. Her power in her heart was diminished. Taken over by this invader of her beautiful body. When it was in a large mass, it was easy to find it. When it was in smaller patches, it was harder because they looked like the same cells, but with just a little tweak. However, that tweak was enough that he could tell the difference. Then he noticed something very important. In Adara's body, everything had a light to it. Each cell had a type of aura to it. The cancer did not. It looked like a blight on an otherwise picturesque landscape.

Melvin prayed silently to Deo. *"Please help me, I have found the cancer, well, most of it. Guide me to where I need to go to find it all. Please help me get it out of her. How do I do that?"*

"Use her own body. She has defenses. They just don't know how to distinguish her good cells from her bad cells. Use what you have learned to identify them and teach her cells to do the same. Multiply her defensive cells and lead them to the cancerous cells. The chemicals in the canbas juice will be able to help. It will take time, but it is possible. I will give you the power to direct them, and they will obey."

"How is that possible?" Melvin asked.

"Every living thing has intelligence. Every cell is a living thing. Every cell in every plant, in every animal, on the earth, in the sky. They all obey Me. I will give you the authority to direct them. Just as you would have had authority over Penelope. However, when you are finished healing her, you will no longer have the authority to direct the cells in Adara's body. However, if there is a need, you may have that authority back at some point."

"Thank you," Melvin responded, *"I understand."*

Melvin did one more comparison between Aria and Adara and told Aria she could go. He needed everyone to leave the room so he could concentrate. He allowed one servant girl, roughly the same age as Adara, to stay and sit on a bench quietly in case he needed something. She was allowed to read, or draw, or whatever, as long as she sat relatively still and remained silent. The servant understood and did as she was told. She was pleased to be able in some way to help heal her princess. She loved Adara, as did the other servants, and would do anything in her power to help her. Even if it meant sitting there and being quiet.

Melvin looked through the scrolls and books one more time to reference what he was looking for, and when he found it, he set to work. Though he had a lack of sleep and lack of nourishment, his mind was laser-focused. He would do what he intended to do, for as long as he needed. He would heal Adara.

Letting Deo lead the way, Melvin put a stream of consciousness into Adara, remembering where he had seen the cancer before. He focused. Then, like with a microscope, he focused smaller and smaller and smaller until he could see the individual cell. He could look at a healthy cell and then could see a cancer cell and knew the difference. He located the body's defensive white blood cells and called on them. He showed them the differences between a healthy cell and a cancerous cell. And they got to work. Melvin then multiplied the white blood cells to a significant amount by dividing them so that they could work together. It was fascinating how the body worked, all the different systems all working in harmony. He also called on the Canbas chemicals in helping identify the cancer cells for the white blood cells. Once they located the cancer cells, the white blood cells just gobbled them up. Encased it in the white blood cell and moved it to the garbage chute. Over and over again, Melvin directed the microscopic cells to the other cancer cells. In time, there were enough canbas chemicals and white blood cells that they could find the cancer cells on their own. Melvin watched and monitored this throughout the night and the next rev. He was amazed at how the body worked. The servant girl was changed out every few hours, but always sat quietly. Once again, Aria sat in the chair. All she noticed was Melvin's eyes moving back and forth in deep concentration. In turn, all three of Adara's sisters sat and watched Melvin. They wondered what was going on and what he was doing.

After another few revs, Melvin was finished. Well, the white blood cells in Adara's body were finished. He charged them to be ever on the lookout for other cancer cells. Anything that doesn't match up with what is already there needs to be taken out. Unless it was, in time, a baby.

When that was done, he looked in her heart and found where her power was. He saw that once the cancer cells had been taken out, her power was starting to return to normal. And it was beautiful. But still, it felt she was barely hanging on.

Melvin called the servant girl who was sitting in the chair to come lie next to Adara on the wide bed. He scanned her from head to toe, he scanned the brain, the throat, the lungs, the heart, other vital organs, and every inch of her body. He scanned every cell, he scanned the uterus, and he noticed something different between the servant girl and Adara. He debated whether to tell her or not, so he decided to ask her a question.

"Missy," he said, "Are you married?" He asked.

"Yes, I am." She responded.

He followed up with another question, "How long have you been married? "A few Annums, Why?" She asked curiously.

"I have some good news for you," Melvin said. While he was still scanning her body. "What news is that?" she asked.

"You are pregnant," Melvin said with a smile.

The servant girl's eyes lit up, and a wide smile appeared on her face. It was a beautiful smile. "We have been trying to have a child ever since we got married."

"Congratulations," Melvin said.

Melvin finished the scan, then let Missy go.

Melvin thoroughly scanned Adara's body one more time to see if there were any of the cancer cells left. He did not see any. He checked Adara's breathing and heartbeat. They were still very slow and shallow, but she was still alive. Barely. He checked her power level, and it was getting stronger. Everything seemed ok. He was relieved. He thanked Deo for helping him through this. He would have never been able to do it alone. He showed the body from the scan of Missy what a fetus would look like in her uterus, and told the white blood cells to leave that alone whenever Adara got pregnant. They effectively said: *Duh, we're not stupid.*

Now all he could do was wait for her to wake up again.

CHAPTER 21

A few weeks later, Melvin was sitting in his chair next to Adara's bed holding her hand. He looked through her one more time, and something seemed off. Her heartbeat and breathing were slower than before, like she was barely holding on to life. He whispered barely audible, "Just hold on a little while longer, you are almost done, don't leave me. You need to stay here. And he started weeping. I can't lose you, Adara, I can't lose you. I promised to take care of you, to protect you. You are healed. Stay with me."

It was a sunny Liten morning. The light was shining brightly through the windows so which lit up the room. Melvin could feel the warmth of the dual suns coming through the windows. He could hear birds chirping. Missy again was sitting in the chair, waiting for orders. Melvin felt Adara tightening her grip. She slowly opened her beautiful, bright purple eyes and saw Melvin sitting there holding her hand. She smiled slightly. She loved Melvin for staying with her this whole time. She was sure there were other things he could have been doing, but she also knew that Melvin would not leave her side. As she would do the same for him.

"Hi, sweetie. How long have I been out for this time?" She asked in a raspy whisper.

Melvin couldn't believe it, she was awake. He was ecstatic. "About a week. I thought I almost lost you. For a bit there, it seemed that your heartbeat and breathing were so faint, I didn't know if you were going to make it through. But you did. You are healed. The cancer is gone. Deo showed me how to use my power to heal you."

"I knew you could do it," Adara said with a slight smile.

"Missy," Melvin called, "go get the family and have them come here."

"Can she do that in a minute?" Adara whispered faintly, "I desperately need to use the restroom, and I'm afraid I can't make it there on my own." So Missy helped Adara to the bathroom, then when Adara was finished, Missy helped Adara get dressed in her night gown again, then she ran off to get the family, and Melvin helped get Adara back to bed. Adara was so light, she must have lost a lot of weight while she was sick. Looking at her face and arms, and legs, he could tell that she had no fat on her body, and some of her muscle was gone as well. When she felt better, they would work extra hard to get her body back into the pristine shape it was in before she fell ill.

While they were waiting for the family. They just held each other. She laid her head on Melvin's strong shoulder. Melvin was so filled with joy that his sweetheart was back.

Missy ran to the meeting room where King Bilby was having another meeting about the affairs of the kingdom.

The guards saw Missy and told her that she was not to be admitted.

I have news about Princess Adara," she said in a hurry. The guards immediately opened the doors for her.

As soon as she entered the room, she made her announcement. "She's awake and asked for their family," was all she had to say, then the King quickly adjourned his meeting. And hurried to Adara's room.

Missy found the Queen watching Anna practice her gymnastics routine and gave them the announcement. Like the King, they quickly stopped what they were doing and ran to Adara's room. In the kitchen, she found Amira eating a bowl of ice cream. When Amira heard the news, she put the spoon down and rushed to the bedroom, which was unusual because she always finished her ice cream. Finally, Missy went to the training fields outside of the castle where she knew Aria would be practicing with her unit. As soon as they heard the news, Aria ran to be by her sister's side. The rest continued their practice. They were all overjoyed that she was finally awake. Once the family was all gathered around the bed, Adara spoke quietly.

"I have something important to tell you all about what happened while I was asleep." Everyone sat close around or on the bed so they could hear. Aria held Adara's other hand while Anna gave her a hug.

"Not long before I woke up," she started, "I died." Everyone simultaneously gasped. "I know this was not a dream. I know this really happened. I left my body. I hovered over the bed, I saw my body lying on the bed, Melvin sitting right there in that chair holding my hand. Pleading with me and with Deo for me to wake up. Missy was sitting in that chair over there, I need to talk to you later about your baby. I flew around the castle, Anne was practicing her gymnastics, and I flew over the grounds where Aria was practicing with her unit. You should have low kicked Major Barnes, He didn't have a counter for that; you would have won the match." She told Aria. "Then I flew over land and the sea, over the land of the dragons. I flew into the sky faster than anything else I could imagine. I went through a tunnel. It was pitch black except for a pinpoint of light at the end of the tunnel. I rushed towards the light. And when I went through the light, there was a brilliant star in front of me. But it wasn't a star, it was a planet. This planet was so bright that it was brighter than the twin suns at mid light. I came down and gently landed on a platform. I looked around, my eyes did not need to adjust. Everything was so bright, so colorful. I saw beautiful flowers, trees, and grass. Animals were off in the distance. They were all singing this beautiful music. It sounded as if everything there was praising Deo. And there was someone there to greet me. He said his name was Frank. He was there as my guide. I was in Heaven. I knew I was home. A place I had been before. We walked in a meadow. Everything was singing, everything was luminescent, shining brilliantly. The flowers were so colorful. The whole place was filled with light. And love. So much love.

"We walked to a stream and sat down on a bench. I looked into the stream, and I saw fish swimming. They were glowing, just as everything else was. I could tell what they were thinking.

They were blissfully happy. As was everything else in that place. Another thing that I noticed was knowledge. Everything I would ever want to know about anything, I could know if I wanted to. I asked about my family, about Melvin, about this war that is coming. I was shown what was and what could be. All the infinite possibilities depend upon the choices that we make here. I knew in that moment the intents of people's hearts. I know now what Empress Kayla feels like. I was told that the only thing we leave our lives with is the knowledge and experiences we gain here. There is more than this life. So much more after this life, so much more life and love and happiness and pure joy after this life. This life is like primary school compared to what is to come."

She looked at all of her family, so much love coming from her soul, and continued. "I learned what I always believed to be true: we are so much more than our bodies. We have a soul, a spirit within us. We know that, but what we do not know is that this spirit is so much more than this body. More glorious, with so much more potential, more wisdom, more knowledge, more power than we will ever know. We are eternal. We have always been, and we will always be. Just in different forms. Our spirit inhabits our physical bodies, and there will come a time, after we all die, that we will all become one with our bodies again. But our bodies will be perfect. Whole." She smiled and looked around the room again. Her voice became stronger.

 "Once we reunite with our perfected bodies, we will never be sick, we will never die, we will know as much as we want to know, there will be no limit to what we will be able to do. We will be in this eternal realm where evil does not exist. Another thing does not exist there. Magic. There is no need for it. For Magic comes from Deo, and in Deo's realm, it is not needed. Deo's word is all that is needed. If it is the will of Deo, it will be done. His word is obeyed by everything. Everything is made up of intelligence. All people, all animals, all plants. Everything. All intelligences obey Deo. And that is a little bit like how magic works. But I will not go into detail on that subject right now. I may discuss it with you later, Melvin."

"I walked with Frank down a path with golden stones. Not the color gold, but actual gold. We came to a place where we saw a man with outstretched arms standing along the path. Frank gestured for me to go up to him. He was dressed in a brilliantly white robe. I knew who he was immediately. Deo. Or that's what we know him by. He goes by many different names." She looked around the room, smiled faintly, and continued. "He had a white aura around him, it was so bright, so magnificent, as if he was glowing. More brilliant than when Reicuas used his power. A thousand times more luminescent."

He embraced me, and all I felt was love. Love more abundantly than anything else I have ever felt before. Perfect love. Sorry, Melvin." Melvin just smiled because he knew that it was true. "I felt his arms around me. Not as a spirit as some suppose, but as flesh and bone. Then he smiled. The most beautiful smile I have ever seen in my whole life. I looked into his eyes. His eyes were nothing I had seen before. They were as white as his aura. I saw knowledge and wisdom, and love in those eyes. I felt accepted. I felt love. I felt that he knew me. He knew me more intimately than anyone else could. I felt at home. I did not want to leave. I just wanted to stay there in that loving embrace forever."

"After a while, he spoke to me. A voice, gentle and soft. He told me it was not my time yet, that I still had work to do. That a way would be provided for me to overcome this affliction, this cancer, that was in my body. He told me that Melvin healed me. He learned how to heal because of me. This would be important at a later time. He told me I needed to go back. That my family needed me, that Melvin needed me, that the Empire needed me. That the world needed me. I don't know why, I don't know what is to come. He has told other people what is happening, and we should trust them." She looked around the room at her family. Everyone had tears in their eyes.

"All I know is that I needed to come back. But for some reason, I did not want to. I was free. I was rid of this mortal, imperfect body, rid of this sickness; I was home. I was surrounded by love, love emanated everywhere, I didn't want to come back, but I knew I had to. I had to for my family, for Melvin, for the Empire. For the people I love, and for the people who love me. As soon as Deo let go of the embrace, I was pulled back into my body, and as soon as I was back, I woke up. So, thank you all. And thank you so much for healing me, Melvin. I owe you everything. I literally owe you my life." With a tender gesture, she reached out and bestowed upon Melvin a kiss of eternal gratitude.

"Actually Adara," Melvin said gently. Looking into her purple eyes that were shining once again, "You healed yourself. Deo gave me the ability to show your body how to do it. I showed your white blood cells the difference between a healthy cell and a cancer cell, and your own body did the rest. Now you will never have that problem again. If you want the gross details on how that process works, I will tell you later. But now you need to rest and regain your strength."

She smiled and said, "I knew you could do it. You can do anything."

"I can do anything Deo gives me the power to do," Melvin responded softly.

Her family gave her hugs and cried happy tears. She took the time to rest and recover her strength, and within a moon's passing, she not only returned to her former self, but emerged even stronger and more vibrant than before. Her love for Melvin increased a thousandfold. Not that she hadn't already done so before, but now she was prepared to move mountains for him. There was nothing she wouldn't do to ensure his happiness and well-being. As long as it was good and righteous. Through this experience, she became closer to Deo and had a burning desire to serve him and fulfil her mission on this planet, whatever it was. She learned so much about Deo and his being from that short experience that he would ponder and hold for the rest of her life.

Melvin pondered about this time as well and grew closer to Deo and improved in his healing abilities, though he had a long long way to go before he fully understood the human body.

Melvin was in a daze about what had happened to Adara. He could not live without her. She was everything to him. He loved her with his whole heart and soul. He was going to make sure that nothing like this would ever happen again. He would do all he could to protect her. One night, when they were alone, sitting on the orange grass in the front of his house, looking at the moon and the stars in the sky, they were talking about the experience they had and what they learned. They became closer to each other and closer to Deo through this experience and sharing it.

Melvin put a stream of consciousness into her body to see if any sign of the cancer was still in her body. As far as he was concerned, there was not. He again instructed the white blood cells and other defense mechanisms in her body to be extra vigilant in detecting and removing any cells that were not exact replicas of the parent cell. Thus, any tumors, cancer, or any other abnormalities would be taken care of. He also made sure they ate healthy foods, and consumed canbas to help monitor for odd cells.

CHAPTER 22
COMMANDER

Now you might wonder how it is that Adara became the Commander of the Armies of the land of Bilby and not her older sister.

Aria, the eldest of the princesses, possessed a rare blend of grace and lethality. She was a master of the blade, the bow, and every weapon in between—scimitars, staves, daggers. Yet, despite her formidable skill, she had no desire to command an entire army. The weight of countless lives, the strategies of war, the responsibility of victory or defeat—it wasn't for her.

Instead, she carved her own path. Special operations, stealth, and calculated chaos—that was where she thrived. If the enemy needed to be crippled before battle even began, Aria was the one to do it.

You may wonder—why were the King's daughters entrusted with the army? If a prince could lead, why not a princess? These princesses were just as capable, perhaps even more so.

And beyond their skill, there was one undeniable truth: the King had no sons. The duty of protecting the kingdom fell to his daughters. They had been trained for this their entire lives.

They could be poised and diplomatic when the moment called for it, the very image of royal grace. But when the drums of war sounded, which didn't often happen in this part of the world, they became something else entirely—lethal, unstoppable, warriors in their own right. And now it seemed inevitable.

So why did the mantle of leading the army fall on the shoulders of such a sweet, caring, loving young lady? Why didn't the King have a big, brooding, muscular, sword-wielding man be at the head of his army? I will tell you. Underneath that sweet exterior, Adara was a Fireball. Literally. As you have read, she commands Fire!! That alone does not make her a commander of an army; however, all her life she had been taught military tactics, diplomacy, and, of course, how to use her talent of Fire. She could also talk to animals. However, she did not develop this part of her talent. If she had, things may have turned out quite different.

There was a war coming. And she wanted to protect the ones she loved. Sure, Melvin would be fine, but the rest of her family she could protect. Yes, she was a princess of a small kingdom at the edge of the empire, and she was ready to take on the greatest threat the Empire had ever seen. Even though Zôltan had gone into hiding, or had been defeated, a greater threat was on the horizon, and she would fight if it came to that. She was the fiancée to the greatest wizard this planet had ever known in 100 Millennia. He was their biggest hope for defeating him, and she planned on being there right next to him. Her courage and determination outweighed her sweetness.

So again, how did she get this position as the leader of the armies at Melvin's side, not only in her small kingdom but of the entire empire? The entire continent of Arion, instead of one of the Empress's mightiest warriors? There were many. She basically told her Father, Melvin, and the Empress that she was going to do it. Then her hair turned to flames, and fireballs in her hands, and they didn't argue. Besides, it was the Empress's plan all along. She knew this was what they were meant to do.

CHAPTER 23
THE INN

It was the heart of Sowing. Fields lay fallowed in preparation, while trees blossomed and wildflowers painted the landscape in bursts of color. The air carried the gentle warmth of this part of the annum.

Inside a carriage, Melvin and Adara traveled toward Lilenhamür, their wedding destination. This time, they were riding in a carriage through the beautiful countryside. Out the window, they saw the orange grassy fields, and the trees with orange leaves as they passed by. It was a 5-rev journey to Wazervīl, then a 7-rev journey to Lilenhamür by carriage from Bilbylund. Melvin and Adara could smell the wildflowers along the road as they headed west.

As they passed through towns and villages, laughter and cheers filled the air. Children dashed after the carriage, waving excitedly, their voices rising in a chorus of admiration. They knew who rode inside and longed to catch even a glimpse of the legendary couple. As they stopped for meals in small towns, they were surrounded by adoring towns people. Melvin would play with the children and Adara would chat with the parents.

As dusk settled over the countryside on the sixth rev of their journey, Melvin and Adara arrived at a small village near Lilenhamür. Normally, they wouldn't have needed an inn—traveling on Penelope cut the journey to mere hours. But at this time, Penelope was otherwise occupied. And truthfully, Melvin didn't mind. The extra time with Adara was a rare gift. Just as the Empress had told him, his status as a Master Wizard had given him extra perks in the inns they had stopped at.

The warm glow of firelight flickered in the hearth and the lanterns, casting golden reflections against Adara's crimson traveling clothes. The inn was quaint, like many others they had visited on their journey—wooden beams, worn floors, and the hum of quiet conversations around the room. There was a large hall for visitors to dine, and a large rock hearth in the middle of the room to keep visitors warm while eating. At this time, it had a small fire in it.

Although the lighttime was warm, the nights were still a bit cool. Tables and chairs were scattered on the floor for patrons to eat at; some were long enough for many people, and some were more intimate. Many visitors filled these tables, eating, drinking ale, telling stories of heroism, etc. The smell of various types of food, fresh-baked bread, and drinks filled the air. A little band was playing sweet music in the corner.

Melvin followed in after. As he stepped in, a hush enveloped the room. Everyone just stared in wonder, as if they were thinking, why are two important people stopping at this inn, in a small town in the middle of nowhere. Lest they forget or possibly do not know, that Melvin himself was from a small town, in a small kingdom. However, since the visit of the Empress to Bilbylund, his fame and Adara had gone far and wide in Eastlund. And as far out to Midland as Lilenhamür, possibly beyond.

"Hi," Melvin says, "We would like a table for three." As their driver stepped through the door after putting the qilins in the stable.

All of a sudden, a large man bustled toward them, his face alight with excitement.

"Your Highness! And—Melvin the Magnificent!" he exclaimed, seizing their hands in a firm shake. "What an honor! Welcome to my inn. I am Ashad, the owner. Please, sit, eat—I will have the finest food and lodgings prepared for you at once."

"Thank you for your kindness, any room will do," Melvin said.

Just then, Adara jabbed Melvin in the ribs with her elbow. And whispered, "Remember what the Empress told you. You are the most powerful wizard in the world after all. You should accept the generosity."

"No, I insist," The innkeeper said.

"Well, then," Melvin responded with a pained smile because of the sudden jab from his sweetheart. "As you say. But we will need separate rooms, as we are not married as of yet. We are traveling to Lilenhamür for our wedding."

"Your Wedding, you say," The Innkeeper said with an expression of excitement. "I have heard that you two were to be married. And you chose our inn to stay the night. For my gift for you, for this most blessed occasion, we shall celebrate your union." Then Ashad smiled widely as he put his hands in the air, "I will throw you the best feast and party that I am able. We will have food and drink and music, and dancing." Then he turned to the kitchen and shouted, "Mahad, bring them your finest meats, and your best ale and wine, fruits and bread. Tonight, we celebrate." He exclaimed, "Zamurad, prepare the 2 best rooms for Melvin the Magnificent and his bride, Princess Adara, who chose to grace our humble inn with their presence. And also a fine room for their driver. Send Zamund to take care of their Qilins."

Melvin took out his purse to pay for the meal and the rooms. The innkeeper put Melvin's arm down as if to tell him to put it away.

"Here is what I propose, Your Magnificence," Ashad said, bowing low.

"Please, none of that," Melvin said with a small chuckle. "I'm no king—just Melvin." He told Ashad while motioning for him to stop bowing.

Ashad continued "My apologies. Melvin. This night will be no charge for you or the Princess. It is a gift, a celebration for your union. However I do ask, just please tell people that you stayed in my inn, and I can say that you and the Princess stayed here, that would drive more business to the inn."

Melvin looked at Adara, and she smiled approvingly. "We accept the offer," Melvin said, and they shook hands to seal the deal. That night, they ate, drank, danced, and Melvin and Adara even performed a song for all those in the Inn. And to everyone's enjoyment, they learned that they both had very good singing voices. They slept in the finest rooms in the inn. They had soft beds, ample covers, and were far away from the hustle of the main hall and the noise. They, comparatively, were very nice rooms, but nothing compared to the rooms at the palace. Before they left the inn, Adara etched on a piece of wood on the wall of the main hall with her magic *Thanks for the Hospitality. Signed, Melvin the Magnificent and Princess Adara.*

In the morning, as they were getting ready to leave, Melvin noticed that part of the corner of the roof was not thatched properly. So, as he always does for people, he decided to help. He collected some tall grasses from a nearby field, then climbed on the roof and mended that corner that was not thatched properly. The fame of this went throughout the town as onlookers came to see Melvin the Magnificent helping the Innkeeper.

When he was through, everyone cheered and applauded.

"It was nothing really," Melvin said "I saw he needed some help and I helped him, nothing anyone else wouldn't do. Isn't that what Deo teaches us, to help thy neighbor? To serve one another? When you see someone in need of help, you help them. Remember when you are serving others, you are also serving Deo." Then he waved to the crowd, they got into the carriage and continued on their journey.

Adara just looked at him and welled up in tears.

"What's the matter, sweetheart? Did I do something wrong?" He asked wondering what was going on with Adara.

"No," She said lovingly. "You did everything right. I am so proud of you. You didn't have to fix his roof, but you did. Out of the kindness of your heart. I love you so much, Melvin, and I can't wait till we are married. Then you can have everything I have to offer." She said with a sly wink. Then she kissed him with all the love and tenderness she could put into it. Melvin couldn't remember the rest of the trip to Lilenhamür.

CHAPTER 24

LILENHAMÜR

"Oh! My! Gosh!" Adara gasped, she punctuated every syllable. Her eyes widening as they crested the final hill before they decended into Lilenhamür. "That is enormous."

Lilenhamür stretched before them, a fortress unlike any she had ever imagined. The seat of power for the Arion Empire stood as a gleaming colossus, shimmering in the sunslight, its gleaming white walls rising like the very bones of the earth.

It was beyond immense—Lilenhamür was the single largest structure Adara had ever laid eyes on. As they rode closer, its towering walls loomed, their sheer height rivaling the tallest trees of Bilbylund.

The walls stretched endlessly in either direction. An impenetrable bastion of iridescent white stone that gleamed like polished marble in the sunslight, a testament to the sheer scale of the empire's might. She knew the fortress was in the shape of a hexagon from her studies back home. Even still, being many Mega-Spans away from it, she could barely make out the shape of it.

Tall towers shimmering in the sunslight rose high into the violet sky. Taller than anything man-made she had ever seen before. The gigantic edifice rose as it got closer to the center. The towers are higher in the center than at the outer edges. As Adara and Melvin came closer to the city surrounding the outside of the wall, she noticed another wall of enormity was being constructed on the outskirts of the city. She thought this was very peculiar. The closer they got, the grander Lilenhamür seemed to be.

While Adara marveled at the sheer size of Lilenhamür, Melvin's focus was elsewhere. He wasn't looking at the walls or the towers—he was sensing something far greater.

Magic.

Raw, unbridled power pulsed from the fortress, radiating like unseen suns. It was unlike anything he had ever felt before—stronger than a hundred dragons combined. The source was unknown, but it was here, woven into the very essence of this city.

He did have a hunch that there were dragons in that fortress, but not all of the magic came from them. He knew, too, that very few people or creatures on this planet would be able to feel or even notice the magic. He, however, was keenly aware of how much there was and opened himself to absorbing as much of it as he possibly could. However, the true source of this magic was unknown to him. He made it his goal, aside from marrying his sweetheart sitting next to him, to find out the source of this magic.

As the carriage rolled past the towering 10-span high gates, Adara let out an excited squeal, gripping Melvin's arm tightly. Her wide eyes darted between the colossal walls and the sprawling city beyond.

"This place is incredible," she whispered, barely containing her excitement.

They were stopped by the guards as was custom. Melvin gave the guard his magical parchment, showing his Master Wizard status.

"There is no need for you to show me this, Melvin the Magnificent," then he bowed a polite bow. "You and the Princess have been expected. You are to be escorted directly to the Empress herself, and may I say what an honor and privilege it is to meet you both, and a privilege for you to meet her. I haven't even met the Empress yet, and I have been working here almost 200 annums. I have always wanted to, though. I have seen glimpses of her coming and going, but have never actually met her."

"Thank you for your hospitality." Melvin responded, "However, we have already met the Empress on one occasion, and she has requested that we are to be married here in Lilenhamür."

The guards' jaw dropped in amazement. They have met the Empress? And the Empress requested that they be married here? That was extremely rare. These must be some extraordinary people.

"What is your name?" Melvin asked the guard. "Jeromy," he answered.

"Jeromy," Melvin said with a warm smile, "I invite you to our wedding as my guest. And you will meet the Empress."

The guard's jaw slackened in disbelief. His voice quivered. "Do… do you mean it? I'm no one special. Why would you do this for me?"

Melvin clasped his shoulder. "I believe that everyone should be able to realize their righteous desires. And this is one, I believe, I can help you with." Melvin said with a smile. He then produced a piece of parchment. An invitation to their wedding, with a special request that the guard get to meet the Empress in person. He gave it to the guard. With this, the carriage continued through the gate. Later that rev he made arrangements for Jeromy to be present at the wedding and to attend the reception as his guest.

Adara was in sheer awe. Not only for Melvin's kindness, but also for the fortress. Just passing through the gates was 5 spans just to get through the wall. This was singularly the widest wall that she had ever been through. No wonder Lilenhamür was famous for being impenetrable. However, she could feel something else as well, but she just couldn't put her finger on it.

The carriage driver gave them a tour of the fortress.

Lilenhamür wasn't just a fortress—it was a world unto itself.

The towering walls encased an entire city, larger than anything Adara had ever known. She had once thought her castle grand, but here, it paled in comparison. Streets bustled with merchants and travelers, sprawling marketplaces stretched beneath massive stone archways, and the scent of fresh bread and roasting meats filled the air.

They passed several more walls within the city, each one just as big and thick as the first one they went through.

They learned that it started off as a farm many, many, generations ago. The original owner, who was an ancestor of the Empress, built a wall around his farmland and lake to ward off the bands of thieves that would steal crops and livestock. That wall is what makes up the center wall deep inside of the fortress still around a farm and lake that produces food for the people living in the fortress.

This was not a single edifice as she had once believed. It had started out as the wall around a farmer's property. Then a town popped up around that wall, so to protect that town, another wall was erected around the town. Then the town spread outside that wall as well, and another wall, bigger and stronger, was built around that town. Larger and larger, taller and taller, the walls grew. As well as fortifying the walls inside the fortress, and building the buildings larger and grander as time passed, hundreds of thousands of annums until what it was now. So it was a hexagon ringed city with many walls around many cities. However, it was always a hexagon.

As they toured Lilenhamür, Adara was amazed at the beauty of this place. The walls were pure white marble, sanded to a perfect smooth luster. She hadn't seen all of it, for that would take weeks, but what she did see of it put her in awe. The ceiling, where there was one, was 7 spans high in most places, where they had a roof. Inside the fortress was like a city in itself. Well, that's because it was. There were shops around the inside of the outer wall, there were inns and restaurants. There were houses and apartments for the citizens. There were large, well-manicured lawns and parks, where children laughed and played. Fountains and rivers ran through the center. There were also quarters for the guards, the soldiers, and the wizards. But the most amazing thing that she saw when they were taken on a tour, when they arrived, was the atrium. The whole middle of the fortress was a farm. Fruit trees, plants, and vegetables grew there, and honey bees were used to pollinate the flowers. There was a lake in the middle where men fished. Water came in from a river flowing through the fortress. It was a truly amazing sight to see. The person giving them the tour said that it took many milleannums to build

Lilenhamür, and the Empress wanted it to be as self-sufficient as possible. She also wanted to be a trading hub for kingdoms throughout the Empire.

As Melvin and Adara toured Lilenhamür, he just couldn't figure out where the magic was coming from. He sent his essence into every area he could find and found nothing. He saw no signs of what could be producing the magic. Where was it located? The configuration? Maybe a spell was put on it? He decided that he would have to ask the Empress at some point during their visit. However, this wasn't the time to worry about it. Tomorrow, he was going to marry Adara; they were here as guests of Empress Kayla, and so he was going to enjoy this time with her and worry about this magic later. He cuddled up to his beautiful fiancée and just enjoyed the ride and the wonders of Lilenhamür. They spent the rest of the rev exploring the fortress. While he soaked up the views, he also soaked up the magic. He could feel himself becoming stronger.

Later that evening, they were sitting in the grass at one of the many parks in Lilenhamür watching the sunsset.

"I made something for you," Melvin murmured, his fingers brushing against Adara's hand. His gaze locked onto her bright purple eyes, filled with warmth and anticipation.

He pulled out a ring from his pocket. Then he sang softly *"This... is your wedding ring," he said softly. "It connects with your engagement ring, strengthening its protection. And through its magic, we will always find each other, no matter where we are."*

"I made this for you last night. I had been trying to figure it out for a long time. I made a lot of it by hand, but needed magic for some of it. But I get the materials the same way I got the materials for your engagement ring. This will add to the protection your engagement ring gives you. In addition, through this magic, we will always know where each other are."

The ring was exquisite. It was a gold ring with a red hue that glowed slightly. It also had a circle of small diamonds cut to perfection that fit perfectly around the center fire ruby of Adara's engagement ring. The diamonds reflected multicolored light so brilliantly in the sunlight that Adara had to avert her eyes. There was no other ring like it in the world. Nor will there ever be.

"Melvin, this is the best ring I have ever seen in my entire life. You should go into the jewelry business.

You could be rich," she chuckled.

"No, Adara, this is only for you. I will only make jewelry for you and our children. Ok, and maybe my mom." He chuckled.

"I love it, Melvin." And she kissed him passionately.

"But I have no ring for you," Adara said, sorrowfully looking up into Melvin's eyes. Melvin held up his finger with the fire ring she had made on it. "I have this."

"I need to upgrade it," she said. "Can you make another gold ring?"

"Of course." And he did so. He sent his consciousness through the Helaeth Mountains near Lilenhamür and found deposits of gold deep under the mountains. He also saw other interesting things under those mountains. But he wouldn't worry about that. He got some of the gold and some other precious metals and as he did with his bride's ring. He combined the metals to make an alloy on the molecular level. Others in the park watched in awe as they witnessed this happening.

When he was finished making the ring, Adara then used her power to do the same thing she did with his ring to her and added a fiery hue to the gold of the ring. "There, now you have an actual ring I can put on your finger."

Melvin smiled. They sat there for a while longer, holding each other. Then Melvin said, "Do you notice anything different about this place?"

"What do you mean?" she asked, curious about what he was getting at.

"I don't mean the size or the grandeur," he continued, "but something else. Magic. Very strong magic. I can feel it all around me. I have been absorbing as much as I can since I have been here."

"I did notice something like that, but I didn't know what it was." She said. "I have felt stronger since I have been here, but I couldn't explain it."

"Wizards can feel and absorb magic." Melvin reminded her. "Remember, I told you about when I saw Penelope hatch. I absorbed some of her magic."

"Yes," she said as she thought about it. "I do remember you mentioning that to me, as well as Reicuas. But you did not absorb a little of her magic. You absorbed a lot of her magic. You looked more powerful, more confident, and your hair and eyes changed color. Your aura was stronger. I never really thought about it since." She said, looking at the dual suns.

"I must teach you how to absorb magic. Then you will also become more powerful." He stated. "If it will help, then yes. Please do." She smiled, then she kissed him again.

It was getting near eventide and they headed to the palace proper to get ready for the night. When they arrived they were greeted by Adara's family and Melvin's mother. They celebrated that evening, then turned in for the night.

Just before Adara headed to her room, her mother caught her arm. "Adara, my dear, I would like to speak to you before you go to bed. She motioned to a bench in the elaborate hallway, and they both sat down.

"Yes, Mother," She responded, "What is it?"

"Adara," The Queen continued "Tomorrow, you will marry Melvin. We have been waiting for this rev for a very long time,"

"I know mother, so have I." She said nervously.

"I know you know this, but Melvin isn't like other men. He has a kind heart, like your father. However, as you know, he is a great wizard. Perhaps the greatest of all time."

She felt like saying *DUH* because she already knew this. But she felt it prudent to be polite. "Yes, mother, I know this as well," She said softly.

"There will be times, my dear," her mother said gently, "when he will have to leave. There will be journeys, quests, and possibly even battles… moments when you will be apart, perhaps for longer than you'd like."

Adara tensed. "Then I will go with him," she said firmly. "I am not a child. I am a strong woman. I am a warrior, a wizardess, the commander of our military—I will not be left behind."

Her mother smiled knowingly. "I'm Sorry, she said soothingly, stroking her daughter's hand. "I do not doubt your strength, Adara. But even the strongest hearts can falter in the face of uncertainty. And when those moments come… You must be his strength, just as he will be yours."

"I know you are all of those things, and I am very proud of you," She continued gently. "What I was trying to say is when those times come, he will maybe doubt himself. We all know he is a magnificent wizard. But does he? Does he know he can do the things that will be required of him?" She looked right into Adara's beautiful, bright, shining purple eyes. "That's where you come in, sweetie. You need to be there for him, just as he is for you. You need to encourage him, love him, push him to be better, and teach him the things he needs to know. But also be meek and humble and let him teach you things you need to know, as well as I know he will do for you."

"Yes, mother, I try to do that already," She said softly.

"That is good." Her mother said, pulling Adara into an embrace. Then her mother told her some other things. Things she should do on her wedding night with Melvin. Adara was surprised. Her mother, of all people, was telling her this. But it was good advice. She would remember these things.

Then they both went to bed, for they had a very important rev the next rev.

CHAPTER 25

THE WEDDING

The rev dawned bright and golden, as if the very heavens were blessing this rev. Standing by the window of the North West tower, Adara gazed across the sprawling city and beyond the fortress walls and the trees beyond the wall. From this height—fifty spans above the ground—she felt like she could reach out and touch the sky.

In the distance, towering mountains loomed, their peaks lost in swirling clouds. She had never seen such majestic heights before. The mountains near home, once impressive, now seemed like mere hills in comparison, and those were pretty big mountains in and of themselves.

She had never seen mountains so large before. She could not see the top of them, for they were covered in clouds. It appeared that they shot straight up into the sky. She couldn't imagine what types of people and creatures lived in those mountains. What beauty they She also had never been this far west before. Being the daughter of a King and the commander of the army, allowed her to go many places far and wide, but she had never been this far west. She had never dreamed of being in the Empress's fortress. For her own wedding, nevertheless.

Adara snapped back from her thoughts to the present. This rev was a special rev. This rev was the rev she and Melvin would become husband and wife. The ladies in waiting came in to get her ready.

Since the Empress had insisted they wed in Lilenhamür, she had also gifted Adara the most breathtaking wedding gown she had ever laid eyes on. The fabric—scampit silk—was spun from the threads of creatures that dwelled deep beneath the earth, their silk rarer than gold and softer than the whispers of the wind.

The dress shimmered in the light, its surface adorned with diamonds so perfectly placed that Adara felt like she was wearing a garment woven from starlight.

She was also given jewels and a tiara to wear, with the most perfect diamonds that were to be found in the land. Well, except for the ring Melvin made. She had her own tiara, but this far surpassed anything she could have imagined. Her shoes were crystal and fit perfectly. And the best thing?? They were hers. She was not borrowing them. The Empress gave them to her as part of her wedding present.

She just enjoyed the moment being pampered and primped and being all made up by the Empress's personal servants. She also watched as her sisters were attended to as well. She couldn't wait to see what they were able to get Melvin into. She knew Melvin wouldn't want to wear anything fancy, but Empress Kayla would probably convince him to do so. She had ways of doing that, but in a good way.

Melvin stood in the grand chamber, shifting uncomfortably. The room was *too* lavish for him—mirrors reflecting his image from every angle, cushions softer than clouds, and... warm running water? Indoor plumbing? He had heard of it before, but never had he seen it so seamlessly woven into everyrev life.

He was certain of one thing—he was far from Bilbylund. He supposed the palace back in Bilbylund had it, but never paid too much attention to it. He would have to install some in his house. Now he had these very beautiful young ladies all over him, getting him ready for his wedding. Well, they weren't that young; they were all around his age, but they were not older women either. He knew he should feel guilty, especially on his wedding rev, but this was a once-in-a-lifetime event, so he just enjoyed the moment. He let himself be pampered, let the beautiful girls wash him, and get him dressed. The Empress told him to relax and enjoy this time, for this was a reward for him and Adara. He could tell that these ladies were enjoying it as much as he was. They gave him a bath in warm water out of a faucet. Then they slowly scrubbed every inch of his body with soft cloths and scented soaps. Some areas they went over a few times with the excuse that they needed to make sure he was extra clean. He knew what they were up to and just enjoyed the moment.

After the bath, the girls dried him off and put some clothes on him that they said were made especially for him, for his wedding. He never did like the wizard's outfits that most of the wizards wore. He didn't like fancy flowing robes or hats that the nobles wore. He looked in the mirror at his clothes and noticed, although they were fine cloth and he thought leather, and some other material, it didn't look fancy at all. He didn't mind this outfit and may wear it often to special occasions.

Finally, after waiting all this time, he would finally be married to his best friend, his soul mate, the love of his life. They would be one. Husband and wife. They would finally be able to share his house. He was invited to live in the castle with her and her family, but he felt his house would be more private, more of a home. He had made it bigger than it was, and with Adara's help, added some womanly touches and cleaned it up a bit. Ok, cleaned it up a lot. Finally, they could live together, share a bed together, and do other things married couples did. Eventually, raising a family with the most wonderful woman he knew. Well, besides his mother.

He thought about these things as the servants got him ready. And he thought also that these girls were enjoying their job pampering him as much as he was enjoying being pampered.

Finally, the time came. Melvin was washed and dressed. Melvin was escorted to the Dias where he would await his bride.

Melvin looked around the gigantic cathedral. The ceilings must have been 10 spans high. Large arches held up the ceiling. Rows and rows of pews were on either side of a wide marble walkway that had a red carpet running down the middle from the back to the dais. Large marble columns accented with gold ran down either side of the cathedral. There was a band off to one side of the dais playing soft music.

When everyone was situated, the band started playing the wedding song. Adara took a deep breath and looked up at the man standing beside her. "This is it, Daddy, I'm finally getting married. I'm nervous, Daddy," she said.

"You will be fine, sweetheart. One step at a time." He said tenderly back to her. "This is supposed to be the happiest rev of your life, well, until the kids come, but one step at a time." He smiled.

"It is Daddy, I am very happy and excited. I have waited so long for this rev. But I'm also nervous." She squeezed his hand.

"It will be ok, sweetheart. Just relish in the good feelings and love of the rev. Of your love for Melvin," he said tenderly and smiled, "Shall we go?" he asked.

"Ok, daddy, let's go." She nodded to the guards. They opened the large doors to the grand hall of the cathedral. It looked like a cavernous space to her. Rows upon rows of pews on either side of them, all filled. Everyone stood. There were more people in there than she had ever seen in one gathering in her life. Not only people but other types as well, fairies, elves, dwarves, etc., even their dragon Penelope and also Percilla, as well as other dragons, were perched on the balcony. She was in awe that all these people showed up for her wedding. Why? Why did the Empress take such notice of her and Melvin? She was just a princess of a small kingdom in a faraway place that most people had never even heard of. As she walked with her father, King Bilby, she started to get overwhelmed with the grandeur of it all. Sure, they had parties and balls and such at the palace, but never anything like this. Now she knew what Melvin felt like. She would never bother him about that again. She missed a step and had to be steadied by her father. She was glad he was there to walk her down the aisle and steady her. Not only physically, but emotionally as well.

As they moved further down the aisle, Adara's breath caught.

There, at the dais, stood Melvin—waiting. Her sisters flanked her side, radiant in their silk gowns, yet when she looked to Melvin's, her heart clenched. He stood alone. No best man. No lifelong friends.

Reicuas, his beloved mentor, had never returned from battle. His only true companions had been his mother, his dragon, and… Adara herself.

She swallowed hard, vowing that from this moment forward, he would never stand alone again.

One look at him and she went weak in the knees; it was a good thing she was holding her father's arm, or she would have fallen.

She had never seen Melvin look so handsome. Sure, he was handsome all the time, but now she was completely blown away. First of all, he was glowing, literally glowing. She didn't know if anyone else could tell, but she could. His Aura was so intense that it shone. Then she noticed what he was wearing. His pants and Jacket were Gold dragon's hide. However, the pants were dyed black. Just like her dress, it shimmered in the light. His boots were also dragon hide and dyed black. He had on an undershirt made of the same silk that her dress was made of. And he was wearing a gold cape made from a combination of the same silk and dragon's hide. He wore a chest piece that was made from gold dragon scales. She wondered how they got the hide and scales, and hoped no dragon was injured to get those. Just then, an image was put in her mind of Penelope's cave with a lot of the scales around, and old skin, or hide, just like any other reptile molts when it grows. Adara was put at ease, and being made from Penelope's hide and scales made it more special. She wondered if Melvin knew. Penelope told her that he did. Penelope also communicated that she was just as much her dragon as she was Melvin's, since she had known her just as long, and since they were getting married, she was just as much hers. Penelope loved Adara just as much as she loved Melvin and was very happy they were finally getting married. This put more of a smile on Adara's face as she continued to walk down the aisle, which seemed to go on forever. '*Wow,*' she thought. '*Am I blessed?*'

To Melvin's surprise, he found himself feeling quite at ease in his new outfit, He was told that Penelope had wanted him to use some of her old scales and leather as part of his outfit. It was part of her gift to him. Since he was there when she was born, had given her her freedom, and they were very close, the magic within these would give him extra power and protection. That wouldn't work for anyone else. Eventually, He would have a whole set of armor made of it.

Melvin stood there patiently watching his love walk slowly up the aisle. He couldn't help but chuckle when Adara missed a step, though he felt bad about it. Was this the same woman he had toured the fortress with last rev? She looked so amazing. He would have to make sure she got all the beauty tips from whoever got her ready. She was radiant. She was quite literally radiant—her skin seemed to glow with an ethereal light, sparkling like stardust, and shimmering with a soft, vibrant pink hue. It was as if she embodied pure joy and magic in that very moment. Everyone could see the white dress sparkling in the well-lit hall. But he, and he was sure others could see, her aura as well shining, and the combination of her red aura and the shining dress, the two made her radiate pink. What was even funnier was that she hated pink. Her long red hair was curled and hung down. She hated putting it up. '*Wow,*' he thought. '*Am I blessed.*'

Adara finally got up to the dais, her father stepped aside. Melvin took her hand, looked into her beautiful, shining purple eyes, and smiled. Adara, in turn, looked into his shining multicolored eyes and smiled. Then looked around and saw Empress Kayla sitting in the front along with the King and Queen, and Melvin's mother. They all looked so nice, her mother and father had on their finest attire and wore their purple capes that they wore to all the important events. She had never seen Melvin's mother look so beautiful. She thought she looked good at the party when Melvin became a Master Wizard, but this surpassed that tenfold. She without a doubt had to get the beauty tips from these people. And she was positive that her sisters would or already have. She was glad that her sisters were standing next to her on this most important event. Her sisters had on different colored silk dresses that matched their personalities and auras. The Elder dismissed them to sit with the family. Everyone sat down.

Then the Elder started the ceremony. "We are gathered here this rev, on this blessed occasion to join this man and this woman in holy marriage witnessed by Deo and these witnesses. Their love has become a powerful bond that has brought us all together this rev. Through this love, they commit themselves to the Father of us all and each other. In body, mind, and spirit, they become one. To share in each other's joys and triumphs and each other's sorrows."

"Rings, please," said the Elder. The maid of honor, who was Adara's sister Aria, took the rings from the little pillows they were sitting on and handed them to the bride and groom. Now you may be wondering, where is the Best Man? Well, there isn't one. But why not, you may also be wondering. Surely an important wizard such as this must have friends. Well, in that assumption, you would be correct. They were Adara and her sisters, and Penelope. You see, Melvin dedicated his life to his studies. Dedicated himself to being the best wizard he could be, to his mother, his Master, Penelope, his dragon, and most of all to Adara. That's all he needed in his life. He loved them with his whole heart, soul, and being. They were his world. He didn't care about having other friends. He did have other friends, but none were as close as these.

Melvin's ring was a simple gold band with a fiery glow to it, and Adara's reflected the light in the room so brilliantly that it cast multicolored shafts of light throughout the great hall.

"I have to get one of those," The empress said, and many of the queens from the different lands whispered to their kings. Then to all of them was projected a thought: *There is only one and will ever only be one of these rings. It was personally made by Melvin for his bride, and it belongs to Adara. There will never be another one like it made.* All the ladies frowned. *However, Empress,* A thought only to the Empress, *if you desire, I am sure we can convince Melvin to make you a ring. But not exactly like this one.* The empress smiled.

The Elder continued: "Melvin and Adara, have prepared vows for each other, please say your vows that you have prepared."

Adara started her vows with a shaky voice. "Melvin, the Magnificent. You are my love, my life. I make a solemn vow that from this time forward, as I have done since we first met, I will love you and honor you and cherish you. I will be by your side, through good times and bad times. Though you don't need it, I will use all my ability to protect you. You are my heart, my soul, my equal. Everything I have is yours. With this ring, I devote my life, my soul, and my being to you." Then she slipped the ring onto his finger.

Then it was Melvin's turn. Since this was a very emotional moment for him, he chose to sing his vows so he would not stutter. "*Adara of Bilby. Deo has brought you into my life. You are the light of my life, you are the shining example in my life, just as you shine, so does this ring. The two circles of this ring represent our never-ending love. Mine below, yours above. The gold and titanium for strength, they make each other stronger, which I give to you, and you give to me. The diamonds for the light that you give me. I promise to love you, honor you, and cherish you. To put you above all others, to protect you and our future family with all my ability. I will be on your side through all our joys, triumphs, misfortunes, and sorrows. You are my heart, my soul, my equal, my better half. Everything I have is yours. With this ring, I devote my life, my soul, and my being to you.*" Then he slipped the ring onto her delicate finger. As soon as it was on, a flash of bright white light flashed through the entire hall. Adara felt a strength, a power she had never felt before. She felt like she was invincible.

When the crying died down, mostly from the queen, Melvin's mother, and the Empress, the Elder was able to continue. "I would like to first give you some advice as you start your lives together as one. As was stated by both of you, your love and devotion to each other make a marriage strong. Never let the feelings of this rev fade, but continue to deepen your love and devotion to each other. Also, remember that there is a third party to this marriage. Deo, our Father, our Creator, should be just as much involved in this marriage as both of you. Like a triangle. He is on top of the triangle, and you two are the other angles, all pointing to each other. When you have hard decisions to make, talk it out, and then take it to our Father. He will be the answer to all decisions, both in family matters and other matters. He has given you great gifts and talents. Use them wisely to serve and bless the lives of each other, and of others around you. Now, I am sure you are anxious to finish this ceremony." The Elder smiled. "So, by the authority of the Almighty Deo, from this time forward, I pronounce you, Melvin the Magnificent, Master Wizard, and you, Commander, Princess, Adara of Bilby, husband and wife. May Deo bless this marriage that it may be long and happy. May you find joy in each other and the family you will someday have."

Melvin cupped Adara's face, his eyes locked onto hers as the Elder gave his final blessing. "You, Princess Adara," the Elder said with a quaint smile, "may now kiss your husband."

And with this, they kissed for the first time as husband and wife. Their lips met, and the world fell away.

Magic surged between them, an undeniable force, crackling like fire and light. Suddenly, brilliant fireworks erupted throughout the great hall—not conjured by spell or command, but by pure, unrestrained joy.

Cheers rang out as colors illuminated the high-vaulted ceilings, showering the newlyweds in a cascade of golden light. And at that moment, they weren't just a wizard and a princess.

They were one.

Everyone cheered for the newlyweds.

Later on at the reception.....

Melvin looked around the great hall, greeting guests. This was a hall in the main palace, but just as big and just as much grandeur. He remembered the party thrown in honor of the Empress's visit back at the palace back home. That was a poor man's party compared to this. Banners hung on the walls and the archways of Lilenhamür, the Arion Empire, and the banners of Bilbylund. A large tapestry of Melvin and Adara hung on one of the walls as well. Elegant tables and chairs were organized along the perimeter of a large marble dance floor. Along the sides of the walls were multiple tables filled with more food than Melvin had ever seen in his entire life in one place. Then there were the guests, Kings, Queens, Magistrates, Nobles, the most important people in the empire of Arion were there, and also from other lands across the ocean. But the most important person on the planet was standing right next to him. His wife, Adara. Melvin stood there in awe and wonder. He wondered, Why? Why all this grandeur? Why are all these people here for him and his bride? Were they there because it was a party with food, drink, and dancing? Were they there because the Empress invited them? Or were they there because of Him and Adara? Who was he? Just a wizard from a small village on the other side of the continent. To himself, he was no one of any importance. His wife, on the other hand, he could see why people showed up to be at a party for her. She was the most amazing woman he knew. Everyone was lined up to shake their hands and congratulate them. Why were they so special?

Adara stood next to her now husband. She couldn't control her excitement and her deep, penetrating joy. She had waited for so long to be married to this wonderful, amazing man, and now she finally was. He was the most handsome, wonderful, kind, humble, yet powerful man that has ever lived. The problem is, is that he doesn't realize this. She will remind him often. Hopefully, one rev he will realize this and use his full potential.

Growing up as a princess, she was used to lavish parties for dignitaries. But this, this was beyond anything she had ever experienced. Take one of their lavish balls, and multiply it by 1000. She was used to parties, food, banquets, people, dancing, etc. But nothing ever on this scale. She has met kings at parties, but they were never a party for *HER*. She was in awe that this many important people came to their wedding. She didn't think that she was that special. But her husband, on the other hand, she could see how people would line up to meet him. He was more important and more famous than he knew. He was the most famous wizard in the history of the planet Estry.

Since Melvin didn't have a best man, Adara's father, King Bilby, gave a speech for the bride and groom. He opened his arms wide as if to embrace them both. "To Melvin and Adara. Melvin, Adara could not have chosen to marry a better man. You have become like a son to me, I know she is in good hands and that she will be well taken care of. Adara, I know that Melvin loves you more than anything in this world. He would do everything in his power to protect you, not that you need it, you would just blast anyone with fire, but still." Everyone chuckled because they knew it was true. "Melvin, Adara has this same devotion to you. What you don't know is that she has waited a very, very long time for this rev. For decannums, she has wondered when you would ask her to marry her, she has cried on my shoulder for hours wanting to be your wife. She was about to ask you herself if you didn't hurry up and do it. But when you did, she was the happiest I had ever seen her. From the moment she met you, those many long annums ago, she was smitten, the more time she spent with you, the more she fell in love with you. I pray that you two have safety and happiness in your marriage. May you live in peace to raise a family."

"Everyone here is glad to see this rev finally arrive. A father's blessing I leave on you two, that you may have strength in each other, happiness with each other, that you will raise your children in peace and love and with a knowledge and great abiding love that our Deo who provides us with everything we have. Now eat, drink, celebrate this most happy occasion." Everyone clapped and cheered and took a drink.

Next, Melvin's Mother, Penelope, stood and gave a brief speech. "Melvin, I second what King Bilby has said. I used to teach Adara at the palace, as you know. And she always talked about you, the whole time growing up. Her heart ached to be with you, she saw in you the qualities she had always wanted in a man. Kind, gentle, humble, loving, etc. Adara, like King Bilby said, the moment Melvin laid eyes on you, the rev at your practice building, he was in love. He ran home and told me that he had just met one of the princesses.

And she was the most beautiful girl in the world. He said that eventually, he was going to marry you. Well, many cenannums, decannums, and many annums later, the rev has finally arrived. May you both have peace, love, and joy throughout your lives."

Next, Empress Kayla stood. She looked regal in her sparkling purple dress and flowing cape. An exquisite crown adorned her head. As she started to speak, a silence engulfed the room. She started slowly, choosing her words carefully. "I usually don't speak at weddings, I usually don't host weddings at Lilenhamür, unless the people are very special to me and the Empire." She looked at Melvin, then smiled. "You may not know this, Melvin, but Reicuas was one of my most beloved friends and teachers. For many, many decannums he taught me. But he had to go back to Bilbylund to raise up a new wizard apprentice. That apprentice, Melvin, was you. When he told me about you and Adara, I instantly looked into your heart. I saw the person you were, and the person you could become. I saw the power that you have inside you. I knew then I must meet you." Then she looked at Adara, her bright blue eyes shining in the light of the hall. "Adara, you as well, you have such power in you, enough power to decimate anything you wanted to. But you would not do that, for you also have but also such compassion for all creatures, and your love and devotion for each other. I knew then that separate you would be a power to reckon with. She held her arms wide, "but together." She then clasped her hands together, interlocking the fingers, "You two would be unstoppable, and you are proving that to be true. Now this rev belongs to both of you—a shared celebration of love, unity, and the journey you've embarked on together. Let it be filled with joy, meaning, and memories to treasure forever. Celebrate, enjoy it. Have fun," She smiled again and then put up her pointer finger, as if her next statement they must remember, "Oh, and remember, when you have children, to bring them to visit. I'm not going anywhere for a long long time." and with this she motioned to the band to start playing and the party and dancing commenced.

The band played a song for the daddy-daughter dance. Adara, glowing from head to toe, danced with her father. A short time later, Melvin joined them on the floor and danced with his mother. This was the best rev of their lives.

Melvin kept his promise and personally introduced Jeromy, the guard at the gate, to the Empress. Jeromy couldn't believe how beautiful she was, and how young. He had heard about this but had never seen her this close before. Then she smiled, and he felt like the luckiest man in the world. Not only did she smile and shake his hand, but she embraced him and thanked him for his service as a royal guard. He was so elated he almost passed out. She motioned to some other guards to have them take him to a seat and let him sit down. She also mentioned that she must make a rev to honor the palace guards. Once every annum, she will have a banquet for them and show her appreciation for their hard work.

Melvin and Adara ate, drank, danced, but both couldn't wait for that night when they could be alone as husband and wife.

That night, when they were finally alone, in a lavish suite, in part of the fortress away from all the others, they were finally able to be together as husband and wife, without any interruptions. And Adara remembered what her mother told her. The next morning, they flew on Penelope to their honeymoon destination.

Adara and Melvin went away on a honeymoon that actually lasted one moon, which was the custom. He and Adara flew on Penelope to what we would call a tropical paradise. It was an island haven on the southern end of the continent of Arion. There, they relaxed, played on the beach, had fun at the nightly bonfires, and just loved being with each other without worrying about things going on back home. They were pampered, catered to, went to lavish parties with lots of food, and had delicacies. They swam in the ocean; most of this they could do back home. But what they did the most was just spend time with each other.

CHAPTER 26

QUESTIONS

As their honeymoon ended, the newlyweds returned to Lilenhamür, where duty awaited them.

Though Melvin cherished the past moon spent with Adara, a nagging curiosity had lingered at the back of his mind. The moment they had stepped foot into the fortress, he had felt it—a deep, ancient magic woven into the ancient fortress. And now, at last, he had the chance to uncover its source.

Now that they were back, he enjoyed seeing the sights and being with his new wife, he just couldn't shake off this wonder about the magic. He was sure other non-wizards did not even know it existed, but it was very noticeable to him. And he tried to absorb as much of it as he could.

After a moon of waiting, Melvin finally secured an audience with the Empress. She was busier than ever, yet when he stepped into the grand hall, she greeted him with a knowing smile.

He bowed. "Empress, I have a question—one I believe only you can answer."

"Melvin," she said, her voice smooth as silk. "You don't have to be so formal with me. Call me Kayla. Now, what is puzzling you?"

"I'm sorry, Empress Kayla," he said as he bowed again.

"Melvin," She responded in a soft voice, and gave him a look that gave the notion to stop.

"And enough with the bowing." She said, frustrated. She gained her composure, and in a softer voice, she continued. "Melvin, let us take a walk in the garden so we can speak privately." With this, she motioned to the guard to open the door to the garden.

As they walked out, she continued. "Your master and I would often take walks in this garden as he would teach me or advise me, so long ago when he was here. How I miss those revs."

Melvin glanced around, momentarily distracted by the sheer beauty of the garden. Roses bloomed in flawless symmetry, their petals rich with color. Ancient trees arched over the cobblestone paths, their branches woven together like a natural cathedral. Even the shrubs had been sculpted into elegant figurines, each one a testament to a master gardener's careful hand. The air itself hummed with an energy he couldn't quite place.

"He told me he taught you, but did not go into any detail." He said as they walked. There was an ornate, meticulously carved bridge that spanned a small stream, which ends he did not know where they it came from or went. They stopped on this bridge to talk.

Kayla motioned for them to sit on a padded bench on the bridge where they stood. Oh, how this brought back memories of a time before, when Reicuas and her would have long talks in this garden. "What is puzzling you, Melvin?" she asked, although she pretty much already knew.

"Magic," is all he said. Looking around the garden. He did not feel that he was worthy to be speaking to the Empress like this, like they were personal friends.

"Magic?" she asked. She could feel the uneasiness of Melvin, knew his heart, and wanted him to feel at ease.

"Melvin," she said, sensing his unease. "I know you feel out of place speaking with me. Yes, I am the Empress—but before that, I am simply a person. And you—" her eyes softened as she studied him "—are no ordinary wizard. You are the rarest I have seen in a lifetime.

You…" she said, looking into his bright, multicolored eyes, "are the greatest wizard I have seen in a long, long time. If it's anyone who should be uncomfortable, it's me. I have heard and seen you do things that no other wizard has ever done. Most wizards have one or two talents, and they take annums to master those. Deo has blessed you with many talents. You have nearly every talent, and ones I don'teven know of, and you wield magic as easily as breathing, talents that take others decades to master. The world will recognize you, whether you seek it or not. Fame, power, expectation—they will find you. But you must decide how to use them."

So please relax, do not feel intimidated. I want us to be friends. I want us to be as family, both you and Adara."

Empress Kayla looked up at the dual suns, as if she was remembering a long forgotten memory "Keep in mind, I did not choose to be Empress, it was put upon me because of my rare ability to know the hearts and intents of people, and can see the future from the actions of people."

She turned again and looked at Melvin. His eyes, a kaleidoscope of color that drew her in, she continued explaining what she knew about him. "You, I see, are pure in heart, you do not like grandeur, you do not like fame, I see that, I understand that. However, it will be thrust upon you. You are an exceptionally rare Wizard, Melvin. You already have fame, you will be recognized wherever you go. Just look at your wedding. Every king and queen and the most noble, the high professors from Wazervïl, all of those people came to see you and your bride Adara get married. And why is that? Because you are an exceptionally talented wizard, and your bride is an exceptionally talented fire wizardess. You can use that to your advantage when the time is right, for good purposes. To serve others, and certainly, to upgrade your room at an inn," she chuckled. "I am sorry, Melvin, I have rambled on and have completely ignored your inquiry. You were wondering about Magic. What about magic are you wondering about? I think you would know a lot more about that subject than I," she said humbly.

With these words from the Empress, he was put at ease. "Kayla," Melvin said tentatively, "When I entered the gates of this fortress, I noticed a power within it, a magic. A magic so strong that I could not escape it, a power emanating from Lilenhamür. However, no matter how hard I tried, I could not find the source of it. I channeled my conscience into every conceivable place in this fortress, and I cannot find the source of it. Even the dragons who live inside Lilenhamür don't compare to the magic I feel. And I hope you don't mind, but I have been soaking in as much as I possibly can."

"Melvin," the Empress said, her voice quieter now, almost reverent. "Not many can sense what you have. Few even know it exists. But I knew you would. This is no ordinary magic—it is ancient, woven into the very bones of Lilenhamür. And I had hoped… no, I had counted on you feeling it."

But yes, you are right, there is magic in this place. You will not find it in a single place or an object within Lilenhamür or within the walls. For it *is* the walls. It *is* Lilenhamür itself. This is one of the reasons why I wanted you to be married here, I knew you could absorb magic. I was hoping that you would absorb the magic here in Lilenhamür. And Adara as well."

"Lilenhamür?" Melvin whispered, his brows furrowing. "The fortress itself?"

The Empress nodded. "Yes. The walls are not just stone, Melvin. They breathe. They **remember.** Every tower, every brick, every path—they were built with magic, carved with runes that pulse with an energy older than the empire itself."

"How is that so?" Melvin asked, amazed.

She continued softly. "Anciently, when the first farmer, my ancestor, built the first wall around his farm, he did so using magic. You see, he was also a powerful wizard, and much like you, he liked the simple life, so he farmed. His main talent was herbology. Growing plants and crops, so it made sense. So when he built the wall around his farm, he did so in such a manner that it evoked magic for protection. He used a certain type of stone that absorbed and then released magic when needed. He also carved powerful magic runes into the stone to add to that protection. He also built the wall in a certain pattern that concentrated this protective magic even further. The greatest concentration of magic is at the lake in the center of Lilenhamür. That's why my palace is closest to the center; it enhances my abilities, as it enhances yours.

"In addition," the Empress continued, "He cast incantations on the walls, the ground, and buildings for protection and prosperity. That anything within the walls would be protected and would also prosper. Each generation, and each wall or building that was added, was built in this same manner by wizards. If you flew Penelope over the top of this fortress, you would see intricate patterns of where the walls and buildings are placed. The Hexagon is one of those magical patterns, but if you look more closely, you will see it's much more intricate than that. I am sure you learned about this from Reicuas."

Melvin's mind was blown. "Yes, we did go over this, but not in great detail. I should have figured it was something like that. Thank you for the explanation. Now that you reminded me of the symbology in magic runes, I can go and modify Adara's ring for better protection for her."

"That is right. I am proud of you for always thinking of your bride first. However, Melvin, I also know that she thinks the same way about you. Do not forget, though, that she is a very talented Wizardess and is very capable of taking care of herself. She did not get to be the commander of the Arion army by being weak. Enable her in her strength, lift her, encourage her. She is capable of more than you realize, more than she realizes. As are you. Use your magic to enhance both of your abilities. Again, I suggest you go visit the elves in Illëngard. I will send them a message to expect you, though it doesn't have to be quickly. I have spent much time with them after Reicuas went to the land of Bilby. They can teach you how to use your magic more effectively, and Adara and Aria as well. They can help you greatly enhance your magic abilities. And, I am sure, you can teach them a thing or two as well." Empress Kayla paused for a moment to look around her beautiful garden and took a deep breath. The gentle afternoon breeze blew her purple hair. She wished she could continue this conversation longer. Being with Melvin invigorated her. But alas, she was the Empress and had matters to attend to. She sighed then continued, "It was a pleasure speaking with you, Melvin. I would have liked to have been able to chat longer with you about history and magic, but I must get back to my duties. You and Adara are welcome to call on me any time, as well as your dragon Penelope. If you ever need assistance in your quest to relieve us of this evil wizard, I will do all I can to help in this effort."

"Thank you, Kayla. I feel honored and humbled that you give your precious time to one such as I, who comes from a small village so far away."

"Let me remind you again, Melvin, that your Master was one of my closest friends, and I can see that you and the princess will do great things for this Empire. Also, as I have said before, I see the magic within you, and it far surpasses anything I have seen in all my life. And as you know, I have had a long life."

With this, they got up, and Empress Kayla went back to the throne room, and Melvin called Penelope for a ride around the fortress. As they rode high in the sky, he could see and understood what Empress Kayla was talking about, the pattern of the walls. They landed on the shore of the lake. The shimmering of the water in the bright noon suns brought a magical sight. The crops being grown next to the lake looked bigger and brighter than any others he had ever seen. The animals looked healthier. Yes, this was truly a magical place. He took a personal note to learn all he could about these patterns, runes, and magic so he could do the same thing to his and Adara's home when they got back.

Melvin sat on Penelope, and he could feel the concentrated magic. Stronger than anywhere else he had ever been. He opened himself up to it, absorbing as much of it as he could. He would have to bring Adara here. But he also needed to go to the Elves, as Empress Kayla suggested. After a few hours, he could absorb no more; he was full as he could be of magic at this point, so Penelope flew him back to his bride. Melvin brought Adara to the lake and explained to her what the Empress had taught him. He taught her how to open herself up to absorb the magic. He taught her an incantation to be able to absorb more magic. She absorbed a tremendous amount of magic that afternoon.

Chapter 27
Rellik Stealing Eggs

"I must have more eggs," Rellik growled, his voice echoing off the obsidian walls. "More power. More dragons. I will be unstoppable." Rellik was standing on a balcony high up on a tower of his black obsidian castle deep in the forest of Nŏrden.

Rellik stood atop the highest balcony of his obsidian fortress, the jagged spires looming over the ancient forest of Nŏrden. Below, the trees swayed unnaturally, their thick branches reaching toward the sky like grasping hands trying to get the slight rays of the suns that pierced through the thick canopy.

"Yes… Master," the advisor murmured, his voice careful, measured. "But dragon eggs are rare in Arion. We have located only a handful…" His words trailed off, wary of how Rellik might react.

"Please continue," Rellik said cooly. His smooth voice, cold and calculating, sent a shiver of dread down the servant's spine.

"Yes, master," his advisor said. "But you know, there are very few eggs here in Arion. We do know of a couple of dragons that live in the desert near the Thrall, and there is one in the swamps to the south. A green dragon has laid an egg. And one in the lofty peaks of the Helaeth Mountains. But besides that, we know of no others."

"Then you shall go get the ones we do know about. Send out your men to get the eggs. If at all possible, I want the adult dragons as well."

The advisor assembled the orcs, trolls, goblins, and warlocks and commanded them to go to the dragons and get the eggs.

The group made their way to where the dragons were reported to be. The first was high atop the peaks of the Helaeth Mountains at the top of the highest peak of Mount Nŏrden. These peaks had a permanently ice-covered glacier. The northernmost peak on Mount Nŏrden was home to a very ferocious white ice dragon. These dragons loved the cold. While red and orange dragons breathed fire, these dragons breathed, well, you guessed it, ice. Not just any ice, but ice so cold, it would freeze you to death in a matter of seconds. This particular dragon had laid an egg. One so rare that an ice dragon egg had not been laid in many milleannums. This particular dragon did not like humans. They captured her mate long ago and ended up taking him to the desert, where white ice dragons could not survive because of the heat. You may be wondering, if they took the mate long ago, then why did she just now lay an egg? The answer is simple. Since a dragon is so large, it takes many annums for the egg to be laid, and then many more annums before it hatches.

She knew that these creatures were coming up the mountain, but what she did know was that they were not going to capture her or her egg. At the top of the ice-covered mountain, the Orcs, Goblins, and Warlocks scrambled up the icy slope. They had spent weeks on their journey and many had fallen to frostbite, sheer drops, or the slow hunger that came with traveling through such a frozen wasteland. The dragon, an ancient frost beast, had sealed the mouth of her cave with a wall of solid ice so thick and strong, nothing could break through it. She had burrowed deep into the glacier itself, carving out a frozen fortress high above the clouds. She was supposed to join the others in Dragonia—but pride and hunger kept her here.

You see, these jagged peaks were home to a rare creature called a *yodum*, a thick-furred animal found nowhere else in the world. And to this dragon, yodums were more than a meal—they were her favorite delicacy. To keep intruders away, she summoned guardians from the ice itself—cold, merciless demons made from frost and shadow. They stood watch, ready to shred anyone who dared approach her lair.

Unfortunately for her, a good amount of the group had made the arduous climb up the mountain and were approaching the cave. They had fire users among the group who would, with no effort at all, melt the ice demons and, in short order, melt the ice wall. The dragon had not faced this kind of opponent before. As they entered the massive cave, she caused massive stalactites made of ice to fall on them. She knew which ones were the fire users, so she used her icy breath to freeze them instantly. They would pose no more problems. Summoning the last of her strength, she encased the egg in an impenetrable ice shell, hardened to the strength of enchanted steel. Frost spiraled from her breath, coating the cavern in layers of shimmering blue. She would protect her unborn child at all costs.

The orcs and goblins came to attack her. She swiped her claws at them and froze them with her icy breath.

While she fought with all her fury, her talons shredding through flesh and ice-cold breath freezing foes mid-charge, she did not see them.

A pack of orcs slithered past the carnage, their gnarled hands grasping at the ice-encased egg. With inhuman strength, they lifted it and vanished into the storm. By the time she turned, her child was gone. A howl of fury and heartbreak shook the mountain.

As quickly as possible, they escaped the cave and slid down the mountain. One of the frozen fire wizards was able to thaw himself and put a fire barrier at the entrance of the cave, preventing the ice dragon from pursuing. They took this egg back to Rellik, where he had the insight to have the ice covering left over the egg because it needed to remain frozen for it to hatch.

The second dragon—a towering green acid dragon—made her lair deep within the heart of the Boglunds, where the land turned foul and the air thick with poison. Her swamp was especially vile, choked with choking vapors and bubbling pits of sulfuric acid that hissed and steamed as they boiled. It was the perfect home for a creature like her.

When the group arrived, the dragon rose from the acid swamp and asked their purpose. They explained they were seeking dragons and eggs to aid Rellik's growing army. She listened, her eyes gleaming with amusement. Spiteful and bitter by nature, she didn't hesitate. Not only did she offer her allegiance, but she also let them take one of her eggs—hardly giving it a second glance. She had no interest in raising it and saw more satisfaction in watching it serve someone else's war.

The last dragon they sought lived deep in the scorched reaches of the arid Sōden Desert. A place so dry and unforgiving that even the hardiest traveler would think twice before crossing it. The heat could fry an egg on a pan without flame, and the air was so dry it seemed to steal the moisture straight from your skin. Without water or the right kind of clothes, a person could dry up like old leather in just a few hours.

Worse still were the winds—fierce and wild—that whipped across the land with no warning. Sandstorms would roll in from nowhere, burying anything three spans high in minutes. The sand got into everything: your clothes, your boots, even your teeth. And it scratched. Scratched like a thousand tiny blades.

Vegetation was rare—almost nothing grew here. But still, life endured. Creatures and people alike had found ways to survive, hidden away in the shade of rock outcroppings or deep in underground shelters.

Among them were two mighty dragons—KLÜG and his mate, Zänderig. Copper-scaled and radiant beneath the desert suns, they were more than beasts of legend. These magnificent dragons were the king and queen of the Sōden Desert. Proud, powerful, and wise, they watched over the land and its creatures like guardians. To them, the desert's people were not strangers—but their children.

Although they were mighty dragons, it was communicated to them that Rellik was stealing dragon eggs. They had orcs, witches, and warlocks who could somehow bypass dragons' defenses. They decided to hide Zänderig and her egg in a cave beneath the sand. They used their magic to cover the cave with many spans of sand and transformed Zänderig's scales to blend seamlessly with the desert sand. With her eyes closed, she was indistinguishable from the surrounding sand. For added security, KLÜG stood guard outside the cave.

Finally, the time came when Rellik's forces came to the desert. Unfortunately for the Dragons, they were not prepared for the arduous trek through the arid desert heat.

"I know what you want, "KLÜG told the leader of the group." She was a particularly evil sort of Sorceress. "You will never get the egg. Run back with your tail between your legs and tell Rellik that you have failed. You will never get to it. And if you try, I will tear your limbs off and feed you to a borlog."

"Are you so sure about that?"-she asked mockingly. "I think we are quite capable of getting the egg."

"Then why don't you try and get it?" The mighty dragon said with a roar. "You don't even know where it is."

"I may not, but we brought someone who can locate it." Then a sorcerer stepped out from behind her. His eyes were glowing red as he used his talent.

"It's underground," he said. "Approximately three spans." Then the sorceress commanded the orcs to dig.

They scrambled over and, with animal ferocity, they started digging where she pointed.

KLÜG snatched them up with his mighty jaws and flung them many spans away. He could have eaten them, but he did not like the taste of orc. His gaze then became laser-focused on the sorceress. What now? He asked mockingly. Two wind sorcerers came up and created a tornado that sucked up the sand and blew it away. In the matter of minutes, the sand was gone, and Zänderig was exposed with her egg beneath her. Quick as lightning, KLÜG snatched up the sorceress and the two sorcerers and ate them. Other orcs that were with the company scrambled to get the egg. Which Zänderig promptly ate. She didn't mind the taste of orc.

A dark incantation hissed through the air, curling around KLÜG like an unseen chain. His mighty form locked in place, his roar turned to a strangled growl as the spell bound him. Paralyzed, he could only watch as the sorcerers turned toward Zänderig.

She saw the fear in his eyes. And she knew—she was now alone.

They could see through her enchantment. Seemingly out of nowhere, many more orcs and gremlins came out and tried to seize the egg.

Zänderig bit and clawed and slashed her tail at the orcs, but there were just too many of them. They climbed onto her, biting and scratching, their little swords swinging. They could not do any damage to her copper scales, but they were able to grab onto her wings, legs, and neck, trying to keep her on the ground.

Eventually, Zänderig was able to break free of the orcs and beat her mighty wings. She flew up into the air with the egg. "See? How are you going to reach me now?" She taunted. She breathed fire, incinerating the orcs and the rest of the warlocks.

Out of nowhere, a green dragon emerged, concealed by the blazing dual suns. In an instant, the sky became their battleground. Zänderig unleashed torrents of fire, while the green dragon countered with streams of acidic venom. Their attacks clashed ferociously, but neither inflicted harm—Zänderig's metallic scales deflected the acid, and the green dragon's tough hide endured the searing flames.

Then, the battle turned savage. With roars echoing across the heavens, talons flashed and spines bristled. The green dragon slashed and struck, yet Zänderig's unyielding copper scales proved impenetrable. But when Zänderig retaliated, her talons hissed and sizzled upon contact with the acid dragon, forcing her to draw back. Their struggle was relentless—a dance of strength, resilience, and ferocity. The sky itself seemed to tremble under their fury.

Finally, the green dragon was able to rip the egg from Zänderigs claws and flew away as fast as she was able. Zänderig and KLÜG pursued, but they were no match for the green dragon's speed. They vowed they would get the egg back or kill Rellik trying.

Back at Rellik's castle, healing and nature warlocks assembled themselves to weave a spell to speed up the growth of the baby dragons inside the eggs.

The leader of the expedition came to speak with Rellik. "We have obtained the 3 eggs. They are now down in the dungeon. Many of our troops were lost fighting the dragons, and I do not think it wise to search for any more dragon eggs."

"We must have more dragons," Rellik said harshly.

"I have an idea, Lord Rellik." Another warlock said timidly, afraid of the wrath of Rellik if he did not like the suggestion, "Why steal eggs when you can create them instead?"

"What do you mean, *create* them?" Rellik asked.

"Not precisely create dragons, but rather breed them to ensure they lay eggs"

"Do you know how long it takes for a dragon to lay an egg, and then wait for that egg to hatch? Many decannums." Rellik said cooly, They could feel the menace come through his voice. "That's why that won't work. Now I am patient, but not that patient."

"We have warlocks, sorcerers, and sorceresses that have the ability to influence animals, maybe they can influence the dragons."

"Dragons are not normal animals, they hold an enormous amount of magic within them. I do not know how we could speed up the process of dragon eggs being hatched." Rellik said snidely. Then he softened a bit and commanded the servants. "However, if there is a way, you must find it."

"As you wish, Master," they said in unison, then bowed and walked backwards out of the room.

CHAPTER 28
HOME

After their time in Lilenhamür, Melvin and Adara soared home on Penelope's golden wings, the familiar sight of Bilbylund's mountains, farms, and rolling hills spreading beneath them.

Once, the town might have erupted into chaos at the sight of a mighty dragon descending upon its streets—but those revs were long past. Now, villagers merely glanced up with knowing smiles, accustomed to the legendary wizard and his fiery bride.

They were married now and settled in the house that Reicuas gave to Melvin. In the annums before their wedding, in the anticipation of Adara living there, they prepared the home and the property for Adara's arrival. However, they continued to renovate the place. They added gardens and more trees to the orchard. They built another room for the children they anticipated having. Melvin didn't want all the scrolls and books in the main part of the home, so he built a study where he could study the books and scrolls that Reicuas left for him, and also other ones that he had collected. He also remembered Lilenhamür and built in such a way that the buildings would evoke magic. He studied and drew runes on the walls and other items in the house. He also had an Elder come and bless the house so that Deos' spirit would dwell there as he and Adara remembered what the Elder who married them said. Marriage is a triangle between Husband, Wife, and Deo.

Adara had spent her life surrounded by towering walls, gilded halls, and servants who anticipated her every need. Now, in their modest home, she found herself waking to the quiet chirping of birds instead of the hum of castle life.

At first, the simplicity had felt… strange. No maids to draw her bath. No cooks to prepare her meals. No formalities. But in this little house, nestled between the trees and the gardens, she discovered something even grander than a castle—a home.

She could have requested a maid if she wanted to, but to be honest, she looked forward to the rev when it would just be her and Melvin. They had their own home and their privacy. No servants are around you all the time. In the annums leading up to her marriage to Melvin, she had learned many things that a wife would normally do to take care of a house. She learned how to cook, to clean, to do laundry, and all the other tasks she would need to know. However, she and Melvin shared in those responsibilities. Melvin was a very good cook. She liked being responsible for a home and keeping it organized. At least that was one thing Melvin had over Reicuas. Melvin was very organized, whereas Reicuas was not. However, when they had children, she thought she would get a maid to help with the chores, so she could spend as much time with her children as she could. But for now, she just enjoyed being married.

Sharing a bed had been a new experience—one she hadn't expected to love so much. Her chambers in the castle had been vast, with silken drapes and golden chandeliers, yet somehow, this smaller room, warmed by the sound of Melvin's steady breathing, felt **infinitely richer.**

And in the quiet darkness of the night, she discovered another secret—the pleasure of whispered conversations, of laughter muffled beneath the covers, of hands seeking each other in the stillness.

She loved sleeping in the bed with Melvin at night. His shallow breathing lulled her to sleep at night. Plus, she was now able to do other things with him that were forbidden before marriage. And they did as much of that as possible.

Melvin also loved sleeping with her at night. He could feel the warmth of her next to him. She usually slept without a blanket, even in Darken, because her core temperature was much higher than a normal person's. Just to be able to put his arm around the one he loved most in this world at night intoxicated him.

Though they didn't need the money, the villagers still hired out Melvin to repair their homes and do other jobs in the towns and villages in Bilbylund. Well, it was mostly the ladies because they loved to watch Melvin work. He mostly worked for supper, and they were happy to feed Melvin, Adara, and Amira as well when she helped. They loved the home-cooked meals the villagers fed them. Sometimes they didn't like being hired by the townspeople, because other craftsmen could do the same job, and they needed the money more than Melvin and Adara did. So they tended to hire them as helpers and paid them wages for their time. Although secretly, they had a deal with the craftsmen that they actually were able to do most of the work and use their skills and talents.

As was Reicuas, Melvin was the wizard for the kingdom and did official wizard duties for the King. Everyone who knew him knew he did not like wearing the fancy wizard robes other wizards wore. Adara didn't just sit around either, remember, she was commander of the army and not just the army of Bilbylund but the army of the Empire of Arion. She spent a lot of time with the other generals and captains coming up with strategies and tactics for the upcoming war. They all knew it was coming, but just didn't know when. And they practiced.

As hard as they worked, they also loved to play. They would take many rides on Penelope or hike the mountain to visit her and her mother in her cave. They would often spend revs at the beach or riding their qilins. They would go to the castle and visit her family. All the things that a normal couple would do.

Although he loved that his bride was finally living with him, he was still saddened sometimes. This was his master Reicuas' house, until he went off to battle Zôltan. He was killed in battle and would never return to his home again. How Melvin missed Reicuas. His heart ached for him every rev. He was like a father to him. Everything in this house reminded him of his master. He vowed that he would get as strong as he could be and rid this land of this new threat. Studying these scrolls and texts reminded him of Reicuas and all he taught him.

One rev, Melvin knew, they would need to build a house of their own—one that wasn't haunted by memories of Reicuas. But for now, they would stay.

Because within these walls, Reicuas still lingered—not as a ghost, but as a memory. A whisper in the crackling fire. A lesson in every rune. A presence in every scroll, Melvin studied late into the night.

And as long as they remained here, they would never truly be alone.

Chapter 29
ANATOMY

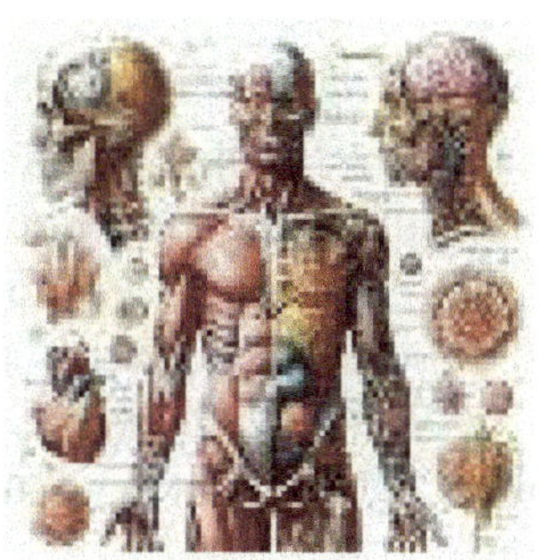

Ever since he had cured Adara of cancer, Melvin's mind had been consumed by a single obsession—the human body. At first, it had been a simple mission: eradicate the disease, save his wife. But now? Now, he hungered for more. Not just healing, but understanding.

When she was sick, he looked into her body just to find and eliminate the cancer, but now he wanted to learn everything he could about anatomy. So he practiced his anatomy.

He began with himself, peering inward as if unraveling the blueprints of his existence. Muscles stretched like woven cords, veins pulsed with life, and bones stood as the scaffolding of his being. With painstaking precision, he mapped each organ, each system, each microscopic detail onto parchment, his quill scratching against the paper in the quiet hours of the night.

He would watch as the neurons and axons would fire off a signal of electricity and watch them go throughout the body via the nervous system. He would find every cell, every part of every cell, the make-up of every cell of the human body, and draw it. He would study down to the very DNA and the chromosomes in the quadruple helix.

He looked at the digestive system, the endocannabinoid system, the circulatory system, the immune system, the respiratory system, etc., and how they all worked together. He watched food being eaten, swallowed, digested, and then the nutrients taken from the food carried off to other parts of the body to build other systems. He watched people breathing in air, the air going into the lungs, then the oxygen molecules going from the lungs to the bloodstream, then to the cells to be used for work. He had already seen the immune system work.

He would look into his wife's body and study her. He would note the differences between men and women and how their anatomy differed.

As he studied further, he noticed subtle but distinct differences between men and women. Not just in their bodies but in their very minds. Some areas of the brain pulsed with a denser network of axons, a greater concentration of neurons. Signals are fired differently, and traveling pathways are unique to each sex. It was not just anatomy. **It was designed.**

Deo had created man, they said, in his own image. Thus, he reasoned, that Deo must be in the form of a man. And noticing the very complexities of the human being, how each system worked with each other, how amazing the human body was, then Deo must be a master craftsman to have created them.

He studied the reproductive system, watched as his wife had her reproductive cycle as her egg went from her ovaries to her uterus, then out of her body when the egg wasn't fertilized. He would look within pregnant women to see how the babies developed over the annum they were in the mother's body. He would look into people with injuries and broken bones, and see how the body healed itself. He would look into the deaf, the blind, the mute, the halt, and people with other physical problems throughout the kingdom, to see what happened to the body to cause this. He learned a wealth of knowledge and wrote it all down.

Melvin was fascinated by the human body and how it all seemed to work together so seamlessly, like a machine. However, he never tried to heal anyone, nor claimed he could. Although he did heal Adara, it was her own body that did that. Maybe someday he would be able to. But now, that was not his purpose. Deo had other plans for him.

Within an annum, he had the most comprehensive book on human anatomy that existed. He had it printed into a book and sent to all the healers in the land and the Empress. This book became the official book on anatomy for the Arion Empire and was the only anatomy book used by healers as a reference and for the teaching of healers from then on. In the annums that followed, he would look into plants as well and draw them out.

Late at night, as Adara slept beside him, Melvin turned his gaze inward—not to flesh and bone, but to something far more elusive.

Magic.

It coursed through him like rivers of light, interwoven into his very cells all throughout his body. His own magic was a tapestry of colors, shifting and flowing in a mesmerizing dance. Adara's, however, was different—a deep, burning red, concentrated in her heart and brain.

Now he understood. Though he knew it before, it made more sense. He had noticed that since being in Lilenhamür, she had way more magic in her than she did before. As did he. Lilenhamür had changed them both. They were more than they once were.

He would also look into animals as well, and notice how they were put together. For the most part, it was all the same: the cells, the organs, etc. Animals were just configured differently with four legs, or wings, instead of arms, feathers instead of hair, and tails. He looked inside Penelope, his dragon, and what he saw amazed him. For the most part, she was the same as any other animal. Basically the same organs, but much, much larger. And her magic particles, there were so many, millions of billions. However, he also noticed that her particles weren't only in her cells, but part of her very DNA. This, he would have to learn to do, but he didn't have that type of power yet. He would have to absorb more magic.

Melvin would experiment on himself. He remembered the first time he caused something to grow. He thought of a rose to grow, and it did. He wondered if that would work for a person. He never thought of changing a person before. Sure, he cured his wife, but he did not change her physically in any way; he just showed her natural immune system how to recognize the cancer cells and take them away. It was her own body that did that. Basically she healed herself. So for now, he did harmless stuff. He tried to see if he could cause more muscle to grow. He looked into his body and found a muscle. He then told the muscle to grow, just a little, and it did. Not enough to notice, but it did. He looked into his wife and caused her hair to grow just a little. And it did. She noticed, though, and asked what he was doing. And he explained it to her. She was amazed. She wondered if he could heal other people besides her. She knew that she healed herself, but maybe he could do that with others as well. Have their natural systems heal themselves. He told her that Deo had not given him that ability. He had allowed him to cure her, but not heal others. He asked Deo when he would have this ability, and the answer was that if he only used it for good, to heal and to bless others, only in times of need, he could use this talent. Also, since he had studied anatomy and understood the body, he was now ready to be able to heal others.

Next, a little more ambitious, he put his consciousness throughout the village and looked for someone with a broken bone. He found a small child who he knew had fallen off a wagon and broken his arm. Just as he did with himself and his wife, he put his consciousness into the child. He looked at the broken arm and then at the good arm and compared the two. Since the healer was able to straighten the bone and splint it, it was straight. He healed the outside, but the inside had to do its own work. The town healer wasn't the most powerful. He usually worked with potions and herbs to cure sickness. Mending bones was beyond his capabilities. So Melvin set to work mending the bone. He used the same process as he did with his muscle singing to the bits of bone in the crack to grow, on both sides, and to join together. When he was finished, he looked at both of his arms to compare them, and he found that the healed arm was actually stronger than the other arm. He knew that this child had small bones and they were more easily broken than other children, so he tried something else. He sang a song and wove a spell, and while that child slept in the long night of Darken, Melvin caused an extra layer of bone tissue to be made on the whole skeleton of this child. Just so his bones would not be so thin and brittle. He left the instructions in his DNA, so as he grew, the new bone would also grow with an extra layer. When he was finished, he smiled and went to sleep. In the morning, he heard shouts that a miracle had happened, that the boy was healed and was stronger than ever. They thanked Deo for this miracle. Melvin smiled and knew that this power was given from Deo, and he promised he would only use it for good to heal those in need if it was Deo's will.

Another thing happened unexpectedly while looking into his and his wife's bodies. Something they had been taught, but no one could ever prove or disprove. While he put his consciousness into his wife's body to study it, he could see something else. It was another body. Not a physical one, but one made up of purer elements. He was fascinated by this. He knew what it was. Now he could see the spirit, or soul, within his wife. It was glorious. A shining white being within her body. He had to focus and train himself to see it. When he had learned how to see it without much effort, he looked into other people and saw theirs as well. When he would kill an animal for food, he could see the spirit leave the body. He told Adara about this, and she was in awe of all the things he could do. He asked Adara not to tell anyone he could do this. But he had the ability just in case he might need it someday.

CHAPTER 30

TRANSMUTATION

One evening, as Melvin sat in quiet meditation, studying the magic woven into himself and Adara, a memory surfaced—one he had nearly forgotten.

Reicuas's voice echoed in his mind, distant yet unmistakable: "Some creatures—dragons, unicorns, the rarest of magical beings—do not merely have magic. They are magic. It is etched into their very blood, threaded into their bones, part of their very DNA."

Penelope had told him the same.

Melvin's heart pounded. What if he could do the same?

He looked within himself again to look for his magic, where it was stored. He looked into Penelope, though she was in her cave, he could still look inside of her, and he noticed that what they said was true, her magic particles were in her very DNA.

He went into the backyard where he had built something similar to Lilenhamür. He had built concentric hexagonal walls from that same stone that he had gotten from the new wall they were building. He studied the runes and copied them onto these new stones. He learned the incantations they used for the walls and enchanted the walls as well. Though this area was not as strong with magic as Lilenhamür, it did an adequate job and absorbed and grew his and Adara's magic exponentially.

He studied Penelope's magic and mapped out how and where they were attached. Then he looked into himself and looked at where the magic particles would be within himself. After gathering as much information as he possibly could, he looked within himself, down to the very DNA, and migrated his magic particles and infused them into his very DNA. This took him a very long time.

Adara came home from practicing with her troops in the evening and saw Melvin sitting in the backyard. In his makeshift power wall, as she called it. He was concentrating as he did when he was using his conscious ability. However, this time was different. He was glowing. She thought that this was not his aura as it was pretty bright normally, but this time it was even brighter, almost as bright as Reicuas was when he used his light magic. But what was odd to her was that not only was he glowing all the colors known to be associated with talents, but it was radiating from inside him. Not only his eyes, but his whole body was enveloped with light. Adara had never seen him do this before. She was so amazed that she completely forgot what she was going to do that evening and just sat there transfixed, watching her amazing husband learn yet another aspect of his magic.

In deep concentration, Melvin continued the transfer of his magic particles from his cells to his DNA.

Melvin drifted into the depths of himself, deeper than ever before. He was no longer just studying magic—he was becoming it.

He went one talent at a time. Looking within the structure of his DNA to see what area matched the type of magic particle. He referenced Penelope and Percilla regarding the pairing and matching. As they were Gold Dragons and used light particles, he started with that for the sequencing. Then, noticing his wife was home and watching him, he looked within her DNA to see what matched her fire particles. And placed this fire particles in that position on the DNA structure.

As he did this, he looked at the atomic structure of each particle and his DNA, and put it together like a jigsaw puzzle. Very slowly, very meticulously, one by one, Melvin studied, compared, moved, and reassessed that everything was in its proper place. With surgical precision, he examined his own DNA, unraveling the threads of his being. Each sequence shimmered before his mind's eye, coiled strands of life itself. Then, carefully, he began the transfer. He aligned them like a master craftsman fitting gemstones into a crown. Magic particles—previously scattered in his cells—migrated toward his very core. Every shift sent surges of power through him, the very fabric of his existence reshaping itself.

As Melvin did this, he felt a surge of power run through him. He felt not only more powerful, but he felt more alive, like he was part of the magic, and the magic was a part of him.

He gasped. For the first time, magic was not something he used. It was something he was.

While transferring the magic, he noticed that there were some places in his DNA that he did not have a matching magic particle for, and he also had other talents that he did not have a place in his DNA for. This was all very interesting, and he would have to ask Percilla or another master wizard about this.

Melvin exhaled, his body still humming with energy. He had achieved something incredible—but he was far from finished.

The elves. They held knowledge far older than any human wizard. If anyone could explain the missing pieces of his magic, it was them. And he would find the answers. No matter what it took.

CHAPTER 31

PRACTICE

During this time, they trained relentlessly. Though their magic made them nearly invincible, they pushed themselves harder, refining their skills beyond limits. Melvin could do almost everything with ease since he transferred his magic to his DNA. Easier than before, he had to merely think about what he wanted to do, and he could do it faster, stronger, with more power.

They practiced their swordsmanship. Every rev Adara and Melvin battled. They knew with their magic shields they could not hurt each other, although they wouldn't anyway. They fought with the intensity of sworn enemies, holding nothing back. They tested old and new battle tactics, pushing themselves to exhaustion, only to rise and fight again.

Not only with each other, but with the guards at the castle, with the army, with Aria and the Special Forces. They also put the military on a workout regimen to increase their muscle mass naturally; they trained to be quicker and more agile. Not only that, but Melvin looked into each of them and caused it so they would have more stamina, be stronger, faster, and not tire so easily. For those with talents, they worked on them using their talents more efficiently and effectively. In battle, they would have to be ready for anything. They practiced with magic. Honing it, discovering new ways to use it. Both suggesting that they try new things. They even practiced battles with one person against many, and many against many. They played kids' games in the woods as part of their training. They played capture the flag, hide and seek, but this time you battled instead of tagged the other. They played sports, they ran on the beach, and they even battled Penelope and Percilla. For they were going to have to battle against the dragon army that Rellik was building. There came a time when all battles ended in a draw. They were all that good. They sent the training regimen to Lilenhamür so those troops could train in the same way and have the same physical and mental training as well.

Beyond battle tactics, they honed the art of escape. If Rellik's forces ever captured them, they trusted that most guards would lack intelligence, making an escape an easy feat. They were shackled, tied up, put in manacles, put in cages, dungeons, cells, and every other sort of means to incarcerate them. They were taught the art of escaping from these devices, the means of picking locks. Some, like Aria, were double-jointed, so they practiced popping their joints out of their sockets and squeezing through shackles and bars of the cells. Adara just melted the metal, Melvin sang to the metal, and it fractured; others just hid lockpicks on their person. To make it more interesting, bets were made on who would succeed and who would not.

One rev, Melvin and Adara were sparring in their backyard. Adara was throwing everything she could at Melvin, and he was deflecting everything easily. Melvin was also throwing everything at Adara, and nothing was touching her. He used all of his talents, some of which were: Fire, lightning, wind, water, and light. He had plants entangle her, she would just burn them to a crisp. He would try to catch her in whirlwinds, but she would just ride the wave of wind. He tried encasing her in ice, of course, that wouldn't work. Everything in his arsenal she had a counter for. As did the rest of the troops.

Frustration crept into Melvin's mind—it was all becoming too predictable. He halted mid-fight, staring at Adara. What was the point? They had pushed each other to their limits, countered every move, and mastered every strategy. They needed something more. They were as good as they were going to get. He walked up to his beautiful wife and embraced her, and kissed her.

"What was that for?" she asked, questioning, breathing hard. "I didn't beat you."

"Yes, I know," he said softly. "And I didn't beat you. And you never will."

"What's this about?" she asked, her hair aflame and her eyes the color of burning coals, looking up into his bright, multicolored eyes. She was still in magic mode.

"And I never will beat you." He replied. "At this point, we are as good as we are going to get with the knowledge and understanding of magic and fighting that we have. We need a bigger challenge. No one in this town or the military can give us a challenge on one or even as a group. Penelope can't even beat us. And she is a dragon. We need someone who can help us improve. I see all this potential in you, all this magic inside of you, and I have taught you everything I could think of to help you improve, and you have done the same for me. We are leaps and bounds beyond what we were when we came back to this house. You have learned so much, improved, but we need more.

We must go to the Elves. Empress Kayla once told me this was necessary, but I wasn't ready—my magic, my skills, my understanding all fell short. But now, everything has changed. We have changed. It's time, Adara. And Aria and the troops must come with us.

"I think you are right, Melvin. My Love," She said softly, still looking into his big, beautiful, bright, multicolored eyes. "We all need to go pay a visit to the elves. I will talk to my sister and arrange the trip. Of course, we will not be able to take all of the troops; some have to stay here."

"I have thought of that," Melvin said thoughtfully. "Now that the people are used to seeing two gold dragons in the kingdom, I will ask if they can watch the kingdom while we are gone. However, if some in the army don't want to go, then they can certainly stay here."

While they were making preparations to go see the elves, disturbing news arrived from the Empress that a band of Orcs, Goblins, Sorcerers, and the like, were stealing dragon eggs and taking over more and more villages and towns west of the Helaeth Mountains. Rellik's army was growing with the most horrible creatures. And now Melvin and Adara felt that they must do something about it.

Melvin communicated with Penelope, and she and Percilla were willing to watch over Bilbylund for them.

Melvin and Adara met with Penelope and Percilla one last time before they journeyed west.

Melvin told them that he knew Rellik was stealing dragon eggs and capturing adolescent and even adult dragons as well. Which were still very rare in Arion, but he was doing it. How, he did not know, but he asked them both something very important. "For your safety, I ask you to bond yourself to me and Adara. I don't think Rellik will dare to come this far east, but just in case. Or if you decide to join in the fight, then I know you will be safe from his power over dragons. I do not know how he does it, but with this bond, he will have no power over you. Please, get word to other dragons as well. Even if they want to stay out of the coming war. They need to bond with another so Rellik will have no power to bind them."

Penelope and Percilla answered without hesitation, we will gladly bind our lives to yours. The four joined in an intricate spell—golden dragons and warriors entwining their fates. Their bond was absolute; only their collective will or death itself could sever it.

Once this was done, they gathered their troops and took their journey to see the Elves.

CHAPTER 32
JOURNEY TO THE ELVES

If it had been just Melvin and Adara, they might have brought Penelope along. But this journey was different—this was preparation for war, and their destination was the Elves' training grounds.

They brought their elite captains and fighters because these were to be the captains and generals of the units. They marched west with Aria and her elite group, all of whom had talents that would aid them in combat, on their journey so they too could learn to use their talents better while fighting. They left those who wanted to stay to protect their home.

They traveled through the Lascar mountains. Now that Adara had seen the grandeur of the Helaeth Mountains, these seemed like foothills. But they were still very beautiful. They stopped in Wazervïl to get some rest. And gather more wizards. These they would also take with them to Illëngard, for they needed all the help that they could get.

On their journey, they passed through Lilenhamür. When they arrived, the Empress summoned Melvin, Adara, and Aria to her. When they came into the throne room, besides her personal guards and the High Wizard of the Empire, the throne room was otherwise empty. They came and bowed before the Empress.

"What are you doing?" she asked sternly. "I said No Bowing." They all stood straight. "That's better." She said in a softer, more familiar tone. "As I have told you before, you three are like family to me, so enough with the formalities." Then she motioned to the guards, "Bring in a couch for them to sit on, then go have a bite to eat. I will be more than safe with them. I think it would be a good idea that you play some sparring games with the troops from Bilbylund. I hear they are the best warriors in the Empire. A special prize will go to the winner." Then she got a piece of parchment and wrote the declaration and handed it to the guards. Hand this to your captains and have it announced." And they did.

Then the Empress gestured to the Wizard standing next to her. "This is Wizard Brennan. He is my personal wizard for the Empire, just as Reicuas was all those annums ago. As you can tell, he is a Nature Wizard. He really is a powerful and wonderful wizard. I would like him to join you on your journey to the elves to help him be able to hone and improve upon his skills, as you are planning to do. I know there is much more ability in him, but he has no one here to teach him, and he has surpassed all the wizards in Wazervĭl. I was hoping he could learn some things from you and the elves."

"That's terrific. It would be our honor to have him come with us," Melvin said excitedly. "I am sure we can learn some things from him as well." Melvin could tell that he was a nature wizard by the way he dressed, and also by his bright, deep green aura, eyes, and hair. I don't believe I've ever met a nature wizard before. I'm certain you'll have plenty to teach me."

"There will be time enough for that," The Empress said. "Now, for the real reason I called you here. You know that Rellik has been stealing eggs to grow a dragon army. He grows stronger daily. I have heard reports that he is breeding dragons. Mating them for the sole purpose of getting the eggs, watching them hatch, and gaining control of them to grow his dragon army. I fear that after you have had your training with the elves, you will not be going back home. You will be needed here to fight Rellik before he builds a large enough army that he will be unstoppable. Please learn everything you can, grow as strong as you can, so you can defeat Rellik, we can free those he has captured, and this empire will be at peace once more. Now let's go celebrate, and soon you will be off to the elves."

As Wizard Brennon listened to the Empress, he looked at the beauty of these two women; he could see their bright auras shining from them and thought that this was no place for these two women to be. But given the situation and who these two women were and what they were capable of, he knew that this was exactly where they needed to be at this time. This was the first time he had ever met the 'Big Three', as they were called. He looked at them and noticed the way they commanded the room. The air of authority that came from them. Not to mention how intense their auras were. They must be really powerful with magic. And there was one more thing that he heard, and could now confirm, the princesses were really beautiful. His heart skipped a beat, he had to get to know Aria better. He knew that Adara, the Great Commander, was married to Melvin the Magnificent, the greatest wizard in the world. But as far as he knew, Aria was still unattached. His mind spun, and a plan was forming in his brain.

The troops from Lilenhamür and Bilbylund played their sparing games in the training grounds. As they came to find out, the troops from Bilbylund could not be beaten. The troops from Lilenhamür were sure that they were cheating. But they knew they were just better trained. They had heard that in the past annums they trained under Commander Adara and Melvin, and they practiced so much and trained so well, that there was nothing else they could learn, and they were so good, they could not be beaten. Even with Melvin and Adara sparing with them. No one could beat another. They did have magic shielding around them so they would not get mortally wounded, but they held nothing back.

At the feast, awards were given out to the winners of the matches. Most are going to Bilbylund. Melvin, Adara, Aria, and Wizard Brennon even participated. The other opponents didn't even have a chance. From this, the Empress had the captains of Bilbylund give the training regimen to the captains from Lilenhamür so all of the troops could be at their peak performance. Then the Empress gave them a great reception. They all cheered, sang victory songs, and prepared for the rest of their journey to the elves. During the celebration, Wizard Brennon got up enough nerve to ask Aria if she wouldn't mind him showing her around Lilenhamür. Being that wizard Brennon was a handsome man, and seemed very kind, Aria agreed. She also knew that they both knew that she was more than capable of taking care of herself if the need arose. She was the captain of the special forces after all.

Though they did not stay long, the next rev, while Aria was on her date, Melvin and Adara went to the lake in the center of the citadel and opened themselves up to the concentration of magic. Melvin looked into Adara's heart, where her power was, and measured how much magic she had within her. And it was a great amount. He noted how much there was, it would be important later.

Melvin opened himself up to absorb as much of the magic as he possibly could. He felt the magic flowing into his very DNA, not only into his cells. This felt very similar to when he opened himself up to feel the spirit of Deo. He could feel the magic flowing into him, lifting him, and he could feel his power grow inside of himself. He felt more confident, more sure of himself. More powerful. Like he could take on any challenge and be the victor.

Melvin taught Adara the same technique as he used. This increased the power they could absorb from when they did this at their wedding. She could also feel the magic particles flowing into her. She could feel them going into her heart, where the rest of her magic was. She could see her aura get brighter, stronger as she absorbed the magic. And she was sure that Melvin could absorb more than she could. When they absorbed as much magic as they could at that time, they were ready to continue their journey to the elves.

Then Melvin did something. He had Adara sit still on the grass near the lake while he looked inside her. Adara, he said, I am going to do something for you that will make you stronger, faster, better. I don't know why I didn't think of this before. But here in the center of Lilenhamür, I think it is the best time and place. He looked into her heart and saw all this power almost bursting out of her heart. He looked into the rest of her and noticed how the cells were. They had magic receptors as well, not just in her heart. Just as he did with himself, he moved the red, glorious fire magic particles from Adara's heart to the rest of her body. He could see her power increase he could see her whole body become more powerful. Now there was no limit to how much magic she could absorb, they were not limited only to her heart. Then he caused his beautiful wife to absorb more magic particles until she could absorb no more at that time.

Adara felt different. She felt more powerful and more confident. She felt stronger, she felt more energized, just more. She felt better than she had ever felt before in her life. She felt more alive. She loved this feeling and wanted to get more and more powerful. That maybe one rev, she would be as powerful as Melvin. And be able to better defeat Rellik and his armies.

Melvin looked into her again at the end of their session and noticed the remarkable change within Adara. Her magic particles almost doubled during this time. Even he could not do that. His wife was a wonder to behold. During this time, the Empress sent word to the elves to expect them.

Wizard Brennon and Aria had a nice time taking a carriage around Lilenhamür. He did not mind that she was clad in her form-fitting black leather armor. He kind of liked it. He was dressed, as always, in his wizard's garb, which afforded them some nice perks. Which, because of both of their statuses, they would have gotten anyway. They saw the dancing fountain, which a water wizard had enchanted. They saw the lake and the gardens in the middle of the city. They had lunch at one of the many restaurants in Lilenhamür. They saw a comedy play at the theater. They sat on the orange grass in the late afternoon at one of the many parks and talked and got to know each other. Wizard Brennon explained the history of Lilenhamür to her, as the Empress did for Melvin. She marveled at the tall, iridescent white buildings. She was in awe of its grandeur, the sheer size of this fortress. A city within a city within a city. Her city back home looked like a poor man's cottage compared to this. She could see herself living here. They laughed and joked and had a great time. At the end of the rev, they both were glad that Wizard Brennon was coming along with them on the journey to the elves. I think there may have even been a kiss somewhere in there. His mischievous plan had worked, although it wasn't all that mischievous.

In the afternoon, they gathered the needed supplies and prepared to head out. As they were packing their supplies, a messenger came from the Empress and handed them a parchment. It read *"Beware on your path, the forest that was once a place of fun and frolic, is now a dark, loathsome place. Take extra care in the forest before you reach the elves."*

CHAPTER 33
SHIELD TREES

"We need to move quickly," Aria urged. "Nightfall is approaching, and these woods are no place to be after dark." As the two suns set in the east, the small group quickened the pace. The princess was right, this was no place to be after dark. A few annums ago, traveling through these woods would have been different. The forest was beautiful. The paths were lit, you could hear the sound of music playing, fairies flew about taking care of the forest, and the wood elves frolicked along the paths. But now, all that had changed. Ever since the Shadow Lord gained his power, in the annums since, this forest has become the home of all sorts of vile creatures. Ogres, Pixies, Orcs, and other foul creatures had moved in. But worse of them all were the Leprechauns because they could use magic.

"I had hoped to make it to Illëngard before nightfall," Melvin said. "This meeting with the elves is most important."

"Melvin," Adara said, "you know you can go ahead of us. It is you who needs to talk to the King, you don't need us for that."

"I don't want to leave you unprotected," he replied.

"Leave us unprotected?" Aria smirked. "What am I, invisible? Melvin, I know you mean well, but sometimes you're too kind… and other times, just painfully clueless. Who are you traveling with? Only the most capable, most trained, elite of King Bilby's army. I am a master swordsman, commander of the Special Forces. My sister here is the commander of our whole army. With enough firepower, yes, pun intended, to level cities. Plus, some of the finest soldiers in the Empire. I know, because I trained them. And let's not forget Master Wizard Brennon here and the other wizards from Wazervïl. So you think we need your protection? I think we will be just fine."

"Calm down, Aria." Melvin said, "Quiet. Who are you to tell me…."

"No, I mean it, be quiet."

"I…" Just then, a loud, fierce, defining growl came from the forest, not too far away.

"Borlog… RUN!!!!!!!!" They all ran as fast as they could. Adara shot fireballs towards where the sound was. They would stand and fight, but in this case, it was more prudent to run. You do not want to fight a borlog. But run where? They would never get to Illëngard on time. Night was fast approaching, and more foul creatures would come out. So they ran. This would have been a good time to have qilins, but they had been lost. As they camped during the night before, shrieker came near to their camp and howled their ear-bleeding shrieks. Everyone had to cover their ears or they would bleed and they would lose their hearing.

This was one thing they were not prepared for. A few of the soldiers were not able to cover their ears on time, so now they have lost their hearing. Since no one could get to the qilins to cover their ears, they were frightened and ran away. Thus, they lost their qilins.

So they ran.

Now, you may be wondering—what exactly is a Borlog? Let me put it in terms you can picture. Imagine a beast as massive as three African elephants, with a rhino-like horn on its snout and a pair of menacing bull horns on its head. Its maw holds three rows of razor-sharp teeth, and its body is encased in thick, armadillo-like armor, with a hide so impenetrable no weapon could pierce it. This was the only animal that the mighty dragons were afraid of. And this was a small one. Oh yeah, they can also breathe fire. And because of their armor and hide, fire did not affect them.

As they ran, they saw flashes of light and heard thunder, their hearts sank, though they would never show it, fear welled up inside of them. That would only mean one thing: Rellik was not far behind. Their forces weren't sufficiently large enough to defeat Rellik's forces as of yet. They still had a lot to do.

So they ran.

Suddenly, a downpour of rain started, and although still running from the Borlog, which they could hear crashing through trees behind them and gaining ground, and bellowing an awful scream, they were relieved. Though Rellik could produce lightning, he could not make it rain, as far as they knew. This was a natural thunderstorm. Even though they still had a borlog, chasing them. Fire spewed from its nostrils.

So they ran.

The borlog was right on their heels. Though it was a huge armored animal, it could run very fast. And was gaining on them. Soon, they heard other sounds behind them. Another type of screech. Shriekers, basically wingless dragons. They can't fly, and they have no magic, but they can run very fast. However, their primary weapon was their high-pitched shrieks. It sends out a sound wave that pierces the ears, it can even make them bleed. The sound and shockwave gives you a tremendous headache, knocks you out, and has other effects on your body and mind.

Great, this was getting even better. A borlog, now shrieker. Next, they heard the yells of Ogres and Goblins. The chase went on, as often as she could manage, Adara would shoot off fireballs that would just glance off the Borlog. Fortunately, some did hit the Ogres. The archers shot arrows, which pretty much did the same thing.

I bet you're wondering—what was Melvin doing this whole time? A fair question. Aria had made it clear they didn't need his protection, so he waited. But he wasn't just standing idly by. As he ran, he projected part of his consciousness ahead, scanning the terrain for a safe refuge. At the same time, he reached out to Penelope, who knew these woods well, and asked for her guidance. She responded by planting an image in his mind—an ideal hiding spot not too far away, along with the safest route to reach it.

Even if Melvin had jumped into the fight, he wasn't sure what he could do against a Borlog—at least not yet. Shriekers, ogres, and goblins? Those would be easy. But right now, his priority was getting everyone to safety.

So they ran.

As they ran, Wizard Brennan caused thick, large vines and other foliage to grow behind the group to stop the pursuers.

Yes, Adara did have the ability to talk to animals, which she rarely used. But what was chasing them was not your common animal. A borlog was known as a mindless brute of an animal that only cared about eating and destruction. So, there was no way that Adara knew of that she could communicate with it.

So they ran.

"Follow me, I know where we can go," he commanded. "How?" Asked Aria.

Melvin and Adara said simultaneously, "Penelope." Aria understood.

After a few minutes, they ran into a clearing. A large meadow with flowers blooming. On the other side, they saw a stand of trees apart from the others, very tall, very large, very old trees. "To those trees!!!" Melvin yelled. The borlog, Goblins, and Ogres were close behind. They didn't get too far into the meadow before the borlog and the Ogres came crashing into the clearing. The vines Brennan was casting up were no match for the borlog. All the while, Adara was shooting fireballs, fire bullets. Trying to pick off as many ogres and goblins as possible. She tried not to set the whole forest on fire.

So they ran.

As they ran through the meadow, the ground became muddy from the rain, and they lost their traction, but the good thing was their pursuers would too. Only a little way off now, and they would be to the trees. Melvin still didn't know why they needed to get to the trees, just that

Penelope told him they needed to get there. One of the guardsmen slipped and caused himself and another to fall. Quickly, they were overcome by the borlog and the ogres. They were trampled, but the pursuers did not stop. Melvin and the others also could not stop to help them. They are warriors, hopefully, their armor will protect them, and they can fight off the ogres enough to get to safety.

So they ran.

The borlog was right on their heels. Finally, they reached the stand of trees. Just as the last man got under the cover of the trees, Melvin felt a warning to stop. "STOP," Melvin commanded.

"Why?" Aria asked. Just then, the borlog stopped as if it hit a wall.

"That's why," Melvin retorted. And pointed to the borlog growling. "I don't know why, but Penelope said we would be safe here." The ogres, as well, were stopped. They were growling and pounding their fists on what appeared to be air. Then Melvin saw it. A shimmer of light, then he knew. "A-a-a magic barrier." He said.

Then out of nowhere came a deep, resonating voice. "That is right, Melvin."

Adara looked around, but saw no one else besides those with whom they came. "Who's speaking?" she asked. "We are the Na'Van, or in your language, The Ancient Trees." The voice resonated. They did not know where the voice came from. It sounded like it came from all around.

"Ancient trees?" she asked.

"Sit, rest, eat." The voice said very slowly. "You are safe here. It will be a while before they leave." "How are you able to create a magical barrier?" Adara asked curiously. "And how come we were able to be protected under your boughs, while the borlog and ogres weren't?"

"While you rest, we will tell you how we came to be. Adara of Bilbylund." "How do you know my name?" she asked, amazed.

"Sit, rest, and we will explain." They all sat down, got their bedrolls out, got their food, and the story began.

"Long before the rise of humans, dwarves, or even elves—long before the age of dragons, when the world of Arion was still young and home to only a handful of creatures—this forest was already ancient. It had stood since the very first seeds touched the earth, scattered across the land after the world was shaped by the Deos. The trees that grew here had witnessed the birth of time itself, their roots tangled deep in the soil of Arion, carrying the weight of millennia in their silent, enduring strength. Eventually, there was an ancient civilization that came from the skies and dwelt here. They started cutting down the forest and mining ore. They built cities, they spread throughout the face of Arion. There was one wise man, Elfin, the first magic user. They didn't believe in magic back then, as you do now, because they had technology. They had machines to do any task you wanted done. Elfin was different, he was a scientist. He studied the flora and fauna. He studied nature. He lived among us, nurtured us. He learned how to commune with the trees in the forest. Learned how to protect us. Learned that we were alive and sentient, could think and feel. He showed us how to communicate with him. He could look inside us or anything else. He imparted us with magic, or rather, showed us how we could use magic from Estry, which was all over; we just had to harness it. Then he, just before he passed to the next life, gave us of all his magic power, that we may protect ourselves from anything that we perceived as being evil or wanting to hurt us. He left us with a spell that has only grown stronger over the millions of milleannums we have been here. His descendants eventually became the Elves, leprechauns, and other magical peoples. This spell creates a shield around us, from the top of our limbs to the bottom of our roots. We can invoke this shield for any part of our forest. The part just in front of you, as you have seen, or the entire forest. This shield will stop any weapon, any magic, anything we perceive that will harm us. So with this shield, that civilization was not able to cut us down. With this shield, we are protected. And anything or anyone who is under our branches is also protected as we are protected. Unfortunately, we cannot extend this protection beyond our borders. That is why we were not able to stop the invasion of those evil creatures that came into the forest you came from. But from here to the end of the Elven lands, you will be safe. Take your rest and you can be on your way to Illëngard in the morning."

"Thank you, Na'Van, for your protection." Adara said in humility, "But you did not explain how you knew who I was."

"The trees know." Said the voice. Just then, a vision came to her mind. Actually, it was Penelope sending her a message. She told the trees of their mission, and if they could help in any way, to please do it. Adara then understood and chuckled.

As the night came on, Melvin walked a little ways away from the rest of the camp to reflect on the revs events. He didn't know why he didn't fight the borlog, he just ran. He easily could have stopped it; it may have taken a little time, but he could have done it. How could he think to defeat Rellik's armies, much less Rellik himself, if he couldn't even fight a Borlog or the Ogres? This just kept bothering him, he should have fought, but didn't. He felt like a coward.

Soft, warm hands gently slipped around his waist from the back. "Are you alright, Melvin?" Adara asked softly. Melvin could hear the concern in her voice. He could feel it through him.

"What am I doing here?" he asked almost in tears. "What do you mean?" Adara asked softly in his ear.

"I mean I-I-I-I just ran, I-I-I could h-h-have fought the b-b-borlog, b-b-but I d-d-didn't, I-I-I just r-r-ran."

"I don't know Melvin." She said softly as she moved around to the front. "You are a great wizard. Trained by the best. You have surpassed Reicuas in every way. He would be proud of you."

Then he voiced the question he had asked himself just moments ago. "How could I-I-I think to defeat Rellik's a-a-a-armies, much l-l-l-less Rellik h-h-h-himself, i-i-i-if I-I-I couldn't even f-f-f-fight a B-b-b-borlog, or the O-o-ogres?"

She took his hand and walked over to a log and sat down with him. "You need to calm down," she said, reassuringly rubbing his hand. "You're stuttering is getting worse. I don't know why you didn't fight the borlog, I think I was doing an ok job slowing it down, but I know that fireballs don't do anything to that thing. I didn't have time either to make an explosion large enough to stop it."

"I think, though," she continued, "that you didn't want to take the time to summon your magic. Some spells, Melvin, you can do by just thinking about it, but this, this would have taken time, time to sing, time to weave a spell powerful enough to stop that thing. You knew you didn't have that kind of time right then. You needed to get us to safety, I know that. Penelope talks to me, too. I knew we had to get to these trees. I didn't know why, but I knew you were trying to get us to these trees. Sometimes you need to know when to fight and when to run. And this time, Melvin, you did the right thing. I am glad to have you, Melvin, and I am sure glad we have Penelope to help guide us, even if she is a long way away."

Then a picture came into their minds that she wasn't actually all that far away at all. Melvin smiled. "I-I-I didn't k-k-know P-p-penelope talked to y-y-you."

"Sometimes she does. Only when it's important."

Melvin tried to calm himself down enough so he wouldn't stutter.

"H-h-h-how long have you been able to t-t-talk to her?" "Since we first rode her together."

"H-h-how come you never t-t-told me?"

"I thought she did, but it's no big deal. Like I said, it's only once in a while, not like you, you talk to her all the time."

"Sometimes we do t-t-talk quite a bit," he said, then he kissed her. "If you don't mind, I would like to be alone for a while."

"I understand. I will see you in a while, huh? I love you, Melvin," she kissed him again.

"Yes, in a little while. I-i-i love you too." He kissed her again, then got up and walked further into the woods.

Adara headed back to camp. When she arrived, the two soldiers who had fallen came stumbling into the camp. They explained that their armor protected them from the trampling Ogres, and the wet mud actually absorbed them as they were being stepped on. While the borlog and ogres were trying to get past the shield, they were completely ignored, so they were able to get up and hide in another part of their forest. When the ogres left, they made their way to the camp.

As Melvin walked again, he heard the same voice call his name.

CHAPTER 34
A HISTORY LESSON

"Melvin," the voice said slowly. The deep voice sounded ancient, like it was coming from a faraway place. "Yes?" Melvin said curiously. "I-i-is this the Na'Van?"

"Yes, Melvin. Sit down, we wish to converse with you." Melvin sat on another fallen log, and pictures flashed through his mind in the same way that Penelope speaks to him. Essentially, it said, "We learned this form of communication from the Dragons. It's a faster way of communicating than with words."

Melvin thought in his mind, "I know how to use this form of communication as well, I have a dragon I speak to frequently."

"Yes, we know. Penelope is her name. We have known her since she was a baby, and we also know her mother, Percilla. We know almost every dragon who has ever lived in this land."

"Is this what you wanted to talk to me about?" he thought.

"In part, but not all. We have been waiting for you to come to us. We knew at some time you would. We are ancient, we have patience, we can wait. Human affairs do not concern us, we are protected from you with our magic. Nothing can harm us. However, you are different. You are not like other wizards who have lived on Arion or even Estry. This is what we speak of. You are a direct descendant of Elfin. You contain his magic."

"I thought you said the descendants of Elfin were the Elves."

"Yes, we did, but not all. Elfin had two sons. One son, Elfes, and his family decided to stay in the forest and carry on his father's work. He continued to live in harmony with nature, and these woods became their home. They kept primarily to themselves, learned to use their magic to help the forest, and grow the forest. They became one with us, and we protected them. They learned to prolong their lives through magic, they were able to live a thousand annums, some even longer. The normal humans on the planet lived a maximum of one hundred annums at that time."

"Galdür, his other son, wanted to live in the city. The city grew, and many other cities rose in the land. A war started, and Galdür and his family went back to live in the forest with the Elves. For many, many annums this war ravaged the world, but Elves and Galdür were safe in the forest under our protection.

"They nearly destroyed all life on Estry during this war. Very few of the people survived. Of those who did, some went back into space, some went into hiding, and came out of hiding much later. All the land after the war was not fit for life. When the others came out of hiding, the residual radiation in the air they breathed and the ground went into the food they ate and into their bodies and mutated them, also mutating most of the animals that were here.

During this time, the descendants of Elfes and their families learned how to live very long lives. Eventually, many thousands of annums after the war was over, they ventured out of the forest to see what had happened. They became subject to the radiation. When they came back, they carried the mutations caused by the radiation within them and passed them onto their descendants. Since they could use magic, they could control the effects of the radiation and use it to their advantage. They stayed in this forest, eventually becoming the wood elves, as you know, thi rev. They learned how to prolong their lives much longer than a Cenannum, even past a Milleannum. Utilizing the natural resources around them, they discovered ways to heal and benefit from nature's gifts. They kept their magic pure, kept it strong. Over time, these two groups became very different, used their magic differently.

Galdür descendants finally left the shelter of this forest and traveled, and they went far and wide. They spread all across the land. Since they left much later, the radiation wasn't as potent as it was when the others came out of their hiding places, or when Elfes left. They mixed with the other survivors of the war. The magic in these descendants became diluted, weaker. This is where the talents you know of came from. More powerful magic users usually have a gene that enables them to use a greater portion of the magic that was in the two sons, or from someone who has seen a dragon hatch or other magical creature being born. This carries through to their offspring.

These other survivors eventually became the humans, dwarves, gnomes, goblins, orcs, ogres, etc, depending on how much the radiation mutated them. Same with the animals. This is where the dragons eventually come from, and the unicorns, pixies, fairies, borlogs, and other such creatures."

"So you are saying that all these different peoples and creatures come from something called radiation?" Melvin asked, not believing what he had just heard.

"In a sense, yes." The Na' Van replied.

"And you were unaffected by this radiation." Melvin assumed.

"Yes, our shield protected us." He answered. "Because the shield surrounds us completely, we and the people who lived beneath our branches were unaffected."

"So, where did magic come from that Elfin learned to use?" Melvin asked. He thought, *This is the key to my power. If I can figure this out, then I will be powerful enough to defeat Rellik.*

"It was already part of this planet. No one knew how to use it until him. Elfin was a scientist and a naturalist. He studied nature, studied particles, energy, and all types of life forms. He discovered this one energy particle that is in the air, in the ground, everywhere. It resembles light, He called it the magic particle. He learned how to harness this energy particle and be able to control it, and over a long period of time he learned to use it to do wonderful things.

Some animals are born with it inside them, such as Dragons and Unicorns, due to the mutations the radiation caused in them. It allowed them to somehow harness it, to store it, and to use it. Most animals do not have any magic within them, as well as most of the people and creatures after the war that eventually became the dwarves, goblins, orcs, etc. They never got the mutation that absorbs the magic particle. With the radiation and mutations, some animals absorbed more of them than others. This radiation caused the very DNA, the cells of these animals, to change, allowing the magic particles to be absorbed. Dragons were not the same then as they are now; they were giant lizards. They did not originally have wings and scales and breathe fire or other things as they can now; these were caused by the mutations in the animals or were caused by others mutating them for other purposes. Some animals absorbed so much, like dragons, it is passed on to their offspring. The ancestors of Dragons, because they were such large animals, got a mutation that allowed them to absorb these particles in such a concentrated amount during their lives that their offspring emit them when they are hatched. That's why if there is anyone in the vicinity, they will absorb magic as well, whether you had the mutation or not. And, if you are already a magic user, such as yourself, you will absorb even more, and that will make your magic stronger and your abilities grow. The type of talent, or type of magic a person can do, will increase. The aura that surrounds you is the particles and the energy that gather around you."

"Why are you telling me this? What does all this have to do with me? Am I supposed to write this history down or something?"

"Melvin, this history has been written many times by many people, and forgotten many times. The elves have this history written. You and your company can go study it at your leisure. But that is not what is important right now. Melvin, you are special. You are an anomaly. Being directly descended from Elfin, somehow you got the ability not only to harness these energy particles in great numbers, and then even more so after you saw Penelope hatch, then after you visited Lilenhamür, but also the ability to use all the facets of them. They respond to your every thought, your every command, when you direct them in a certain way. That is why your aura, eyes, and hair are multicolored. That's why you can use any kind of magic. Your father was a great wizard; he carried a lot of the same ability as you, and your mother is also a great Wizardess. But you surpass them all."

"I never knew my mother was a Wizardess."

"Her talents aren't as manifest as others. Hers is the ability to teach, to know where and how the student is struggling, and how to teach them in a way that they can understand the concept. She has the ability to help others learn. She can also learn to retain knowledge and recall it in an instant. This is a rare talent. Because of that, you can learn things easily and learn magic more easily than others. But she also has inactive magic abilities that have been passed down to you, and for you, these have been unlocked. Your father is very rare indeed. He was a very powerful wizard. He had magic particles flowing through him. Although those abilities were recessed. Both of your parents are very powerful."

"And who is my father?" Melvin asked, wanting to know the answer since no one ever told him.

"Who your father is will be revealed in time, but it is not for us to say. Now on to more important matters. We have noticed that you have the ability to magnify. The ability to see inside things, to see how things work at a cellular or molecular level. The only one we know of who had this ability was Elfin, and very few of his descendants, always elves. You can put your consciousness inside things. Like when you healed Adara. No one has that same ability. Yes, there are healers, but they cannot put their consciousness into someone or something and heal them at the cellular level like you can. This is the reason that you have every ability any other magic user has ever had. Even if you don't know how to use it, even if you don't know you have the ability now, you will learn it. You have the potential to be the greatest wizard who ever lived. Because of this great ability, we suspect that one of your parents was of the lineage of Elfes, and your other parent was a descendant of the Galdür. You have both halves within you; that's why you can do any type of magic. Though we do not know who one of your ancestors was or is, an Elf. As is your bride. We see that she is a direct descendant of Elfis as well. This is the reason she is so powerful. Any children you have will be more powerful than you can imagine."

"Wouldn't Adara's sisters be just as powerful as she is?" Melvin queried.

"Not all children get the same or the same amount of abilities. Although Adara's sisters are powerful in their talents, as are the King and Queen. Just as with any trait, even if the parent has it, it does not always mean that the trait is passed on to their children. In your case and Adara's case, your traits were dormant. Waiting for the right time to reveal themselves. Alas, we have kept you away long enough; you should go back to your group. And to your wife. Though she is strong, she needs you."

"Can I tell Adara what you have told me?"

"Yes, but only her, for now. There will be others as you journey, whom you can share this information with as well. Yes, one of them is the Empress, though she has known this for a while, through her talent. This is why she came to talk to you that night. Another is Penelope. Both your mother and your dragon. Est'iän Arnatuilë already knows this, you may also tell the King of the Dragons, NöGard, if you have the chance to talk to him and the need arises."

Melvin went back to the group and told Adara all that the Na'Van had told him. They just sat and held each other for a long while, deep in thought, and discussed these things.

That night, they all slept well. They needed no watch, for the Na'Van protected them.

CHAPTER 35
Est'iänArnatuilë
Lord of the Elves

The path they walked now was unlike any they had walked before. Lined with glowing, luminescent plants, the way ahead shimmered softly in the twilight. Fairies danced in the air, their delicate wings flickering like stars, while luminescent butterflies flitted from flower to flower, their soft glow adding to the enchantment. Strange animals, too, roamed through the forest, their forms barely visible in the mist, yet all of them seemed at peace—protected by the magic of the Na'Van.

Though they were still a long way off, they could already see the walls of Illëngard rising in the distance. The gates and towering walls were unlike anything Melvin had ever seen before. They weren't made of stone or metal, but of ancient trees—giant, living trees growing so close together that they formed an unbreakable, living wall. The trees rose impossibly high, their tops lost in the mist and sky, as if reaching toward the heavens themselves. Melvin could feel the deep magic pulsing through them, a powerful force that seemed to hum in the very air.

These had the same magic as the Na'Van. For in fact, they were part of the Na'Van. As they got closer, Melvin could tell these trees were very old. They were over a decaspan wide. That would equal 100 feet to you. As they approached the gates, they could see elven warriors on the walls and at the gate. The guards opened the gates to let them pass through, and as they passed, bowed their heads to show respect for the Great Wizard Melvin, the Princesses, and the Commander of the Arion forces.

An elf wearing shining armor with the traditional nature patterns of leaves and trees etched into the armor greeted them inside the gate. "Master Wizard Melvin," he said in an honored tone. "And Princesses Adara and Aria. We are honored that you have come to us; we have been expecting you. My name is Malfinnor, Emissary to the King. Est'iän Arnatuilë, the *Lord of the Elves,*" has asked me to bring you to him as soon as you arrive."

"Thank you," said Melvin. "That is part of the purpose of our visit." As they walked, Mclvin looked around at the interesting city of the elves. There were no buildings or houses as he was used to; there wasn't even a castle for the king. All he saw were trees, large ancient trees. Trees so big around that it would take one hundred men, fingertip to fingertip, to encircle one. Melvin noticed that they used the trees for their buildings. For their houses, for businesses, workshops, schools, libraries, etc. The trees were also extremely tall, like the Na'Van. Then Melvin thought they were part of the Na'Van. These trees were so tall that he could not see the tops of them. They must be millions of annums old. He wondered how the trees still lived with the elves using them for their edifices. He must ask the king, or someone, this question.

The rest of the army was taken to an "inn" for food and rest, to get their armor repaired. Melvin, Adara and Aria continued to the King's "palace" to have an audience with the king.

The three climbed the stairs of an ancient tree that was far larger than the rest. The stairs did not look as if they were cut from the tree, but had grown that way. The wood was polished smooth to a shine through many milleanniums of traffic in and out of the tree. Once inside, they were in a room the size of the great room in the castle Adara and Aria live in. Along the back was a throne. An intricate set of branches woven together, there the king sat. Guards stood on either side of the entrance. As they walked, Melvin could hardly believe how immense this tree was. As they approached, Est'iän Arnatuilë stood to greet them. The king was tall, very tall. He was lean, but also well-muscled. His dark green hair flowed to the center of his back. He had on a silky blue robe and pants with the same intricate leafy design on them as the emissary. But what stood out the most were the eyes. Shining green eyes. He hadn't seen too many people with those eyes. The same eyes that nature wizards have. Like Wizard Brennan has. He wore a gold crown on top of his head in the pattern of leaves. His long elf ears pointed upwards.

"Welcome, my friends," Est'iän Arnatuilë said with a soft, airy voice. One that invites you to listen to him. "I have been expecting you. Let us find a more comfortable place to converse. You have been on a long journey and must be tired." With a wave of his hand, two servants brought in a leaf orange sofa with branches woven to make the back, arm rests, and the frame, just as the throne. Large cushions sat on the frame. They also brought in a chair for the king that was the same design as the couch, but was in purple. Melvin was relieved because he didn't feel like standing. Once everyone was seated, the King continued.

"News of your travels have reached my ears, the Na'Van, and others have told me of your mission. We here have felt the great evil that is being spread across the land. We have seen the vile creatures that have infested our forests, but we do not have sufficient numbers to continue to drive them away. I know you come to ask us for aid in this fight against Rellik and his armies. The Empress has sent word to us that you will be coming. I will send as many troops and magic users as I can spare, but unfortunately, it may not be as many as you require. However, we do have other information and resources that will be a benefit to you in this fight."

"We also know you would like to train using magic with us. However, we think that we are the ones who should learn from you."

Commander Adara responded "That is very kind of you Est'iän Arnatuilë. Any help you can give us would be greatly appreciated."

"It is our honor to help you in this war against the darkness." The King said, "It will not be easy. We feel his strength grow, his influence spread throughout the land. We are safe here with the Na'Van, but the rest of Arion is in great peril. For any troops that pass through this land, we offer sanctuary and rest as they travel. And other means that we can help. If you have anything else to discuss, I will be happy to converse with you."

The King told them about a manner of instant communication between the commanders and the troops, and different battalions in different lands. Dragons. Since this is a war which involves dragons, they would be able to use many abilities that dragons had. Like instant communication. Flight from place to place, and many other uses. Melvin said that they had already used Penelope and other dragons to talk, but he had never thought of a coordinated network of dragons.

Melvin asked about this marvelous city they had in the trees, and how they were able to live inside living trees, how they were able to grow so tall and be hollow. Est'iän Arnatuilë told him about his ancestor Elfin and how he communed with nature. It was the same story that the Na'Van had told him. And then added that since the elves and the trees lived in harmony, they shared the same magic. He explained that they could help the trees grow in such a way that the outer rings are extremely hard, almost like steel, and all the water and nutrients for the trees move along the outer rings. The inner rings were not necessary, so the trees moved and compacted all the inner rings to the outer part, leaving the centers hollow. If they needed a window or a balcony or to shape the tree in a certain way, they would sing what they called the "Song of Estry" and use the magic particles to shape the tree as they desired, as long as the tree's ability to live was not affected. In this manner, they could grow new trees in whatever shape they needed to. Over the millions of annums they had perfected this ability. Melvin told the king that he had found, as he sang incantations, that his magic became stronger. He would like to learn more about this skill from the elves.

The King also said that he had contact with some dragons that lived in the forest, and they would be happy to help, they would also contact other dragons to help in the fight. There was a dragon egg soon to be hatched, and they would like the three to be there for it so they could absorb some of the magic. And Rellik could not get to it. Est'iän Arnatuilë would also be there. All control of the dragon would be left to its mother, just as Melvin had done with Penelope. Melvin agreed.

After the visit, Melvin and the princesses went back to the Inn to wash, eat and rest. While Melvin was resting, one of the Kings servants told Melvin that the King wished to speak to him privately. Later that evening an escort brought Melvin to another tree into a room high above the city, which was glowing with light from shining orbs floating in the air. The King was standing on a balcony overlooking Illëngard.

"Melvin," the King started somberly, "I wish to speak to you privately so as not to alarm your friends any more than they already are. We all know this is a very grievous time for these lands. The Empress, as you know, can foresee events before they happen, can see into the hearts of people, and the Na'Van also converse with her; they told me that you were the only one who could defeat Rellik. I do not know why. But I think it has something to do with what the Na'Van told you about your heritage.

"Yes, they told me I am a direct descendant of Elfin, and that I am descended from both sons, and I have like all the talents known."

"That is correct, Melvin, I don't know how you can use all of the talents, it must be some recessive genes that have allowed you to use these talents. I am sorry to inform you that many know of your talents. Good people as well as bad. You may not know it, because you like to keep to yourself, but you are famed far and wide for your magical ability. It is unfortunate, though, that you do not fully know how to use your talents. Your wife, Adara, as well is just as known. We know you have been learning, progressing, and can do many things that no ordinary wizard can do. However, you do not know your full potential. We will teach you what we can so you will be able to defeat Rellik. Do you have any questions?"

"I have been trying to learn all I can since Reicuas taught me all those decannums ago. He said I could do more amazing things than he had ever seen before. Most wizards have a specialty in one area, sometimes two, but I can use magic in all areas. I do have a few questions. How are you able to teach me and hone my skills and abilities, when I don't even know myself what all I can do? And something completely different. How are the elves able to talk to and use magic to manipulate the growth of a tree? How do they grow into the shapes you want?"

"Melvin, we elves are descendants of Elfin, as you well know. We have been preserved and have preserved the magic of Elfin. I am sure the Na'Van have told you the history of our people, albeit very slowly." The King smiled. "Since we have a long history of using magic, collectively, we probably know more than anyone ever will know about magic. However, like other people, wizards, and magic-using creatures, we have mostly a talent for one aspect of magic, nature. However, some of us have other types of talents, such as healing, metalworking, etc. But mostly tied to nature. You, however, can use all aspects, thus we will have multiple teachers for you in different disciplines, then try to infuse them all together so you can use multiple aspects all together. I have noticed you have done this before, somewhat effortlessly. I have seen your bride's ring. It would take a Master Wizard many annums to be able to create a ring like that, with the powers you put into it. But," He paused. "You did it with no effort at all. In one night. We could also use you to learn things from you."

"Thank you Est'iän Arnatuilë. You honor me. Thank you for offering to teach me how to learn to control and use my magic further. If I can teach your people, I will do so, but I feel so inadequate compared to the elves." He said reverently.

"As I have said, we cannot combine talents, however, you do it effortlessly. I also ask if I may have one of my physicians study you and see how the magic particles interact with your body? That may give us some insight into how you can do what you do."

"It would be my pleasure. And maybe I could teach them some of how I can look into the body and heal from the inside out.

"That would be very welcome. Now, about the trees, no, I have not forgotten. Ever since Elfin protected this forest, his descendants have been able to talk to the trees. We Elves have a special relationship with the Na'Van. We just ask them to do something for us, and they do it out of respect. In return, we take care of them, nurture them, and strengthen them. They do not speak to anyone else but us and the Dragons."

"But they spoke to me," Melvin said meekly.

"Yes, they did. They said you are a descendant of Elfin. May I ask, who is your Father?"

"I don't really know," Melvin said as he thought about it "He died when I was a little boy. My mother has never told me anything about him, except he was a great wizard. He went off to battle and somehow died. At least that's what my mother told me."

"I was just curious because, one: you are a descendant of Elfin, two: you can use all of the magical abilities, and three: I have noticed something interesting, your eyes. They are multicolored. I have never seen that in anyone else before. But your eyes weren't always like this, were they?" asked the King.

"No, they were just normal bright b-b-blue. Before," he stuttered. He mostly had his stuttering under control, except when he was extremely nervous or excited.

"Yes, bright blue eyes show that you have magic." The King said, "Then when you learn your talent, they change, when you use that talent, they glow."

King Est'iän Arnatuilë noticed that Princess Adara had brilliant purple eyes. And Princess Aria had yellow eyes. Melvin explained that Adara's eyes were purple because of her natural blue eyes being overpowered by her enormous amount of fire magic within her. Aria's hair changes from blonde to yellow when she uses her talent. Est'iän Arnatuilë also inquired about the parentage of princesses.

"All I know is their Father is King Bilby. He doesn't have those eyes, nor does the Queen. You would have to ask them, I guess."

They talked some more about other aspects of magic and the elves' history. The King also said that they could make new weapons for them, infused with magic for their protection and special abilities. Of course, he said that Melvin could already do that, but they would teach him how to further his abilities in all areas of magic.

And with a customary slight bow of respect, Melvin departed to his temporary room.

CHAPTER 36
TRAINING WITH THE ELVES

The next few weeks were anything but a vacation for Melvin, the princesses, or the rest of the troops. Training was relentless. They pushed their limits rev after rev, sharpening their skills even further for the battles ahead.

Though Melvin primarily relied on magic, he was also a highly skilled swordsman, though he rarely chose to wield a blade. Under the guidance of the Elves, he and Princesses Adara and Aria learned to seamlessly combine their magic with swordplay, turning their combat abilities into something truly formidable. To deflect blows without effort, to hit their target every time. To make the sword an extension of themselves, become one with it as they use their arms. They also taught Princess Adara how to hone her skills with using fire, new aspects of using fire, or just heat as a weapon, or for comfort when it's cold. They were in awe the first time they saw her hair flame up when she used her powers, for none of them had that ability. Fire users, she learned, were very rare in Arion.

They started off showing the elves what they could do. Melvin, Adara, Aria, and the rest of the army they had brought with them, including Aria's special forces, held mock battles with each other and the elves. They used every tactic, every method, every magic trick they had, and always, like before, ended in a draw. Some battles had lasted for hours.

"This," Melvin said, nearly exhausted after a, long, strenuous battle, "Is why we came to you. We are as good as we are going to get on our own. We need to learn more, we need to get better, we need to improve our fighting skills and our magic skills, if we ever hope to beat Rellik."

One of the captains of the Elvin army responded by saying, "Since you can stand toe to toe with the elves, you can beat any other army out there. You have the quickness, the agility, and the stamina to outmaneuver and outlast any other army out there."

"That may be true." Melvin replied, "But Rellik has Ogres, Orcs, witches, sorcerers, leprechauns, a borlog, and a lot of other nasty creatures, which a lot of them are a lot bigger and stronger than we are. And..." he stressed this part, "He has dragons."

"That does make a big difference," the captain said. We will teach you all we know.

The Elves also taught Melvin many more aspects of magic to explore and use. A lot he already knew by experimenting himself, but even more that he didn't know.

Melvin taught the physicians how to see inside the body. To look into the body, look into the organs, into the cells. Showed them how to mend broken bones and muscles. How to heal from within. He said that this could also work for animals, trees, and plants. They were very appreciative, for they could heal in general, but they could not see inside the body to heal any specific thing.

After learning this, Melvin allowed them to examine his body down to the very core of his DNA, observing firsthand how the Magic Particles interacted with him. What they discovered left them baffled.

In typical magic users, Magic Particles resided within the cells, interacting with the host and enabling them to perform magic. When a magic user witnessed a dragon hatching, some of these particles were absorbed into their cells, increasing their magical reserves. However, what they saw within Melvin defied all known understanding. They discovered that Melvin did not just have magic in his cells; his very DNA was infused with the magic particles. Each different type of DNA was also a different type of magic particle. His body *WAS* magic. Since he could do many types of magic before he saw Penelope hatch, he was already infused with different particles, but when he absorbed a tremendous amount of particles from the hatching, some of the cells doubled up. Instead of having one magic particle per cell, some had two or three. Then he told him about that rev when he transferred the magic particles to his very DNA. This was also why he could absorb magic so easily. The Empress was right. He had more magic within him than all the wizards combined. The Elves looked into their own DNA, something they had never been able to do before. They saw that their cells were infused with magic particles, but not their very DNA. Melvin was, without a doubt, an extraordinary exception. They also looked into Adara as well, and saw a tremendous amount of fire particles within her, especially in her heart and head, that of a great Wizardess. Within her, the elves saw great power. More than some of the elves. Melvin saw that power long ago when he made her engagement ring, and then again as he studied her anatomy while healing her. They all were determined to teach her how to unlock, harness, and use that power within her, but also make sure she did not harm herself from the inside out. She already could use her magic extremely well, but they wanted to teach her how to use it to her maximum potential.

Melvin showed other elves how to look into plants and trees and rocks, and metal. All the way down to the molecules and atoms. How the various parts were aligned and how the pieces fit together. He showed them how to move these molecules around to make different shapes. Make a blade that never dulled, make stone split a certain way.

They showed him how to make trees and plants grow in a certain pattern, like they did for the trees for their homes and the furniture. But their magic with the forest was more respect between the elves and the forest than making the forest do certain things, so that's what Melvin learned. Melvin even made himself a chair by interweaving young vines, and caused them to grow together as the elves had done.

He showed Adara how to take a bit of her consciousness with his into her body to show her where her power lies, how to use it more effectively. How to channel it. She could do some of this before, but not to this extent. They showed him many more things. And he showed them many things he could do that they couldn't.

Melvin had an idea to help Adara's magic become stronger. Melvin took a closer look inside

Adara's body. He noticed that her magic was within her cells, but it wasn't a part of her, like the Elves or himself. So he looked within her cells to see what he could do about it. And he did something he had never done before.

"Darling," he said to Adara. "I think I know how to help you unlock your full potential."

"That's great, how?" she asked curiously. She would love to be as powerful as she could, to defeat Rellik and his armies.

"I am going to infuse your magic into your very DNA, like me and the elves."

"Are you sure about this?" she asked. "I am not like you and the elves. You have way more magic than I do."

"Not really, they just have magic within their DNA," He said, reassuring her. "It will be like that rev at our house when I infused my magic into my DNA. You have more magic in you than a lot of the elves, and you have absorbed tremendous amounts from the lake in Lilenhamür. I know this will make you stronger and enable you to use your magic better."

"All right, Melvin, I trust you. Do what you think is best," she said with a hesitant smile.

Despite her words, worry gnawed at her. What would happen if he went through with this? Would she burst into flames? Turn into a fireball? A storm of uncertainty and fear swirled inside her, but she pushed it down, choosing to trust him.

Out in a meadow, Melvin opened up her cells in her heart and head to be able to release the magic particles, then he opened up her very DNA throughout her whole body. He looked into her DNA structure and found out where to insert the magic particles. He called upon the magic particles to go to those places that where they were supposed to go. Then Melvin infused Adara's DNA with the magic particles, the particles moved to those locations in the DNA where they were meant to go.

In a flash of fire, her hair ignited, she became a pillar of fire, her eyes turned as red as glowing embers, then they turned white like the internal part of a flame. Power rushed through her body, and she screamed so loud and strong that the sound pierced the forest. She had become something entirely new. Melvin did not expect this to happen. He was afraid he had done something terrible to her. She stayed like this for an hour. Melvin was worried for her. He asked if she was ok, but she didn't answer; she just continued to scream. Brighter and brighter she became, her whole body was consumed in blinding white fire as bright as the suns at mid light time. He had to do something. This was not what he had intended. He looked within her. He connected with her consciousness.

"What is happening?" She asked, "What did you do to me? I feel so much power now, I don't know how to control it. Please help me."

"I am trying to," he said to her mind. Melvin looked into her DNA, her body wasn't ready for this much power. He had trained many annums to control his power. And this was just thrust on her. He found where he had gone wrong. He had attached the magic to the wrong part of her DNA. He looked inside himself and noticed where the fire magic particles were infused. Then he looked at Adara and attached the particles in the same areas. The part of the mutation of DNA that was responsible for using magic, for using fire. He could tell that she and Aria were descendants of Elfin as well. That's why they had the bright blue eyes behind the colored irises. After Melvin changed the location of the magic particles in her DNA, the pillar of fire died down, and she stopped screaming, and her hair returned to normal. Except her eyes were still bright, fiery white. She lifted her arm and blasted Melvin with a blast of fire so strong that it threw him back 50 spans. Adara's eyes turned back to their normal bright purple color.

"I deserved that," Melvin said as he got up and dusted himself off.

"Don't you *EVER* do anything like that to me again!!!" she screamed seething, and stomped off. Over the weeks of training, they became more powerful, more expert in their respective fields.

Aria was very good with a sword and all kinds of weapons; however, the elves taught her how to be an expert with them. How to aim better, throw farther, block better, and strike more accurately. All this, with her ability to dance. They taught her how to draw from her power within to dance with a blade. Not stiff repetitions, but fluid motions like a dance. She could see where she was, where she wanted to be at the same time. Where her opponent's weapon was and where it would be, how to move fluidly to counteract a move, and make a strike of her own. They taught her how to use her power to see not only her target with a bow, but also how to zoom in on the target, how to know precisely where the arrow would hit. After she learned how to do this, she never missed. She became more deadly, as did the other troops.

They named her **"Taila-Atria"**—*Blade Dancer.*

To honor her skill, Melvin and the Elves crafted special, enchanted leather armor and weapons for Aria. The armor was so impossibly light that she barely felt its presence, yet it fit her like a second skin, moving seamlessly with her every motion. Her weapons, forged with Elven precision and magic, were both lighter and stronger than anything she had ever wielded before.

They linked her weapons and her armor to her magic within her, they could act and react without even thinking about it. It took her ability to dance and enhanced it several hundredfold. She could dance and dodge and strike in fluid motions. She could anticipate even better what the enemy would do and counteract it flawlessly. She was truly a blade dancer. The Elves worked with her in the large meadow where she was transformed. The Na'Van erected a special force field around it so she wouldn't burn down the whole forest. Melvin studied this force field to learn how to improve his. They taught her to use heat without fire. They showed her how to create everything from a tiny spark to a towering inferno, well, that she could do already. How to shoot fire like arrows, lob fire balls accurately, create a type of fire that, once it caught something on fire, it would not go out until it consumed the whole thing. They called it Dragon Fire because it was similar to how dragon fire worked. Since her fire particles we not only in her heart and head, but now throughout her body, in her very DNA, not only could she shoot fire from her hands, but also through her legs. Her whole body would erupt into flames if she wanted it to.

 She learned how to heat things from within, and she could make one heck of a barbecue dinner. They also taught her how to use her power for good. How to keep herself and others warm in the cold by heating her body just slightly. She learned how to wear clothes or armor to keep the ones wearing them warm, without burning them. Melvin and the elves showed her how to use her full power. Just watch out when she gets mad. People thought she was powerful before. Just wait till they can see her now. As their power grew, the enchantment on their rings grew. Adara's ring protected her before, but now it would be an impenetrable visible shield if Adara so desired. As long as Melvin and she were alive, nothing could touch her, unless she allowed it. Although he didn't need it, Adara and Melvin created a shield for him as well. She got magical form-fitting bright red leather armor as well. It would resist the intense fire without burning. It was the same red hue as her ring. And had the same spell on her armor as on her ring. But she wasn't expected to wear her armor all the time, only during battle; she had another set of leather armor for traveling, with the same enchantments.

The final thing that Adara, Melvin, and the Elves made for her was a sword. Even with all of her magical fire ability, you would think she didn't need a sword. Well, in that estimation, you would be correct. However, she was a master swordswoman, and she loved using one. This sword, like many things she had, was one of a kind. It would only work for her. Just like her ring, it worked with her magic. If anyone else tried to use it, it would just be like any other perfectly balanced light sword. While making it, Melvin taught the Armor smith elves how to work with the molecules of the metal, how to form it in a way to would never get dull. The molecules would align perfectly instantaneously if knocked out of place. Since the elves were more nature magic oriented, they could only find one with the ability to do it. Then, when the sword was forged, as with the other weapons and armor, they put an incantation on it that used Adara's magic to flame up, just as Adara's hair, and now body, does while in battle. Not only could it cut through anything, but it would cauterize the cut at the same time. However, Adara could also send fire through it as if it were a flamethrower. She didn't need to, but it was fun to do.

With the help of the Elves, Melvin forged special magical weapons for Aria and the elite guard. These weapons were designed to amplify their strengths while minimizing their weaknesses, making them deadlier in battle.

To ensure their protection, they also crafted enchanted shields, each imbued with defensive magic. As Melvin deepened his understanding of runes, he and the Elves meticulously etched them onto every piece of weaponry and armor, layering them with powerful enchantments and incantations. The result was near-indestructible gear that not only enhanced their abilities but also gave them an undeniable edge in combat.

CHAPTER 37
DRAGON EGGS

As promised, the elves took Melvin, Adara, and Aria deep into the forest to watch another dragon hatch.

Fortunately, the dragon also lived under the protection of the Na'Van. She was friendly with the elves and helped them whenever possible, and in return, she was helped by them when needed.

They walked along a winding path through the heart of the enchanted forest, surrounded by towering trees that had stood for countless millennia, their gnarled branches stretching high above, reaching toward the sky like ancient, wise guardians. In some places, the forest was so thick with leaves and vines that the sunsss' light barely touched the forest floor, casting everything in a shadowy, mystical glow.

Soft, glowing orbs floated gently along the path, lighting their way with an ethereal, calming light. As they moved deeper into the woods, the air grew thicker with magic, and they glimpsed creatures of legend—unicorns with coats that shimmered like silver in the dim light, fairies with wings that sparkled like tiny stars, and gryphons with eyes full of ancient wisdom. But even in this magical place, there were creatures of the forest—graceful deer, majestic mandras, and other wild animals that wandered freely through the shadows.

The elves set up a couple of tests for Melvin along the path. They came to a large river, with no way to cross. Actually, there was a way to cross, but it had just been disassembled the rev before, but they made it look like the bridge had been broken. The elves asked Melvin how they would be able to cross it. Melvin thought for a while and remembered some of the training that he received with the elves. He would just fly over by compacting the air beneath and around him and using wind to push him across. They had taught Adara how to shoot fire from her palms and feet to give her a sort of thrust to propel herself. She thought that would work to propel herself over the river.

However, he knew the others had no way to cross. Searching the ground, he found a handful of seeds. With a deep breath, he sang an incantation, channeling his magic into the earth.

Before their eyes, the seeds sprouted and stretched upward, their branches twisting and weaving together, forming a living bridge. The vines thickened, strengthening with each passing moment until they reached the other side. One by one, they crossed safely over the river.

The Elves stood in awe, witnessing magic unlike anything they had ever seen.

It would have taken them weeks to grow a bridge sufficient enough to cross over. Melvin did this in a couple of hours. Truly, he was amazing to behold. They walked for a few more hours, then camped for the night.

They walked along the path for a few hours and saw that a large tree had fallen over the path. It was too large to climb or jump over, the elves said, although they could do it, and so long it would take hours to go around. Ok, that was an exaggeration, however, the Elves wondered what Melvin would do in this situation. Adara offered to do a controlled burn, but Penelope, who always kept an eye on them during this time, reminded Adara that although her solution would work, it would also take a very long time, and this was a test for Melvin from the elves, so to should let him figure it out.

The elves asked him again to solve this dilemma. He thought a moment, then sang a song so low that even the elves with their superior hearing had trouble hearing it.

Drawing upon what he had learned from the Elves, he manipulated the tree's wood, guiding it outward until a tunnel formed through its center. The archway seamlessly blended with the tree's natural structure, allowing them to walk straight through without straying from the path. What took him mere minutes would have taken the Elves several hours—a display of power that left them silently impressed.

The small group traveled through the dense woods along the path lit by orbs floating along the path. Melvin had never seen anything like these orbs before. He asked the Elves how this was done. They said that it was ancient magic, however, Reicuas, his master wizard at one time, had shown them how to do it. Since he was a light wizard, he could do it easily. They concentrated the light and put a force field around the light. Very few of the elves could do this type of magic. Melvin decided to give it a try. Since he could use all types of magic, this should be easy. He had seen Reicuas do this type of magic, make magic balls of light. He lit his House with them. He had tried to teach Melvin how to do it once before when he was much younger, but he couldn't quite get it. However, part of Melvin's magic was controlling light, so he concentrated and formed a ball of light in his hand, then, as the Elves told him, he formed a force field around the ball of light. He had done it. Then he practiced making it brighter and brighter. He set it along the path, and they continued onward. His light was a lot brighter, and the color of the yellow suns. For without realizing it, he had made sunslight. A few hours later, they came to an area of trees that was denser than those around them. This was where the dragon lived and had laid her egg.

As they walked into the grove of trees, Melvin saw a majestic purple dragon. Her scales shimmered in what little sunslight came through the trees. She was larger than his dragon, Penelope, but smaller than Penelope's mother. Remember, Penelope was still a very young dragon, as far as dragons go. Either way, to Melvin, she was Ginormous.

The Elves greeted the dragon and communicated with her. Then she turned her attention to Melvin.

"Melvin. I have heard many things about you, I know that you are trying to stop Rellik and his minions. I wanted you to be here to see my eggs hatch, so he could not get to them. Although we are in the shield of the Na'Van, Rellik has many dark wizards and other creatures that could trick the Na'Van and steal the eggs. And you, Princesses Adara and Aria, I am honored that the leaders in this fight against this evil wizard are here as well."

"We had just encountered some when we were coming to visit the elves," Melvin said, then asked. Then asked, "Eggs?"

"Yes," she replied, *"there are two eggs. Dragons of my type usually have two eggs versus one egg. Penelope and the elves told me about when you saw Penelope's hatching, and gave the control back to the mother. That was very generous of you. I am not concerned whether you keep control of my babies or not. I know you will not cause them to do anything against their will."*

"Thank you," he said. "But I don't even know your name."

"Lila Drache" She said. *"Come now, the eggs are about to hatch."*

Melvin approached the two massive eggs, each standing as tall as he was—impressive by human standards, though still shorter than the Elves. Suddenly, a sharp crack echoed through the air. Tiny fragments of shell crumbled away, revealing streaks of glowing purple light seeping through the fissures. The magic radiating from the twin dragons was undeniable, filling the grove with an overwhelming presence.

Sensing the power, Melvin began weaving a spell through song, ensuring that he, Adara, and Aria could absorb as much of the magic as possible. As the shells continued to splinter, their luminous energy intensified, surging outward in brilliant waves. The trio absorbed the magic hungrily, though Melvin remained cautious—he needed to leave enough for the Elves, for Adara and Aria, and, most importantly, for the dragons themselves. If too much was taken, the newly hatched creatures could be left weak and vulnerable.

While Aria excelled in combat and dance, she could not regulate how much magic she absorbed. Nevertheless, she managed to take in enough to significantly enhance her skills. Despite the presence of several onlookers, the sheer strength of the dragons' magic ensured that each person received their share, though the more individuals present, the less each could claim.

Being the strongest wizard among them, Melvin had absorbed the most magic. Now, he faced a crucial decision—should he maintain control over the baby dragons, or allow their mother to guide them until they were mature enough to fend for themselves? He reflected on his experience with Penelope and, in the end, chose the same path.

"I will give control to the Mother." He said, "Until such a time as they can be on their own. However, I request that at such a time that I should need their assistance, they come to help me, especially in defeating Rellik."

At this, Lila Drache was relieved. *"We would be honored to help you in the fight against Rellik."* Then flashes of pictures came to their minds. They saw Rellik stealing, hatching, enslaving, and torturing dragons. He absorbed so much of the baby dragon's magic that they barely survived. Then, after it had hatched, he enslaved them. Melvin and Adara could feel the cool hatred Lila Drache had for Rellik.

"How do you know of these things? Adara asked.

"I know these dragons. Every dragon in these parts has a connection to one another." "How come Penelope doesn't have this connection?" Melvin asked.

"She was born on the other side of the continent, so she is not part of the connection." Lila Drache replied. *"Although I could easily add her."*

"Would you please do that?" Melvin asked politely. "It would be of great help to know what dragons are being taken. And where?"

"I will do that." Lila Drache replied. Then added *"And also, I will tell you where each of the dragon eggs are, and when they are about to be hatched, so you and your forces can get there before Rellik does, and get them before Rellik. The egg does not need the mother or father there to hatch, so you could take it to a safe place to hatch, weather you want to watch the hatching or not is up to you, but if you do, you will have more power to defeat Rellik, and if you don't, at least Rellik won't have them."*

"If that is alright with the other dragons, we will gladly do this. Would it work to take the eggs to Dragonia?

I am sure they will be safe there."

"You would think that, wouldn't you. Unfortunately, the Dragon King NöGard will not take them. He thinks the dragons who do not live in Dragonia are outcasts and lesser dragons. No, they must stay here. We must fight this evil sorcerer before we all become slaves."

"Then we will take them to Lilenhamür, to be under the protection of the Empress," Adara added. *"Thank you,"* he heard not only Lila Drache say, but also other dragons that were connected to her. And then he cast an enchantment of bonding and protection over them. That Rellik or any of his wizards could not have any control over them. And they could not be captured by them.

He expressed his hope that they would stand with him against Rellik should the need ever arise. Though he believed in their strength, he wished they would never have to fight. In response, Lila Drache vowed that they all would.

After getting acquainted with the new baby dragons, Melvin and the elves went back to Illëngard without incident. After long weeks of training and a few revs of rest, it was time for the small band to be on their way and head for the Jïgabuji.

CHAPTER 38

A CALL FOR HELP

Rellik had amassed a great army either through coercion or by force. Every imaginable evil creature came to his side. Orcs, ogres, goblins, leprechauns, pixies, witches, warlocks, bandits, and most of all, Dragons. They razed and raided cities, towns, and villages. Some were promised great power and wealth. And others were forced to serve him. And thus he went on, taking possession of many cities, the port city of Pyne in the north, and the city of Ündarhaven, and Hammoth-Dōr on the west slope of the Helaeth Mountains, the city of Lăncaster, the city of Banaldür, and the lands of the Jĭgabuji in the grasslands. He also took the cities of Stüdenhiem, Sēsīd, Schiffen-Heim, on the west sea, and the port city of Heisenvad on the south sea, all of which were on the west borders on the seashore. So Rellik obtained, so many cities west of the mountains, all of which afforded strongholds for the armies of Rellik. He also took many small towns and farms. Forcing them to produce food and weapons for his vast army. In a remarkably short span of time, Rellik, through the sheer power of his armies and dragons, seized control of all the lands west of the Helaeth Mountains.

In the ancient land of Eldoria, nestled between towering mountains near a shimmering lake, lay the Dwarf city of Hammoth-Dōr. Known for its majestic architecture, the dwarves were known as master stone cutters and masons, and their workmanship spread throughout the Empire. The Empress had even used their services herself in the buildings in Lilenhamür.

Hammoth-Dōr, once a beacon of prosperity and peace, bustled with vibrant markets and thrived as the central trade hub between the western Helaeth Mountains and the lands to the east. But dark times had come. Rellik had laid siege to the city, threatening to annihilate everything its people held dear.

Among Rellik's most formidable generals, there was one known as Vargath. He was no ordinary man, but a hybrid—a product of arcane experimentation. Rellik had fused the cunning and intelligence of a human with the brute strength of an ogre, encasing it all in the impenetrable armor of a borlog. The result was a creature both awe-inspiring and terrifying to behold. He thrived in causing destruction and mayhem. And did so with great enthusiasm.

The Magistrate of Hammoth-Dōr sent an urgent call to the Empress of their plight and pleaded for urgent help to defeat the forces of Rellik. They would hold them off as long as they could, but they prayed that they could hold on long enough until aid came.

When news of Hammoth-Dōr's plight reached The Empress, she knew she could not stand idly by. Rellik had taken too many cities already, and it was time they started taking them back. She sent word to Melvin and Adara and tasked them with leading the army to save the city. One of the Empress's greatest Generals was Thalion.

General Thalion was a seasoned warrior with a heart of gold. He gathered a formidable force of knights, archers, and wizards from Lilenhamür. The army's resolve remained unshaken, driven by the knowledge that the fate of Hammoth-Dōr—and all of Arion—depended on them. Their mission was clear: to rid the world of the dark sorcerer Rellik. He felt a surge of excitement at the honor of serving under the legendary Princesses and Melvin the Magnificent.

Chapter 39
Through the Mountains

The group traveled from the ancient forest toward the mountain's base. Penelope sent word to the Empress, instructing the remaining troops to rendezvous at the entrance to the pass. Only then did they realize just how much time had slipped away in the company of the elves.

Here it was, late Harvest. Leaves were changing from Purple to green, and orange to teal, and many other colors, ready to fall off the trees for a long Darken which would come sooner. The nights were getting cooler, however, they needed to get across the mountains as fast as they were able to help the people on the other side. They knew leaving this late would get very cold in the mountains. Being very tall mountains, freezing temperatures came early, and with that, snow and ice.

When Melvin and his company arrived at the entrance to the pass that led through the mountains, they were met by General Thalion and an army of one hundred thousand soldiers, footmen, and three thousand archers waiting for them. All of these soldiers were sent from the Lilenhamür. Many wizards from Lilenhamür and Wazervïl also volunteered for this assignment. It would take several weeks to get to the other side of the mountains. He asked that the troops bring plenty of supplies to keep them warm on their journey.

A few revs into the journey through the mountain pass, temperatures were freezing. They didn't realize that it got that cold so soon in the mountains. Aria, though very skilled with weapons, was no match for the cold. The slow pace of the march, as well as sitting on a qilin, didn't allow her to exert herself and stay warm. Even though she had a cloak on, she could tell that something was wrong.

Her feet and hands turned numb, but she refused to complain. She wouldn't allow herself to be a burden to the company. As a leader, she was meant to set an example for her unit and the entire army. Melvin and Adara were slowly walking their qilins up the pass when, all of a sudden, they heard a thump. They looked around and saw that Aria had fallen off her qilin. Adara became very frightened for her sister, this had never happened before.

They raced to her side and noticed her skin was blue, her hands were cold as ice. She was getting frostbite. Something had to be done quickly. Adara immediately sent a shot of fiery warmth through her body to warm it up from the inside. Melvin then went through the ranks and asked the captains for reports on how the soldiers and wizards were doing.

Even though they had on leather and skins, and fur under their armor, they were still very cold. They started becoming sluggish. Some had their fingers and toes starting to go numb. Some were on the verge of frostbite. If they were attacked, how were they to fight in these conditions? The wizards were also having problems keeping warm. They would be of no use if they were too busy trying to keep warm. Adara was worried for the troops. What could she do? Being the commander of the army, she had a responsibility to keep them safe, well, as safe as she could; this was a war after all. She could at least keep them warm—but how? There were over a hundred thousand soldiers, wizards, and animals pulling the supplies. She didn't have the power to sustain warmth for each individual. She needed a solution—something that could envelop everyone at once, require minimal energy, and wouldn't demand her constant focus.

She talked to Melvin about this and they came up with a solution. Along with Melvin and Penelope's help, Adara put a small spark inside everyone's armor, or robes if they were a wizard. With that spark, Penelope put a small flame of Dragon Fire into each of those sparks, contained so they would not catch on fire. They produced heat but no flame. They heated the armor and the clothes, but did not burn the wearer. For the animals without a heavy winter coat, she put a spark of warmth within their bodies to keep them warm as well. She learned some anatomy from Melvin and learned this technique from Melvin and the elves.

They managed to cross the pass without freezing to death, but that didn't mean they were free from trouble. Adara could only hope that if Rellik's army dared to enter, the bitter cold would claim them instead. They were winding up the road that led along the river when they saw a nice flat spot with a large number of trees. There was no snow on the ground due to the tree cover. "General Thalion," Adara said. "We are going to rest here for the night. Get the men's tents set up and get them fed. Your unit is going to take first watch tonight. You know the drill."

"Yes, Commander," he responded with a salute, then went to perform his tasks. They set up tents and fires to cook food to keep warm. Melvin and the other wind wizards caused a breeze over the trees to blow the snow off so it wouldn't fall on the troops.

CHAPTER 40
WATCHER

Later that night, Melvin jolted awake, a deep unease settling in his chest. Something was wrong—he just couldn't pinpoint what. Then, a piercing shriek shattered the silence, slicing through the night like a blade. The entire camp sprang to life, chaos erupting as screams of terror and agony rippled through the ranks.

"Shrieker?" Adara asked, for she was awake as well. "DRAGON," the cry rose up.

The large dragon flapped its enormous wings to stay aloft. The firelight reflected off its dark red scales.

It shot fire from its enormous maw.

Adara immediately saw the dragon with the light of the fires surrounding it and started shooting fireballs at it. They just bounced off its scales. "My attacks are useless." Use the catapults and the nets, and let's see if we can capture it."

The dragon screeched, and it was so loud it felt as if their ears would burst.

Aria's special forces went to work. They strategically placed the catapults and shot nets at the dragon.

Before they were even near the dragon, it burned the nets with its fire.

"We should have known that wouldn't work. Get the steel nets," Aria commanded. Then she got the wizards to put a spell on the net so it would fly true and not melt. Other magic users tried to cast spells on the dragon, to no effect. The water wizards tried to drench it with water, to no effect. Nature wizards caused the roots to bind its legs so it could not fly away. Ice wizards tried to encapsulate it with ice. It just breathed fire, and the ice melted.

They shot the nets at the dragon, and it was still able to avoid the nets. It screamed again and bellowed fire at the troops. They were able to avoid the fire using their shields. This was a young dragon, but still very large and powerful.

Melvin got a message from Penelope. "Remember what the Na'Van told you, and the elves taught you?

Put a force field around the dragon."

Melvin strained to recall the exact enchantment. As he raised his staff high, the multi-colored gem at its tip pulsed to life, casting shimmering hues into the darkness. With a steady breath, he sang, weaving the magic into a protective force field.

Air and light combine, surround the dragon, encircle it with your strength

Let neither strength, fire, nor magic penetrate

Then a force field surrounded the dragon. It thrashed and screamed and fought for a long while. Then, realizing it could not break free, it calmed down, and Melvin brought it to the ground. It laid its enormous head on its sharp claws that were as long as a man's arm and glistened in the firelight, and just glared at Melvin.

"Congratulations," a voice was heard throughout the camp. *"You have captured one of my dragons. No matter, I have plenty left. Be wary and watchful, because you will never know when I will attack. I have many dragons and armies. Next time, I will send more than just one, and it will be a lot harder to defeat them. You will not win this war, I will rule Arion."*

That warning by Rellik set everyone on edge. But as soon as it came, it was gone.

"Stay on high alert," Adara commanded. "You never know when or where this monster will attack again.

As he said, next time it will be more than just one dragon." "Penelope, can you talk to it?" Melvin asked.

"Yes, I can, but so can you and Adara." She responded.

"I think it would be better if a fellow dragon talked to it, besides, you know what it's thinking," Melvin said. *"Have you learned nothing from me all these annums? You have the same ability, you can do it just as well as I can. You just have to concentrate. Look into her eyes, they will reveal all."*

"Very well, I will do as you ask," Melvin said. He slowly walked up to the dragon and commanded its attention. It tried to resist but couldn't. He looked, penetrating into her blood red eyes, and saw that yes, it was a female dragon. As he gazed at this magnificent creature, pictures began flooding into his mind. He simultaneously shared these with Adara. Penelope could already communicate with the dragon.

She was scared and alone. Under the rule of Rellik, she was kept in a cage and tortured repeatedly. Nearly starved to death. She was taught from her youth to fight. Her egg was stolen from her mother, high in the mountains, and brought to Rellik's castle. There it was watched over until it hatched. They had sped up the hatching, she was not given enough time to fully develop.

While she was hatching, Rellik stood near in a sealed and otherwise empty coldstone room. As she emerged from her shell, he greedily drained nearly all of her magic, leaving her weak and vulnerable. A twisted, maniacal laugh echoed through the chamber as power surged through him.

"You are mine now," he sneered. *"You will obey me. There is no escape. I own you."*

His laughter rang out once more as his minions seized her, dragging her to the dungeon—a dark, cold prison where she would remain until she grew strong enough to serve him. When the time came, she was transferred to a towering stone fortress, devoid of windows, devoid of light. There, she was starved, left with barely enough food to survive.

The dragon raised its head.. *"I am scared,"* she said. *"I do not want to have to serve him. But I have no choice. I do not want to go back. Please kill me so I do not have to go back."*

"I will not kill you," Melvin told the dragon. "How many are in your situation?" He asked.

"At least a dozen," The dragon responded. *"There are others, but they are evil like the Shadow Lord and like destroying things. They are happy with their situation. They are treated better than those like me."*

"I will try to help you be free of the bond. However, if I cannot, will you help us defeat him?" Melvin asked, "Penelope, can you help me?"

"Of course, my friend, what do you wish?" she responded.

Then he communicated that he needed to know how the bond between a dragon and a human worked. Since they did not have one, like she and Rellik did, he couldn't examine his. She said that they are connected with the heart. This bond is very difficult to break. She has known only one wizard and dragon be able to break it, and both have to be willing to break it. Usually, the Dragon is willing, but its master is not. With this, Melvin set out to find if he could break the bond.

"I am going to look inside you, to see if I can break the bond," Melvin told the dragon. *"Yes, please."* She begged.

Melvin asked for a chair to be brought to him as he worked. Once he sat down, he sent his consciousness inside the dragon. He looked into the heart of the dragon, in the middle of where she held her magical power. He had never seen so much magic in his life. If she had this much magic, and she said that Rellik absorbed most of her magic, then he could hardly imagine how much a normal dragon, like Penelope, had.

He looked deeper into the Dragon's heart, and then he saw what he supposed to be the bond. It was a shining strand, invisible to the naked eye, that went out from the heart, out to where he supposed Rellik was. He was not able to see the end of it. Melvin tried with his magic to sever the thread. It would not work. He then tried to look further at the molecular level. He noticed that the bond was tied into the very molecules of her heart and could not be disconnected. He brought his consciousness out of her.

Shaking his head, he told the dragon he was unable to break the bond, it was a stronger, more ancient magic than he knew how to use. However, he did have an idea. He told her that he could make another bond with her, not a bond of control, but a bond of communication that would be hidden from Rellik and would enable her to communicate with Melvin, Adara, and Penelope over long distances. In essence, she would be a spy. Letting them know where Rellik was and what he was doing. The dragon was thrilled with the idea and would love to get back at Rellik for her harsh treatment her whole life. She would also see if the other dragons would join her, but she would be cautious.

Melvin once more looked into the dragon. However, instead of looking into the heart, he looked into the brain, and looked to where the communication part of the brain was. There, he put a piece of magic that opened up her thoughts to them so they could communicate. He told her to live as normally as possible. If she was sent to fight them, then do it; if she was told to raze a village, then do it. But to let them know what was going on beforehand, so they could prepare. The dragon agreed. He asked for one last thing. What was her name?

"I don't have a name, I was never given a name." She communicated sadly.

"Then I shall call you Watcher." He told her. Then he lifted the enchantment off the net. "Escape." He

Told her acting as if he were trying to attack her, in case they were being watched.

The dragon then roared and struggled and thrashed and finally ripped the net from over her and flew off into the night.

"Thank you," she communicated back graciously, *"I will never forget your kindness. How will I ever repay you?"* She asked.

"Just help us defeat Rellik," he communicated.

"I will do what I can." She replied, then flew off into the night.

Under the cloak of night, Rellik and his Shadow Dragon, Skügge, descended upon the unsuspecting Arion army, unleashing a suffocating wave of thick, acrid smoke. The toxic cloud rolled over the camp like a living nightmare, seeping into every crevice, every breath. Soldiers awoke in panic, coughing violently as their lungs burned with each desperate inhale. Cries of confusion and terror echoed through the night, their voices choked and rasping. The once roaring fires that illuminated the encampment were snuffed out, plunging the army into an impenetrable darkness. Panic spread through the ranks as the soldiers stumbled blindly, unable to see their comrades or the enemy. The air was thick with the <u>stench of sulfur</u> and the sound of coughing and wheezing. It seemed as though the Arion army would be suffocated by the relentless smoke.

Adara was disappointed that her magic could do nothing to dispel this smoke. Any attempt to conjure fire would be smothered by the thick, oppressive smoke. Just then, they heard snarls and wails and gnashing of teeth. Not only were they suffocating from the dense smoke released by Rellik and his dragon, but now the enemy was upon them. Not being able to see was a disadvantage to the army. How could they fight what they could not see? Fortunately, Aria's forces had honed their skills to be able to adapt in this type of environment. Melvin and some of the wizards were able to see in the darkness because of their talents. They went to work on dispatching the enemy.

Cries of anguish and agony swept through the ranks as the unseen foe dealt deadly blows to the unsuspecting army. Everyone stood at the ready, guarded in case of attack.

Amid the chaos, Melvin and his fellow wind wizards gathered their strength. Channeling the power of the wind, they summoned a mighty gust. The wind howled through the darkness, sweeping away the suffocating smoke and clearing the air. As the smoke dissipated, the stars reappeared in the sky, and the encampment was once again visible.

Now, with the smoke beginning to clear, they could finally see their enemy. The battlefield was illuminated by the eerie glow of embers still floating in the air. The soldiers of Arion were ready to fight—yet many still struggled, their lungs raw from the acrid fumes, barely able to lift their weapons.

Aria and her team, protected by masks covering their faces, remained unaffected. Wasting no time, they moved swiftly, cutting down the enemy with precision. Amidst the chaos, Adara took a different approach—her eyes glowed with raw power as she ignited a spark within each foe she set her sights on. One by one, they convulsed, flames erupting inside them, their bodies consumed from within.

This took but mere seconds, for her it was effective, although the smell of cooked orc was putrid. Another wave of the enemy attacked. Hundreds of cross-bred goblins and gremlins called gormlins jumped and hopped into the camp. Jumping on the army, scratching, biting, and wreaking havoc wherever they went. They toppled tents, set things on fire, and their shrill laughter rang in the air. The army didn't know what to do against these creatures. They tried to swing at them with their swords, but they were too fast. Archers were able to hit a few, but they usually dodged the arrows.

It was up to the wizards to stop this threat. Melvin had a dilemma. Although he was very powerful, these creatures were small, and they were all over the other soldiers and the wizards. They had to be careful not to harm their own men. Adara unleashed precise fire bullets, each searing through the air and striking down the Goremlans with deadly accuracy. She focused on her aim, ensuring every shot hit its mark. Meanwhile, the water wizards drew upon the lake's reserves, sending torrents of water crashing over the creatures, extinguishing their burning forms and forcing them back.

Air wizards were air punching them up into the air.

Nature wizards would cause vines to grow out of the ground and entangle them. Earth wizards were opening up holes in the ground and swallowing them. Aria and her team were dispatching them one swing of their sword after another. Aria did however admire these little buggers for their mayhem and distruction. She would try to use these same tactics on Rellik's army. She wished she could have them fight for their side, however, these little buggers were filled with mischief and malice, and could not be contained.

What was Melvin doing this whole time? Nothing that you could physically see. He looked into them in rapid succession and mentally severed an artery, which stopped their heart. They were dropping like, well, goremlans. Once they hit the ground, they were swallowed up by the earth. In a matter of minutes, the whole swarm of these little things were taken care of.

Just then, lightning struck. Melvin held up his staff and directed the lightning into it, then shot it back out into the sky, dispersing what smoky clouds that were still lingering in the darkness.

The Arion soldiers, now free of the goremlans, and the smoke looked around in relief and awe at the power of Melvin, Adara, Aria, and the other Wizards.

Melvin stood tall, his eyes glowing with determination as he surveyed the battlefield. They had won this battle, but the war was far from over. Rellik had been driven back—for now. Yet, the shadow of his dark power still loomed, a reminder that the final confrontation was yet to come.

CHAPTER 41

HAMMOTH-DŌR

The Arion army finally made it through the mountains. They traveled along the lake town of Hammoth-Dōr.

As they descended from the mountains, Hammoth-Dōr came into view. The once-great and thriving city was now a shadow of its former self, smoldering from dragon fire —its walls battered, its people weary. Smoke curled from the ruins, the aftermath of dragon fire. A city built of stone should have been resilient, but dragon fire did not merely burn; it clung, seared, and melted even the strongest stone.

One of Rellik's fiercest captains, Captain Vargath, and his forces had invaded and surrounded the city, their dark banners fluttered ominously in the wind. Adara's armies set up base camp overlooking the city, thus they would have a better vantage point.

Melvin had Aria scout the city to see the extent of the damage and the situation there. They snuck in through the grate that went to the lake. They proceeded to find the magistrate as stealthily as possible, silently dispatching any opposition along the way. They finally located the Magistrate, locked up in the prison awaiting public execution.

"Magistrate," Aria said softly. "I am Aria with the Arion Army. We have arrived to help you defeat Rellik's army. We are here to get you out. We need as much information as we can get to defeat them."

Shaking, the magistrate responded. "Thank Deo, you finally arrived. We had almost given up hope."

Aria thought he had a very interesting voice. It was high-pitched, but still definitely masculine. It was not what she expected to hear from this middle-aged dwarf, but when she thought about it, it did seem fitting.

"Yeah, about that, we had some trouble in the pass. With cold and a dragon." She said softly, shaking her head, "But we are here now, what can you tell me?"

"I do not know the extent of it. As soon as they arrived, they threw me in here. All I could do was listen." The small dwarf said sorrowfully. "I heard dragons razing the city, women screaming, men shouting. My army fought as valiantly as they could, but they were no match for Vargath." I wish I could be of more help, but as I said, I have been stuck in here for moons with little food."

"You have been more than helpful." She said as she unlocked his chains and they slowly made their way back to the base camp, making sure not to be seen by the troops patrolling the still-smouldering city.

Melvin, through his bond with Watcher, asked her if she knew anything about this. She replied that she did not. She had not been part of it, but all she could tell him was that a mighty red dragon named Bloodlust had razed the city before Vargath took control. Bloodlust was not subject to Rellik—he had done it for the sheer pleasure of destruction.

Adara, Melvin, Aria, and the other generals formulated a plan. The magistrate told them about secret entrances where they could sneak into the city. A direct head-on attack would not be the best idea. They would need troops strategically placed to combat from behind and the sides, while another army comes through the front. There, they would be surrounded and cut off many of the enemy's troops from reaching the gates of the city, which were now flung many spans away thanks to the dragon who had razed the city.

Adara took one group, Melvin took another group, Aria took her special team, and one of Adara's best generals, General Thalion, would head the main group through the main gate. He was a large man, a man of valor. He was the Empress's best general. He had studied the art of war. His strategies could not be beaten in battle. His use of tactics enabled him to use many strategies against the enemy. His men adored him for his bravery and fortitude. He had a good nature when not facing an enemy, but when he was in battle, he was all business. What gave him an advantage was that he could read his enemy. He had a talent for seeing a person's strengths and weaknesses. Thus giving him the ability to know what his opponent was going to do, what move he would make, and he knew exactly how to counter. He taught this method to the rest of the troops from Lilenhamür. Most did not have this talent, but could, in some ways, learn the same techniques with enough time and practice.

The teams stealthily snuck into the city and took down as many enemy troops as possible. Arias's small force was expert at taking down the enemy quickly and quietly. Aria, called "*Taila-Atria*" by the elves, which means the "Blade Dancer", literally dances with blades. She made it look effortless. It was as if the blades were extensions of her body; she twisted and turned, spun, jumped, ducked, pivoted, and pirouetted—all while cutting down enemies at every turn. Watching her fight was like witnessing a deadly dance. The aftermath was nothing short of a bloodbath.

Adara used what she learned from the pass and caused a spark of fire within the armor of the enemy, but she did not contain it; she let it burn, and it cooked the enemy from the inside out. It was possibly not the best idea, because charred orcs and goblins did not smell very pleasant, but it was efficient. While the rest of her team used whatever method they could to eradicate the enemy.

Melvin's team consisted of some of the elite guards that they had brought from Bilbylund. They efficiently dispatched the enemy as well. Their unparalleled swordsmanship and archers killed an enemy with every blow. Even Melvin chose to use his sword against the enemy. There were civilians all around, and he did not want to take a chance at hurting someone with his magic. As we know, he was just as talented and just as lethal using a sword as he was using other types of magic. He did not like killing anyone or anything. But sometimes it must not be helped.

However, Most of the enemy were near the city gate in anticipation of the Arion Empire coming to save the people of Hammoth-Dōr.

With a mighty roar, General Thalion led his men into battle. The clash of steel and the crackle of magic filled the air as the Arion's fought valiantly against Vargath's horde. The knights' swords gleamed in the sunslight, the archers' arrows flew true, and the wizards' spells crackled with energy.

The citizens of Hammoth-Dōr, inspired by the bravery of their saviors, joined the fray, determined to reclaim their home. As a city known for weapon manufacturing, arms were readily available, allowing them to fight with fierce resolve.

Vargath's forces managed to hold the gates of the city. Despite being heavily outnumbered, General Thalion and his men fought valiantly, buying precious time for the rest of the army to regroup and launch a counterattack and make their way to the front of the city.

The battle raged on, but the tide began to turn in favor of the Arion Army. Thalion, with his unmatched skill and unwavering determination, confronted Vargath in a fierce duel. Their swords clashed with a fury that shook the ground. Thalion knew every enemy had a weakness, and he had found one with Vargath. He knew every move Vargath was going to make. Though Vargath was covered in borlog armor, his face was not. In the end, Thalion's blade found its mark. He thrust his sword through Vargath's eye and through his skull. Vargath fell, and with his defeat, his army scattered like leaves in the wind.

The people of Hammoth-Dōr roared with triumph as the Arions raised their banners high in victory. Their city, once on the brink of ruin, had been saved. For the first time in what felt like an eternity, hope flickered in their hearts. The Empress's army had not merely fought for a city—they had reignited the spirit of a land that had nearly lost its will to fight.

The defeat of Vargath and the dispersal of his forces marked the end of a dark chapter in Hammoth-Dōr's history. The city, with the help of the Arion Empire and the bravery of its defenders, began to heal and rebuild, emerging stronger and more united than ever before. A detachment was left in the city to help in its defense should Rellik come against it again. However, darker revs would come in the future.

After the defeat of Vargath and the scattering of his forces, the surviving members of his army faced a grim fate. Many of them, demoralized and leaderless, surrendered to the victorious Arion army. General Thalion, known for his sense of justice and mercy, offered them a choice: to lay down their arms and swear an oath of loyalty to Hammoth-Dōr and its people, or to face death. However, not all of Vargath's forces were willing to submit. A number of them fled into the wilderness. These remnants of Vargath's army were hunted down and captured, and some were able to avoid capture and went back to the main body of Rellik's army.

And so, the tale of Adara, Melvin, Aria, and General Thalion and the army of the Arion Empire became legend for the people of Hammoth-Dōr, in a story passed down through generations as a testament to the power of courage, unity, and the unbreakable spirit of those who fight for what is right.

CHAPTER 42
THE THRALL

A few weeks had passed since the liberation of Hammoth-Dōr. In that time, they had freed several other towns and cities before returning to Lilenhamür. However, their campaign was halted—Rellik had anticipated their moves and fortified his armies in the surrounding towns, making further liberation impossible, for now.

"*Melvin,*" Penelope communicated, "*The Empress has a mission for us and Adara.*"

"What is it?" Melvin asked.

"*I am not entirely sure.*" Penelope responded, "*All I know is that we need to go there.*"

"Where? And when does she want us to go?" Adara asked.

"*As soon as we can,*" Penelope replied.

They suited up in their armor, and Penelope carried them southeast. They had never been to this area of Arion before. They flew southeast over forests and plains and a humongous lake, and finally, they flew out to a desert. Brown and sand and desolate as far as the eye can see. They flew over small towns and houses out in the middle of the desert. Melvin looked at the mega spans of dry red and brown dirt and sand, the bleakness, the emptiness, the nothingness of the landscape.

The endless dunes stretched before them. Melvin turned to Adara and asked, "Why, in all of Estry, would *anyone* want to live out here? It's nothing but brown, barren, and lifeless. How does anyone survive in this wasteland?"

"Melvin," Adara said, "People live everywhere on Estry. They adapt to the climate. They live in the north in the cold and snow, They live down here in the desert, they live in the mountains, prairies, the forest, the jungles, the bogs, and everywhere in between. Just because you don't like it, doesn't mean other people don't."

"I guess you're right," He said humbly. "But, I'd never live out here." He mumbled under his breath.

Penelope found the right place and landed. They were in the middle of a canyon. Steep multi colored sandstone walls climbed up each side. Many hues and colors from deep brown to red, copper, and light sand.

As they dismounted, Penelope, a figure in a hooded robe, came walking towards them. Penelope communicated that it was ok.

"I am Serina," the woman said with a heavy accent that Melvin didn't know the origin of, and a slight bow. "I am the leader of the Thrall. We have petitioned the Empress for your help."

"How can we be of service?" Melvin asked.

"Come, I show you. You will understand." Serina responded.

The three walked into a cave. Penelope stayed outside; she was too big to fit through the opening. *"I will be of no use to you, I will visit an acquaintance of mine who lives here in this desert. I will monitor you through our link. Stay safe,"* With one giant bound, she leapt into the air, spread her wings, and was gone out of sight.

In front of them was an awe-inspiring sight. Carved into the sandstone were two giant figures about 30 spans high.

"These are leaders who brought ancestors here," Serina explained. They walked through an opening between the feet of the carvings, and all they saw was a long, wide tunnel going down underground. For being underground, it was unusually bright inside the tunnel. As they descended, Serina told them a story.

"During the great war," Serina stared out, trying to pronounce the words right, "that gave rise to current civilization, were people who came down to caves, and escaped war and radiation. Before the war, their ancestors were taught by Elfes how to use magic, they could manipulate the earth and the ground. They grew crystals, and these crystals enhanced magic."

"Yes," Melvin replied "We know of the Na'Van, and Elfes. We know the history. We know of the great civilization that destroyed it's self with war."

Serina smiled. Few knew the true history of the last civilization. As they reached the bottom, the passage opened into a vast underground cavern—larger than anything they had ever seen.

In this cavern, way below the surface, there was a civilization. Much like Lilenhamür, they had a lake, gardens, animals, and a whole city underground. Serina gave them a tour of the city. She showed them where they grow and harvest the crystals. She also showed them a lake and a spring flowing into that lake. "The spring is living water, helps us live very long lives, 5000 annums or more." She said.

Their source of light was glowing crystals. She also explained that this is where the Empress got the diamonds for Adara's wedding dress, tiara, and jewelry, and the Elves got the multicolored jewel for Melvin's staff. Adara was even more impressed now.

She told them that they needed help from Melvin because Rellik came and wanted a bunch of crystals. And if they didn't get a certain amount of crystals he would essentially enslave them.

They couldn't grow the crystals fast enough, so they needed him to either help accelerate their growth or defend them against Rellik. She also revealed that Rellik had kidnapped several children. He had warned that if they failed to deliver the crystals, the consequences would be far worse.

As they stood near some of the glowing crystals, Serina saw the brilliance of the light and colors reflecting off Adara's ring. She had never seen anything like that before, and they were experts in crystals and gems.

"Where did you get ring?" she asked.

"Melvin made it for me," Adara replied, admiring her ring.

"Where did he get diamonds and rubies?" Serina asked in amazement. She had never seen diamonds so brilliant and exquisitely cut.

"He pulled them out of the ground, along with the ore. With his magic, he made the ring, shaped the stones, and put the stones on the ring."

"He must teach us!" she said matter-of-factly. Then she called some other ladies over to look at the exquisite gems on the ring. Every one cut perfectly. As they looked at Adara's ring, they admired its craftsmanship. They also looked at the glow from the inside and had never seen anything like that before.

"Can you take off so we can examine better?" she asked.

She looked at Melvin for approval. You see, this type of thing was normal for them. Everyone wanted to see the ring. But she never took it off. With a shrug, Melvin said that it was up to her. As she took off the ring, Melvin turned because he thought he heard something, just as he did, a knife penetrated Adara's side, where Melvin had just been standing. Now, they don't know that the ring has powers, the assassin was aiming for Melvin, and since Melvin turned just at the right time, the assassin got Adara instead.

Melvin instantly knew who the person was and blasted him with lightning and sent him flying about 10 spans back. He didn't know he could do that till just now. He had never used lightning before.

Melvin asked Penelope to ask the Empress to see if there were any spies in their midst. The Empress checked, and there were, and they were identified, and the Serina was one of them. They were all rounded up by Melvin and Adara. Serina explained that Rellik took their children, and her daughter was among them, who is especially talented at growing crystals. And unless they killed, or delivered them two to him, they would never see their children again.

"It would have been a lot easier if you had just told us that in the first place," Melvin said.

Melvin put his hand on Adara's side where it had been punctured by the blade. She hadn't felt pain like this since she had cancer. Melvin looked inside her and saw how she was wounded.

As he worked, a wave of warmth surged through her, spreading from the wound outward. She could feel her body knitting itself back together, the pain fading as the healing took effect.

Serina, said how sorry she was that this had happened, but they saw no other way to get their children back. Penelope communicated to Adara and Melvin that everything she said was true. They only wanted their children back and saw no other option.

Melvin told them that he could teach them how to grow crystals faster, but he didn't want them to give Rellik any more power than he already had. As they stood by the lake, he could feel the magic coming from it. Just like the lake in Lilenhamür. He soaked up as much as he could; he had Adara do the same. This magic felt different, more ancient than the lake in Lilenhamür. It even felt more ancient than the magic in Illëngard.

So then they devised a way to rescue the kids.

CHAPTER 43
RESCUING THE CHILDREN

In the vast, shimmering expanse of the desert, Penelope sought counsel with her trusted ally, KLÜG, the copper sand dragon. His scales glinted like molten bronze under the relentless suns. Despite his wisdom and keen senses, KLÜG could offer no insight into the whereabouts of the missing children.

However, he did tell her that Rellik's armies did steal his mate's egg several decannums back, and they fought them off from taking it as well, but they still got away with the egg. He would do anything to exact revenge on Rellik.

Undeterred, Penelope reached out to Watcher. She was equally in the dark.

Desperation mounting, Melvin, turned to his essence, he sent his essence throughout Arion. He discovered that the children had been taken to the dreaded Boglunds, It was a land of dark swamps and dangerous ground, where every step could sink you into the muck. The air smelled like something long dead, and strange noises echoed through the thick rancid fog. Twisted trees reached out like claws, and the shadows moved with things best left unseen. This place belonged to the hag witches—ugly, wicked creatures who brewed their foul potions in blackened cauldrons. Melvin had only heard about them in stories, mostly from Reicuas, who once ran into a few on one of his risky adventures—and barely made it out.

With urgency, Melvin and Adara mounted Penelope, her wings spread wide as she took to the skies. Their destination: the Boglunds, a land shrouded in mist and danger. They soared over the desolate landscape, their hearts heavy with determination.

They went over the sea, as it was vastly easier to do so than to go over the mountains. The suns were high in the sky as they flew over the ocean. All of a sudden, out of nowhere, they were attacked by some of the vilest flying creatures in Arion, the dreaded morcëgo. Like giant bats, they let out a screech that was deafening to the ears in a similar way the shriekers did.

They came at the trio with fangs barred and claws ready to strike. Unfortunately for them, they were not immune to fire. Adara with a mighty blast of fire hit them squarely in the chest and sent them spirling into the ocean, a trail of flames following them as they fell.

Right behind them was a gigantic red dragon. Larger than anything Melvin or Adara had ever seen before. Many times larger than Penelope.

"His name is Bloodlust," Penelope communicated. *"He is the mightiest dragon in Rellik's army. I cannot defeat him alone. He is a fire dragon, so unfortunately, Adara, there is nothing you can do to him."*

"She may not be able to, but I certainly can. I have all this power. I might as well use it." Melvin said. He looked at his surroundings to see what was available to him. Air, light, water. To drive the morcëgo away, he first summoned his power, feeling the surge of energy course through him. Focusing intently, he condensed the air before him and unleashed a shockwave of concentrated air towards the morcëgo. It hit them square and sent them hurtling uncontrollably into the sea. It made no impact on the dragon. The mighty dragon stayed his course as he headed straight towards them.

The dragon breathed fire at them, at the same moment Penelope unleashed a beam of light aimed for the opposing dragon's eyes, momentarily blinding him he flapped his mighty wings and rose higher in the air.

"I do not want to fight him," Penelope communicated, *"But I do not think we are going to outrun him, and he is not going to stop. So we must fight him."*

"We can do this," Melvin said. The mighty red dragon turned around for another pass and headed for them again. "Fly low, close to the water. As low as you can. I have a plan." Melvin commanded. He searched the sea to see if there were any ships in the area. There was one, but it was far enough away that it wouldn't be impacted by what Melvin was planning to do.

Penelope plunged toward the sea, skimming just above its surface. Waves rolled beneath her as she soared—guided by the wind, the pull of the current, and the magic flowing through her. She hovered barely a hand's length above the water, moving fast and free. Behind her, the giant red dragon had shaken off the blinding spell. With a furious roar, he locked onto them once more, his massive wings slicing through the sky as he gave chase. He came at Penelope from behind.

"Stay your course, I've got this," Melvin assured her. As Bloodlust opened its massive jaws to unleash another torrent of fire, Melvin conjured a massive stream of water from the ocean that surged into the dragon's mouth, effectively neutralizing its fiery breath.

Losing his main weapon, Bloodlust, was at a loss as to what he could do. He was amazed. No wizard had been able to do what Melvin had done. He still had his sharp teeth, claws, and tail he could get to his dragon. He lunged towards Penelope to bite her tail. She swung her spiked tail at the mighty red gragon, but it did no good. It just glanced off his scales.

"Do Something, Melvin," Adara screamed in terror. She felt helpless as her fire would do nothing to this giant dragon.

"Penelope," Melvin said. "When I say so, rise as fast as you can." As bloodlust was coming in for another attack, Melvin gave Penelope the signal to rise. Penelope flapped her mighty wings and rose into the sky in an instant. Bloodlust didn't respond as fast and was still low to the water. Melvin caused a huge wave to come up from the sea. The huge dragon could not rise in time to avoid it, and the wave crashed right into him, causing him to be pulled underneath the current. Unfortunately for him, he didn't swim very well.

"Let's get out of here before he resurfaces," Melvin called. For good measure, he churned the water into a turbulent frenzy, ensuring the red dragon would not escape its watery prison anytime soon. From then on, they did not have any problems the rest of the way to the swamp.

They landed in a small clearing near where he sensed the children.

"Be ready for anything, this is most likely a trap, just like the Thrall and the attack over the ocean," Adara said. Just in case, her hair turned to flame, and her eyes changed to the color of burning embers. Her sword, when drawn, would be aflame and the color of glowing, red, red-hot steel. She was ready.

Upon reaching the Verdwyn swamp, they scoured the area, their eyes sharp and senses heightened. At last, on a secluded island amidst the murky waters, they found the children, huddled and in a crudely made hut, frightened but unharmed. The rescue had begun, and the heroes' journey was far from over.

The Verdwyn swamp was not a place any decent person or creature would want to be. Many evil creatures lived in the swamp. Swamp hags who brewed their potions in crudely built huts, Imps, and other swamp creatures that would think you would be their next meal. And Dragons. These Dragons were especially suited for this environment. The water contained acid, perfect for the green dragons who lived here. For they were acid dragons. Instead of spewing fire, or water, or ice, you guessed it. They spewed acid. A nasty sort that would burn a hole right through anything.

"Are you ok?" Adara asked the children, worried.

"Get out of here," one of the children said. "It's a trap."

"We know, she said softly. Just then, a magical shield was cast around them, and inside there appeared many numbers of Witches, Warlocks, Ogres, Goblins, and other evil creatures.

"You are not going to get out of here alive, Melvin." One of the wizards said with loathing. "There is no escape, nowhere for you to run, and if you try to do anything, we will kill these children. You don't want them to be hurt, do you?"

Melvin paused for a second, analyzing the situation before devising a quick solution, at least for part of the problem. Silently, he sang a song and wove an incantation, crafting a protective shield around the children, just as he had for his beloved wife. Now, nothing the enemy did could harm them. Then, he whispered to his sweetheart, "Now, dear."

Adara unleashed a wave of fire so intense that it obliterated everything and everyone within the warlock's protective shield that wasn't protected by Melvin's shield. All that was left of the enemy were the charred remains. In an instant, the shield disintegrated. The children stood in awe of Adara's immense power.

"Very Good" a voice came to them. "You have defeated Rellik's pet warlocks and witches, but I will not be so easy. Just then a large green dragon rose out of the boiling acid swamp. She looked as big as the island they were standing on.

One of the kids spoke up. "This is what I was warning you about."

Melvin looked straight at the dragon. "You can let us go, or suffer the consequences. You have seen what Adara here can do. If you don't want to end up a pile of ashes like they did."

"Don't be so naive," she mocked. "Her fire cannot hurt me. I am Malice, and your little parlor tricks cannot hurt me. However, you will melt just like she made the witches and warlocks melt." And at that, she spewed green acid at Melvin and Adara.

"This is going to be hard to get out of my tunic," Melvin said, wiping the acid off his tunic, otherwise unscathed.

The dragon was astonished. "How did that not melt you? My acid is stronger than anything." She said.

"Magic." Was all Melvin replied. Malice did not know about the shields protecting Melvin, Adara, and the children.

Just then, a beam of light so intense lit up the bog for the moment blinded the mighty green dragon. She clawed at anything she could with her long, sharp talons and swept her tail as well. Unfortunately, Melvin was not fast enough dodging the tail, and it hit him squarely in the abdomen, its spikes penetrating Melvin's stomach. He flew back 2 spans and landed hard on the ground. Adara used the same wave of fire on the dragon as she did with the warlocks and witches.

Melvin was down but not out. Fortunately he was not knocked out. Since he had the shield protecting him, the damage was not as bad as it otherwise would have been. He quickly started the repair of his body and left it to do its work, then concentrated on the task at hand.

By this time, the dragon's sight was coming back. "I told you that fire does not hurt me." She said with malice.

"So you did," Melvin responded with a wry smile. "But you never said fire inside you wouldn't hurt you."

"What are you doing?" The Dragon asked, afraid. Her abdomen felt a warm sensation she had never felt before.

"You see, I have lit a fire inside your body, and it will burn you from the inside out. The animals in the bog will have a dragon feast tonight, unless you cease and desist."

Malice's body began to feel uncomfortably warm, a clear indication that something was wrong. Could this wizard truly be performing the spell as he claimed? If she wasn't experiencing it firsthand, she wouldn't believe it. The heat within her intensified, spreading throughout her entire being, accompanied by sharp, excruciating pains. She reached her limit. She could take no more —these children, these two wizards, were too much for her to endure. It wasn't worth being cooked to death to kill them or hand them over to Rellik.

"I yield," She said. In obvious pain. "Take the children and go. I know when I have been defeated. Rellik will not like the news, but at least I will live to see another rev."

They gathered the children, placed them on Penelope's back and they headed back to the Thrall's underground city.

As they were flying, Adara asked, "How did you do that? Did you actually light a fire within the dragon like I did when we were crossing the mountains, and I killed those little pesky goremlin buggers?"

"No, actually, I didn't," He responded with a chuckle. "It was a trick."

"A Trick?" one of the children asked.

"I have studied the anatomy of humans, elves, animals, even dragons. And all I did was pinch some nerves. It gave the dragon the sensation that she was hot and being cooked from the inside. It gave her intense pain, but she really wasn't. He looked inside the child and pinched the right nerve with his mind, and made the child's arm go numb. The child was dumbstruck. "I wouldn't want to harm a magnificent, magical creature like that when there is another way to get out of the situation without harming it. In a few hours, the effects will wear off, and she will be back to her normal malcontent self. As will the effects of your arm."

Once they arrived back at the Thrall underground city, the children were reunited with their parents. The people of the Thrall were so happy that they made a pact to stand by the Empress, Melvin, and Adara, any services that they could provide, they would willingly provide, in the fight against Rellik. The children spoke of Melvin and Adara rescuing them, and their fame spread throughout the Thrall, and the desert people, then eventually Arion.

On the flight back to Lilenhamür, Melvin discussed the situation with Adara and Penelope. "Rellik is trying to separate us and attack us with his most powerful weapons. Before, the little goremlins, now, a huge Dragon, and his sorcerers. He thinks he can take us out and then take over Arion. We just defeated both. I think that will show him that we are a force to be reckoned with." Melvin said.

"You are right, sweet heart, we may be able to defeat one or two of his many minions, but we can not take on his whole army at once." She said.

Although her power grew a thousandfold since going to the elves, and Melvin's power grew an unfathomable amount, she thought just the two of them could not possibly defeat Rellik's army. Yet. She knew, if it really came down to it, Melvin would find a way, but his problem was still that he didn't know that he could. He didn't think he was able to do it. However, she tried to convince him that he could.

"I don't know, with your fire, power, I think you could decimate everything within a megaspan radius. What you did back there was just a small taste of what I know you can do."

"Thanks for your confidence." Adara smiled her beautiful smile, then she took a graver tone.

"But I don't know about that. That fight took a lot out of me. I may be a human flame thrower, but using that much magic, that much power, takes a lot of energy. I need time to recover. Maybe at some point with more training, I would be able to, but not now, not yet."

She paused for a moment to think. "We need a bigger army," she finally said, "better-trained wizards, and a whole lot of luck to defeat Rellik. And by Deo's grace, we will be able to win this war." Her voice grew softer, more intimate, more reassuring. "But I believe you, Melvin, you could probably solo this war if you knew how remarkably powerful you are and truly knew your full potential and how to use it. You could do it."

She put her arms around him and continued, "Rellik will return. Now that he understands what he's up against, he'll strike harder, with greater numbers and more powerful warlocks, sorcerers, and other magic users. Instead of one dragon, he'll unleash many. In a sense, he's infiltrating the eastern side of the mountains. Even if it's only a few, he still has forces here. Though he may not have his full army, he has spies working for him. We need to be prepared for that possibility. The training we received back home, combined with the lessons from the elves, has greatly enhanced our powers and abilities. But we still don't know how to fight this kind of war."

"Then we will learn. Rellik must be stopped." Melvin said with definite assurance.

CHAPTER 44
TO SEE THE DRAGONS

They hadn't been in Lilenhamür long when Penelope contacted Melvin.

"*Melvin,*" Penelope said, "*I have a message from the Empress.*" She had learned human speech. She could talk to them in their minds and verbally. In their minds, it was much easier for her. She was able, through their magic, to speak to both of them at once.

"*Go on,*" he replied.

"*She wants us to go talk to my kind. The dragons, in Dragonia. She wants us to enlist their help in defeating Rellik. She says it would be in their best interest if they helped us. If they knew what he was doing with the dragon eggs, and building a dragon army. She can see two possibilities. If they do join us, Rellik can be defeated; if they do not, he will find more hatching eggs, control more dragons, and eventually this land will be under his control, and it does not fare well for anyone.*"

"*Yes, I can see what you mean. Who does she want to go with? And when?*" Melvin inquired.

"*She wants me to take you and Adara to them.*" Penelope communicated to him. "*But the journey will not be easy.*" She showed him flying over forests, plains, wind, and snow-swept mountains, flying through stormy seas, long hours on her back with no place to land till they reached the island nation of Dragonia in the middle of the ocean.

"We must go as soon as possible," Adara said.

They gathered supplies for the journey and set off. As a magical creature—a dragon no less— she could fly much longer than most birds or other animals. They headed east, just as Penelope had been shown in her vision.

They flew over forests, plains, mountains, then eventually over Melvin's town. This part of the journey was not a problem because they had made it many times. They stopped long enough for Melvin and Adara to get some things from their house, and for all of them to eat, then continued on over the ocean. They didn't bother to ask why they couldn't take a boat, they all knew the answer to that. It would just take too long.

Penelope flew for a long time over the vast ocean. Melvin had never been over the ocean before. He did, on occasion, take trips in a boat in the ocean, but that was still relatively close to land. Now, even being high up in the air, he could not see land anywhere.

"You do know where we are going, don't you?" Melvin asked. *"You have never been to Dragonia before."*

"Yes, you are right," Penelope communicated while soaring on an updraft. *"But all dragons have like a homing beacon within us, that we can always find our way home to Dragonia."* She flapped her mighty wings that shone in the sunslight like a thousand diamonds. *"I have an idea, I will need your help with Melvin."*

"What is that?" he asked, intrigued.

"If I go higher, I can go faster. However, if I do go any higher, you and Adara may not be able to breathe. The air gets thinner the higher I go. Though we have flown high before, we have never flown as high as I can."

"Will you be able to breathe?" Melvin asked.

"I am a Dragon, I am meant to fly high in the sky." She said.

"Then let's do it, we need to get there as soon as possible," Adara said.

Penelope stretched her powerful wings and pushed them hard against the air, lifting them higher and higher into the sky. They climbed above the tallest clouds, where the world below looked soft and distant. Up here, the sky darkened, and the curve of the planet began to show itself—reminding them just how far they'd come, and how small everything else truly was.

Adara started to get lightheaded. "I can't breathe," she said nervously.

"We need to go down," Melvin exclaimed frantically. He did not know what to do. His wife was in danger.

Adara's breathing got shallower. Her body went limp as she passed out from the lack of oxygen, and Melvin got incredibly worried. Penelope plunged towards the sea. When she knew they were in a safe area, she leveled out and glided on the air currents.

"What do I do?" Melvin asked "I-I-I-I Don't know w-w-what to d-d-do" he stuttered getting very nervous. "She needs oxygen" Penelope communicated.

Melvin had an idea. Though he didn't know if this would help, he tried it anyway. Melvin looked into her body. He looked into her lungs, her blood cells, and her brain to see how much oxygen was there, and then he looked into his own to compare the amount of oxygen. He noticed that hers was a lot lower than his; the fire in her heart was also diminishing because it needed oxygen in the blood and in the cells to keep burning. While he did this, he took the water molecules around them in the air and caused them to separate, creating oxygen that she could breathe in.

He gathered the oxygen around Adara, guiding her to breathe it in deeply. With a subtle push of his magic, he made the muscles in her jaw relax, her diaphragm tighten, and her lungs expand with each breath, one after another. He carefully monitored her internal levels to ensure she was getting enough oxygen.

Slowly, he noticed her levels rising, and soon, she was breathing on her own again. Her inner fire was returning to its normal strength. Once she was steady, he withdrew his consciousness from her body.

She opened her eyes, looked around, and asked, "What happened?" "You just ran out of air," he then explained what he had just done.

She gave him a big hug and said, "You just saved my life, Melvin. Again. You keep doing that. Without you, I would have died."

"It was nothing," He said tenderly without stuttering. Penelope flew down to a safe level. You would h-have been ok anyway."

"Even though," she responded, stroking his cheek, "You are marvelous anyway." Then she kissed him and they held each other for a while as Penelope found the fastest air current she could find to take them to their destination.

Once Adara had recovered, Penelope rose into the sky again, but this time, they were ready. Melvin had created shields, each containing oxygen separated from the water. He also put shields around Him and Adara so they could breathe the oxygen within the shields while they were high in the sky. This would last them quite a while, so Penelope could go higher, farther, and faster.

After about 6 hours, their oxygen ran out, and they were forced to go lower. Plus, it was time for them to eat. Evening was coming on, and it would be dark in a few hours. Penelope put her gigantic claws into the ocean and brought up a large fish. She threw it up in the air and caught it in her maw and ate it whole. Melvin and Adara got out the supplies they brought with them. Adara asked if Penelope could catch another fish. Penelope caught one and tossed it onto her back. Melvin caught it.

"What's your plan?" Melvin asked.

"I think you know" she said with a smile. With her magic she put a flame in the fish. She cooked it from the inside out, just as Melvin threatened Malice he was doing.

They ate their meal and prepared for the long flight through the night.

"*Melvin,*" Penelope communicated, "*I sense something coming in our direction from the left side."*

Melvin cast his mind's eye towards the direction Penelope was referring to. He saw nothing. *"I don't see it, it must still be too far away. Keep monitoring it."*

"I will," she told him back.

As they flew on the object came closer and closer in a direct course to their location. *"You should be able to detect it now,"* Penelope said.

Melvin once again cast his mind's eye in the same direction. This time he saw it. Something was definitely flying towards them. However he couldn't make it out just yet.

"It's a dragon," Penelope communicated, showing both of them the image she could make out.

What's another dragon doing way out in the middle of the ocean? He wondered. We aren't even close to being near Dragonia yet, but we are also far from any other land. They flew on.

"Do you think it's a scout from Dragonia?" Adara asked.

"I don't believe so," Penelope responded. *"They are secure on their continent. No one would dare fly out in the open ocean like this. Only a dragon could. They are not afraid of dragons or any other creature. They feel no one can get through their defenses. They are the mighty Dragons. No one can attack them."*

"Are there any water dragons in this area?" Adara Asked.

"I do not believe so," Penelope responded, *"if it were a water dragon, he would have communicated that to me. This one is silent."*

"Could it be another creature, like one of those morcëgos?" Adara asked. *"No, it's clearly a dragon."* Penelope responded.

"Then be ready to expect anything," Adara said.

Penelope put out all her spikes, except the ones Melvin and Adara were sitting on. Adara flared up, ready to hurl fireballs; however, on some dragons, this would have no effect. Melvin put up a magical barrier. The other dragon finally came into sight. No wonder they had a hard time seeing it. It was partly there and partly not. It was a Shadow Dragon. Not just any Shadow Dragon, but Rellik's Shadow Dragon Skügge.

Suddenly, it became very dark. Penelope dived to get away from the dark mist Skügge was spewing.

A dark, sinister, however very soothing and calming voice, pierced through the darkness. "Melvin, Adara. How nice to see you again. Give up on your futile attempt to recruit the dragons. They care not what goes on outside of their realm. They will not join you in this fight. I am stronger, wiser, and command more armies, witches, warlocks, and dragons than you can imagine. Give up now or be destroyed."

Melvin couldn't see where the voice was coming from, but he knew exactly who it belonged to. He was certain Rellik was hiding in the shadow cast by his dragon, knowing he would never venture out in the sunslight. But with night falling, Rellik felt safer, especially as he was concealed within the dark smoke cloud.

"You don't know me very well," Melvin said.

"I know you better than you think," Rellik said. Then cast a simple spell on Melvin. Fortunately for him, it bounced off the magic shield Melvin had created.

"Since you erected that shield, you cannot cast spells at me either. You are defenseless against me. For if you lower your shield to cast at me, you will be vulnerable."

"We'll see about that. Melvin called out." Then turned to Adara. "Hold on" he said in almost a whisper. "*Evasive Maneuvers*" he communicated to Penelope.

Melvin and Adara held tight to their saddles. The enormous gold dragon did a barrel roll out of the darkness, then, with a dragon's war cry, she slashed her tail at the mid-section of the shadow dragon. It went right through. "*Penelope, that won't work unless they are solid, and when they are solid, any attacks they make on you will hurt you, so just be careful, alright?*" Melvin told her.

"*Understood,*" she responded.

Rellik Laughed. "You fools," he called out, "Don't you know that weapons cannot harm us. We are shadow, it will pass right through us." Then he laughed his deep cynical laugh. By this time night had fully come so Rellik could be at his full power.

"Melvin, lower your shield," Adara whispered. He obeyed. A fiery inferno erupted from her hands, her hair blazing with flames. The heat was so intense it burned Melvin's arm, but he quickly healed it. Though the fire dissipated the darkness around them, it had little effect beyond that. Unfortunately, it passed right through them.

Rellik laughed again. "Is that all you got?" he asked. Then shot a lightning bolt at the Golden Dragon.

Penelope rolled and the lightning bolt hit her in the stomach. She concentrated it, and redirected it through her tail and shot it back at Rellik and his dragon.

"How did you do that?" Melvin asked.

"*Remember,*" Penelope communicated "*I am a gold dragon. I have gold metal scales, I am conductive, I am a conduit for lightning, I can redirect lightning.*"

Just then, Melvin remembered something. Penelope, since she was a gold dragon, she could breathe out light.

Light scatters the darkness, dispels shadows. Maybe she can defeat Rellik now. Once and for all.

"Breath light", he told his dragon. She summoned up an intense beam of light. And shot it forth towards Rellik and his dragon. At the same time, he used one of the spells Reicuas and the Elves had shown him. He made balls of light, the brightness of Helios. He also shot them forth towards Rellik. He created another shield that surrounded Rellik and his dragon. Surrounded by light, Rellik and his dragon shrank into nothing and were gone. The trio celebrated. Melvin and Adara celebrated with a kiss as soon as her hair had gone out. Melvin let the balls of light go out and dissolved the shield. Then the voice came again. "You may have won this battle, boy, but you will not win the war. Then all was silent."

How did he know we were out here? How did he get here during the lightime?? Adara wondered. She was determined to find the answers when they got back to Lilenhamür.

Penelope was tired from the battle and could not have flown all the way to Dragonia. Penelope continued on her course to Dragonia until they found a small island to stop and rest for the night. Melvin looked up at the stars. There were millions of stars in the night's sky. He didn't know much about the sky, but what he saw was awe-inspiring. Seeing all these stars out there made him realize how small and insignificant he was in the grand scheme of things.

After traveling all of the next rev, they landed on a sandy beach. It was nighttime and nearly pitch black. A multitude of stars were shining, but that's all the light she had; it didn't help much. Penelope was so tired she could fly no longer, especially carrying Melvin and Adara on her back with their gear. Which wouldn't have mattered in a short flight, but a long flight such as this made a big difference. Once they landed, Melvin made a campfire, and immediately, Penelope was asleep. As was Adara.

CHAPTER 45

In front of them were very tall cliffs that must have been hundreds of spans high. Beyond that was a ring of large mountains that surrounded the continent sized island of Dragonia. Within the island were contained all types of climates. Every sort of climate for every sort of dragon from deserts to jungles to forests to plains, to snow covered mountains and everything in between. Or so they heard.

For most creatures, there was only one way in. That was a narrow passageway, more like a maze, through the mountains that took weeks to go through. That is, if you ever made it through. But if you happened to be a dragon, or had a dragon, a Pegasus, or a giant eagle, you could fly over the mountains to the interior of the continent. But most dragons wouldn't carry you over.

Once Penelope regained her strength, they resumed their journey to talk to the King of Dragonia. The cliffs of the mountains went straight up, nearly 200 spans. With the mighty flaps of her wings, she bounded high into the air, they were airborne once again. Once she reached the tops of the cliffs, they saw what they were up against.

Tall mountain peaks, their snow-capped tops reaching into the clouds, stretched endlessly above. This range was far more massive than the Helaeth Mountains near Lilenhamür. As far as the eye could see, there were mountains. It took nearly an entire rev to clear them.

As she flew over Dragonia, they realized it was much larger than any of them had ever thought. They thought it was just an island, but this was not just an island. It was a continent. Through magic, the dragons manipulated the outer shores of the land and sent up mighty mountains to great heights. As they flew, they noticed that Dragonia indeed does have many different climates, just as Arion does. It has mountains. They flew over forests, deserts, plains, bogs, large lakes, every type of landscape you could imagine. As they flew, they also saw many types of dragons. Red Dragons in the mountains and forests, blue dragons in the lakes, White snow dragons in the snowcapped mountains, green dragons in the forests and bogs, copper dragons in the rocky mountains and deserts. Purple and yellow dragons lived in the prairies. Not only did they see dragons, but they also saw buildings, farms, cities, etc. And not all of the dragons were large like Penelope was, or her mother. But there were many different sizes of dragons, from very large red dragons to small yellow dragons. Some lived in caves, and a lot lived in villages and cities. Something they had never supposed before. They all sure had a lot to learn about Dragonia. But what was more to their surprise was also the diversity of other animals and creatures that lived in Dragonia.

There were pixies, unicorns, elves, and even humans, to name just a few. Along with them, countless non-magical creatures and animals roamed the land—unicorns and blasmoths in the plains, lions, deer, rabbits, mandras, birds of every kind, and everything in between. They had assumed Dragonia was home only to mighty dragons, but they were mistaken. It was a civilization just like any other.

This had surely opened their eyes. Finally, they came to a grand castle, almost as large as Lilenhamür. But they figured it needed to be large for NöGard - King of the Dragons to live in, for he was the largest and mightiest of all the dragons.

Chapter 46
NöGard
King of the Dragons

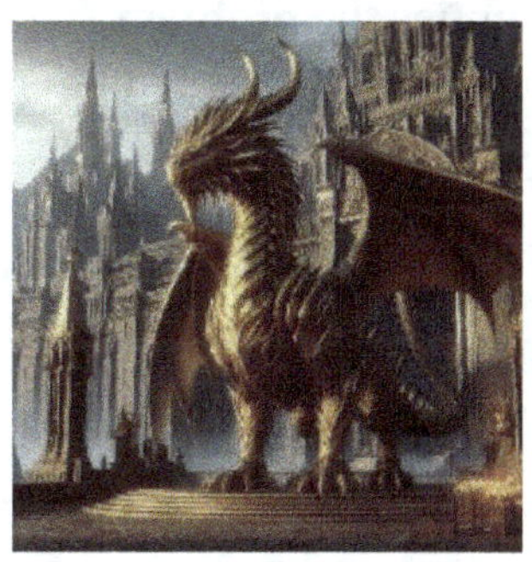

Penelope landed just outside the castle—a golden fortress larger than any they had ever seen. As soon as her claws touched the ground, two massive dragons, even larger than Penelope, approached. They were clad in what appeared to be gold plate armor. "Who are you, and why do you dare land on NöGard's royal castle grounds?" one of the guards demanded.

 "We were sent from Empress Kayla of Arion to see King NöGard," Adara said.

"Wait here," one guard said. "I will inquire of the king what he wants to do." Adara was surprised that he spoke their language. Most dragons communicated the way that Penelope did.

The guard came back a short while later, and the guards took them before the king.

"Who are you, and why are you here?" King NöGard asked. He was very large, larger than any of the other dragons. He must have been five times the size of Penelope, and she was a large dragon in and of herself. He was also bright gold, just as Penelope. Spikes ran along the ridge of his massive body, his scales sparkled as if polished to a reflective luster. His talons were easily more than a span long and sharp as swords. They looked as though they were blades from a gold scythe.

"I am the Wizard Melvin, and this is Princess Adara, Commander of the Arion forces. We are an emissary from The Empress Kayla of Arion." Melvin replied.

The mighty dragon turned his head in amusement. "I have heard of you. Supposedly, you are some sort of great wizard," he said thoughtfully. "However, we have nothing to do with your kind, we want nothing to do with your kind. We have brought ourselves here and have lived here throughout several millions of annums to stay away from the affairs of men."

"I understand that, great king," Melvin replied, "but what is happening in our land will affect your kind as well. Eventually."

"Nothing that has ever happened in your lands has affected us, and I doubt it will now. You see, just like the Na'Van, we are protected by magic. The only way in or out is on a dragon or other flying creature, which obviously you have, but pretty much no one else does, or through the maze through the mountains. Which, without a guide, would be impossible to complete."

"Yes, your majesty, however, therein lies the problem. There is another wizard who possesses control of a dragon. Several hundred dragons. His name is…"

"Lord Rellik." He said cutting Melvin off. Then paused. "I have heard of him." He said sarcastically. "He does not scare me or the dragons. Just because I live here, does not mean I don't know what is going on in your lands. Rellik cannot defeat us even if he brings a thousand dragons."

Then he said something Melvin did not expect. "Remember, we *are* magic, we bring magic into this world. You merely use the magic we bring. There is more magic here than you humans will ever see in thousands of your lifetimes."

Melvin could feel this as well. He could feel the profound concentration of magic. With so many dragons so close together made the magic particles within him went into over drive. Although no baby dragons were being hatched in the vicinity, he could feel himself absorbing more and more magic. He didn't know how this was possible or how he was doing it. He wasn't even trying to do it on purpose. However, he could tell that even Adara was absorbing some magic.

He could feel his power growing with each passing moment. Maybe this was what the Empress had wanted—him absorbing the dragons' magic. He pushed his body into overdrive, determined to absorb as much magic as possible. To aid the process, he sang a low song, helping both himself and Adara absorb more. Later, he would transfer it into his DNA, making it a permanent part of him. But for now, his focus had to be on the meeting with NöGard.

Melvin remembered what the Na'Van had told him in the woods many annums ago. "Great king, I can feel the magic on this island. It seeps into my very DNA without me even trying. Just as the Elves, I am a direct descendant of Elfin who long ago discovered and learned to use the magic particles. I have the magic particles in my very blood, in my DNA, just as he had. So as you are," and this part he sang a powerful song, "I AM MAGIC!!!!"

NöGard could feel the power of Melvin's song. "You are a very powerful wizard, Melvin indeed. I can see that you are one of a kind, an anomaly, but your magic can't even compare to ours, even if you have seen a dragon egg hatch and can absorb our magic."

"Yes, that is correct. However, Rellik breeds dragons and then takes the eggs. Then, upon watching the dragons hatch, he absorbs most of their magic, and he also gains control of these dragons. He has watched many dragons hatch and has absorbed their power. He is building a dragon army." Then he turned to his dragon. "Penelope, could you please show the great Dragon King what the Empress has shown you?"

Penelope communicated to NöGard what she saw from the Empress. Rellik amassing a great dragon army, not only that, but also an army of the vilest creatures in the land. She showed him laying waste to the mainland before turning his dragons and army toward Dragonia. She revealed his witches and warlocks riding these dragons, ready to wage battle on Dragonia.

Melvin could see that the King was troubled by these images. "This will happen unless you can help us stop him before he can get that far. He attacked us on the way here. We were barely able to fight him off and escape, but he will be back, and this time with greater numbers."

NöGard knew this to be a true vision. All of the Empress's visions came true if nothing was put in motion to alter it, this much he knew. He then looked at Melvin and said "I will take council with the Elders and we will come to a decision whether to aid you or not."

NöGard continued. "One thing you do have in your favor is, you are a direct descendant of Elfin, and we can tell how much you love your dragon. We know you gave control of Penelope back to her mother until she was able to be on her own. This act of kindness is not often found among humans, who thirst for power, such as Rellik."

"We also know that you rescued dragons that Rellik gained control of, and that is also appreciated. We know that you, Melvin, and you, Adara, are true friends to dragons. We will let you know of our decision through Penelope or the Empress." Then the king told his servants to get some food and supplies for their journey back to Arion. "I know this has been a long journey for you, Penelope. You must be very tired. Take time to eat and rest, you, the wizard, and the princess may leave in the morning."

Penelope communicated her sincere gratitude for his kindness and the servants led them to some chambers where they could rest before the long trip back. While there, Penelope was treated to what was the dragon equivalent to a spa treatment. As were Melvin and Adara by small yellow dragons and fairies that also lived there.

After a restful night and resupplying the next morning, they received a message just before departure from the king, inviting them to visit anytime and sending his regards to the Empress. He was the one who had given the elves the idea for the anti-aging spell. The trio bid farewell to the dragons and fairies who had attended them and set off for the Lilenhamür.

CHAPTER 47

WIZARD BRENNON

"Empress," Wizard Brennan said humbly with a slight bow "May I ask of you something?" "You know you can, Brennan." The Empress replied. "What is it?" she asked.

"I want to go help with the fight" He said. "I can't just stay here and know they are going to defend our home, and not go with them, I need to go."

"Brennan, I need you here." The Empress said pleading, "You have been the Empire's Wizard for over 200 annums. I know you love the Empire, so you must stay here to defend it. Besides, I don't know if you would be able to make the journey."

"That is why I have to go, Empress. Because I love the Empire, I have to defend my Empire. I have to defend my family and friends, and most of all, my Empress." He said emotionally.

"That is very noble of you, Wizard Brennan, but if you go, you may never come back." She said with tears in her eyes. "You are one of my dearest friends. When Reicuas left for the Land of Bilby, it nearly broke my heart to see him go, but I knew why he had to go. Brennan, I don't want my heart to break again. I don't want you to go. But you are one of the best, most talented wizards in all of the Empire. You would be a great asset to the troops. Your magic would deal a great blow to the enemy, and your humor will keep the troops' spirits high." She said with a smile. "But if you must join the ranks, I will have the elves make a special staff for you that will increase your abilities and protect you from attacks."

"That is very kind of you Empress, I don't know what to say" He said with a huge smile.

"I am making you, High Wizard Brennan Baily, the head wizard of our wizards from Lilenhamür. You will be treated as such and have a council with the leaders of the other forces to coordinate with them. You are very wise and have a lot of good counsel you give them. However, remember that Wizard Melvin and his wife, Commander Adara, are still the head of the military, and they will make the final decision on any course of action to take."

"Yes, Empress. I feel the same way. I do not have experience in war, so I would feel inadequate making any decisions." He agreed.

Very well, go and prepare for your journey. I will inform the captains of our armies to expect you. Wizard Brennan gave a slight bow. Just then, the Empress wrapped her arms around him in a warm embrace.

With tears in her eyes, she whispered. "Take care of yourself. Come back in one piece. I lost Reicuas, I don't want to lose you as well."

Brennon was taken aback by the embrace. She had never hugged him before, nor had he ever seen her hug anyone, though he was sure she had. Her embrace warmed his soul; she had this effect on people. He silently vowed to return from the war, not just for himself, but for her as well.

CHAPTER 48

WAR COUNCIL

Several Annums later, Melvin sat in a large room in Lilenhamür, with Adara by his side, and Aria was on the other side. They were surrounded by other military leaders. Piles of tactical notes and maps were scattered across a broad table.

"That's why we have to strike here and now!!" Aria was saying. "They have laid to waste too many towns and villages."

"I-I-I don't kn-n-n-now," Melvin stuttered.

"Melvin" Adara said as she put her hand tenderly on Melvin's strong muscular shoulder, "You need to calm down. You are stuttering again. We thought you had that under control."

"Sorry," he took a long calming breath "I know I can do many things, but this, planning for battle is not one of them. This is your expertise. You two." he said looking at Adara and Aria "All of you, were trained your whole lives for this sort of thing," He said looking around at the other captains and generals of the army, "and I was just sort of thrust into this because, I am supposedly the greatest wizard in the world, ever. Well, I don't think that I can do anything that all of you, or our team of talented wizards, can't do. Look at Brennan over here, he won two battles almost single-handedly, I mean, having giant man-eating plants sprout up and gobble up the other army like that, GENIOUS!!!"

"Yes, that was good. Great job, Brennon," Adara said, smiling. Brennon smiled in return. "However, that trick can only work once. They'll be expecting moves like that and will be ready. They have some very clever warlocks in their ranks as well."

Aria slammed her hand on the table to get their attention. Melvin had never seen her so mad before. "We have to take the offensive. We are never going to win this war if we just defend. Unfortunately, they have more numbers than we do, albeit most of them are unintelligent brutes, but they can kill just the same. We have to make some concerted, decisive attacks on them, or this is going to be a very, very long war. And they will win. We have to go to the heart of their land and take them out."

"You do make a point, Aria," Melvin said. "As long as we stay on the defensive, we will never win this war. But I am no strategist, I don't know these things. I will leave that to you guys and the other leaders. Make a plan, then we will run it by the Empress and the other leaders, and see what they think. If it is agreed, then we will do it."

"Yes, Melvin, that is good," Aria replied.

"However," Brennan interjected, "Many times in battle decisions have to be made without the approval of the leaders, a lot of the time, there isn't time, and you just have to go by your gut instinct."

"Also true," Adara said. "So here is what must be done. We'll make an overall plan of attack with room for contingencies. Room to let Aria do her specialties, and room for general assaults. As the saying goes, we need to be able to think on our feet."

They spent the next few revs coming up with plans for attacks on Rellik's army. The problem was, they needed to go into their territory again. However, they did not know the territory as well as Rellik's army did, who lived there. And unfortunately, Rellik had many more dragons under his control than did the army of Melvin and Adara.

In one particular meeting, they were discussing this fact when Brennan, who was usually quiet and kept to himself, spoke up unexpectedly. "Pardon me for interrupting, and it might not be my place to say so, but I was thinking something."

"Not at all, Brennan, any idea you might have that would help would be appreciated," Adara said.

"Ok, Milady. But as I recall, you told me a long time ago, you mentioned that you can talk to animals?" "I talk to Penelope, yes" She answered.

"I don't mean Dragons, A lot of wizards can do that, but to regular animals. Bunnies, dear, Borlogs, when they aren't trying to eat you, and other animals." Brennan responded.

"Yes, I can," Adara said thoughtfully. "Come to think of it, I haven't done that in a long, long time. I have been so busy with this war that that ability had completely slipped my mind. You sneaky little devil, Wizard Brennan." Adara smiled. "This brings in a whole new advantage for us."

"Do you think the animals will cooperate?" Melvin asked.

"We can check," Adara said. Adara communicated with Penelope to have some animals from the forest meet her outside the back gate of Lilenhamür in an hour.

Adara and Melvin descended to meet with the animals while the other leaders remained in the fortress to avoid startling them. They were greeted by a massive buck, a mandra, and a unicorn—those were the closest animal leaders who could arrive on such short notice.

Adara spoke to the animals. Humans would hear it in their language, however, the animals would hear it in their language, whatever it happened to be. The magic would translate it.

"Thank you for coming on such short notice," she told them.

"We are honored to be able to meet such esteemed humans." The buck said, "How may we be of service?"

"As I am sure you are aware, we are in the middle of a war among the humans. I pray it is not affecting the animal kingdom, but to win this war and have peace in the land again, we call upon the animals for assistance."

"We know of your war, we are in the middle of it, as are you. Rellik captures and enslaves not only dragons but also other animals. Borlogs for one. We know that the borlog that was chasing you near the Elves' forest was one captured by Rellik to dispose of you. Though generally nasty, they aren't completely unreasonable. And the Goblins and Orcs, while they may have a human appearance, are more animal than human."

"I did not realize this war was affecting you as well. I am so sorry," Adara said tenderly "I should have figured this earlier. I am surprised none of the Dragons told us."

"We didn't want you to worry about us as well, you have enough to worry about trying to stop Rellik and all the vile creatures he has at his command."

"I thank you for that," Adara told them thoughtfully. "I just thought of something, dear," Melvin said.

"What?" The buck said.

Adara's eyes opened wide, and Melvin smirked, confirming his suspicions. "Did the Buck understand what you just said?" Adara asked.

"Unbeknownst to humans, we do understand human speech." The Buck replied, "We just are not able to reproduce their sounds."

"And, you know, Adara, I understand them. I guess when you have every magical ability, you discover you have the same ones your wife has."

"Melvin," Adara said, annoyed. How long have you known you had this ability?"

"About a minute," Melvin said. "I never thought about talking to animals. That was your ability, so I never bothered to try. But now, I find it to be rather intriguing and helpful."

"Can we please get back on topic?" the Unicorn said. "Although we are animals, and don't build large castles and write or speak the human language, we are intelligent. And we are capable. We know you need help with this war, we know that Rellik will never suspect animals being spies and other such things. We have had our own network for a while now. There are more animals than you even know about. And if we all work together, we can defeat Rellik. Granted, some of the animals are on his side, but mostly the ones that live there in the rain forest and the swamps. Like Snakes, Ogres, which are also more Animal than Human, but many, many more are fighting against Rellik."

"Thank you." Melvin said with a smile. "We will set up a council with your leaders to discuss how we, together," He nodded to the Unicorn "can defeat Rellik."

Back in the war room in the castle, for the rest of the rev, they planned on how thcy could use the animals to sabotage Rellik's plans, use them as spies, and generally wreak havoc among their ranks. That was also Aria's specialty. They would bring these ideas up at the council with the animals in a few revs. That would give the other animals enough time to reach the meeting place.

Chapter 49
Animals

They gathered in the heart of a beautiful valley in the Helaeth Mountains, a place the animals often used for meetings. It was secluded, surrounded by cliffs. The only way in was through a tunnel or by air, similar to Dragonia, though much smaller.

Representing the humans were Melvin, Adara, Aria, Brennan, and a few other generals and wizards the Empress had selected.

They had talked to the Empress, to read the hearts of all present, to know their intents, to see if there were any spies for Rellik present. As well as any other human or animal that might be in the vicinity, also as a spy. She would communicate any findings to Penelope, who would then take care of the problem.

One of the wizards could also tell the presence of other people or creatures, but could not tell the intent of their hearts. This was a talent that very few possessed. There was also another wizard from Wazervĭl who could talk to animals. She, Melvin, and Adara would translate for the other humans.

Representing the Animals were the Stag, Unicorn, and Bear, from the first meeting, also a Lion, Gorilla, Hornswollop, Beaver, a weasel, a Giant Eagle, and, believe it or not, a Borlog.

Penelope represented the dragons, able to instantly broadcast the meeting to all other dragons who needed the information.

Before the council got started, Penelope bounded into the air and landed on the far side of the meadow. Moments later, she came back with a gnome in her jaws and deposited him in the middle of those present.

"It looks like we have us a spy," she communicated to the rest.

"Please don't hurt me," The little gnome pleaded. "You don't know what it's like."

"What is it like?" asked Adara, concerned.

"Rellik, He came into our peaceful town in the mountains, his orcs and ogres ransacked our town. They took us all captive. We work for him now. He threatened that if we don't do what he says, he will feed us to the orcs and goblins. We live in cages. We dig all rev long for gold and silver. For ore to make weapons. He feeds us very little. We are tired and sick. When one of us dies, we are food for the goblins and orcs. Maybe death would be better."

"We know what you mean," the beaver said. "We have reports of other creatures with the same predicament. He even takes animals into servitude."

"This is worse than I imagined," Adara said, horrified, eyes wide. "I knew he was capturing Dragon Eggs, watching them hatch and controlling them, but this I did not know about. Dragons are bad enough, but animals as well?"

"This isn't the worst part." The Hornswollop adds. "Even those vile creatures, he has control over. Orcs, Goblins, Hags, Sorcerers. A lot of them follow him willingly, but a lot of them are forced, threatened, or bribed."

"What do we want to do with the Gnome?" Aria asks.

"If he doesn't return, then Rellik will know the gnome was found out," Melvin said. "But at least Rellik won't know what went on at this meeting." The Unicorn replied.

"Please, let me go. The only reason I came here was to ask you for your help." The little gnome said pleading. "Rellik has my wife and children, and my friends. He will kill us all. Please save us, and we will help you. We will be spies. He doesn't know I'm here."

Melvin looked at Penelope, She instinctively knew what he wanted. Penelope communicated to the Empress to look into the heart of this little guy to see if he was being honest. The Empress relayed through Penelope, who relayed it to the rest of the group, that indeed he was telling the truth. He faked his own death in the mine. When he was put on the pile of the dead, he escaped and got as far away from the camp as possible. He hid in holes in the ground for Revs while making his way east. One rev he heard about the meeting from the beavers, and decided to follow the beavers. He had just gotten through to the valley through a small hole when he was captured by Penelope.

"So, he can't go back now," Melvin told the group. "He faked his death, so if he shows up again, he will be noticed."

"Not necessarily." Said the gnome. "To Rellik and his minions, we all look the same. He wouldn't know if I were me or someone else. So if I did go back, he wouldn't notice I was gone, except we are counted when we go into and come out of the mines. Then, if someone doesn't come out, they search the mines, and find those who are hiding and bring out the dead and put them in a pile to be eaten by the orcs, goblins, ogres, gremlins, and gormlins. And the living, well, the same thing happens. Fortunately, that rev, there were quite a few dead. Unfortunately, there were quite a few dead. So I was able to escape."

"We aren't the only ones he has in the mines." The little gnome said sadly. "What is your name, little Gnome?" Adara asked.

"Piper," he replied in a shaky voice. "I make pipes for smoking. Or at least I used to before Rellik came."

"OK, Piper," Adara said tenderly, "We may just have something you can do for us. Sit tight while we have our meeting, maybe you have some information we can use." Adara turned to the rest of the group and, with the air and authority of command, she spoke to the rest of the group, Animals and Humans. "Now that we have that squared away, let's get on with our meeting. I would like to hear from the animals. What have you encountered dealing with Rellik and his minions?"

The lion spoke up. "I am Hemsforth," the lion said. "I am the king of the plains animals west of these mountains. Many of our animals have been taken to be used by Rellik's armies. But that is common among humans, but how he treats them is reprehensible."

Adara and Melvin took turns calling on each of the animals for their report of what was happening during this war.

"What do you say?" Melvin gestured to the Borlog.

"We have gotten a bad rap from the humans, Dragons, and most other animals," he said matter-of-factly. "We may have a tough exterior, may be used to rampage and destroy, but that is not in our nature. Evil men like Rellik, and before him Zôltan, have used us for their purposes. I barely escaped getting captured by Rellik and his armies."

Melvin could see the wounds in the neck and sides of the Borlog. "I can see what they have done to you he said mournfully. "I can heal those wounds if you would let me."

"These are but scratches to me. They will heal, but others of my clan have gotten much worse, not only physically, but emotionally, mentally. They torture you, not only animals, but humans, and the mighty dragons, even their own armies of orcs, goblins, and witches. He spares no one. Unfortunately, many of my own kind are in league with him. If you are loyal, do your job well, and do what he says, he will reward you. That's why a lot of humans, animals, and even dragons serve him willingly. Because he promises great wealth and riches, he gives the spoils he takes to his underlings. His thirst is for power, not for material things. I have seen it firsthand. Both the cruelty and the rewards. My brother was coerced to join Rellik's forces. He was the one who was chasing you in the forest. He was promised his heart's greatest desire, but because he failed at his task, he was shackled and forced to pull the carts with the cages containing the Dragons. Full-sized dragons."

"Thank you for telling us this, Borlog. I would have never known this if you had not told me. I have a whole new appreciation and respect for the Borlogs and other animals and creatures of this land."

"I, too, am sorry," Adara said. "I knew I had this talent to talk to animals, but I never really used it, never improved it. Not for this purpose anyway. If I had thought about it, I could have counseled with you a long time ago, and perhaps this war would have been over by now."

"Don't worry about the past, that is over and done and there is nothing we can do to change it. All we can do now is prepare and shape the future" The Unicorn said.

"Rellik must be defeated, we must combine our forces to defeat him." The Lion said. All the animals were in agreement, the humans were as well.

"And of course, the dragons will continue to fight by your side," Penelope communicated. "Then it is agreed," Adara said. "We will meet again soon to start planning strategies."

"We should start planning as soon as possible; every rev that passes by Rellik's army grows stronger," The Hornswollop said.

"If it is all agreed, we shall all travel to Lilenhamür and make our preparations there. It is the most secure place I know." Melvin said to the group.

They all agreed. Penelope relayed that the dragons would fly them to the fortress. However, they would need to find an exceptionally large dragon to carry the borlog, as he was nearly the size of a small adult dragon, extremely large compared to the others present.

CHAPTER 50
REFLECTIONS

The spies returned to the fortress with news: Rellik was no longer stealing or capturing dragons. Instead, he was mating them—specifically the ones he controlled and the ones that willingly came to his side, not the dragons he had captured. He mated the females as soon as possible. Using his wizards and warlocks, he cast growth spells to accelerate the dragons' growth and maturation, much like how Melvin had hastened the trees' growth on his way to see Penelope hatch.

When the dragons laid eggs, the warlocks also cast spells for them to hatch earlier. He watched every egg hatch and gained power over them, and also gained their magic. Week by week, Rellik grew stronger and stronger. With the dragons, he experimented with breeding different kinds of dragons together to get different qualities in dragons. Such as breeding fire and ice dragons together, acid and water dragons, and mixing their abilities.

Melvin was concerned by this news, but not for his or Adara's sakes, but for the sakes of all the others in the army, and on Arion. Melvin often went to the lake in the center of Lilenhamür. There he could get away from all the hustle and bustle of the city, could get away from the war, and everything else. But there was another reason. There, in the solitude of the lake, was the center of the fortress. Melvin could soak in that magic, without having to watch dragons hatch, without having to go to Dragonia. More and more dragons were coming to Lilenhamür to build their own army. Some even flew in from Dragonia to help. Melvin soaked in all of this magic, and he became more powerful every rev.

But not for the power itself—instead, it was to protect the empire, his family, and those he loved. There were countless things he could do. He could probably single-handedly win the war just with the sheer amount of power he possessed. However, he didn't think that way. He didn't fully grasp the extent of his power or all the things he was capable of. He still saw himself as the newly commissioned master wizard, with much left to learn. One thing he was glad to have learned, though, was to stop stuttering. Although when very anxious or stressed, he still occasionally did. But he continued to sing his spells to give them more strength and power.

Then he thought of Adara. How she had grown in her power and ability, from where she was when they went to see the elves the first time, to now. She had grown by leaps and bounds in her power and ability. She could do things that she never thought possible. Sure, fireballs and fire arrows were one thing, but now she could make a towering inferno, a giant tornado of fire. She had been learning to concentrate her fire ability so much that she could make a fireball that could get as bright and hot as Helios at noon rev. That would burn someone's retinas. He chuckled because he knew how to do the same thing when he was still an apprentice. He was trained by a light wizard, you know.

He taught the other wizards how to soak up the power in the fortress as well. They would never have to worry about it running out of power, because of the spell and configuration of the walls, and what they were made out of, it concentrated the magic. Some of the Elves came as well to teach and to train the other wizards how to better use their power. More recruits came, rev by rev, to join the Army of the Empire.

This wasn't Melvin's army, nor Adara's—it was the Empire's army, united to rid the world of the threat that sought to destroy the freedoms they enjoyed. Sure, it was ruled by an Empress, and many lands were governed by Kings, but in general, they were a free people— free to travel where they pleased, free to do business with whomever they wished, and free to achieve as much, or as little, as they desired.

The Empress made sure no one was held back if they wanted to excel, and she made the leaders of the lands adhere to that. However, there was a man who was trying to destroy those freedoms. Taking over lands, putting them in bondage, ruling them with an iron fist, and making them do his bidding. That's what they were fighting against. That's what this war was about. They were protecting their homes, their families, their freedom, and even their religion.

One rev Melvin had a thought, something he had not thought of before. His Mother. Sure, he had thought of his mother quite often, in fact, but this thought was different. He was scared for her safety. Sure, she lived on the other side of the continent, in a small, obscure town. But there was a small possibility that Rellik would find out about her, would know where to find her, would be able to get to her, and use her for leverage. He *had* to protect her.

Melvin called on Penelope. "I need to go back home immediately," he told her. "I understand" was all that Penelope said.

"Do you want me to go with you?" Adara asked concerned.

"No," Melvin answered "It's ok, There is just something I need to do." Melvin and Penelope immediately took off for his small village in Bilbylund.

When he arrived at his mother's house his mom was very surprised to see him. "What are you doing here?" his mom asked. She gave him a warm embrace.

"I just thought of something, and I came here to take care of it so I wouldn't worry about you." He said looking in to her orange eyes.

"I am ok, Why would you worry about me?" She asked still wondering why he was there.

"Rellik may find a way to use you to get to me, like take you hostage or something."

"I will be ok Melvin" She said "The war is far away, am I am here in a small obscure village on the other side of Arion."

"I know, but it would still be better if I knew you were safe." He said the concern was showing in his voice and face. Melvin then took out a necklace from his pocket. A plain gold chain with a letter P pendant on it. "This looks like nothing special. The P is for your name, Penelope. But it is enchanted. I put an enchantment on it to keep you safe. Anyone who doesn't know you and who you are will not see you or notice you. So if somehow Rellik's spies find out you are living here and come to take you, they will not be able to know you are here. If someone you know happens to be working for Rellik and comes to bring you to him, or shows his spies where you are, they will not be able to find you. I will also put a shield over this house, so anyone you do not know, or has mal intent, will not be able to find your house or will forget the reason they came here."

"Melvin, you don't have to do all that. You may not believe it, but I am quite capable of taking care of myself. I am a Wizardess, you know. Reicuas was not the only one teaching the princesses magic. How do you think Aria and Adara got so good with weapons and the use of their magic?

"I assumed it was Reicuas that taught them that. Or the King's army," Melvin said in surprise.

"No, dear, it was me." She said with a twinkle in her eye "You may not believe it, but I was pretty Bad Ass when I was younger. When I went to teach the princesses their lessons, it wasn't only math and reading I taught them. It was also defense, use of weapons, strategy, etc. Sure, they may have also been taught by Reicuas, King Bilby, and the others of his guard, however, a lot of it was me."

"Then why didn't you go on Reicuas's quest with him to defeat Zôltan?"

"I was needed here," she said, "and other reasons that you would not understand."

"You would be surprised what I can understand. I'm not a child anymore, you don't have to protect me." He said.

"I know you're not a child anymore. Perhaps I'll tell you when the war is over, and you return—if you choose to come back to this small village after seeing the grandeur of Lilenhamür."

"You know I don't like all that grandeur. I would rather be back in my house with Adara, raising a family. But unfortunately, that has to be put on hold for a while."

"I know, dear." She said, taking his hand, "Talking about Adara, you should probably go visit her parents and give them an update, then get back to the war."

"That was the plan. I will be going there now." Then he gave his mother a long hug, and he and his dragon flew to the castle. Melvin visited with Adara's parents and sisters. He updated them on the war and assured them that everything was fine with Adara and Aria. He then put an enchantment on her family, the same as he did with his mother, so that to other people they did not know, or to people with mal intent, they would not be seen. He told them that this would only last till the end of the war, but did not know how long that would be. The family understood and was appreciative.

CHAPTER 51
PLANS

All the military leaders gathered around the large wooden table, maps and notes scattered across its surface. The Empress and the others listened intently to every word being spoken.

"We have had a spy network among Rellik's forces for quite a while now. We can pretty much determine every move that he makes." Said the Lion. Adara and Melvin would translate for those who couldn't understand the animals. "We mostly use birds and small animals to infiltrate the camps, because they are the least noticeable. We tried insects, but they tend to get squished or eaten too easily. We will keep you informed of the movements and plans of the army. We have also hindered them quite a bit, not as much as you have, but broken wagon wheels, chewed ropes, small sabotage like that, prolonged the supplies getting to his armies. Although we haven't come out in open rebellion against his armies, because he thinks animals have no intelligence, and we like to keep him thinking that way. He also has warlocks and witches, and other humanoids who can also speak to, or at least understand, animals, so we try to keep the chatter between us and the spies to a minimum while we are in the vicinity.

"Thank you for the update," Melvin said. "We greatly appreciate your help. We would like to keep using your spy network as it is already in place, as an addition to our own through the dragons. Penelope, could you please report?"

"Of course." Penelope had learned how to communicate with Humans through their language, though it wasn't as easy as it was to communicating their normal way, but in the long run, it was more efficient for a larger group of people, especially those who couldn't communicate with Dragons. "We dragons have our own network as well. Watcher and her siblings are among them. There are many who are forced to serve Rellik because he watched them hatch and controls them; if there were any way to break that bond, they would gladly have it done. For now, the only way that the bond can be broken is if one of them dies, preferably Rellik. But since he is in control, neither can break free. There are other dragons he's captured who serve him, though not willingly. Still, some dragons serve him voluntarily, drawn by the promise of great riches and power once this war is over. Those are the ones who are taking pleasure in ransacking towns and villages, even cities, just because they can. If we could break that bond, a good majority of those dragons would revolt against Rellik. They also keep us informed of the happenings around the camps, their plans, movements, etc."

"So what is he planning next?" Adara asked.

"He has taken over the whole west side of the mountains. He is slowly moving east. These mountains are so vast that it will take him several annums to get to this side of the mountains. But we cannot let him advance any further. He does not have sufficient forces to take on Lilenhamür directly, yet, but by the time he gets through the mountains, he will. We must stop him before he gets that far."

"Agreed, what is our plan?" Adara replied

"As we know, he has recently taken over one of the Gnomes' villages on the west slope, so he hasn't gotten very far yet." The Unicorn said, "He has taken over several other gnome villages and a Dwarf town as well. He has been searching for the Miners' Tunnels under the mountains, he could get here much faster by using the tunnels. We must stop him from using the tunnels."

"Can we use the tunnels to get to the other side of the mountains quicker? Melvin asked. "Yes," Said the Lion

"Rellik has dragons, he could fly over and attack." The Unicorn said.

"Yes, he does; however, he does not have sufficient to fly the entire army over. They are mostly being used for razing villages and cities." The lion said

"Yes, and we have been trying to prevent him from doing that at every opportunity, but it is difficult from here," Melvin said. "We need a base either in the mountains or on the other side of the mountains that we can attack from."

"I know just a place," said the Hornswollop.

"Where?" asked the Empress. Her bright blue eyes drilled into him.

"The same meadow valley we held our first meeting at." He said feeling the pressure of her gaze "The only way in is through the tunnel or over the mountains, easy to defend. It is actually a crater of an inactive volcano I believe. The wizards or Elves can put a magical barrier around it to keep those who are inside from being seen by eyes from above. Maybe the same type of barrier as the Na Van has."

"I can do that," Melvin said.

"Let's move our forces there at once." The Empress said to everyone there. "Scout the area and make sure it is cleared. At this time, I do not sense any creature with mal intent in the area, let the dragons and other animals go in first to secure it while we move the rest of the military."

"Yes, Empress," They all said in unison. Then got to work.

"Melvin, Adara, Aria, Brennan and Lion, and Penelope." called the Empress "You stay back I would like to speak with you alone. They rest of you, get everything ready to move out at first light."

"Yes, Empress," they said and saluted, and got moving.

The Empress turned to those who had stayed behind. "You are the leaders of this entire army," she said solemnly. "Melvin," she continued, taking his hand, "I know you don't like being in the spotlight, and I know you don't want to be in charge. You're a simple man from a village in the east. You'd rather tend to your garden or walk along the beach with your beautiful wife, collecting seashells." She glanced at Adara. "But I see what lies within you. You are much more than that. You possess more power in your little finger than all these other wizards combined."

She smiled and continued tenderly, "You are still trying to understand that and use it. But this army needs you, they need you to figure it out. You can do many things already. You have surpassed your master Reicuas in every way, but there is so much more in you. I can see it, I can feel it.

You need to learn to use it."

Then she took Adara's hands in hers and was amazed at how warm they were. "Adara, you are literally a fireball. You have so much power in you, you still don't realize it. Not only in your magical ability, but in your person, in your ability to take charge and lead. You were raised and trained for this your whole life. Now is the time to step up and lead this army and defeat Rellik."

Then she turned to Aria, "Aria, just like your sister, you have been training for battle your whole life. You have the art of dance, combined with your sword training, the Elves taught you how to dance with a blade. They call you *Taila-Atria, 'Blade Dancer'*, you and your special forces have made some decisive blows to Rellik's armies. I expect more great things out of you. All three of you."

Then she looked at all three of them. "These men adore you, they would follow you anywhere, do anything you ask, fight till the death for you. Hopefully it won't come to that. So there is one thing I ask of you. If you can," with tears in her eyes, almost pleading, "Bring them home. As many as you can. Bring them home to their wives and children. I know many will die during this war, that is inevitable, but if there is any possible way to save as many as you can, please try."

She turned to Wizard Brennan, next tears were in her eyes. "Brennan, you are in charge of the Wizards, as you know. Use them wisely. Use their talents and abilities in the best ways possible. "You have been my wizard for many, many annums. I know you can do this. You've also won us countless battles." But remember, your strength is not in strategy. Listen to these three, work with them, counsel with them….." Then she hugged Brennan as if she were saying goodbye to a dear friend for the last time.

Then she turned to the lion. "I admit, I do not know the Kingdom of the Animals as much as I should. I had always left them to do their own thing, not even looking to see if they needed help, and for that, I am sorry. I promise from now on to be more attentive to your needs. As far as I can tell, you are the one to lead and represent all the Animals. I will leave it how you to do that. However, please counsel with these four, and with the dragons as you have been doing. The animals can do many things that humans cannot do. I expect that you will work closely with Aria and her special forces. If you know of any animal that can do any task better than any human, or dragon, or other creature, please do not hesitate to say so. If a wolf or a fox, or a mouse can infiltrate and get information, use them, please. I'm sure Rellik will be doing the same. If you need to use a Borlog to disrupt his supply line and create chaos, havoc, and mayhem, have them do so. I'm sure they'll be more than willing. Whoever is best suited for the task at hand, and whoever will ensure more of this army can return home to their families in the end."

Finally, she looked at Penelope. "Penelope. You have been Melvin's greatest friend and ally since birth. You have been by his side since you were born. He has asked you to help him during this time, and you have chosen to do so. Not because you have to, but because you want to. I am officially making you the leader of the Dragon Army from Arion. Since you have been here from the beginning, and have been a great aid to us. I can not say that you will be the leader of the dragons from Dragonia, if they choose to join our fight, but that will be determined when and if they decide to help."

She opened her arms with the warmth of a mother, as if to gather them all into her embrace, and smiled. "Please be safe. And please, please. Rid this world of that awful man so we can once again have peace in this land. Now go and get to it."

"Yes, Empress," they all said, saluting her before heading on their way.

Chapter 52

Into the Mountains—Again

By the next morning, they had all the supplies ready to move out. As per the Empress's orders, dragons and other animals were dispatched to scout the path and the mountain meadow valley where they were to set up their base. Since dragons were more visible, they flew higher. Birds and insects, though slower, flew lower to inspect the terrain closer to the ground.

The domesticated animals pulled the supply wagons as the warriors marched alongside the wagons. Before and behind the wagons marched 20,000 swordsmen, 15,000 archers, and 7,000 pikemen. Aria had special troops of 25 men, but could wreak havoc on ten times that number. And a relatively small number of wizards and wizardesses also rode in wagons. They had already lost many men in previous battles and knew they would lose many more. Many of these soldiers were barely getting into their manhood and had no training but the few weeks at the fortress or other training camps scattered throughout the empire. Many were older and should have been at home tending their gardens. As they marched through or near towns on their way to and through the mountains, they gathered more who were eager to fight for the Empire. These recruits had a gleam in their eyes, a hope for grandeur and importance, and the promise of a reward when they returned home.

Though the army had had many battles and skirmishes before, this time it was for all or nothing. This time, they were taking their entire force to the mountains, except for small forces to protect the fortress and other cities and towns on the east side of the empire.

Rellik controlled the west side of the Helaeth Mountains, which ran relatively down the center of the continent, dividing the continent in half. The mountains themselves took up quite a bit of the continent. Rellik had already conquered the lands of the Gnomes, the Nŏrden Forest, home to another clan of Wood Elves, and the plains inhabited by the Jĭgabuji. Also, the coastal cities of Pine in the northwest and Heisenvad in the southwest. He razed Banaldür the *City on the River*. Which was the most important trading hub in the west, and the cities on the slopes of the mountains, Hammoth-Dōr, Ündarhaven, Schiffen-Heim, and all the towns in between. Those inhabitants he turned into slaves, and they made his weapons and armor, with metal mined from the mountains. The farmers were forced to grow food for their armies.

Did the people of the West cry out for deliverance? Of course they did. The Empress sent an army to defend them with Melvin, Adara, soldiers, and Wizards. However, they were insufficient and were beaten. Adara's army won a few battles, but grossly underestimated the size of the armies of Rellik. And the Dragons. He had hundreds of dragons, and Adara's Army, at the time, had a total of three.

This time was different. This time, they had a sufficient number of men, many more dragons, and now, the animals. Plus, they had one more advantage that they didn't have before. Melvin.

I know what you are going to say, Melvin was in those past battles. And you would be correct, However, this Melvin is different. This Melvin is stronger. He has spent much time at the Fortress, soaking up as much magic power as he possibly can these past few moons. He has trained, learned to use his magic from great wizards from Wazervĭl and the Elves. He has more abilities than he had the last time. He possessed the abilities; he just didn't know how to wield them properly. Always learning, always improving, he was constantly growing in both skill and power. The wizards were astonished at how advanced he had become despite lacking formal training at Wazervĭl.

And the Elves, they were impressed that he was so much better at his magic than when he stayed there and learned from them before.

Adara has grown more powerful as well. And had also improved on her abilities. The whole army in general is better trained and better equipped than last time. Plus, there are more of them.

You may ask, Well, if the Empress has foresight, why didn't she know that the armies of Rellik would defeat her armies? Well, she knows the hearts of men and other beings. She has visions, but she does not have the ability to know the size of someone's army. And she cannot tell the future. She only sees the possibilities of what can happen, Those visions can change.

This time, they were more prepared.

The army began its journey through the mountains. Last time, they had made the mistake of traveling in Harvest season, forgetting how cold it could get in the high altitudes. Adara had expended most of her power just to keep the troops warm. This time, they set out in late sowing when the weather was warmer. It would take several moons to get all the personnel and supplies through the mountains to the meadow. There had to be a better way.

Adara was thinking about this. She saw Penelope fly overhead. Dragons. She communicated with Penelope if she thought that the dragons could carry some of the equipment to the valley.

"Dragons are noble creatures. Not beasts of burden." Penelope told Adara matter-of-factly.

"I know, but this is urgent. We need to get to the valley as soon as possible, and this is the only way I can think of to do it. Pegasi could fly 2 people at most at a time. And all the other land animals would still take just as long, with all the back and forth they would have to do. Dragons are the only way I can think of to at least get the main equipment into the mountains."

"Let me communicate with the other dragons and see what they say." She said. Moments later, she came back with an answer. "You need a leaper."

"A leaper?" Adara asked. "What is a leaper?"

Penelope put a picture in her mind of someone who can "leap" from place to place.

"Oh," she said, grasping the idea. "Someone who can teleport. We will search the wizards for one. Thank you."

"But you may not find one." Penelope added, "For they are extremely rare."

She called out to the generals to search out the Wizards for one, or maybe more, who had the talent of Leaping, as Penelope called it, or Teleporting.

They found one—a young girl in her third term at Wazervĭl, who believed she had a special ability that could aid the Empire's army. Adara had her brought to meet with her and Melvin.

Melvin could tell that the girl was nervous. She looked very young, probably no more than 150 annums, if that. He took her small, slight hands in his. She looked up in wonder with big brown eyes behind thick, round glasses. The school robe she wore looked three sizes too big. And looked like hand-me-downs. He could tell she had blond hair beneath the hood of the robe.

"What's your name?" Melvin asked reassuringly. "M-M-Marlie," she responded timidly.

"Do you have a Stutter?" he asked.

"No, I'm just nervous." She said looking down. "Why are you nervous" Adara asked.

"Because it's *YOU!!!* And *YOU!!!*" she said, pointing to Adara. "The two most famous wizards in the whole world. I have always *dreamed* of meeting you." Emphasizing the Dreamed part.

"We're nothing special," Melvin said.

"You are the great Melvin the Magnificent. You can do anything." She said. "And you, Princess Adara," looking at Adara in awe. "You are the greatest fire Wizardess there has ever been," and she made as if to bow down to them.

"Wait a minute, young lady," Melvin said as he held his hand up to stop her. "There will be no bowing here. There is only ONE person you should bow down to, and that is the Almighty Deo!! We aren't any more special than anyone else in this army. Just because Deo chose us to have these talents and lead this army doesn't make us any better than you or anyone else. Now," he took a breath. "Why are you here?"

"I wanted to help the Empress defeat the Evil Rellik." She said more confidently.

"That is very brave of you, Marlie. I hear you have a special talent. Why don't you tell me about it? What is it you can do?"

"I can teleport myself, and anything I touch. But I'm not very good at it yet. Just small things." She said with her head down, almost a whisper.

"Do you know of any other wizards who can teleport like you?" Melvin asked.

"Not that I know of," Marlie replied sadly. "There may be others at school, but if there are, I don't know them."

"Neither do I." He said, shaking his head. "And that makes you very, very special. You have a very special talent. And right now we need that talent." Melvin said reassuringly.

"Like I said, I'm not very good." Still, she almost whispered with her head down. She didn't feel like she should be in the presence of the commander of the Arion Forces, or the greatest wizard in the history of this planet.

Melvin could see her hesitation. Could see that she was very anxious and nervous. He gently lifted her head with his finger and looked her in the eyes. "There was a time when I wasn't very good with my magic either. But I trained and practiced, and bit by bit I got better and better. I know something, or someone, that could help. But first, could you show me an example of what you can teleport and how far?"

"Yes, distance doesn't matter." She said, "I just have to be able to see the place and I can go there, instantly." She was mesmerized, captivated, and enchanted by Melvin's eyes. She had never seen multicolored eyes like his. Sure, wizards have different colored eyes, and they glow when they use their magic. She had seen this from her teachers and other students, but never had she seen multicolored eyes as deep as the universe that just drew her in like his did.

"Can you teleport people?" Adara asked.

She could barely understand what he said. She had to withdraw into herself again, turning away from those amazing eyes in order to focus. Looking at Adara, she said, "I haven't tried. I've attempted to teleport animals before, but it hasn't gone too well."

"What about inanimate objects? Like a doll?" Melvin asked.

"Oh, those are easy. As long as they aren't alive." She stated with a bit more confidence. She realized how truly nice and wonderful Melvin was.

"How big of an object can you teleport?" Adara asked softly.

"I don't really know. Once, I teleported my brother's clothes chest to the girl's dormitory because I was mad at him. After all, he took my doll. But don't worry, I teleported it back when he gave me my doll back."

Melvin smiled and then pointed at some barrels of food not too far off. "If we showed you a picture of a place in your mind, do you think you could teleport one of those barrels to the place we show you?”

“I can try,” she said, excited to be helping.

Melvin led her over to the barrels and asked Penelope to show her a picture of the mountain meadow in her mind so she could visualize what the place looked like.

“Do you think you can go there with a barrel?” He asked. “And then back here?” “I think I can.” She said.

He told Penelope to keep an eye on her and to see if she could teleport the barrel there. Marlie touched the barrel, closed her eyes in concentration and in an instant she and the barrel were gone. As soon as she left she was back. Without the barrel. Penelope confirmed that she had left the barrel in the meadow.

“Wow, Marlie, that was GREAT!!!” he said excitedly. Now you only have to do it two hundred more times.” Marlie’s eyes grew wide. “Just kidding, but you will need to do that a lot, but I know something that may be able to help, like I said before.” He turned to Adara and told her his plan.

“Do you think this will work? We’re already on a tight schedule,” she said.

“Right now, it’s our only option unless you have a better idea,” Melvin replied.

“I don’t have any better ideas,” Adara responded.

“Marlie, have you ever been to Lilenhamür?” Melvin asked.

“No,” she said, “but I’ve always wanted to go. I hear it’s remarkable.”

“Yes, it is. And we’re going there now,” Melvin said.

“Now?” she asked, wide-eyed with wonder.

 “Yes, but we aren’t going there for a sightseeing tour, we are going to a specific place for a specific purpose.” She nodded. Then he communicated to Penelope in his mind, *“Penelope. Can you communicate with those wizards still in Wazervïl, and see if there are any others with this talent among the staff or students? Or something similar. We need as many as we can get. Put into their minds the shore of the lake in the center of the fortress, please. And tell them to go there, I will meet them there. That’s where we will be. Also, put the image into Marlie’s mind as well. Thank you.”* Then he thought to her, almost pleading, *“Penelope, I know Dragons aren’t beasts of burden, but can you please see if you and the other dragons can transport the army to the mountain meadow. It would help us greatly.”*

“Yes, of course I will. You know that. When I was hatched, my mother promised I would help you when you asked and when there was a need. That is my bond. And there is absolutely a need. Besides that, you are my dearest friend, I will always do anything I can to help you. I cannot guarantee the other dragons will help, but I will try.”

At that, Penelope told Adara to gather all the soldiers together and the wizards into mixed groups. Melvin told all the troops to organize all the weapons and equipment, and supplies into groups as well. He would be back the next rev with Marlie and any other wizards that showed up. Adara already knew that Penelope would take the soldiers and wizards to the mountain meadow. She just didn't know how long it would take.

Just before they left, Adara turned to Marlie. "Thank you," she said sincerely. "We need wizardesses like you. I saw you earlier, Marlie." She lowered her voice to almost a whisper, then added, "Don't worry, all the ladies get transfixed by his wondrous eyes. You'll get used to them."

Then she smiled and chuckled. Marlie leapt to the lake in the center of Lilenhamür, and Melvin flew.

CHAPTER 53
LEAPERS

Melvin and Marlie stood on the shore of the lake in the center of the fortress. , waiting for the other leapers to arrive. A few minutes passed, and one by one, a few others showed up—a male teacher and two students, one male and one female. Not that it mattered.

When the others arrived they were in awe that the Great Melvin the Magnificent was actually there. They were actually in Lilenhamür. Melvin was partly happy that there were only four of them, but also sad that there were only four of them. Because doing what he was about to do, he had never done before, he wasn't even sure it would work.

"Ok," he started. "You have all been drafted into the Army of the Empire, effective when you leaped here. Is that what they call you leapers?"

They nodded in unison.

"I do not have a lot of time to explain what I am going to do, because we need to get going." I will explain as I go along. I will start with your teacher. What is your name?" Melvin asked.

"Sadrick," he responded.

"And what are your names and what term are you in?" he asked the other students. "I am Gwendell, 4th term" said the red haired girl.

"My name is Cameron," said the boy. "I'm in 4th term as well." Both of them looked to be not much older than Marlie.

All of a sudden another person leaped appeared by the lakeside. She was a very pretty young lady who looked to be about 180, with purple hair. Melvin looked at the newcomer with shock.

"No, no, no, no, no." He said softly to himself. "Amira, what are you doing here?" Melvin asked.

"There was a communication from Penelope that they were looking for Leapers, and I want to volunteer. She showed me the lake and I leapt here. I want to fight against Rellik. Just like you guys." She answered.

"You need to go home right now, young lady. Where you will you be safe?" He responded in a harsh tone. "No, Melvin. I have a talent that will help, and I am going to use it to help you fight Rellik." She said defiantly.

They others were in shock that this girl would have the audacity to talk back to Melvin the

Magnificent. One of the leaders of the Empresses army. The most powerful wizard the world had ever known. This was getting exciting.

Melvin turned to Sadrick and asked him if he could leap people from place to place. He said he had done it once or twice. He told Penelope to show him the caravan and for him to leap there. "Could you please go to the caravan and bring back Aria and Adara. Tell them that they are needed here. It's very urgent. They will find out why when they get here." Just then, Penelope put the image in his mind of where the caravan was.

"Yes, sir," he saluted, then Sadrick leapt to the caravan. He found Adara and Aria deep in discussion, strategizing how to get everyone to the mountain meadow.

Sorry to interrupt." He said timidly. He was in awe that she was in the presence of these two princess warriors.

"Who are you and what do you want?" Adara asked in a commanding tone, her eyes starting to turn red.

Sadrick cleared his throat and gave her the message. "I am one of the leapers who leapt to the lakeside in Lilenhamür. Melvin the Magnificent needs you to come to the lake in Lilenhamür. Immediately," he said sharply, like it was a command.

"Can it wait?" Aria asked more harshly.

"He said it is very urgent and cannot wait. You will know when you get there. I am to take you straight there." He said in a more confident tone.

"Well, if Melvin says it's important, then it must be," Adara replied. Both princesses grasped Sadrick's hands, and together, they leapt to the lakeside.

As soon as they arrived, they knew exactly what Melvin meant. "What are you doing here?" Adara and Aria said in unison." To the others, this was getting more interesting. Not only was Melvin the Magnificent here, but also Commander Adara and Captain Aria. This was getting even more exciting. They still didn't know who this girl was.

"Like I told Melvin, I have a talent that will help, and I am going to use it to help you fight Rellik," Amira said.

"Amira. You go right home this instant." Adara demanded. Pointing to the east. "This is no place for you."

"No. I am not a child any more," She stated. "I have as much right to be here as you do. You let these other leapers come and join, but not me?" she asked harshly?

"Wha.. When, How? What is happening?" Aria asked, "How can you do this? When did you find out? I'm confused." Confused was an understatement.

Sadrick being the adult leaper in this group decided some things needed to be cleared up. Like, who was this girl, and why did the leaders want her to go home? He had an idea, but didn't know for sure. So he asked. "Who is this girl, and why does she need to go home? She does have a point though. "We're all here, mostly children. If it's okay for us to be here, why not her?"

"I'm sorry," Melvin said, sighing. "I should have told you who she is before."

Aria interjected, glaring at Amira. "This is our sister Amira."

A collective AAAHHH went over the group. Now they understood.

"Amira, we have had decannums of practice to hone our skills. And from what I can tell, you just barely found out about yours. When and how did this happen anyway? We did not even know you could leap."

"You guys have been away so long, how would you know? I have been able to do this for a few annums now. Not long after you left for the elves. I was thinking that I wanted to visit a friend in town, I could picture myself there in her living room, and next thing I know, I was there. I didn't know how it happened. So I told mom and dad, and they asked the wizards in Wazervĭl since our wizard for the kingdom is off to war," she said, looking at Melvin, "and they said I could leap. Which was rare. So I practiced. I leapt all over the place. Never very far, though. Until one rev, a wizard from Wazervĭl came to talk to me. He said there was no limit to the distance I could leap, as long as I could see where I wanted to go in my head. He also said that if I held something, I could take that with me. So I practiced more. I was leaping all over the place with objects, then I tried it with animals, and then with friends. I discovered I could leap with people. Then I heard that you were looking for leapers. So I figured I would come. I know I can help. I can get in and out without anyone ever knowing I was there. I was always playing jokes on Mom and Dad and Anna and the servants. Until they figured out what was happening, and I got in big trouble. But now I know I can put my talent to some good use. I want to help you against Rellik."

"We don't want anything to happen to you," Adara told her lovingly. "Mom and Dad already have two of their girls in this war. Three is too many."

"Well, in case you haven't noticed. One of those daughters just happens to be the commander of the Empress's armies. With literal firepower so strong that she could annihilate any enemy. Who also has an enchanted sword and ring, and armor so that nothing can touch her. Who is also married to the other commander of the army, who just happens to be the greatest wizard who has ever lived. And the other daughter just happens to be the leader of the Special Forces of the Empire's army, who can dance with a blade and is so deadly that nothing can touch her. She and her squad can decimate any enemy before they even know they were there. So, I don't think the King and Queen are worried about those two poor little princesses." She smiled and batted her eyes innocently.

Melvin said, "Well, she's not wrong."

Adara told Melvin she needed a minute to talk to her sister. So they walked a few spans and discussed the matter. When they came back, they told the group what they concluded.

"Ok. Amira can stay. However, we are putting her in Aria's group so she can keep an eye on her." Then she came and hugged her sister. "You be careful. Although we can take care of ourselves, I am more cautious about you."

"I will be fine," she responded. "I am sure you two and Melvin will take good care of me. But I don't want any special treatment. You two are my sisters, we have the same blood running through our veins. I am as tough as you two are. We all have the same parents and have had the same teachers. I am more capable than you think. I have also been trained in how to use weapons and strategy." She hugged both her sisters. They knew she would be able to take care of herself, she had been trained by the same people who had trained them, though they still worried about her.

Now that that was taken care of, Melvin started with what he was planning to do. "Why don't you two stay here and absorb more magic. We are going to need all the help we are going to get." So they did. Adara, being taught by Melvin how to absorb magic, absorbed a tremendous amount of magic. She became more confident in her abilities and felt strong and invincible. She should come here more often. Aria was taught when they visited the elves to absorb magic, so she too absorbed as much as she could, and same as Adara, she felt more confident in her abilities and felt stronger and invincible.

"Good. OK, Sadrick, I am looking inside your body for your power." He told him as he actually did it. "This place is concentrated magic, There is a spell in this fortress that concentrates magic, it is strongest here at the lake. Open yourself up to it, I will help you if you can't. Try to absorb as much as you can." While he was looking inside Sadrick, he found his power. Bits of magic were jumping around inside of him. He had never seen anything like this before. He looked inside himself and didn't see anything like that. "I guess that is one talent that is so rare, I don't even have it." He smiled. "Well, I can't do everything you know," they laughed.

As he looked inside Sadrick again, he tried to notice how his magic was stored, attempting to observe the magic particles flowing into him. He focused on the places where he knew magic was stored in both himself and his wife, but there was no trace of magic in the same spots within Sadrick. It was not in his heart, his chest, or his brain. He noticed it was not in one place but jumped from place to place within his body. Well, that made sense. Melvin supposed it was different for everyone. He communicated with Penelope to communicate with the elves for anyone with this ability, and who could also help him teach them how to absorb magic and grow their abilities. Shortly, two elves popped into the lake area.

"Thanks for coming on such short notice." Melvin said to the elves, "What I am trying to do is help them absorb as much magic as they possibly can in as short a time as we can, and also grow their abilities exponentially so they can leap as many people and supplies as possible in as short a time as possible. And by the way, both of you are drafted as well."

The elves immediately understood what he was trying to do. They located the stores of magic within the leapers, as well as where their abilities lay, and helped them absorb as much magic as possible. At the same time, the elves absorbed more magical power themselves, which allowed them to assist the students in absorbing even more and enhancing their abilities.

After helping Sadrick, Melvin looked into Amira to find her magic particles that helped her abilities. As with Sadrick, her particles were bouncing all over. However, unlike Sadrick, she had around triple the amount Sadrick had. He showed her how to open herself to the magic and absorb as much as she possibly could. While they were absorbing the magic, something happened to Marlie, actually to all of them except Aria. Their hair turned purple. Several people could have the same hair and eye color. Though faint, Melvin and Adara could see that they had auras as well.

After several hours of this, they all became more powerful, more confident, and more in Awe of Melvin and the Elves, for they never knew such a thing was possible. Actually, neither did Melvin until he tried it. Another thing he tried before he left Lilenhamür. Just as his ancestor Elfin did several millennia ago for the Na'Van, he sang an incantation while creating a force field around Lilenhamür. Such that no evil could enter into it. It penetrated the ground underneath the lowest part of the fortress and went above the highest tower. Now that the fortress was protected, he communicated this to Penelope, who communicated it to the Empress. Melvin could feel her warm smile and Gratitude.

Later that rev, after absorbing as much magic as possible and growing their abilities as much as possible they leaped back to the army. Most of the personnel had been moved by the dragons to the Mountain Meadow. When the leapers got there, they tested their abilities. They found that they could leap with much more than they were able to before. Melvin even showed them the physical makeup of living things so they could take people and animals as well. They were able to take not only one barrel at a time, but many barrels. They could leap over the large weapons and the supply wagons.

Usually, after they leapt, they would feel exhausted and needed to rest. But now, they were invigorated and no longer required rest after leaping. What would have taken several moons to cover on foot, or several revs by dragons, or many revs before the training, now took only a matter of hours to move all the people and equipment to the Mountain Meadow. And this ability would come in handy in many ways during the war.

Finally, by the end of the rev, all the troops and gear were moved to the mountain meadow. The leapers had discovered something. If a group of people were holding hands or touching in some fashion, the leapers could take the whole group. It didn't matter how many there were. The same thing with inanimate objects. This sped up the process of moving personnel and equipment exponentially.

Chapter 54
Mountain Meadow

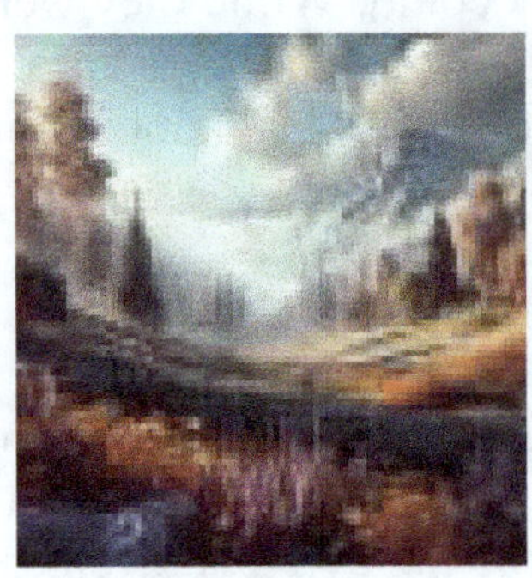

All the men and supplies had been leapt to the Mountain Meadow. The troops were busy arranging supplies and weapons when they were shocked to hear from the scouts that near the mouth of the cave system leading into the meadow, there were buildings—structures that had been built at some point in the past. Melvin examined them closely and immediately recognized that these buildings had been constructed by Reicuas and his troops when they passed through the mountains during their first battle with Zôltan. The battle that Reicuas did not come back from. Melvin and Adara felt a tinge of sadness from the loss of their master and teacher those many annums ago, but they needed to put that behind them for now. They had a war to win. These buildings would save them time from having to build these structures. However, they were going to need more, because this army was much larger than Reicuas's army was.

The troops started building other structures. The spot where the animals, humans, and dragons had first met was where they built the war room. A large round Dragon stone building where the leaders of this army would discuss matters and plan strategies.

Dragon stone was made by fire dragons heating the lava rock, which was plentiful in this valley, till it was molten again, and they would shape bricks in molds from the lava rock. Then the bricks would cool to be very strong. No mortar was needed because the dragons heated the top of the top layer of rock, and the next layer was placed on top of the molten rock, which, when it solidified it was as if it were one rock. Though this method seemed labor-intensive, it proved to be an incredibly efficient way of constructing buildings. Other structures, such as barracks, armories, a mess hall, and a hospital, were also being built from dragonstone and timber sourced from the valley. Once all was underway, Melvin and Adara decided to scout the valley to see what was in the area. They could have taken their dragons, but this gave them a chance to be alone for a while and take a little time off from the troops.

As they rode, they noted characteristics of the valley meadow. Noted where certain types of rock formations were, Melvin sent his consciousness into the ground to find any metal deposits for making weapons. There was plenty. Stands of trees for wood. Lakes and streams for water, and anything else. They rode to the far side of the valley. There, he saw something they had never seen before. They saw a town. But not like anything he had ever seen before. Though there was no life there. It looked like it had once been a thriving community. Most of the buildings were still intact. In fact very well preserved. They looked as if they were made of metal. As Melvin and Adara explored this town, they noticed something very interesting. There were multi-story homes, stores, restaurants, etc. Food was still on the shelves, in these metal containers in the stores, furniture was still in the stores, and metal homes. Melvin thought of who might have lived in this town. Then it occurred to him. He remembered what the Na'Van and the elves had told him about an ancient civilization. This must have been one of the settlements that wasn't destroyed by the war. Somehow, all these annums, this town, being in this valley high in the mountains, must have preserved it. They walked down what they supposed to be the main road of the town, which was even made of metal. They saw poles up high, which must have given light to the street. Melvin noticed ropes going from one to the other and wondered what they would be for. They followed the ropes to a building. There was a very large lever on a metal box with writing he could not read that looked like it could be pushed the other way. There was a label on the top and the bottom of the lever. The handle was close to the label that said OFF, though he didn't know what it said. He pushed the lever towards the label that said ON. Suddenly, there was a bang.

They smelled something in the air, a familiar scent—the unmistakable smell of lightning, the very same that Rellik had once unleashed toward them. Instantly, both their defenses were on high alert. However, at that very moment, every pole on the street flickered to life, and the lights in the shops, stores, and homes flickered on.

Melvin was baffled. He knew that Rellik could unleash lightning and that it was bright, and he understood how fire produced light. But he had never imagined that lightning could be contained in poles, switched on, and off. He turned to Adara and told her he needed to study this further—he might never get another opportunity like this again.

Adara nodded and told him she would explore more of the town while he finished his study. Melvin agreed, his mind already racing with possibilities.

Melvin was in awe of this discovery. He sent his consciousness inside one of the poles. He could look underground for metals and rubies, he could look into the human body, why not look into a metal pole? In there, he saw lots of thin metal wires. He looked further. He saw that there were these little devices in these lights that lit up when the lever was at the ON position, and weren't lit up when it was at the OFF position. This was very interesting. He turned the lever to ON again and looked into the lights again. He went deeper into the components. He sent his consciousness to look into the wires, just as he had done with his anatomy studies.

Melvin felt a strange sensation, something he couldn't quite explain. He focused on the wires stretching between the poles. He examined them more intently, moving closer, his focus narrowing. As he continued to observe, his sight adjusted until he could see the wires at the molecular level. Something was happening within them, something elusive, but he couldn't yet decipher what it was. Determined, he pushed further, down to the atomic level, hoping to uncover the mystery.

Then he saw something amazing. He saw electrons passing from one atom in the wire to another all the way down the line. They were traveling at an amazingly high speed. He pulled out most of the way, he causedcausing one of the wires to break and looked at the poles. Poles on one side of the break closer to the building with the box and lever were still lit, while the ones on the other side of the break were not. He mended the break in the wire with magic and put his consciousness back in.

What he saw then was incredible. The electrons that were passing from one atom to the next were glowing. They were light. However the wires weren't lit. He thought, Maybe there had to be a concentration of these electrons to light up. So he looked into the little devices on the poles to look for a concentration of these electrons. Maybe that's how lightning worked. However he did not find any concentration of electrons. The electrons went into these devices and somehow they emitted light. Melvin did not want to spend any more time on this he wanted to explore the rest of the town. Though he told himself at some time in the future, he would come back and study this.

Melvin called to Adara through their link and told her he was done. Once she came back they continued to explore. Adara told Melvin about what she had discovered. Clothing shops with garments still hanging neatly on display, food stores stocked with supplies, and restaurants where dishes remained set on tables as if the people had just left. Although everything was covered in over plant growth, it looked like when who ever lived here left, they did it in a hurry and they didn't take anything with them.

CHAPTER 55
COVENANTS

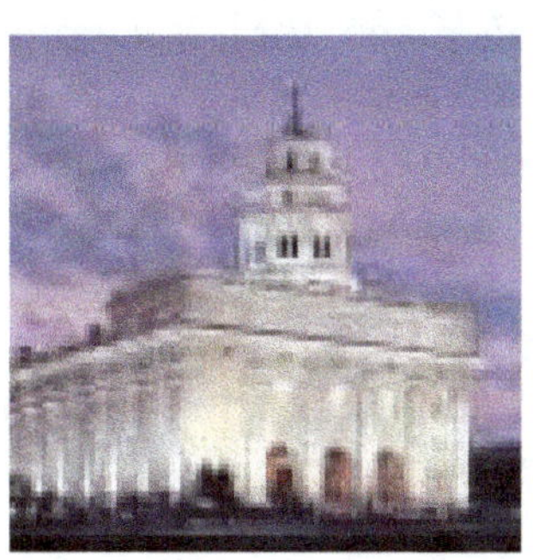

Melvin and Adara continued down the road until they reached a hill where a building stood before them. This one was different. Unlike the others made of metal or wood, it was constructed from stone—stone similar to that of Lilenhamür. What struck them even more was that it was glowing. The structure stood nearly five spans high, ten spans wide, and twenty spans long. Two sets of windows, spaced about two spans apart, ran down the length of the building. At the top front, a tall stone spire rose, giving it the appearance of a cathedral.

As they walked up the steps to it they stopped in sheer awe. A feeling came over them. This was very similar to the way Melvin felt when there was a large concentration of magic, but at the same time it was different. A feeling of peace, a feeling of calm, a feeling of reverence, a feeling of love. Intense love washed over the couple. As they looked above the high doorway there were letters engraved in the stone. They could not read them, but somehow they knew what it said.

The engraving said, "**HOLINESS TO THE LORD. THE HOUSE OF THE LORD.**"

Melvin and Adara knew that this was a holy place, a sacred place, and thus must be left alone.

At that time, a gentle voice came into Melvin's and Adara's minds almost like a whisper. "Melvin, Adara." They didn't know who it was, but they could feel the power behind it. They knew it wasn't their dragons or Rellik, nor the Na'Van. Was it another group of trees, or such as the Na'Van? They did not think it was any sort of magic. It felt different.

Melvin was in shock who ever this was knew their names. Tough they were well known, no one was around that they could tell.

The voice continued. "Reicuas has visited My Holy House, but out of reverence, he did not enter."

Melvin couldn't believe that Reicuas was there. The voice continued. "He left an enchantment on this Holy House, more like a blessing. He said that this temple would be protected, and that no one would even see it unless I deemed them worthy."

"Who is this that puts these words into my mind?" Melvin asked reverently.

"It is I, the Lord I AM Deo. This is My Holy House," the voice answered. Then continued. "Only those I deem worthy may even see this place, for it is sacred unto me. You and Adara have been found worthy to enter. You are pure in heart, your only desire is to do good. If you wish, you may enter the House of the Lord and make covenants with Me that you must keep always. And I will give you knowledge and wisdom. And a place with me after this life."

This Melvin would like because he was always in pursuit of knowledge and wisdom, and to be with Deo after this life. He tried to do Deos will at all times. Reicuas and his mother always taught him to put Deo first, Adara reminded him also. So it was an easy decision for them both to make.

Adara's upbringing had been similar in many ways to Melvin's. Reicuas had been her wizard, just as he was Melvin's, and his mother had been her teacher. Like Melvin's parents, hers had instilled in her a deep sense of duty to Deo—a commitment to keep His commandments and always do what was right.

Melvin and Adara climbed the stairs to the large doors. Melvin thought they would be hard to open, but they opened very easily. When they stepped in, they did not know what to expect.

Light shone through the open windows. It was very light inside, almost lighter than outside. As they stepped over the threshold, the feelings of peace and love intensified. Deos' love for them, their love for each other, and also their love for others. They looked around the edifice it looked much like the cathedral they had been married in, but everything was white.

 They noticed that their clothes had changed. Instead of the leather traveling armor they were wearing, they now wore white robes. As they walked further, they saw rows of white cushioned benches on either side of a center aisle. In the back of the large hall, there was a white altar made from the same glowing stone as the outside of the building. The floor looked as if it were the same polished stone as the altar. Tall white pillars rose up along the benches. The benches were carved with ornate carvings along the sides and back.

The edges of the hall, where the walls met the ceiling, had ornate carvings of what were adorned with ornate carvings of what appeared to be angels. Around the altar, a ring with a rune was etched into the polished floor- the symbol for eternity.

Melvin couldn't help but marvel at the contrast: while the town's other buildings succumbed to nature, this Temple—so aptly named— remained untouched, a beacon of purity and devotion.

"Please walk to the altar," the voice said gently in their minds.

Melvin took Adara's hand in his and they proceeded down the aisle. Not even questioning.

"Please kneel at the altar." The voice said.

They knelt.

Then, suddenly, a man in a white robe appeared in front of them.

Adara thought this to be strange, but at the same time, it seemed perfectly normal for this place.

"I am Aurulien. I was a prophet to the people who lived here long ago. Before they returned to the stars. Almighty Deo, whose house this is, has found you worthy to enter into covenants with him. Would you like to continue?"

Melvin and Adara looked at each other and knew this was right. They both nodded their heads and said "yes."

"Raise your right arm as if you were asking a question. Then repeat after me." They did "I, Say your name, and." and they both said their name and repeated what Aurulien said. "Covenant to use all my powers and abilities, all my strength, for the betterment of man and the Glory of the Almighty Deo. I covenant to devote myself to my spouse and my Deo. And to rid this world of the powers of darkness." They both repeated what Aurulien said.

"It is done," Aurulien said. "You may lower your arms." They did "You have received promise of knowledge and wisdom, and a place among the Deos after this life, as long as you keep your covenants. You may rise."

They both stood up.

"Please take a seat on the bench." Aurulien motioned to the bench behind them, and they sat.

The Angel continued, "Deo has given you these talents for a reason." He looked at Melvin, "Melvin. You have almost every ability that anyone else has, except for a few, but he has given few others those abilities. He has given them to you for the very reason you are using them for. To do good, to help and bless others, to heal others, to rid the world of darkness and evil. Use them well. Learn all aspects of your abilities. Hone them, improve upon them, strengthen them. Use them wisely."

Melvin nodded.

Then he directed his comment towards Adara. "Adara, you have been given special gifts as well, not many in this world have. You can use fire. Remember that fire is not only for destruction, but its main purpose is warmth and light. Be that warmth and light for others. Not only physically, but emotionally and spiritually. Be the beacon of light in the darkness for all to see. You also can talk to animals. Use this gift. Use it to defeat evil and help and bless others."

He continued directing his comments to both with his arms open as if to embrace them both. "Even if Rellik is defeated, there will be others who will rise up to spread darkness. They may or may not desire to take over the world, they may want to spread falsehood and deceit. Or bring others under subjection as Rellik is doing. These, too must be defeated. Go and do well, give glory to Deo in all you do. And in these efforts, Deo will bless you and be with you."

With these final words Aurulien vanished and Melvin and Adara were left alone. They just sat there on the bench and pondered what had just happened. They spoke to one another about this experience. One that probably no one since the last civilization that lived here had had. They held each other and discussed what had just happened.

They had never experienced anything like this before—the overwhelming feelings of peace and love that now filled them. Their love had been strong before, but it deepened a thousandfold after this experience. They could sense that something within them had changed for the better—something profound had shifted, a transformation that elevated them. Their devotion to Deo intensified, their bond with each other grew deeper, and their compassion for others expanded beyond measure. They only wanted to do good, to be good. All they wanted was to remain in this state of love and light for as long as possible.

But they knew they needed to get back to the army. After a few hours, they got up and headed outside. As soon as they stepped outside the doors, they were again dressed in their armor. This war would make it hard, but they would try. As they walked down the street, the temple vanished. They mounted their qilins and rode back to camp. As they rode, they discussed more about the spiritual experience they just had. And decided it would be best that they keep it sacred and only talk about it to certain people if it was necessary. They noticed that they are both very tired after that intense experience. When they got back, it was nighttime time so they slept well.

Chapter 56
Melvin's Crisis

Adara stepped into the dimly lit room, her footsteps making the worn wooden planks creak beneath her. The air was thick with sorrow, pressing down on her like an unseen weight. Her eyes immediately found Melvin. He sat hunched on his cot, a shadow of his usual self—shoulders slumped, head bowed, his red-rimmed eyes betraying the tears he had shed.

Adara had never witnessed Melvin like this since Reicuas had died many annums ago. His grief was palpable, etched into every line of his face. She approached him cautiously, her hand finding its way to his muscular shoulder. The touch was meant to offer comfort, but something felt off. A subtle shift in the air, a tremor beneath her fingertips.

Their love had weathered storms, and Adara knew Melvin better than most. She remembered the times they laughed together, shared secrets, and leaned on each other during difficult moments. But this—this-this broken version of Melvin—is unfamiliar territory.

As she settled beside him, she wondered what lay beneath the surface. Is it guilt? Regret? Or perhaps a hidden vulnerability he's never revealed? Adara wondered what secrets lay hidden behind Melvin's sorrow. Perhaps grief wasn't the only emotion he carried.

There was more to this moment, and Adara vowed to uncover it—to be the wife he needed. As she placed a gentle hand on his shoulder, the touch carried both comfort and an unspoken promise: she would stand by him, even if it meant walking through the depths of his sorrow.

 In this dimly lit room, Adara's heart ached for her husband. She hoped that by sitting beside him, she could offer solace and unravel the mystery that shrouds Melvin's emotions. He needed to get his head on straight before anything bad happened. Adara was concerned. He could heal the body, but not the mind.. She knew she had to help Melvin get his mind in order so they could defeat Rellik. She remembered this had happened once before. When Reicuas died in battle, Melvin fell into a deep depression.

Adara's voice was tender as she asked, "Melvin, what's the matter?" Still with his head lowered, Melvin mumbled, "I can't do it."

"Can't do what?" Adara asked, softly rubbing his shoulder.

"Be what everyone expects me to be," he continued. "Everyone expects me to be this great wizard, to save everyone from Rellik, lead the armies to victory, and be their savior. But I can't. It's too much."

"What makes you think that?" Adara pressed gently.

"I'm just a simple man from a small town in a small kingdom on the fringes of the empire," Melvin replied between sobs. "I don't know how to do everything everyone is expecting of me."

Adara put her head on his shoulder. "I know how you feel, Melvin. Remember, I have always been right there with you. One rev, we are planting flowers out front of our house, and the next, we are planning strategies to take on the greatest evil this world has ever known. I don't think any of us wants to be here. I would rather be back home with you, planting flowers, fixing things, watching you studying anatomy, studying my anatomy." She gave him a sly wink to lighten the mood a little

"But for some reason, God has chosen you to bear these extraordinary talents, and you stand as the greatest wizard the world has ever known. And I ended up commanding the armies of the empire. Not just our little kingdom, but the greatest empire on Estry. For some reason, Deo saw fit to give us these powers, and even more thought that we needed to be together. To tell you the truth, I am perfectly content with the second part of that arrangement."

"I like this arrangement, too. And I am glad I have you by my side, but I still don't know if I can do this. There is something else." Melvin paused. Then said softly, "I don't want to hurt anybody."

Adara knew what he meant. She did not want to hurt anyone either. Didn't Deos' word say you shouldn't kill anyone? But in these circumstances, sometimes you have to break the rules. "Melvin." She said soothingly, "I don't think anyone in this army wants to hurt anyone, I don't think anyone wants to even be here. But I can't say that for our enemies. They will hurt and kill as many as they need to take over this land. Then put everyone in bondage, just as he has the west side of the mountains." Then she took a more forceful tone. "Rellik needs to be stopped. And it just so happens that you are the only one who can do it."

"Everyone keeps saying that, but I don't know if I can." He said sorrowfully.

Adara knew she had to do something. How could she make him see that he could do this, and that he was not alone in this? That he had friends, powerful allies, and he had her. She moved in front of him and knelt, gently lifting his chin with her finger so that his eyes met hers. "Look at me, sweetheart," she said tenderly. "Now really look at me, Melvin. What do you see?"

As she gazed into his eyes—those marvelous eyes, she had lost herself in thousands of times before—she noticed something different. The light that once radiated from them had dimmed. What had happened to Melvin to make him feel this way? She silently prayed to Deo, asking for the wisdom to help him see his strength, to make him believe that he could rise to the challenge.

Prompted by his wife's gentle nudge, Melvin lifted his head. His eyes locked onto hers—the woman he loved. Her irises shimmered like amethysts, unshed tears threatening to spill. "I see you," he whispered. "I see my wife, and I see the beauty in your radiant purple eyes."

"Melvin, darling," she said with a little more force, her eyes locked onto his, "That's superficial, look deeper and tell me what you see, look at *ME*."

Melvin thought for a long moment. What was his wife getting at? What did she want him to see?

Adara knew Melvin wouldn't understand without a visual demonstration. She rose to her feet, the worn wooden floor creaking under her weight, and took a few deliberate steps back. Clad in her crimson leather armor, she assumed a commanding stance—a warrior unyielding, fueled by purpose and defiance.

The air around her thickened, charged with latent power. Her aura grew more intense red around her as she gathered her power. Adara's fingers trembled as she drew upon her magic, but Adara was now a master of control, and she restrained it, allowing only a fraction to escape. It surged through her veins, a tempest seeking release. She couldn't risk incinerating the humble hut that sheltered them.

Her hair, once a cascade of red waves, erupted into flames. The flickering tendrils danced, casting an otherworldly glow upon her face. Her eyes followed suit, irises smoldering like glowing embers. They held secrets—the weight of battles fought, lives saved, and sacrifices made. The sword at her side—forged by the elves and imbued with power from ancient enchantments—absorbed the same fiery hue.

Adara's voice cut through the tension. "Tell me, Melvin," she commanded, her words edged with urgency. Adara's transformation was nothing short of mesmerizing. The small, dimly lit hut seemed to shrink in awe as she stepped back, her armor creaking with each deliberate movement. The air thickened, charged with anticipation, as if the very elements held their breath.

Her red leather armor clung to her form, accentuating her strength. Adara's stance shifted, and suddenly she was no longer just a woman; she was a force of nature. Her aura changed. It was not just red, but her whole body was surrounded by fire. She was fire. Her sword also aflame.

And then she demanded again, her voice cutting through the charged atmosphere. "Tell me, Melvin," she said, her words both a challenge and an invitation. "What do you see?"

Melvin's gaze shifted from the flames dancing around her body to the flaming sword in her hand. He saw not just a woman, but a symbol—a beacon of hope. Adara was more than a wizardess; she was a testament to resilience, a living embodiment of courage. In that moment, he understood: he was not alone in this fight. Love, loyalty, and the unbreakable bonds they shared—they were their greatest weapons.

The hut's walls seemed to lean in, as if eavesdropping on their conversation. The flickering flames cast shadows that danced across Melvin's face, emphasizing the furrowed lines etched there. His eyes widened, pupils dilating as he looked at Adara's transformation. She was fire and steel, a living paradox—a protector who could ignite the world or quench its flames. Although Melvin had seen this a thousand times, this was different for some reason.

Now he truly saw her power—not just her magic, her fire, her abilities—but her spirit, her unwavering strength, her unshakable will. This was what she wanted him to recognize. Her resilience. Her determination. Her indomitable force. She was not just powerful— She truly was a force to be reckoned with, she was unstoppable.

"Adara," he whispered, his voice raw with awe. "You're not just a wizardess. You're a symbol of hope."

She smiled, a hint of sadness in her eyes. "Hope is born from necessity," she said. "And right now, Melvin, we need some."

He reached for her hand, fingers intertwining. "Then let's be their hope together," he vowed. "For Arion, for Ēstlund, Bilbylund, for love."

And as the flames flickered, casting their shadows upon the hut's walls, Melvin knew that their story—their defiance against darkness—had just begun.

Melvin smiled. Not for himself, but for his wife. She had grown into her power. She had learned to control it, master it. She now had become what he knew she could become and she finally believed it.

Adara reeled in her power. She extinguished her hair, her eyes turned back to purple, and her sword returned to normal. She sheathed it and returned to Melvin's side.

Adara's voice softened. "Sweetheart," she said lovingly, "I know you're afraid. We all are. None of us has faced anything like this before. No one wants this war. I'd rather be back home in Bilbylund, planting glowing flowers with you." She smiled, ran her fingers through his hair, and continued.

Her voice regained strength. "Melvin, you're a kind, gentle, wise, Deoly man. Do you know why all these people follow you? It's not because they're forced to, like Rellik's minions. It's not for power, glory, or gain. It's because of love. We love you. We love what you stand for— your humility, your unwavering commitment to doing what's right, no matter the cost. That's why we stand by you."

"Thank you, sweetheart," Melvin replied. "This means a lot to me. You mean everything to me. I'm doing this for you, for our future children, for Bilbylund, for Ēstlund, and for the Arion Empire. We need to live in peace. But Rellik is so powerful, and he commands countless dragons and armies. I don't know if I can overcome them."

She smiled, running her fingers through his hair. "But you're not alone in this. You have me. Remember the vow I made when we first met? Remember the vow I reaffirmed when we got married? I promised to always be by your side. And I stand by that—then, now, and always. As the commander of the Arion forces, I have 200,000 troops ready to lay down their lives for you. My sister and her team are wreaking havoc on the front lines in support of you. We have hundreds of wizards, Penelope, and other dragons—all standing by your side. And I know you know what I can do. You are not alone!"

"But they are counting on me. They say I am the greatest wizard this planet has ever known.

But I don't know if I am enough."

"I know, Melvin," Adara said, her fingers still running through his hair. "Remember, you have all of us. You're not alone." She gave him a sly smile and a wink. "But even if you were alone, as the Empress told you many annums ago when we were married—and it's even truer now— you have more magic in your little finger than all the other wizards combined. Yes, including me, and you know what I can do. You can perform feats effortlessly that others struggle with. Although we all know you can single-handedly wipe out Rellik's army, you need to know that. Your problem, mister," she said in a sharper tone, "Is that you lack confidence in yourself. Despite all your abilities, you still see yourself as that geeky, bucktoothed little boy back in Bilbylund."

"That's about right," he said, still wrestling with the idea that he is that powerful.

Adara's voice softened. "Melvin, I love you. More than anything in this world. I adore your humility, your simplicity. You've taught me so much about the world, about myself, about magic, and most importantly, about Deo. I know you can do this, Melvin. The whole world knows it. You just have to believe in yourself. Okay?"

Adara's eyes sparkled with determination. "Melvin," she said, "you're not just a wizard; you're a beacon of hope. Your humility, your unwavering commitment to doing what's right—those are your true powers. Rellik may have dragons and armies, but we have something more potent: love, loyalty, and the unbreakable bonds that tie us together."

Melvin's gaze shifted from the floor to Adara's face. "But what if I fail?" he whispered. But what if I'm not enough? "What if I can't live up to their expectations?" Melvin's voice cracked.

Adara cupped his face in her hands. "Listen to me," she said, her eyes boring into his. "You are enough. More than enough. Remember what Deo told you? He gave you these powers. This is what you were meant to do. Save the world from this evil. And any other evil that comes."

Melvin's breath hitched. "Adara…"

"Melvin," she said, "You're not alone. We'll face Rellik together. And when the battle rages, remember this: you're not just a wizard. You're my heart, my hero, and the light that guides us all. You are the Champion of light. You're the melody in my heart, the fire in my veins. When you doubt yourself, remember our love—the love that defies kingdoms, time, and even the darkest magic. You are here to vanquish darkness." She smiled slightly and chuckled. "That's funny coming from a fire wizardess."

With that, she leaned in and kissed him, pouring all her love, all her faith into that kiss. It was more of a kiss of consolation, encouragement, and confidence. It tasted of courage, of promises whispered across starlit nights. A kiss to remind him that she'd always be by his side, now and forever. No matter what happened. When they finally pulled away, Adara rested her forehead against his. "I love you, Melvin the Magnificent. Now let's go kick Rellik's ass."

"I don't even know if he actually has one," Melvin said, amused. They both laughed.

CHAPTER 57
A DRAGON ARMY

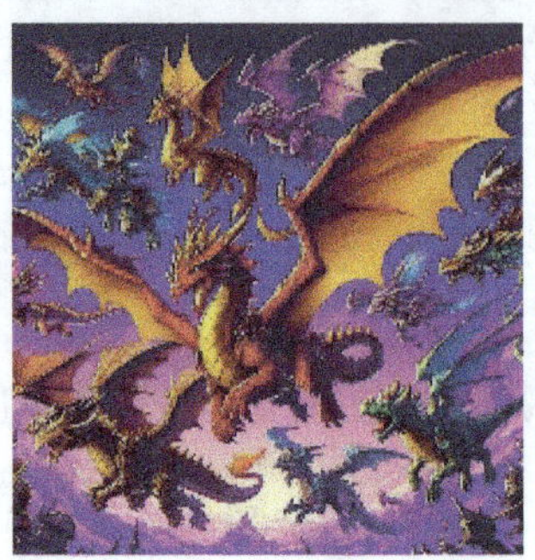

A few moons later Melvin was going over some plans on taking back more cities from Rellik. "*Melvin,*" Penelope communicated, "*NöGard wishes to communicate with you.*"

"Are we going to fly back to Dragonia?"

"*No, Melvin, there is an easier way. He will communicate through me directly to you. There are ancient ways of magic that you still do not know about. He will do this now.*"

Just then, Melvin's' mind opened to a scene. He was standing in front of the Dragonian King's castle. Two humans were standing in front of him. One was a large man, handsome. He had on shining golden armor with the Dragonian crest on the chest piece. Long blond hair ran down his back, and he wore a golden crown on his head. His golden eyes pierced him to the soul. Next to him stood a very beautiful woman. Almost as beautiful as Empress Kayla. Neither one is as beautiful as his bride Adara.

She stood in a long golden dress that shimmered like woven strands of gold. Her hair, too, gleamed as if spun from gold itself. Her blue eyes rested on him with compassion, and her radiant smile filled him with warmth. It reminded him of Princess Anna's smile back home.

Then he realized something in his peripheral vision. Adara and Aria were also there, as was Penelope. This was all very strange and new to him. How was he instantly here in Dragonia? Seconds ago, he was in a field in the mountains.

"Melvin" the man said gesturing to himself. "I am King NöGard. You may not recognize me in my human form. I am a shape-shifter. I can take on a human form and many other forms." In his human form, he had a deep voice with what we would call an Irish accent.

"This is the Dragon Queen Loraine." He introduced her by gesturing to the queen. "The council and I have spoken in depth about this situation. I have also spoken with the Empress, and she has shown me her visions of what is to come, with the possible outcomes of this war.

I will have Penelope show them to you."

Just then another scene opened up to Melvin, Adara, and Aria's minds. They were standing on a hill looking over a large valley. Destruction filled the scene. Trees were chard towns were in ruin and smoking. A dark cloud of smoke was in the air, it was hard to breathe. Then the scene shifted. They were flying as if on Penelope's back.

The black smoke still hung low over the land. Dragons soared above, ransacking towns, their fiery breath reducing entire villages to ash as they snatched up treasure. Imps, ogres, and witches reveled in their victory. Below them, the Empress's fortress lay in ruins, mirroring the devastation of the surrounding city. Bilbylund fared no better—its once-thriving streets were now nothing but charred remnants, unrecognizable in the wake of destruction.

Then another scene came before them. This time it was annums into the future. They saw people starving, women, men, dragons, all sorts of creatures in chains. Darkness covered the land. The Empress was in the public square in the gallows, bloody, she wore tattered rags, skin and bones, the determination and life in her eyes gone. They saw Lord Rellik on his shadow dragon giving orders to his minions to feed the humans to the dragons. Foul creatures ran amok.

They flew over other areas in Arion, and the same scene was there, repeated time and time again. The elves' forest was burnt and desolate. Na'Van forest was charred. It reminded Melvin of what the Na'Van had told him about the previous war in the time of Elfin. Next, they flew over Dragonia, and the same scenes that were in Arion was before their eyes. The great castle of King NöGard was in rubble, destruction was everywhere.

Then, the vision shifted again—this time, it was the complete opposite. They stood on the same hill as before. However, the Valley was orange, crops growing, villages prospering, the suns were shining brightly. They flew over Lilenhamür, the fortress was shining brightly in the high mid rev suns. They flew over the same places as in the first vision, all were prospering.

Then, as suddenly as it started, the vision ended. Melvin, Adara, and Aria were back in their own time and place. They were in shock. King NöGard was in front of them again. "My friends, I have seen the same vision. I know it is a true vision. The first one was if Rellik wins the war, the second is if he is defeated."

"Is this actually going to be what happens if Rellik wins the war?" Aria asked in disbelief.

"Unfortunately, it is, or something very similar." The King replied in a somber tone, looking at the ground. "I have known the Empress for a long, long time, and although I do not much care for the affairs of man, and disagree with the Empress from time to time, we are friends, and I do respect her tremendously. I can tell you that her talent to see into the future is rare and precise. Every time she has had a vision in the past, like this one, if we hadn't done something to change its course, it has come to pass."

"I do not wish this future on dragons or humans, or any creature." King NöGard continued in a somber tone, "Therefore, I will gather my armies to join forces and we will defeat this evil together."

"Thank you King NöGard" Adara said. "This is greatly appreciated. We have made a covenant with Deo to rid the world of evil and darkness."

The vision closed, and they were back in the Mountain Meadow. Actually, they had never left.

Melvin said, "Why couldn't we have done that the first time, instead of flying all the way there?" Penelope laughed. Melvin never heard her laugh, it was interesting to him, he didn't know dragons laughed.

"It is very powerful magic, very old magic. I do not even know this magic." She responded *"But some revyou may learn it."*

I have one other question "How did the shields break? The one over the Na'Van and the one over Lilenhamür?"

"I do not know." Penelope said, *"But the way to make sure it doesn't happen is to defeat Rellik."*

CHAPTER 58
TO WAR

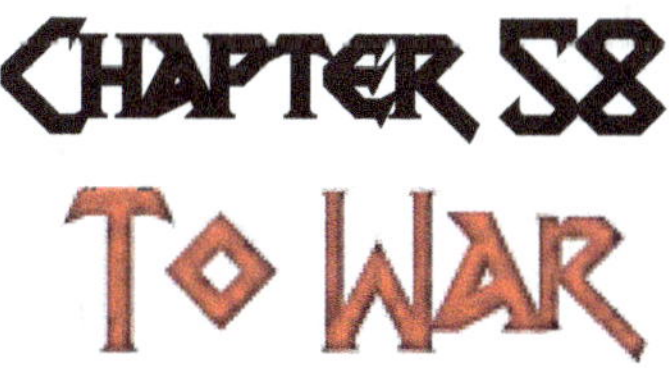

"Gather the generals and the captains!!!" Melvin called out.

In no time at all, all the generals and captains were standing at attention, ready to hear Melvin's orders.

"As you were, Gentlemen." Melvin said. "I have just received some disturbing news," he said and proceeded to tell them about the vision that he was shown by Penelope. "However, there is some good news. NöGard, King of Dragonia, has pledged a dragon army to help in this fight. We will no longer be outnumbered by Rellik's dragons." A cheer went up among the troops.

"Go tell your troops. Let's give them some hope in this war. Dismissed."

Later that rev, Aria's special team set out on a mission. Their objective was twofold: locate Rellik's armies and sabotage their supply lines, creating as much havoc and chaos as possible. According to reports from animal spies, the enemy had not yet reached the mountains. With this in mind, Marlie leapt them to the far side of the mountains.

Normally, it would have taken weeks to get there, but with the leapers, they could do it instantly. They didn't think Rellik's army had anything like this. You might think they would have trouble getting in and out of the shield. But remember, it works by magic. Melvin intertwined the bio signatures of his elite group into the shield so they could pass right through where others would not be able to.

Aria's animal spies of her group found a supply train headed for the main camp for Rellik's army on the west side of the Helaeth Mountains. They could not believe how large their army was. Not only were there troops of varying types of creatures, but also all the support wagons and other trades. Weapons makers, armorers, cooks, and many more. It was like a small city. The Empress's army wasn't even close to this size. Something had to be done.

Instead of directly attacking the army, they targeted its support system. A dramatic explosion would have been a bold statement, but it would also alert Rellik's forces to the Arion Military presence. Instead, they opted for a more covert approach—one that would cripple the enemy while strengthening their army.

Aria told Marlie to go get the other leapers. Marlie left and came back a few minutes later, soon after the other leapers came to their position.

"You see those barrels of food on those wagons?" Aria asked. "I want you to leap over there, then leap over the barrels to our camp. Then come back here."

"Yes Ma'am" they said. In a flash they were gone and back again. "Great job" Aria told them. "What else can we do?"

Marlie said "We can get in there, pull the pins that hold the qilins to the wagons. If it doesn't free the qilins at least it will slow down the supply wagons."

"Not a bad idea." Aria said, "But it may prove a bit difficult to pull those pins while the wagons are being pulled. However, we could send in the ferrets or mice to chew the reins and supporting harnesses, to give you time, also while they are busy with that, we can have the beavers chew the wheels. While that is going on, get some more of that food and take it back to our camp. I don't want them to know that we know where they are."

"Why not?" one of the team members asked.

"Element of surprise. Because then they would possibly get more anxious and move forward sooner, we need to stall them as long as possible. We cannot fight such a large army straight on. We need to whittle them down. Starve them, make them sick, and beat them at their own game. I need a nature wizard, can you bring me one? She asked the leapers."

"I will," Sadrick said.

At once, the plan was set in motion.

Wizard Brennan came with Sadrick. Aria said with a sly look and a wink. "I need some poisonous plants. Preferably ones that don't kill you right off, but make you sick over time. I'm sure there will be healers there, so I need to overwhelm them. Possibly eliminate them."

"I know just the thing," Brennan said. "Rotroot. And I know where to get it."

"Sadrick, you are with Brennon, take him where he needs to go to get it. Meet back here." Just like that, they were gone. Just then, they heard a scream and a crash. Qilins ran from the wagons, wheels fell off the wagons, and men went flying. The animals were able to escape without being noticed. While the men were dealing with the qilins and the wheels, the leapers took as many supplies as they could without it being too noticeable. When Sadrick and Brennon returned, they carefully mixed the poisonous plants into the remaining food supplies.

"It won't kill em right off, but it will give them the runs and an awful bad stomach and headaches for a few revs. They will wish they were dead."

"Excellent. What we need to do is get to that camp and cause some more havoc." Aria told her group. They went from supply wagon to supply wagon. Each time either stealing their supplies, breaking or weakening their wagons, or poisoning their food.

They traced the supply chain to the enemy camp and assessed their next move. Vastly outnumbered, they faced an overwhelming force—hundreds of thousands of troops gathered in one place. There was no way to engage them all and remain undetected. Instead, they sent a message back to the main camp, detailing their findings and requesting guidance.

"Raze the camp," someone suggested in her mind through the link through the dragons.

"What??" Aria asked. "Raze the camp? I understand what you said, but that would be suicide. I know we have Dragons, but they have 100 times more than we have. He has been breeding them."

"So have we." The voice answered. "We have been breeding dragons for many millennia." "King NöGard?" Aria asked. "Is that you?"

"In the flesh," He replied. "Well, not really, I am here though with Melvin and Adara. And my dragon Army is on its way. We are here to give you our support. I know Rellik has hundreds of dragons, and hundreds of thousands of the most vile creatures; he bred those as well. But they are infants compared to us. I have a trained army of dragons at my command. Many more than Rellik could ever hope for. Far better at combat than Rellik could ever make."

"Thank you for coming." Aria said. "Now we have a chance to defeat Rellik and save Arion and Estry from his future."

Another voice popped into her head. "Do what you can to the supplies, and then get everyone back here." At once they started wreaking havoc on the supplies and support. They broke wagons, stole or poisoned food, the small animals ran around camp scurrying up the legs of soldiers causing them to run all around falling into tents and fires, the animals were having a great time of it. Once they were finished, Aria's team leaped back to the camp in the meadow while the animals scattered into the wilderness.

For the last blow of this attack, in the dead of night, they got a borlog leaped inside the camp where the animals were being held. He rampaged through the animal cages, freeing many, they scattered and ran for safety. He zigzagged throughout support camp burning and, knocking down or destroying everything he could. He made sure to stay away from the main army. Fortunately there weren't many troops or dragons on the outskirts of the camp, so he was able to get away. On the way out he took the road where the supplies were coming in and rampaged through them as well. Most of the supplies and wagons were destroyed—except for those that were either stolen or poisoned. The Borlog ensured that only the ones with the poison remained.

As this was going on. The Dragons were heading towards Rellik's camp. Just as the Borlog was heading out of camp the Dragons came in. As well as the leapers and animals. Their job was to free the prisoners and the other animals or creatures who didn't want to be there. The intel came from the animal spies with in the camp. There was a coordinated effort in areas of the camp to get them out. As they were being freed, the main army was being attacked by the main dragon force of Dragonia. Not only were they fierce fighting dragons well trained in battle, but they were also wearing dragon armor. To add to that, a spell was cast on them by Melvin to repel any weapons or magic cast on them. There was not much he could do about other dragons attacking them. However, they were many times larger than the dragons bred by Rellik, though the natural dragons tended to be the same size.

The Dragons came and razed the camp. Setting fire to everything in sight. Now Rellik knew what it was like for other towns and villages. Rellik sent up his dragons to contend with the Dragonian Army. They were no match. The dragons captured a few of the dragons that were sent to fight them. They killed the ones that were serving Rellik of their own free will, they let escape the ones bred by Rellik. There was a plan for them.

Animals, humans, and other creatures ran and screamed as the camp burned. As they fled, the flames consumed them, igniting nearby tents, wagons, and makeshift structures. The blaze roared, visible for many megaspans around. Those who lived in the surrounding areas cheered, for they knew exactly what was burning.

And if there is fire, you know who else would be there? That's right, Adara!! For she was not only immune to fire as you know, she creates it. She was like a kid in a candy store. During the commotion she was leaped close to the middle of the main camp, then she walked right to the exact center of the camp where the highest officers' tents were located. She did not know if they were there or not, nor did it matter. She knew however that Rellik was not there, but that was ok, Adara would deal a severe blow to Rellik's army. When Adara got to the center of camp, a signal was sent out for everyone else to vacate the area. She dug deep into her power, as the elves and Melvin had taught her. She brought the power forth and concentrated it. If you would have looked at her, it would appear that she was glowing as bright as Helios in mid rev. She told the dragons who were not immune to fire to get to safety as quickly as possible.

Hotter and hotter, brighter and brighter she burned—just like the rev with the elves when Melvin fused her magic with her DNA. But now, she was stronger. She controlled her power. Nothing could get near her without turning to ash. Drawing on the fire within her very essence, she summoned it forth, concentrated it, layer upon layer, letting it build and intensify. Then, all at once, she unleashed it.

A wave of heat and fire erupted from her, so explosive, so devastating, that it was as if a nuclear bomb had detonated in the heart of the camp.

Wave after wave after wave of intense heat and fire decimated everything and everyone in its path for many mega-spans in every direction. When she was done, and her energy was spent, Penelope came and picked her up and took her back to their camp. The view from the air looked like a massive bomb went off. Charred ruins as far as you could see. Black burnt bodies, charred buildings, fires burning. You know, it kind of resembled the vision that NöGard showed Adara, Melvin and Aria. But in not so grand a scale. If one extremely powerful fire wizard and some dragons could do this to a military camp, imagine what Rellik's army could do if unstopped.

CHAPTER 59
TAKING THE OFFENCE

During the moons that followed, their mountain camp expanded beyond Reicuas's original settlement. They built additional stone structures—sturdy, fireproof, and lasting. What once resembled a temporary outpost now took on the appearance of a small mountain town rather than a mere military base.

Melvin's army grew. The more people that heard about the victory over the base camp of Rellik's army, the more people gained some hope and wanted to join the fight. Although Rellik's main base camp was completely destroyed, some of the troops and dragons did manage to escape, with the help of some of the wizards. They also knew that there were more of Rellik's army out there. More camps, more dragons and more evil creatures to defeat.

Some of those creatures and troops and dragons from Rellik's army came and joined the Army of the Arion Empire, the only reason they fought for Rellik is because they were forced to. Now they knew there was a way out. The Empress looked into their hearts, and if any was hiding their true intention, like being a spy for Rellik, they were found out and taken to the war prison that was set up. It was impossible to hide anything from the Empress. All the others were verified their true intent was to help the Army of the Arion Empire.

However, at the same time, Rellik's armies had been taking over more towns and cities on the western side of the mountains, and capturing more prisoners and looking for tunnels through the mountains to get to Lilenhamür quicker. Heli was waning, Harvest would soon be upon them, and they did not want to try to cross the mountains in the during Harvest.

Though they had dragons to carry them over, Rellik knew the Empress's army had dragons as well. However, he didn't know how many, nor did he realize that the dragons of Dragonia were also stationed at Lilenhamür.

At the same time, Melvin had been working on something important that could change the way this war would be fought in the future. All of the dragons they caught were ones born when Rellik was watching the eggs hatch. Thus, gained control over. Although he had control over the dragons, and the dragon had to obey him, most of them did not want to. They were being forced to do Rellik's bidding. Melvin searched within them, seeking the strand of magic that bound them to Rellik. He studied the bond between himself and Penelope to study this bond. He studied the bond between himself and Adara to see how it was attached. He tried to find how the bond worked and how to undo it without killing the dragon it was attached to. Melvin didn't mind if it killed Rellik. He linked new bonds to those dragons who were willing to himself for multiple reasons. Not to control them, but mostly for information, and it helped lessen the control Rellik had on them.

As time went on, they continued to run skirmishes. Continued to steal supplies from Rellik's armies, and continued to wreak havoc on their supply lines. But Rellik was getting wiser and had more caution. Troops always moved with the supplies.

Dragons patrolled the skies constantly while guards remained vigilant through the night. Melvin, Adara, Aria, and their fellow leaders had to devise new strategies to defeat Rellik's troops without engaging in direct battle. Despite their efforts, Rellik's armies still vastly outnumbered those of the Arion Empire.

Little by little, they were able to free towns from Rellik's grasp. The Gnome town at the base of the mountains that Piper had come from was liberated, and smaller towns of Humans, Dwarves, etc. were also freed from Rellik's grasp. Melvin put up magical barriers so Rellik's forces could not take them again.

Rellik had fortified other towns and cities that he held the captives in, and posted more troops therein. He caused the prisoners to build up walls of earth and put a breastwork of stone around the two. He also made them build high stone walls around the perimeter. He commanded the Earth wizards to locate and cut the stone with their magic, but the prisoners were the ones forced to move them and erect the very walls that kept them captive. These would be harder for Melvin's troops to liberate. Although Empress Kayla and Adara knew Melvin could probably defeat Rellik's army himself, Melvin himself did not have the confidence in himself to do it. Melvin did think, though, that after Adara's show of power, she could probably wipe out Rellik's armies herself. She often told him there wasn't anything any of the wizards could do that he couldn't. Except leap.

The leaders came together in a council meeting in the Great Council hall in the meadow base camp. This was the largest edifice in the camp. Oval in shape, made of large stones that were made from dragon stone. It had a domed roof with ornate woodwork surrounding the building.

Inside, it was a single large room with carpets covering the ground. Arion Empire tapestries and maps adorned the walls, and in the center stood a large round table. All the leaders gathered around it.

"It's time we take the offensive," Aria demanded. "We have been waiting long enough. Sure, we have freed a few cities and towns, but as we do, Rellik takes more every rev."

"You have a point," Adara responded. However, his army still vastly outnumbers our own. He has more troops, more dragons, and hostages. How do we fight against that?"

"We have the Dragonian Army," Aria said very aggressively. "Use them to raze the towns he controls." "Then how would we be any different than him? Razing a base camp is one thing, but razing towns and cities that have innocent people in them who just happen to live on that side of the mountains. We need another plan." Adara responded.

"Then we need a strategy," Aria said. "Rellik is coming closer and closer to finding a way to get through these mountains and to Lilenhamür. He knows there are tunnels through these mountains, and he is very close to finding them. However, if he doesn't find them, he has already been creating his own tunnels to send his troops through. What do you think they were doing with the Gnomes? He has to be stopped. And we can't stop him by taking the defense. We have to take the offense."

"She is right." Wizard Brennan said, "We have to stop him. Melvin, have you figured out how to break the bond between Rellik and the Dragons? If we can break that bond, most of the dragons will refuse to fight for him; they probably even fight against him."

"I have tried," Melvin said, shaking his head. "But to no avail. I have tried every spell I could think of, even made up a few. I have looked into the dragons to see where the string of magic attaches to them. It connects to their very DNA. If I try to detach it from their end, they will die. If it detaches from the host, it will survive. It is impossible to free them without killing them. However, some prefer that to their current state."

"Then I know what we need to do." The Lion King said with a growl. "We should have done this from the very start. Let me ask you a question. Where is the Empress?" The lion asked.

"Lilenhamür," They all said in unison.

"Exactly my point." Said the Lion, "The Empress is in her stronghold, far away from the battle. Has anyone seen Rellik lately? It has been reported that after he captures a town or city, he goes back to his castle and plans his next move. He isn't always at the front of the war. He sends in his troops, comes to deal the final blow, threatens the people, then splits. So, if we go straight to the castle and fight Rellik Himself and avoid all the unnecessary fighting of the troops, we chop off the head, and the rest of it just falls apart."

Adara spoke up. "That makes sense. He is the only commander. He has no one who will continue the fight if he falls. Most of his army is forced to fight, the others do it for the spoils of war, but I don't think any of them have the vision or the drive to keep on fighting if Rellik falls."

"Let's take a vote." Melvin said, "All in favor of taking the fight straight to Rellik raise their hand." They all raised their hand. "It looks like we are all in agreement." He announced. "One last thing. Let's run it by the Empress and see what she sees." All agreed with this as well.

"Penelope, will you communicate with the Empress to see her thoughts on this matter?" Melvin asked. "*Certainly*" was the reply. Penelope counseled with the Empress on this matter. The answer was affirmative. Time to end this war. They would need to get King NöGard and the dragons from Dragonia involved. They had some of the Dragonians fighting alongside them, but not all. Most of them went back home after that first battle. But if they were needed again, they would come.

Plans were made and set in motion. You don't just fly over there and kill the second most powerful wizard in the world. You have to plan. First of all, they didn't even know where the guy lived. They knew it was in the west, but they didn't even know what part.

They used their spy network of animals and the dissenters from Rellik's army to find the location of his castle. One knew exactly where it was located because he had been there for a long time. They would have to get their army there somehow without anyone noticing.

They had some of the dragons that Rellik captured as well that came over to the Army of the Empire. These dragons did not have the bond with Rellik. Melvin supposed that Rellik did not know how to make a bond with a dragon other than watching it hatch. They were already adolescents or adults when they were captured. Which was a bonus for Melvin, who did. One of them also had been at the Castle where Rellik lived. She knew the way.

"This is what we are going to do." Melvin started, "Can Blue communicate with Humans?"

"Of course he can. All dragons can." Penelope said. "But not all humans can communicate with dragons." "I want Blue to show Sadrick an image of a place for them to go. I am going to send a Leaper to the area surrounding the castle with your special team. I want you to scout for a place to leap the troops to."

"How about this, you can send me as well," Aria said.

"Or how about this?" Adara added. "How about the Leaper take Melvin to the area, and he can erect a shield around the area so the troops inside cannot be seen. Like the ones he erected around Lilenhamür and this base."

"Now you are taking all the fun out of it." Aria chimed in. "If Melvin does all the work, then what are the rest of us going to do?"

"We could go home and live the rest of our lives," Brennan said, looking at Aria in a certain way.

"That would be boring." She retorted, "We all know that Melvin and Adara can decimate Rellik's armies all by themselves, though they don't think they can. Just look at what Adara did at their base camp. I have trained all my life for this. I want some action."

"And you will get it," Melvin said. "But for now, I think Adara's plan is the best, with a few modifications. Aria and I will go with Sadrick and scout out a place for our troops and erect a stealth shield. Then we will all leap there. Get everything ready."

They broke up and started preparing for battle.

Chapter 60
To The Castle

Sadrick leapt Aria and Melvin to a spot near Rellik's castle before immediately returning to the meadow. They had no idea what to expect upon arrival. While they believed they were far enough away to avoid detection, they still felt uncomfortably close. Bringing their entire army here would be impossible without drawing attention.

They landed in an ancient forest—one that might have been just as old as the great Na'Van woods. Towering trees stretched high like mountains, their massive trunks thicker than wagon wheels, climbing toward the sky. Their limbs reached out wide, tangled and heavy, trying to catch what little sunsslight filtered through the thick canopy. The light from the twin suns above barely made it to the forest floor. Though it was mid-Rev, it felt like twilight beneath the trees.No wonder Rellik had chosen this place. It lived in shadow. Always dim, always cloaked. Yet despite the darkness, the forest was rich and alive. Orange leaves dripped with moisture. Vines curled along tree limbs. It was raining steadily now, and the air was thick with the scent of wet bark and earth.Off to the southwest, flashes of light split the sky, followed by the low rumble of thunder. It wasn't surprising—Rellik was a lightning wizard after all. This was his kind of place.As they scanned their surroundings, they saw all sorts of plants. Some were familiar. Others were strange, with twisting leaves or glowing veins—like nothing they'd seen before.

The trees and rocks were draped in phosphorescent moss that shimmered with an iridescent purple glow, casting the entire forest in a surreal light. Purple ferns dotted the forest floor, their delicate fronds swaying gently in the cool, moist air. All around them, flowers of every shape and color bloomed in wild abundance—violet, glowing, and iridescent blossoms sprung from a plant Melvin had never seen before.

Vines hung down like jeweled curtains, adorned with glowing pink flowers that pulsed softly in the dim light.

Strange animal sounds echoed through the woods—hushed whispers of creatures Melvin couldn't recognize, their calls blending with the wind and the rustling leaves. A light fog rolled across the ground, thick and mysterious, adding to the sense of hidden wonder. It wrapped around the trees like a soft veil, hiding their movements from prying eyes.

Melvin climbed a small hill to get a clearer view of the surroundings, but even as they did, he summoned more fog, thickening it to shield them further, making sure their presence remained unseen by whatever magical creatures roamed nearby.

As they were climbing a hill to get a better look, very large and powerful arms seized them from behind. "What do we have here?" a very menacing but not very intelligent voice said from behind. To Melvin it sounded like an Orc.

The other one said, "I thinks we found us some spies. What should we do with them?"

"Why don't you forget you ever saw us, if you want to live?" Aria said while struggling against the hold of the orc, trying to get free. She calmed herself and remembered her training on what to do in this situation.

"I thinks we should eat you for dinner," the first orc said.

Before anyone realized it, Aria dropped down out of the orcs' grasp, spun around while drawing her blades, and chopped off the orcs' legs then head. Then, she lunged the second one through the back with both blades, and he fell to the ground.

"Gross, now I have to clean orc guts off my swords." Wiping the blade on some glowing moss on a rock. "See, I told you to bring me along. Now it's starting to get exciting."

"You're right, Aria, although I would have handled it differently, you did well," Melvin said with a smile. "Let's get on with looking for a place for our troops," Aria said. Then started walking up the hill.

"I think we should dispose of the bodies. If they are part of the army, and they don't report, someone may find out that we are here. And that would not be good." Melvin advised looking down at the now decapitated orc.

"That's your department, Melvin," Aria said as she walked away.

Melvin then, with his magic, dug a hole in the earth, rolled the dead orc corpses into it, and covered it back up. No one would even know that the ground there was disturbed. While they continued their hike, Aria thought of something. She asked Melvin why he didn't just send out his essence to find a place for the armies. The answer was, he hadn't thought of it. This was a good idea and would save a lot of time. He sat by a tree, while Aria stood watch.

It was fortunate that Aria wore her black leather armor. In the darkness of the woods, she was nearly invisible until it was too late. Melvin extended his essence to explore the area. After about half an hour, he discovered a clearing roughly two thousand spans away—open yet concealed by overhead branches and dense ground cover.

"I found a place." Melvin said, "It's about two thousand spans from here, away from the castle."

"Good. Let's get going." She said as if in a hurry. She didn't really want to run into any more orcs, or any of Rellik's troops.

Since they didn't have qilins, they had to walk. They walked through the foliage to the place Melvin saw in his mind. They were careful not to make noise. Aria had mastered the art of stealth, able to move undetected. Melvin, however, had not. Melvin, on the other hand, had not. He thought of something that might help. So he flew. It never ceased to amaze Aria the things he could do.

A few hours later, they arrived at the clearing. It must have been 80 spans wide, nearly in a circle. They looked around. It was far enough away from Rellik's castle not to be noticed. But close enough that they could get to the castle walking at a rapid pace in a few hours, instantly with leapers. The tree canopy was dense enough that it would be hard to be seen from the air. It appeared to have the ruins of some ancient building in the clearing. But mostly all that was left now was a few crumbling piles of rocks.

They explored the area and made sure there was nothing there, except for animals.

"This will make a nice place to set up camp," Aria said, looking around. She had found a part of a corner of what was once a wall. This would give them protection in the back, so they would only have to guard the front.

Then Melvin communicated with Penelope to have a leaper bring Adara to the clearing. Seeing through his eyes, Penelope transferred the image into the leaper's mind, guiding them precisely.

Moments later, Marlie and Adara appeared in the clearing.

"What do you think?" Melvin asked Adara.

"I wouldn't build a summer cottage here, but I think this will do just fine to stage our troops." She then communicated with Penelope to communicate with the empress so she could see if there was anyone else around. The empress looked and didn't notice anything out of the ordinary. None of Rellik's troops were this far out, nor were any of the dragons. The area was safe.

Just as a precaution, Melvin put up a shield of concealment around the perimeter of the clearing and a bit further beyond, just in case. It was like camouflage. If anyone looked at the clearing from above or from the sides, it would appear empty; no sounds, no smells would go through the barrier. Immediately, Marlie leapt back to the mountain meadow and started bringing in Arias' special troops and supplies.

They didn't need to bring everyone in at once; troops could be transported directly from the mountain meadow to their needed positions. From this vantage point, they set up camp and began strategizing for the final assault on Rellik's castle.

Aria and her team were sent out to scout out the area. They were leapt to the same spot Melvin and Aria came to before, then stealthily came as close to the castle as they dared. They knew that Rellik did not have many troops here, but he had sufficient to defend the castle. They were surprised at what they saw. It was not what they expected at all. Instead of being a rundown, dark, sinister castle, though it was built from dark black Obsidian stone, it looked well taken care of. The castle was large. The outside had well-manicured grounds. It seemed odd to be in the middle of a dark forest.

At the heart of the great wall stood the main keep, nestled securely within. In its center rose a large round room with a domed roof surrounded by several buildings that stretched outward like spokes from a wheel. Towering above it all were massive black towers—one at each corner of the wall, and one in the middle of each side—each rising four spans high. They stood like silent sentries, watching the land beyond.

The entire castle was enclosed by a thick, towering wall made of polished black obsidian stone. Every block had been shaped and set with expert care, gleaming with a dark, glassy sheen. High atop the towers, flags of many colors fluttered in the wind.

There appeared to be only one entrance—a large gate at the front of the gate tower. As expected, it was heavily guarded. Troops were stationed along the walls, their watchful eyes scanning the surroundings. The guards were a diverse mix of beings: goblins, orcs, humans, leprechauns, sorcerers, and other malevolent creatures, all united under Rellik's command. What they didn't expect was that on top of each corner tower sat a very large, very fierce-looking dragon.

They would need a good plan if they were to get inside. About then, they saw two goblin guards walk past. Aria quickly disabled them, and she and another member of the team, named Mo, put on their armor to disguise themselves. Fortunately, the armor sort of fit, and the helmets covered most of their faces.

However, the stench was unbearable. While the rest remained hidden, Aria and Mo scouted the castle. With their stolen guard uniforms, they hoped slipping inside wouldn't be too difficult. Mimicking the sluggish, careless stride of the other guards, they approached the main gate. To their relief, they walked right in. The guards barely spared them a glance. It seemed intelligence wasn't a common trait among Rellik's forces. Inside, the castle wasn't heavily patrolled, and the few guards they did encounter appeared just as dull-witted. They appeared as large, mindless brutes. Some were orcs, some were goblins, and some were human. They were all arrayed in some sort of mismatched armor, and it looked like it did not fit properly. It looked like it was the armor of the armies they had defeated. The one thing they did have in common was a big R on the shoulder piece. Aria supposed it stood for Rellik. Aria and Mo were careful not to be seen.

Once they got inside, they were surprised at what they saw. This, too, was well taken care of. Gardens with well-landscaped areas, rose bushes, and other shrubs and flowers lined paths that meandered through grassy areas. A small pond was situated in one corner with fish swimming in it. There was even a large fountain with exquisitely carved fish with water coming out of the fish's mouths.

Once they managed to get into the castle proper, they saw that tapestries and murals were hung on the walls, of wizards, beautiful paintings of scenery, and battles depicting wizards blasting their opponents.

The furniture was well-maintained, dusted, and polished. Vases of freshly cut flowers adorned the tables in the hallways and rooms, while red and black carpets stretched across the floors. It bore a striking resemblance to Aria's castle back home. No matter how twisted Rellik was on the inside, he had an appreciation for beauty, aside from the chilling screams that echoed from the dungeon. Yet, despite its elegance, the castle exuded an oppressive darkness. There was hardly any light. The light it did have was from dimly lit torches. There was no natural sunslight. Of course, being in the shadows of the tree canopy, there wouldn't be any sunslight anyway. Despite this, he must still be defeated.

CHAPTER 61
TO THE DUNGEON

While searching the castle, Aria and Mo discovered a stairway leading down to the dungeon. The deafening screams from below sent chills down their spines. They followed the spiraling steps as they descended into what appeared to be a cavern.

The sight that greeted them was staggering. Unlike the structured elegance above, this was a vast, hollowed-out expanse carved from bedrock. The air was thick with moisture, stale and heavy. Luminous moss clung to the cavern walls, casting an eerie green glow, while droplets of water dripped rhythmically from the ceiling to the uneven stone floor. The cavern stretched beyond sight, towering nearly four spans high, with its far end lost in shadow.

Lining both sides of the cavern were countless cells, each carved into the rock. Inside every cell was a fully grown dragon, their immense forms crammed into enclosures too small for them to stand. Dozens—perhaps more—were shackled to the stone by massive iron chains. Aria clenched her jaw. Her swords couldn't cut through them, and the sheer number of captives was overwhelming.

Then, her eyes fell on a familiar figure—Watcher. The dragon who had spied for them on Rellik now lay in one of the cells, her once-proud form reduced to a frail shadow of itself. Though larger, she looked emaciated, a tragic remnant of the mighty creature she had once been.

As stealthily as they could, they snuck over to Watcher, hiding behind crates and in the shadows. Since the cells were for dragons, the bars were far enough apart that they were able to walk right through the bars. At once, Watcher took the defense and started "growling" at Aria and Mo, supposing them to be Rellik's guards. Looking around to see if any guards were looking their way, Aria quickly lifted her helmet, showing her beautiful face, yellow hair, and bright yellow eyes, in stark contrast to her surroundings. Immediately, Watcher recognized her and calmed down.

"What are you doing here?" Watcher queried using her dragon's communication with her large head lying on her enormous claws.

"We followed your directions on where to find the castle," Aria replied. She had learned this technique from Penelope. *"We are taking the offensive and bringing this war to Rellik. We are going to end this war once and for all."*

Watcher lifted her mighty head. *"Finally, this war will be over. And I can be set free. I would help you if I could, but I cannot. Rellik keeps us locked up down here. Not only that, he feeds us very little and chains us up. The only time he lets us leave is when we are to raze a city or attack an army. I can sometimes eat a cow or two before he calls us back. Then he brings us right back here. And we cannot defy him because of that awful bond. We MUST obey him."*

"I am sorry this is happening to you. You do not deserve this. Have faith in Deo, that he will give us the power, well, Melvin, the power to defeat this great evil, and you all will be freed. However, I am also sorry that he will have you fight us, and not all of you will survive. However, you may help us with information."

"I understand. Death would be a better alternative than this. I will give you what information I have, which is not a lot." She communicated. It seemed to be the consensus of all the dragons in the cavern.

"Hey Creyol, what are you doing down here?" a gruff voice came from the darkness.

Mo answered because it was easier for him to sound like a stupid, gruff man. He quickly thought up a retort. "We are making sure this dragon isn't causing any problems."

The other guard said, "How could these dragons cause any problems? They are in cages, chained up by magic chains. What could she possibly do?" as he walked into the cage with his partner close behind.

Aria quickly communicated with Watcher. *"Eat him!"*

"I would love to," she responded. And she did. While this happened, Aria spun and in one swift sweep, took out her blades and sliced the other guard into three pieces faster than the guard even knew what was happening.

"Another snack for you," Aria communicated. And the dragon ate him, armor and all. Then Aria swung her blade at the large chain. It bounced right off.

"That isn't going to work. These chains are enchanted. Nothing can cut them or break them. They will only open if Rellik opens them with magic." Watcher thought sadly.

"What happens if you do not return to the castle?" Aria asked.

"Pain, terrible pain." Then Watcher conveyed just a little of the pain that the dragons felt if they did not obey. Arias, whose body was in sharp pain. Like all of her muscles cramping at once. In an instant, it was gone, and relief flushed through her body. *"Sorry to have done that to you, but that's what it feels like, but not for just a moment, but for a long time. Sometimes revs."*

Aria now knew first-hand what the dragons went through, and this was just a small part. She must tell Melvin and her sister about the atrocities he commits against the mighty dragons. She asked if she could convey all this to Melvin so he could convey it to Penelope, then to the Empress, then to NöGard.

"That is not all. He does even worse things with other creatures and animals, even your own

people. He has them locked up all over the place. Some are in other areas of the dungeon. He MUST be stopped."

"Show everything you know to Melvin. And show him I have come and talked to you. We will be back as soon as we can," she communicated with even more disgust for the one they call Rellik.

Watcher said that she would, and she instantly did.

Megaspans away, Melvin received the message from Watcher, and was horrified at what she was conveying. But also relieved that they were ok. Then, instantly relayed it was relayed to Penelope, who in turn relayed it to the Empress, who relayed it to King NöGard. Something like this, you would call a game of telephone. But in this instance, it was pictures, not very easy to distort. And they felt the pain, just as the dragons do, just as Aria did.

Aria said her goodbyes to Watcher and told her that shortly, this war would be over, and she and the other dragons would be free. Then they continued exploring the castle.

As they continued to explore the large castle, they discovered one room that seemed pretty odd. It was a large, round room with a domed ceiling about 5 spans high. What was odd about it was that the ceiling was covered in copper plates, shined to a perfect, brilliant luster. Mirrors were hung on the wall in every direction. Aria didn't want to imagine what went on in this room. Soon, they headed back to where the rest of the group was hiding. The problem was, they weren't there. Aria and Mo searched the grounds for them, but they were nowhere to be found. Aria knew these to be expert fighters, probably the most capable fighters in the whole army. She knew this because she trained them.

Not only had Melvin and Adara trained them, but they had also been part of the elite group that trained with the elves. They were skilled, disciplined, and not easily defeated. A surprise attack seemed unlikely—yet there were no fallen enemies anywhere.

The absence of any signs of struggle was unsettling. Something was wrong.

With no other options, they turned back toward camp, their unease growing with every step.

This was no easy task. As soon as they reached the place where their team had gone missing, they were attacked by numerous guards. Thanks to their annums of training, Aria and Mo were able to defeat the incompetent guards easily. Aria danced around the guards, light as a feather on the balls of her feet. Her blades easily sliced through anything that came too close. As fast as the guards came, they fell. Twirling, ducking, and slicing, the blades followed through every motion that Aria made. She jumped and flipped over one falling guard as she pierced another through the heart. Mo was no less effective in dispatching the enemy as well. By the end of it, the bodies of the enemy were strewn all around the area.

"We better get out of here before more come," Mo said, breathing heavily.

"Yeah, I think they know we are here," Aria replied.

Then they stealthily made their way back to the camp, continuously making sure they were not being followed. They took a different route back to the camp, just to be sure.

When they got back to camp, they told Melvin, Adara, Brennon, and the other leaders what had happened. They told them about how large and immaculate Rellik's castle was, about the caverns underneath, and about how their team went missing. They also told them about the attack.

"Rellik knows we are here, or at least someone is here. He will increase his guards and troops around the castle. He will probably expect an attack." Melvin told the group. However, they already knew that.

"About time we get this war over with," Aria said. "I'm ready for some more action. Plus, we need to get my team back."

"Don't be in such a hurry, we need to see what we are dealing with." Adara retorted.

"From what you told me about your team going missing, there are only two possibilities that I can think of that would lead to this outcome. One is, your team fled." Melvin chimed in.

"I don't think so," Aria said. "They are highly specially trained, elite fighters, they wouldn't have gone down without a fight. It's not in their nature. You know firsthand how well they can fight."

"Yes, I know that, that's why I am ruling out that possibility," Melvin reassured her. "The second is Rellik has leapers as well."

"I never thought of that," Adara said. "They are so rare that it was hard to find the few we have."

"Marlie, can you go to the meadow and have all the leapers come here?"

"Yes, sir." She saluted and she leapt. Moments later, she came back. As did Sadrick, Gwendell, Cameron, and the two elves. Where is Amira?" Melvin asked.

"I didn't see her," Marlie said.

"I haven't seen her for a couple revs. I thought you may have sent her on a mission," Sadrick added. "No," Melvin said. "But she does like exploring."

"Let's double check," said Adara, who liked giving everyone the benefit of the doubt. "Have everyone check the meadow. Maybe she leapt back home until she was needed; she is my sister after all. She probably missed Mom and Dad."

"We will find out," Melvin said, gritting his teeth. Just like Adara, Melvin did not get angry very easily, but when he did, you better watch out. "Sadrick, do you know where the Palace is??"

"Yes, I do. I have been there a few times with Reicuas," He said.

"Good, go there and see if she has been there. The rest of you, go to the meadow and search for her." Melvin said.

All the leapers went to their destinations. About 10 minutes later, Sadrick came back to the clearing. "What's the news?" Melvin asked.

"Not good," Sadrick replied. "She wasn't at the Palace, but neither were the King nor the Queen. But she had been there. And no one saw them leave in a carriage or anything. I asked a few of the servants if they had seen them. No one has seen them for a few revs.

A chill ran down Melvin's spine. Fear crept in—a rare sensation for him.

"This is not good," he muttered, his voice tight with unease. "Go see if there's any information at the meadow."

"Yes, Sir," Said Sadrick. He saluted, then leapt.

"I think I know what may have happened with your team, Aria. If your sister is working for Rellik, either by her own volition or against her will, she probably leaped each of the members of your team to the dungeon, or all of them all at once. It takes a fraction of a second to touch someone and leap them somewhere. Then leap out. Even with your team's skills, it would be hard for them to stop her."

"We need to get them out!!" Aria said, seething. "I can't believe Amira would do something like that."

"I know she wouldn't. Something must have happened." Adara reassured her. "But remember, Mom and Dad are gone as well. No one saw them leave the palace. We will get them out."

CHAPTER 62
RESCUING THE TEAM

The rest of the leapers returned from the meadow, their expressions grim. They had searched Amira's bunk, the lake, and all her usual haunts. They questioned everyone they could find.

No one had seen her in several revs.

A sinking feeling settled over Melvin and Adara.

They were almost certain they knew what had happened, though they desperately hoped they were wrong.

But how could this happen?

They communicated with watcher to see if she, or any of the other dragons, had seen any sign of Arias' team. They said that they had not, but they had heard that some new prisoners had been locked up. They then talked to the leaders of the animals to see if anyone in the spy network had seen anything. The animals said that the team had been captured and sent to the dungeons with the other prisoners. There were many prisoners in the dungeons. So they weren't sure which part of the dungeon they were in.

They made a plan.

Aria smiled sadistic looking smile. Her eyes lit up. "Jail break. Sounds like fun."

Sadrick said, "If a leaper got them in, leapers would get them out."

Aria replied. "You are going to need all the help you can get. I have been in there before, I know what you would be up against. Plus, if their chains are enchanted like Watchers was, then we will have a hard time getting them out quickly."

Adara spoke up. "Aria, you have a knack for havoc, destruction, and mayhem."

"My specialty," she declared sadistically with a mischievous sparkle in her eye as she rubbed her hands together with palpable anticipation.

"But we can't break that chain. It's enchanted." Melvin added. "We need a magical weapon to break those chains."

"The Elves," Adara said. "They enchanted my blades, they can do the same for Aria's blades as well."

"Sounds like a plan." They all agreed.

One of the elf leapers leaped Aria to Illëngard and they enchanted her blades that would enable them to slice through anything. Any metal, dragon scales, and any magic. And they would always be sharp. They used the same method Melvin taught them.

However, Melvin couldn't do it—the Elves had forged the blades, and only they could enchant them so they could break the enchanted chains binding the prisoners.

Sadrick and Aria, wearing the armor they took off the guards, leapt into Watcher's cell in the dungeon to scout and find out where her team was being held. It was so dark in there that they could barely see. They had the Empress scan the area for any immediate threats. No one was hiding in the shadows.

Watcher was severely tortured for eating those two guards. She had cuts all around her body that were bleeding, and they had put a clamp on her mouth so she could not eat any more guards. Watcher conveyed the horrors inflicted upon her by the guards, igniting rage in both Aria and Sadrick. She then shared that she hadn't seen the rest of her team, but other animals might have. The mice and rats in the dungeons were part of the animal spy network. Sadrick leapt out of the dungeon to the base camp. He told Adara what was happening and that he needed her help to talk to the animals. He leaped back with Adara so she could talk to the animals. The mice told Adara where her team and the other prisoners were and that they would lead them there. Adara also saw the sorry state that Watcher and the other dragons were in, and vowed that they would kill Rellik and set them all free. She relayed this information to Penelope and the other dragons. Aria cut Watchers' chains and muzzle with her enchanted blades, but told her to appear as if she was still chained. Sadrick leapt Adara back to the base, then leapt back. Aria and Sadrick then followed the mice through the labyrinth of dungeons until they found her team.

Aria took off the goblin armor and felt much freer in her own leather armor. Since it was black, she could easily hide in the shadows. And since it was so dark in there, that would be easy. The team looked like death rolled over. They were cut and bruised, dirty, and looked as if they had been tortured. They had been stripped of their armor and their weapons, and most of their clothes which were in a pile about 3 spans from them. They were chained with the same enchanted chains that Watcher and the other dragons were chained up with. They dangled precariously, almost brushing against the ceiling of the shadowy, dank cavern. Their shackles were tight and cutting their wrists. Blood was running down their arms.

They informed Aria that it was Amira who had taken them. The revelation hit her like a gut punch, making her feel lightheaded and nauseous. Struggling to steady herself, she turned to Sadrick. "Go back and report to Adara," she ordered. Without hesitation, he leaped back to camp, relayed the situation to Melvin and Adara, and then returned to the dungeon.

There they found not only her team, but also others who had been captured. In cells cut into the walls of the cavern.

Aria used her enchanted blades to free her squad. She told them to go with Sadrick to base camp. They refused and said that they would make Rellik pay for what he has been doing.

They went over to the pile and put on their armor and took their weapons. While they were doing this Aria freed the other prisoners.

Sadrick leaped the other prisoners back to the mountain meadow, but they were detained until the Empress could look into their hearts to see their intentions. One was found to be a spy in case they were freed. He was dealt with promptly. The rest were treated for their wounds and could either stay with the army or could return home. Most chose to stay. Sadrick then leapt back to the dungeon.

Aria found Amira was shackled up in another cell by herself. The sight of her was too much to bear. Amira's once shining purple hair was grungy and matted. Her face once full of color, was now pale. She, too was shackled to the ceiling, but her shackles were different. Hers had a rod that went through her ankles and wrists, so she could not leap out of the dungeon, or it would rip her hands and feet off.

The princess, once regal and resplendent, had been diminished to mere tatters, a shadow of her former self. Her garments stripped away, to leave her scarcely clothed. Cuts and bruises marred her skin, and filth clung to her like a second skin, a cruel reminder of her suffering.

"What Happened?" Aria asked Amira with a sneer on her face.

"Rellik took mom and dad." She said through sobs "He said if I did not do as he said, that he would feed them to the dragons. So I did what he asked."

Aria knew Amira wouldn't betray them, so she calmed down. "Where are they?" Aria asked softly. Amira started crying uncontrollably.

"Let me guess, He fed them to the dragons anyway." She said with seething hatred.

Amira howled and screamed and cried and affirmed that that is what happened. "And made me watch." Then she screamed in rage some more.

No one in the castle thought anything of the screams because they were used to screams coming from the dungeon. Aria communicated through Watcher to the rest to have the Empress see if Amira was telling the truth and had any malicious intent. It was communicated back that there was none; she was telling the truth. Aria swiftly cut the chains off her little sister. Then had Sadrick leap her back to the staging camp so Melvin could take the rest of the chains off from through her wrists and feet and heal the wounds.

This infuriated Aria. She was enraged at this sadistic warmonger before, but this blew that right out of the water. Seeing her sister in this condition, as well as the other prisoners, not only that, but the mighty dragons and other animals that he had tortured. It just broke her heart. But the news that he essentially kidnapped their parents and fed them to his dragons was just too much. In that instant, something inside her broke, a switch had flipped. She was playing at being sadistic before, but now complete rage had taken over. Rellik was going to pay for what he had done and what he was planning to do. Revenge was the only thing on her mind. Nothing was going to stop her from killing this asshole lunatic and destroy his army.

She was skilled at stealth, and her black leather armor would help her blend in with the darkness. She quickly released any other prisoners she found. Those who would not or could not fight, Sadrick leaped back to the mountain meadow. Those who could fight were given weapons so they could fight back. With Aria in the lead, they swept through the dungeon, cutting down anyone who would oppose them. Since she somewhat knew the layout of the castle. She led her team and the others out, slicing their way through any enemy who came their way.

They called it *Dancing with Death*. Aria and her team carved their way through wave after wave of enemies, blades flashing in a lethal rhythm. Pure hatred burned in Aria's yellow eyes as she moved like a whirlwind of steel blades, slicing and weaving through the chaos.

Heaps of corpses—goblins, orcs, humans, and creatures of darkness—littered the blood-soaked carpets of the shadowed castle. Yet, despite the slaughter, Rellik was nowhere to be found. If she had seen him, she wasn't sure she could have struck the final blow—her enchanted blades still could not kill a shadow. That was Melvin's burden. But she could do the next best thing. Aria and her squad obliterated anyone and anything that came their way. They were close to the outside gate. Aria made sure her squad was out, then followed behind. Just before she could escape, she was struck by lightning.

Aria opened her eyes. A figure in a cloak stood before her. Well, it appeared to be a man, he did not have a face, or arms or anything, just swirling dark mist.

"Hello Aria." He laughed maniacally. "Did you really think you could escape?" His voice was smooth and almost calming.

"You will die you SCUMBAG!!" This was the man, the evil monster they were after. She thought quickly and sent a message to any dragon available to relay a message, and hoped the animals were listening as well. She intended to find out what this sadistic monster was planning. *What are you planning to do with me?* She thought to herself.

"Eventually I will die, yes, but not this rev, and not by your hands." Then Rellik said coolly, menacingly. "I let them escape. They are nothing. Bait. What I was after was… Well, you will do. One of the big three." He laughed again. Interestingly enough, he had a soothing voice. It sounded like someone she knew, but she could not put her finger on who. "Do you not think I know your plans? You plan to attack my castle, my home. Which is fine. I am going to attack your base in the mountains, and your camp is not far from here. Then you will have nothing left. Your little insurrection will be over. I will then take Lilenhamür and make the Empress my slave. Then I will be the ruler of Arion and then the world. You cannot stop me."

"No, I can't, but Melvin can." She said matter-of-factly, the hatred burning in her eyes.

"Do you think so? Do you think he has what it takes to defeat me? The greatest wizard who has ever lived?" he said calmly. Like, all this was just a nuisance. Like they were opponents in a children's game.

"He has more power than you will ever have!" she spat, blood dripping from her chin. Only then did she notice the warmth of it, the sting of her wounds. And the cold bite of shackles around her wrists, just like the others.

 "Yes, so I have heard. But he does not know how to use his power. He is afraid to use his power. If he even hesitates for one split second, I will end him." Then he laughed again. "I want you to do something for me."

"I will never do anything for you." She said her hatred was boiling over.

"Oh, I think you will." He said softly the coldness of him filling the dark dungeon. "Scream!!" then he let his magic flow through his shadow body and lightning shot from where his hands would be.

This hit Aria like she had been kicked in the gut by a borlog. All of her muscles cramped up at once. Her heart felt like a thousand needles had punctured it. This was more pain than she had ever felt before in her life. How was she feeling this? Wasn't her armor supposed to protect her? Then she noticed it. She wasn't wearing her armor. Or any of her weapons. She wasn't wearing anything. "Oooh," she said softly, "You are going to pay when I get out of here." He did not know she was also a master of escape.

Rellik had mastered the art of torture, wielding lightning with surgical precision, enough to inflict excruciating pain without delivering death. He could break anyone, force them to spill their deepest secrets. But Aria was not just anyone. Little did he know that this would not work on Aria. She had practiced scenarios for this very reason. The agony only fueled her fury, sharpening her resolve to destroy this monstrous being. She gritted her teeth, rage burning hotter than the pain—until the darkness finally swallowed her, and she lost consciousness.

CHAPTER 63

ARIAS REVENGE

Aria woke to darkness. The dim light barely illuminated anything beyond a span in front of her. A dank, putrid smell burned her nostrils. How long had she been out? Minutes? Hours? Revs? Moons? She had no way of knowing.

Water dripped in the distance, the only sound breaking the eerie silence. The screams had ceased— she had freed the other prisoners. But were the dragons still caged?

A chill ran through her as she became aware of her state. She was clad in nothing but ragged scraps barely covering her breasts and loins. Her clothes and weapons were gone. Perhaps the guards had finally learned their lesson and hidden them.

Aria's shackles were pulling her swollen, bleeding wrists from the ceiling, causing her arms and torso to stretch in agonizing pain. She thought of the positive, at least she would be limber. The shackles on her ankles were stretching her leg towards the ground. Her muscles felt like they were tearing. Not only that, but it felt like some of her ribs were broken.

Agony consumed her. Searing pain shot through her arms, legs, and torso, each pulse of it more unbearable than the last. Her heart felt... wrong.

Damaged. The lingering effects of the lightning coursing through her had left something broken inside her, something she couldn't quite name.

She could only imagine what her team—and her sister—had endured.

Then, through the haze of pain, a memory surfaced. The training they had back home. Most dismissed it as unnecessary, but Aria had insisted they be prepared for anything.

Now, that preparation was all she had.

She forced herself to breathe slowly, deeply, fighting against the instinct to tense up. She willed herself to relax, to focus inward, to shut out the agony. She concentrated on her muscles, her bones—on regaining control of her own body.

She practiced her flexibility. It was a good thing she was double-jointed. She dislocated her thumbs from their sockets, making her hands narrower, and pulled them through the shackles, scraping a lot of her skin from her hands. She clenched her jaw so she wouldn't scream, but her captors would expect that. She wouldn't give the satisfaction. When she freed her hands, they throbbed, but that would not stop her. She was able to do the same with her feet. Slowly and carefully, she maneuvered her feet so they would come out of the shackles. When they were free, in the darkness, she felt her way with her hands and crawled to the front of the alcove cell. Even with the glowing plants on the far walls, she could barely make out the bars. She located the door of the cell, and it was locked. She did not have any way to pick the lock, so the only thing she could do was squeeze through the bars. They were just wide enough that she could get through.

Aria steeled herself. This would not be easy, but she knew she could do it.

Taking a slow breath, she positioned her head carefully. She flattened one ear, then the other, inching forward. The space was too tight, but she forced herself to stay calm. With a final push, she barely managed to squeeze her head through.

Slowly, she dislocated her shoulders out of their sockets and slipped her arms and shoulders through. There she stopped. Her ample breasts would be a challenge. She gently pushed them as flat as she could. One by one, she squeezed them through scraping her skin, causing them to bleed. Finally, she shimmied the rest of her thin, lean, though muscled torso through the bars. Then she twisted around the bar, dislocated her hip joints, and squeezed them through scraping her hips, buttocks, and thighs as she went. She had to grit her teeth not to scream from the pain. Then she squeezed her legs through. Finally, out of the cell, in tremendous pain, she put her ball joints in her arms and hip joints back in her sockets. She was free. Her eyes had adjusted to the darkness, and she could see about 3 spans around her. She found another alcove without any bars, so she crawled into the darkness and caught her breath. As she rested, she calmed her mind and thought of what she could do. She got an inspiration.

Aria contacted Watcher and asked her if she was still in her cell. The answer was affirmative. Then Aria asked her to communicate with the animals to help her find her armor and escape. About five minutes later, some rats came up to her and motioned for her to follow them. She supposed that these were the same ones that led her to her team. The rats led her through one cavern to another, then to an alcove. She saw her clothes at the back of the barred alcove. It was locked. She asked the rats if they could get her her swords, and they did. She asked them if they knew if anyone was about. They chittered and shook their heads. She used her enchanted swords to cut the lock off of the door and went in to get her armor and other weapons. Once she was dressed, she thanked them. Was she imagining, or did they seem to smile at her? Since she had explored this dungeon before, she sort of knew where she was. She stealthily made her way back to Watcher's cell. Since she wore black leather armor, she could remain relatively hidden in this dark dungeon. When she got there, she thanked Watcher for her assistance and asked her if all of the dragons here were bound to Rellik.

Watcher told her that not all of them were. Some he kidnapped after they were born he even kidnapped adolescent dragons. Those he used for breeding. However he would still always keep them chained up.

Aria was horrified. She asked Watcher where they were located. Watcher stated that they were all over the caverns. But mostly in the breeding area. Aria thanked her again and said that she would free them. Watcher said that most of them would appreciate that, but not all. Some of the male breeding dragons didn't mind what Rellik made them do. But the females would love freedom. Watcher told her that she would let her know which ones to free and which ones not to.

As Aria Stealthily snuck through the cavernous dungeon, Watcher would tell her which dragons to free. Watcher notified them of what was happening before Aria arrived at their cells. Aria cut the bars and chains with her enchanted swords, and the dragons escaped. If they wished, they could join the Arion Army, which many did. Finally, when all the prisoners that could be freed were freed, she headed up through the castle. This time, she would be ready if Rellik attacked her again. With the adrenaline rushing through her body, like a whirlwind of blades, she advanced through the castle, dispatching any enemy that came her way. Though her body was tired and in agony, her adrenaline and her hatred for Rellik kept her going. She danced through the hallways, becoming one with her weapons as if they were extensions of her arms, spreading death and dismemberment as she went. She looked into the throne room and saw Rellik standing there. Even though she wanted to kill this man more than anything else in the world right now, she knew that she was no match for him.

Even her enchanted blades couldn't kill a smoky shadow. Rellik was beyond her reach, for now. She would have to leave him to Melvin.

At last, she reached the great door at the front of the castle. Every step was cautious. She expected Rellik to strike again. But he didn't.

As she exited the castle, she saw Melvin standing outside. A sadistic smile spread across her lips.

"He's all yours, he's in his throne room," she said, voice cold, full of hatred. "Use the domed room."

Without another word, she turned and sprinted toward the base camp, cutting down any enemy that dared cross her path.

CHAPTER 64
ANSWERS

Back in the clearing, while Aria was escaping the dungeon, Melvin examined Amira's predicament. He contemplated how to remove the shackles restraining her.

The rusted metal rods pierced her wrists and were attached on the other side. This was something he had never encountered before. It wasn't like an arrow or knife, or javelin that could just be pulled out. The rusted metal had to be cut out, not only that, it was still magically enchanted, so it could not be cut by an ordinary implement or saw. The only one he knew that had one was Aria. And he was sure she was busy escaping the castle. This had to be done delicately.

Amira was very distraught, so Melvin had to calm her down so he could get the manacles off. First he had the healers very delicately wash away the blood and grime off of her wrists and arms. Then he studied the manacles. There was no break in them. It was like they were one piece of metal, welded at the molecular level.

Melvin knew what he had to do. He calmed himself and focused on the metal. He examined it down to the atomic level, studying how its structure held together. Carefully, he broke the bonds at the rod, then the ones securing the round part. With precision, he removed the manacle and slid the rod through Amira's wrist.

He repeated the process for her other wrist and ankles. Though he was gentle, the process still caused Amira great pain—but she would gladly endure it if it meant shedding these vile restraints and taking her revenge on Rellik.

Then Melvin healed Amira's wounds. This would take some time for the nerves, tendons and muscles to regrow. This intricate healing required precision, and he didn't think that other healers would be able to get down to the cellular level of the human body as he was able to. Plus, this was one of his dearest friends and would not leave this to anyone else. After several hours, the healing was complete. He silently thanked Deo for the ability to do this.

Once Amira was healed, had a bath and a fresh set of clothes put on, Adara came over to her. She was very upset with her sister.

"What Happened? I need some answers." She said sternly.

Amira broke down and cried and cried. Melvin came up to Adara and put his hand on her shoulder, and whispered in her ear. "I am very upset with her too, but I don't think this is the time or the manner to talk to her. She has been through a lot."

Amira explained what happened through sobs. "I was visiting mom and dad for the weekend, and a strange man came to the castle. He said he was a wizard from the Empress and had some important news for them about the war, but needed to see them in private.

This was an immediate red flag for me, and I told Mom and Dad as much. I didn't see what he looked like—he was completely covered by a hooded robe. For some reason, I was allowed to be there. The meeting was going fine until, suddenly, everything went dark.

 "Next thing I know I woke up shackled to the wall in Rellik's Dungeon. Mom and dad were there too. They were shackled as well. Rellik tried to get information from them, but they didn't tell them anything, so he said if I didn't help him, he would feed mom and dad to the dragons. So I did because I didn't want anything to happen to mom and dad. He knew Aria's team was there, so he made me leap them to the dungeon where he imprisoned them as well. He was really after you two. But he said Aria would do as bait. After I got her team, he fed mom and dad to one of the dragons anyway. A really big nasty one they called Bloodlust. They were but a small snack to him."

Then she started sobbing uncontrollably again. Adara comforted her sister. "We have had a run in with Bloodlust. Nasty bugger, but we defeated him in the end. But I have another thought. How was he able to see past your enchantment? If he can get Mom and Dad" Adara said seething "Then who knows who he can get to next. Maybe your mom or even the Empress."

"He would not be able to get to the Empress. She will know if anyone on his side gets anywhere near Lilenhamür. As for my mom, I put an enchantment on her as well. Besides, as she told me, she knows how to take care of herself. All of this was to get to me and you, because he thinks he can get rid of us, and if he does, he thinks that our forces would just stop fighting him." Melvin said deep in thought. " We defeated his largest dragon and the goons that kidnapped the Thrall children. So he knows we can beat him. So he has to resort to kidnapping little girls. However, I was thinking dear," he looked at Adara, "With all of your ability honey, I don't think you can do much to him. Shadows and smoke don't burn. Sure you can make light, but he can always slink into a corner shadow somewhere. He has to be defeated another way."

"I think you are right" Adara said, putting her hand on his broad shoulder. "I am not much good in a fight against him. I will lead the troops here. You go defeat him. This is what you were born for. This is what you were meant to do. Only you can defeat Rellik. Hopefully Deo will grant you the knowledge and power to know how to do it."

"So if he wants me, he will get me. This ends NOW!!" Melvin had had enough. This went from protecting the Empire, to personal. Melvin was done strategizing, done with planning. Now it was time for action. He loved the King and Queen like they were his own parents. And what Rellik was doing to everyone else had to stop.

Not only did Melvin feel this way, but so did Adara and Amira, and from what was communicated to him, so did Aria. And everyone else in the Empire. You thought Adara had a fire in her heart before, but now, it was a burning inferno.

The animals said that Aria had escaped the dungeon and was on a warpath through the castle. Dead bodies lay everywhere. Melvin smiled. That sounded like Aria, alright. Rellik had messed with the wrong family.

Melvin called on Penelope, to call the dragon army. He told the leapers to leap in the rest of the troops and weapons and be ready for a battle. Then, because it was a long journey from Dragonia, he was going to have the Leapers leap in the dragons from their as well and told Penelope to show them where NöGard's castle was.

Penelope informed him that that was not necessary; they had other ways of traveling great distances in a short amount of time. He informed the animals that they were going to attack.

Whoever was going to fight, they better be ready. He was going to pay Rellik a visit. He was going alone. He already knew no one was left in the castle. This was War!!!

Chapter 65
Rallying The Troops

Once the troops were assembled, he addressed them. He climbed on top of a supply wagon so he could see the majority of the troops. There were warriors, wizards, leapers, animals, and even some dragons. Adara stood by his side.

"Men, and Women. Soldiers. Wizards," He called out loudly using his magic to amplify his voice. Another thing he learned from Reicuas. "We are about to go into battle against a most formidable foe. We are not going to sabotage supply lines, not going against a weakened foe. We are going against a vast army of the most vile creatures. Orcs, Goblins, Ogres and the like. Some much larger and more powerful than our own troops. Warlocks and witches, some which have more magic than our wizards. He has hundreds of Dragons at his command. Fortunately we have the dragons from Dragonia on our side. Which are vastly larger, and superior to his.

But we also have something he does not have—a cause. Melvin paused and looked over the vast army assembled there. The message was being relayed to the troops' minds still in the Mountain Meadow via the dragons.

"Rellik thinks he has a cause. He thinks that Wizards should rule the world. He thinks that *HE* is the greatest wizard, so he should rule. And cause everyone on Arion to be subject to him. Well, I do not agree. I think he is a tyrant. His cause is NOT just." He raised his voice, he raised his staff in the air, his Aura shone brightly. "We also have a cause. Ours is a righteous cause. We fight, not for tyranny, but for freedom. We fight for our families. Mothers, fathers, wives, husbands, and children. We fight for our freedom—to be free from tyranny. We fight for our religion. And we fight for Deo." Cheers went up from the crowd.

"I am going to go face Rellik alone. That is my destiny, it is what I am here for. My lovely wife, Commander Adara, will lead you in the fight against Rellik's vast army. Be valiant."

Next Adara stood front and center. Her red leather body armor hugged her body and gave her the look of power. Just standing there the troops were in awe. The mighty Adara was about to lead them into the most important battle of their lives, of the history of Arion. She commanded their attention, not by her words but by her actions. She stood straight and tall. She willed her magic to flow through her. She told her magic particles it was time to use her power. Magic flowed from her DNA to her eyes as the took on the look of burning embers.

Next, her magic surged through her hair, turning it into flames. She looked like a human torch. Then she told Melvin he might want to jump down from the wagon—and he did so. Her whole body erupted into flames, just as it had when Melvin was having his crisis.

"Troops," She said in a commanding voice. "You all know who I am. And during this time I have gotten to know many of you. Many of you are my friends. What Melvin said is correct. We are in a fight for our families, our Empire, our homes and Deo." She looked around. The faces in the crowd were of awe. Many have heard of the power she possessed, but very few had actually seen it.

Adara put out her flames and continued. "We are about to face one of the most terrible armies in the history of the Arion Empire." She spoke loud and strong. The women in the army were inspired by her strength. "I will lead you in this fight. Unfortunately many of you will not make it through, though I will do my best to enable as many of you as possible return home to your families. Remember what we are fighting for. May the power of Deo be with you as we rid our land of this evil tyrant." Then she hopped off the wagon and gave her husband a kiss for good luck, though she knew that he didn't need it. "Go. Defeat Rellik. I will take care of things here." She said. Then Melvin ran off towards the castle.

The troops cheered as Melvin left, chanting his name. They all knew he was the only one with power sufficient to defeat Rellik and bring an end to this war

CHAPTER 66
THE FINAL BATTLE

Sadrick leapt with Melvin to where he had leapt into Aria's group. Then, Melvin walked up to the castle. No one tried to stop him—they knew they couldn't. He passed the guards, walked through the gates, the gardens, and into the castle proper. He thought to himself, *For an evil tyrant, this sure is a beautiful castle.*

As he was about to knock on the door, Aria came out of the door. She looked like she had been through a war. That's because she had. Her yellow hair was all in disarray, she was bruised and bleeding. Scrapes were on her face and she was bleeding through her black leather, so the rest of her must be wounded as well. As she stepped through the doorway she smiled sadistically and said. "He's all yours, He's in his throne room, Use the domed room." Melvin didn't know what this meant, but he was sure he would find out. Within her gaze, he discerned not mere anger, but a tempest of unbridled loathing. It was kind of how he felt at the moment. Then, she ran off and continued to slay the enemy as she went.

Melvin walked through the huge doors. It was dark, very dark. Only lit by a few torches on the walls that emitted a soft eerie purple glow. Of course, Melvin thought, Rellik is a shadow, he needs it dark. Melvin adjusted his sight to see in the dark. He saw the aftermath of Arias' revenge through the hallways. Humans, orcs, goblins, ogres, warlocks, witches, leprechauns, and every other evil creature lay dead, dismembered, or decapitated. Somehow he knew where the throne room was, as if he was being led there. As he walked towards the throne room, Melvin stepped over and around or through dead bloody bodies strewn throughout the castle. *She does her job very well*, he thought. He entered the throne room. It was not what he expected at all. It was lavish.

Tall, dark obsidian pillars flanked both sides of the large hall. Large tapestries lined the walls, depicting scenery—wizards, woods, mountains, meadows, and mighty dragons. A dark blue carpet ran the length of the hall up to the dais. Melvin walked straight to a robed figure standing before a meticulously carved wooden throne.

"At last you come. I wondered how long it would take you to come." The figure said smoothly, his soft voice lulling Melvin in. He thought he recognized the voice, but couldn't remember where from.

"You will pay for what you have done." Melvin said as his anger rose. "You fed Adara's parents to your pathetic dragon, that we defeated once already. And that was after, Amira did what you asked. You do not deserve to rule anyone or anything. Rellik, your reign of terror ends here." He said seething.

"Reign of terror you say?" the saying just rolled off the tongue. "All I want is peace. It's you who oppose me. If those I took by force would have joined me willingly, and acknowledge me as their lord and master, there would have been no need for bloodshed. Your wife's parents were casualties of war, collateral damage, a means to an end. Are all the lives that your sister in law took, are those worth any less than a king and queen?" He spoke softly still.

"What kind of coward kidnaps people, especially children, and enslaves others? And you call razing cities and towns with dragons peace? You call enslaving people, animals, mighty dragons, and other creatures to do your bidding peace? You think the countless lives that you sent to the afterworld weren't just as precious? I call it psychotic!" by this time Melvin's blood was boiling. How deranged must this man be to believe everyone must serve him.

"I do not share your beliefs in that matter. If they would submit peacefully, there would have been no bloodshed." Rellik said calmly. "Now give up your feeble little uprising. You cannot win this war. I will annihilate your pathetic little army with my vast numbers. I out number you 100 to 1. I have hundreds of dragons, and hundreds of thousands of warriors and sorcerers who out match your wizards from Wazervĭl, who at this moment are surrounding your little camp and will destroy every single one of them. As I told your sister in law, there is no way you can win."

"We will see about that. It looks like Aria did a pretty good job with the ones in the castle."

Rellik laughed manically. "Those? Those weren't warriors, those weren't fighters, those, were servants. The weakest of the bunch, the ones who were afraid to go to the front lines. A child could have defeated them. Wait till she, or any of your other army comes across my real warriors. You wouldn't stand a chance." Then Rellik laughed again and said softly but more firm with malice in his voice. "Give up or die."

"Never. You fight for domination. You fight to rule and subject those you conquer to slavery. We fight for freedom. For our homes, our lands, our families. And our Deo!!" Melvin responded.

"It is my right to rule. Wizards should rule over the less powerful, and I am the greatest wizard." Then he showed a fantastical show of lightning in the throne room. Lightning struck all over the room, loud claps of thunder echoed throughout the hall. Then a tremendous BOOM shook the castle. Then darkness filled the room. Dark smoke and shadow reached every crevice. Melvin could not see anything. "Your pitiful army will be defeated. I pulled my vast army here to contend with yours. Once you are wiped out, I will send my forces back to the cities and towns that we occupied. And take back the ones that you think you liberated. You did not liberate those towns, I let you have them so I could use my forces in other places."

"That was a mistake, Rellik. We have infinitely more power and ability than your forces do. Besides we have the mighty dragon warriors from Dragonia. Your ill prepared dragons are no match for them."

Now this whole time Melvin was thinking strategy. He had never faced Rellik himself before so he didn't know what to expect, but now that he faced him he was formulating a plan. Rellik was arrogant, that was for sure. Confident in himself and his army. But he didn't know

Melvin's abilities. Didn't know his armies abilities. And most of all, didn't know Adara's and Aria's abilities. If this is how he wanted it, this is how it was going to be.

Melvin knew he couldn't use most of his abilities because they would simply pass through Rellik. However, as he sent his consciousness through the shadowy figure, he sensed something—somewhere within that smoke and darkness, there was a man. Under the right conditions, the shadow and mist would coalesce into a solid human form.

"WOW, I'm impressed." Melvin said sarcastically with a smirk on his face. Then immediately dispersed the darkness with light from his staff then produced his own lightning just as Rellik did. "What else do ya got?" Melvin asked taunting. He sent a whirlwind toward Rellik, that surrounded him.

Melvin heard Rellik laughing and said "Is that all you got? Is that the best you can do? I thought you were Melvin the Magnificent. More like Melvin the Moron." Then lightning shot from the smoky whirlwind. Melvin expected this and absorbed it with his staff. He thought about what would work. The only thing that dispels a shadow is light. So he formed a light orb, like a bomb, and threw it into the whirlwind where it exploded into a fantastical display of bright light. Then the whirlwind disappeared and there was a scream, then silence.

Did I really defeat Rellik? Was it really that easy? Melvin wondered? Melvin stood a while in the silence. Then all of a sudden he heard maniacal laughter. "You won't defeat me that easily." rang through the halls. The game of hide and seek had begun.

Aria finally arrived back at the base camp. Sadrick watched as she ran toward the camp, then leapt the rest of the way. Once she landed, she turned to her sisters. "What did I miss?"

"Nothing much yet," Adara said. "Melvin got the manacles off of Amira and she was healed. She told us everything that happened with mom and dad. Then Melvin and I rallied the troops and Melvin headed out to face Rellik."

"Yes, I know. I saw him at the door of the castle." Aria said with a sinister look on her face.

"By the way," Adara continued "How exactly did you escape that dungeon? I was sure you would, but how did you? I thought you might be chained up like Amira was."

Aria responded in a cold tone towards her younger sister. "I didn't have rods going through my wrists."

"Cool it," Adara commanded her sister. "As I said, she told us what happened and it was not her fault."

"Yes, I know. She told me when I rescued her."

"Go get healed" Adara commanded. "We need you healthy so you can go kill more of his army."

"Yes, Sir." Aria saluted. Then headed for the healers tents.

An alarm rang out. Warlocks and dark wizards were casting spells at the barrier Melvin erected around the base camp. Orcs and goblins tried to slash their way through the barrier to no avail. The leapers brought in the rest of the army from the mountain meadow and they surrounded Rellik's Army. General Thalion said in a loud voice, to whom the thought were the leaders of Rellik's armies, "We have you surrounded, and more are coming as we speak. Lay down your weapons and we will let you to go in peace. This is not your war, but Rellik's pursuit of domination. If you wish to fight we will slay you until you are extinct."

Though he knew most of these troops were mindless brutes, their leaders were intelligent—driven by the promise of great wealth and power they craved. And for these reasons, they fought.

The leapers leapt in the rest of the troops and armaments. All the soldiers put their hands on their fellow soldiers' shoulders, and they all leapt in at once.

Adara was out front. Her hair was ablaze, her eyes shining brightly the color of burning coals, the rest of her body aflame from the powerful magic surging through her casting an eerie glow that illuminated the darkness around her. She emerged as if the fury of Hell itself had been unleashed upon the world. And indeed, it had. She wore red leather battle armor that hugged her form, each piece intricately designed and etched with ancient runes that pulsed with energy. Now I told you you didn't want to see Adara mad, because this is what happens when she is mad. Her troops had to stay clear of her wake. She exuded raw, untamed power, and the ground seemed to tremble beneath her feet as she advanced—a harbinger of doom and destruction. This was why she had been chosen as the Empire's commander.

Adara started with fire darts and fire balls. Those she could fire off in rapid succession and could aim them so as to not accidentally hit her own troops, but she could not get enough to make a dent in Rellik's forces. Warning her troops to stay behind her, she switched tactics and sent out wave after wave of dragons fire and caught the enemy on fire, that they could not extinguish. That, in turn, ignited others, and the fire swept through the ranks of Rellik's troops. As if that weren't enough, she unleashed flames from her hands like a flamethrower. Rellik's troops fell by the hundreds. But then, they sent in their larger brutes, who were somewhat immune to fire. Just as she had done in the mountain pass, she ignited a spark within their bodies. This time she caused it to grow, and she cooked them from the inside she did this all while the battle was raging on around her. On and on through Rellik's troops she blasted, heated, exploded, and any other fire method that came to her mind. When she was tired of using fire, she pivoted and drew her crimson fiery blade and began a blood bath to match her sisters.

Aria, with hatred in her eyes, threw caution to the wind. She danced. Blades swirling, striking blow after deadly blow. Her yellow hair flew in circles as she dismembered any that would come against her. Her form and speed were so quick, you could not see how fast her enchanted blades were slicing through the enemy. You would think it was a beautiful art form if it wasn't for the fact that once again she was leaving dead, bleeding, bodies in her wake. She was, at this moment *Taila-Atria"* as the elves called her or *Blade Dancer,* the Master of Death.

Once Amira was done bringing in Arions' soldiers, she leapt by the enemy, touched one or two and leapt them into Rellik's dungeon, or the middle of the ocean, or a lake, or the top of a mountain. She did this in rapid succession. She was so fast that the enemy did not know what was happening and did not have time to react. She tried to leap the larger of the orcs far away from the battle. She even managed to get some of Rellik's dragons. She tried to focus on the fire and acid breathing dragons. These, she left in the middle of the ocean. And I mean *IN* the ocean, about 20 megaspans below. The other leapers were doing the same as well.

The wizards were not faring well. Wizards were casting spell after spell. Which were mostly being counteracted by the warlocks, witches and hags. Some earth wizards were able to open up holes in the earth and swallow up the enemy. Water wizards blasted the enemy with water, air wizards caused them to be taken away in cyclones, or blasted them with compressed air. But on the other hand, Rellik's sorcerers and witches were doing the same types of things.

Dragons clashed in an aerial battle above. The seasoned, battle-hardened dragons from Dragonia tore through Rellik's dragon army, which consisted mostly of adolescent, untrained dragons used primarily for razing cities. However, Bloodlust was an exception—he dominated most of the Arion dragons, sending them crashing to the ground.

The wood elves from Illëngard were shooting arrows from the trees dispatching many of Rellik's ' troops, till nature wizards on Rellik's side turned the wooden arrows into flowers. Others were fighting toe to toe with enchanted weapons and armor with the other warriors.

Wizard Brennon was fighting the warlocks with his nature magic. He was growing plants and vines and having them grab the other magic users and tie them in vines, and others, he caused roots to grab and pull them under the earth. He caused giant man-eating plants to grow that would capture the enemy and slowly digest them. One group he decided to turn into, of all things, sunflowers. However, to his sorrow, one warlock wielded reflective magic. Many were transformed, but the spell bounced back, turning him into a sunflower as well. In the future, people came from far and wide to seek wisdom from the wise sunflower. During the battle, Arion's troops advanced towards the Obsidian castle. Outside the castle, the battle was raging. The Ogres were advancing on the cavalry, swatting them like pesky flies, sending them flying.

Chapter 67
Girl Vs. Dragon

After a lengthy battle that lasted most of the rev, the majority of the enemy forces were either subdued or dead, except for a few dragons and those who had pursued Melvin to the castle. Bloodlust, the mighty red dragon, twice the size of the others, was locked in aerial combat. Aria fired enchanted arrows at it, but they bounced harmlessly off its scales. The Arion Army shot nets and fired harpoons at it to no avail. This was the monster that had eaten her parents. This was the monster that had razed so many cities and villages and killed so many people. Her sole purpose was revenge. She hated this dragon with everything she had, she would kill this dragon or die trying. When they finally got their attention. Aria stood in a clearing and yelled at it.

"Hey, you stupid dragon, come and get me. Then I will kill you." Aria screamed, her voice full of loathing, her anger at its peak.

The dragon was not afraid of a puny human. He had eaten hundreds of them in the past few revs. The dragon swooped down to catch Aria in its claws. She dodged its claws, rolled to the right, and with her amazing agility grabbed the dragon's tail spikes and swooped up onto the tail, avoiding getting impaled by the other spikes. Slowly, carefully, she climbed the dragon's massive tail. The dragon, knowing what she was doing, beat his mighty wings and climbed higher into the sky, weaving and swiping its enormous back and forth, trying to get Aria off. Drawing upon her expertise, rigorous training, and natural talent, she not only maintained her grip but also ascended the formidable dragon's spiky tail and back, deftly navigating from one protruding spike to the next. Pain shot through her body from her recent escape from the dungeon, but it would not weaken her resolve to exact revenge on the beast.

Still climbing, the dragon beat his mighty wings. He tried to reel back and see if he could bite or breathe fire at Aria. She nimbly hung onto the spikes and climbed to the side. The fire barely missed singeing the top of her hair. Throughout her arduous ascent, Aria's limbs ached with the exertion of each precarious step. Her muscles screamed in protest, and her fingers throbbed from clutching the massive spikes. The relentless wind whipped against her. With each labored breath, the sting of cold air filled her lungs, and the lactic acid build-up in her weary muscles was a constant reminder of the physical toll the climb was taking. Yet, it was the sharp sting of pain that kept her alert, the fatigue that tested her resolve, and through it all, she thought of why she was doing this. For her family, for her home, and now for Wizard Brennan—whom she had come to love since meeting him at Lilenhamür—Aria's spirit refused to falter as she climbed up the dragon's back toward its head. In the end, harnessing her talent and the knowledge imparted by the Elves, she ascended the beast's neck to confront its colossal head. Having gleaned the rudiments of the draconic language from Penelope, Melvin, and Adara, she was not yet their equal but could communicate the essentials. With a commanding presence, she addressed the dragon.

"I am Aria, Commander of the Empress's elite guard. If you do not stop your attack, I will be forced to kill you. You killed my parents. Prepare to die!!" She said with malice.

The mighty dragon replied with a smirk, *"I know who you are, tiny human. You do not scare me. I am Bloodlust, the fiercest dragon in Arion. You cannot hurt me. I have destroyed towns, villages, and even large cities. I have sent many people, animals, and even other dragons to their deaths. Many have tried and failed to kill or even capture me. My scales are resistant to fire and harder than diamondite. You cannot stop me! Even your fire user cannot stop me. What do you think you are going to do to me?"*

Then Aria recalled a memory. And conveyed it to the dragon. She was with the elves. They had made a special sword for her, light but strong, perfectly balanced. She remembered the elves enchanting it. This sword would penetrate anything. Any armor, any metal, any enchantment. Aria conveyed another memory of her slicing through dragon Golden dragon's scales with the sword. Then, through the black dragon, the green dragon, red dragon. All pierced through and sliced easily with her sword. *"And you were saying Bloodlust? Nothing can penetrate your scales? I can assure you that this sword will penetrate your scales. Not only that, but your skull as well."*

She could see that there was no reasoning with him. He shared the same appetite for conquest and power as Rellik. He believed dragons should rule the world. The only course of action was to stop the threat now. Bloodlust began to convey another message. *"You do not scare me with your little threats, I am the Mighty Bloo...."*

At that, Aria had had enough. She thrust her sword through the skull of that mighty, proud dragon. She twisted her sword and slid it down the middle of the skull, slicing the brain in half, killing the dragon instantly. However, since her talent and adrenaline took over, she forgot one important thing.

They were several hundred spans above the ground, Aria clung to the lifeless dragon. She couldn't call out to the other dragons, nor could she fly. The dragon plummeted uncontrollably, spiraling and tumbling at an alarming speed. She couldn't summon the other dragons, nor could she fly. Maybe if she timed it perfectly, she could jump and roll at the last second. It could shatter every bone, but she would survive, and Melvin would be able to heal her. She hung on to the dragon with all her might, trying not to be flung off, just as she did on the ascent. Closer and closer they got to the ground. Aria braced herself, relying on her speed and agility. At the last possible moment, she jumped.

At that exact moment, the dragon's tail hit the ground and bounced up, catching Aria by surprise and pushing her under the crashing dragon. Trapped under the dragon, she was impaled by the sharp spikes on the dragon's massive back. She lay bleeding, her torso and legs pinned under the dragon. The remnants of the army, that survived the battle, rushed to her aid. They could do nothing to save her. In a weak voice, she said to those who gathered around with her last breath, "Win this war. Eliminate Rellik." Then she died a hero who sacrificed herself to save others.

CHAPTER 68

BATTLE IN THE CASTLE

While the battle raged outside, Melvin and Rellik clashed inside the castle. With bursts of light, Melvin drained Rellik's power as they fought from room to room, half-destroying the castle. Blast after blast, Melvin unleashed his light, forcing Rellik to retreat into the shadows each time.

"Melvin, give it up. You know you can't beat me." Rellik laughed manically.

"I wouldn't be sure about that." He retorted. Sending another blast of light towards Rellik. "You fight like Reicuas, he was defeated as well." Came a retort from the distance.

Melvin thought about that. He fought Reicuas. There was only one person he knew of whom Reicuas fought, and that was Zôltan. Could this be him using another name? He had to keep his mind on the task. He followed Rellik into a dark room. The door shut behind him. "That may be true, but I have more abilities than he di…" Just then, a cloud of dark smoke filled the air in the dark room. Melvin choked on it as he talked. He tried to catch his breath and summoned a gust of wind not only to clear the air, but also to throw Rellik back. Since Rellik was in shadow form, it did not affect him. It seemed to Melvin that the only thing that worked was to dispel the shadow. And the only thing that worked for that was light. Good thing his master was a light wizard. But since it was so dark in this castle, it was hard for Melvin to cast enough light to cause any damage to Rellik. He would just slip around a corner where the light would not reach. Since they were in a small room, there was nowhere for the smoke to go. It just swirled around the room. Rellik created more dark smoke. It was getting hard for Melvin to breathe. Melvin was choking; all he could breathe in was smoke.

Melvin had to get out of this room. But he couldn't see the door. He hurled light ball after light ball, but they were instantly swallowed by the darkness.

Was this it? Would he be defeated by Rellik?

Even though the room was already pitch black, his vision blurred further. His breath came in short, desperate gasps as he collapsed to the floor. Despite all his abilities, he couldn't think of a way out. His mind raced. To be beaten by smoke—of all things.

Then it hit him. The smoke needed somewhere to escape.

Summoning every ounce of focus he could manage in his fading state, he concentrated.

Melvin heard maniacal laughing from a distance. But it only seemed from a distance. He was coughing, gasping for air, but there was none in this small room. Fading into unconsciousness, he heard a smooth voice. "You, the so-called Magnificent One, thought you could beat me. I told you you did not have enough power, enough skill to defeat me. Now look at you, lying on the ground, falling into unconsciousness. Because of what? You can't breathe.

All the magic in the world won't save you now," Rellik sneered. "You're suffocating in this tiny room, powerless. You've lost. The war is mine. *I* have won. His voice dripped with cruel satisfaction. "I will conquer all of Arion. I'll make the Empress my slave. And then—the entire world." Then he laughed, dark and menacing, the sound echoing through the suffocating void.

Just then, Melvin summoned his remaining power, his eyes glowed brightly, his aura grew, casting a multi colored light directly around him. "Not if I can help it," he said in a scream. His power was summoned, coursed through his body, and shot out of his palms. A huge blast of everything he could. Air, water, fire, earth, light, lightning, all directed at. The wall. He blasted the wall, and it shattered outwards into the next room, and the smoke dissipated from the room. He called forth fresh air from the outside, and he breathed in the life-giving air. He maximized his lung capacity. Made sure the oxygen got from his lungs to his blood, then to his cells. His head cleared, he was energized, and said in a commanding voice, "Is that all you got? Smoke? Let's finish this." He did not know where Rellik was, but he knew he could hear him. He shot a death glare in all directions.

Maybe the reports about Melvin were true. He would have to be more careful.

He considered his options. How could he defeat Melvin? Smoke had *almost* worked, but somehow, he found a way around it. Lightning was useless—Melvin could harness it just as well.

Whirlwinds...

Rellik was awestruck. He had never witnessed anyone with so much power, anyone with so many talents and abilities all at once. Whirlwinds? Melvin could counteract everything he could use on him. Rellik was beginning to be afraid. All he could do for now was stay clear of Melvin until he could think of something that would work. However, he knew that Melvin knew the only thing that might work was light. So he always had to have an escape route, a place to slip into the shadows.

They battled on through the castle. Rellik summoning lightning and smoke and Melvin casting balls of light in every direction. Rellik would cast dark smoke to obscure the balls of light. then hit them with lightning.

Melvin and Rellik came to the round room that Aria saw that had mirrors on the walls, and shiny bronze plates on the domed ceiling reflected the what little diffused light of the late afternoon suns the came in through the thin slits in the walls. *So this is what she was talking about.* Melvin thought to himself. This gave Melvin an idea. He knew Rellik couldn't tolerate direct sunlight. Rellik can always hide in the shadows and escape, so Melvin called on his magic and sang a powerful song. He closed the door and emitted a strong, blinding light, similar to sunlight, which filled the room. The shafts of light bounced off all the mirrors and the shiny bronze-lined domed ceiling, and light permeated the room. There was no darkness in the room for Rellik to escape into. He was stuck. His power was draining from him, there was no escape. The light diffused the shadow. Rellik could not stay in shadow form, so he transformed into human form.

Rellik tried to cast smoke, but it was swallowed by the light. Rellik next tried lightning, but to no avail; the light weakened Rellik to the extent that he could not use his lightning magic.

Melvin then erected a shield around Rellik. If he turned off the light, even in this solid form, Rellik would not be able to escape. But just to make sure, he created several bright balls of light and spread them around the room to shine on Rellik, to keep him bound and to make sure there is no shadow for him to slip into. He doubled and triple-layered the shield and light so it was impossible for Rellik to escape. It was interesting that he had learned this technique from his Master, Reicuas, whose talent was using light. Just for good measure, Melvin created a magical rope and bound Rellik in it, preventing him from turning into a shadow, and using the same idea he did with Adara's ring, he enchanted it, that whoever was bound by this rope could not use magic. And magic could not be used on them. Except Melvin, because he is the one who created the rope.

Then, he erected another shield within the dome. If, by some improbable means, Rellik managed to slip past the first, second, and even the third shields, there would still be no escape from the final barrier.

Each shield contained several orbs of light, strategically placed to eliminate any shadows where Rellik could hide or shift into his shadow form. This final shield was a technique he had learned from the Na-Van—an ancient and powerful magic, impenetrable to all.

Melvin strode up to Rellik, since he created the shields, they did not affect him, however, Rellik could not escape. Melvin was anxious to see who was under the hood. What did the actual man look like who caused so much death and destruction in Arion? Melvin removed his hood and mask to give him the finishing blow. He wanted to see his face before he killed him. This man had caused so much destruction, so much sorrow, grief, and pain in this land for so long. He lifted the hood and recoiled from the sight. No, this man was not ugly or disfigured, exactly the opposite. Rellik was a very handsome man, large, strong, with piercing blue eyes. Melvin recognized this man, he couldn't believe it. He knew him, knew him better than almost any other person, besides his mother and Adara.

Melvin cried out in sorrow. "How could this be?? How could this have happened? How could he have turned from how he once was to this?"

Melvin looked into the man's eyes and saw pain, excruciating pain. Pain deeper than he could have ever known. Not only physical pain, which Melvin supposed was from the light, but also mental anguish. Something was not right about him. Tears filled Rellik's eyes. Rellik was helpless to move, being bound by the light surrounding him and the rope, and the shields. Melvin decided to do something he had rarely done before, but he just had to know.

He then called upon one of his rarest talents. Channeling his energy, he focused it with precision, directing it straight into Rellik. His consciousness seeped into Rellik's mind, delving into his thoughts, his memories—searching for the root of what had led him down this path.

What he saw there was horrifying. He didn't see any of the man he knew before. His memory started on a night with lightning flashing. He was bound on some sort of alter with a blind fold on, however, it slipped just enough that he could see. He saw a black dragon egg. A man dressed in dark wizard's robes was standing on a platform, two other wizards were on either side, all were chanting something in an ancient language. He saw the dragon egg hatch, black smoke rising from inside. He saw the magic from the baby dragon hatching flow into him. Then, all of a sudden, a bolt of lightning hit everyone in the room, and all went dark. The next thing he knew was in excruciating pain, his eyes opened, and there was sunslight shining on him. He had to get into the shadows, he needed darkness. He didn't know why. Somehow, he fled into the shadows, he had turned into a shadow. In the darkness, the pain subsided. He heard the baby dragon cry out, and could hear its thoughts. The baby dragon was scared, it too evaporated into smoke.

All he could feel was fear and confusion. Where was he? Who was he? He couldn't remember. A burning desire for power consumed him—a craving to rule the world. But where had these feelings come from? Had he always been this way? He didn't think so.

Something felt… off. Something wasn't right. Yet, no matter how hard he tried, he couldn't recall anything from before. His mind felt clouded, broken—like a puzzle with missing pieces.

That was all Melvin could take. He pulled out of the mind of Rellik. Now he understood. He felt sorrow for what had happened to this man. Melvin couldn't kill him now, he had to try to help him, try to undo the damage that was done to him on that fateful night.

Melvin hummed a song and concentrated, focusing intently on the brain. He scanned it, then compared it with his own, observing where memories reside and how they were organized. He proceeded to the corresponding location in Rellik's brain and noticed extensive damage. Some areas of his brain were missing, while others had been rewired around the absent or damaged parts. His brain was not how it was supposed to be. He scanned the rest of Rellik's body. He saw where other healers had fixed other parts of his body. From bones to organs, some were healed well, and some others were a complete mess. He had healed people before. He healed his wife of her cancer, but never faced a challenge this complex. Thousands of neurons needed reconnection, rewiring, and healing. New areas of the brain had to be created. Plus, he had to repair the other attempted healings.

He was confident in his ability to do so—but not here, not now. The repair would require a significant amount of time and an immense amount of magic. He needed to transport Rellik to a safe location.

Melvin sang a potent incantation, weaving an impenetrable shield of magic around the orbs, Rellik, and the room. He anchored it deep beneath the ground, as he had learned from the Na-Van, and extended it up to the dome's ceiling. Using the brass reflecting plates on the ceiling and the mirrors on the walls, he ensured the light remained constant, trapping Rellik within its glow. He reinforced the shield in three layers, just as he had done with the previous barriers, each one infused with light from the orbs, ensuring that nothing could penetrate or escape.

He made this shield so nothing could penetrate it. No weapon, no magic, from the smallest particle to the mightiest dragon. The only thing that would go through this shield was what Melvin himself allowed.

Melvin left Rellik bound in the light, shields, and the rope and found his way back outside the castle, where the war was still raging. Many on both sides lay dead. He was so caught up in stopping Rellik that he didn't pay any attention to the battle raging on the outside of the castle. Now that Rellik was defeated and trapped in light, the rope and shields, Melvin was angry.

The sky was ablaze with the fury of dragon fire, as well as lightning, ice, water, and acid, as the mighty dragons tore through the air, their roars echoing like thunder. The dragons were engaged in a titanic struggle, their colossal forms clashing against the backdrop of a tumultuous sky. Each one, a master of flight, using their aerial agility to outmaneuver and their elemental breath to overpower one another. They twisted and dove, evading claw and maw as they vied for dominance against their foe. It was a spectacle of raw might and primal fury, each dragon struggling to assert its supremacy over the other.

Wizards, their robes billowing in the tumultuous winds, being soaked by rain in the dark, ancient forest, chanted incantations, sending arcs of lightning and spheres of arcane energy hurtling towards their targets. Other wizards used nature to entrap their opponents in vines. Others opened up the earth to swallow their enemies. Infantrymen, locked in a dance of death, clashed with the hulking forms of Ogres and the menacing Orcs, and all sorts of other vile creatures, their swords slicing them down with lethal precision. The ground became a scene of the fallen, as Adara, her figure silhouetted against the inferno, conjured wave upon relentless wave of scorching fire, carving a path of destruction through Rellik's armies, scolding and scorching anyone that came within several spans of her. Exhaustion etched on their faces, muscles tensed in defiance, they stood, a bastion of hope amidst despair, their resolve unyielding, their courage the last light in the encroaching darkness. They were going to rid the world of this dark threat with every last ounce of power that they possessed.

Melvin had had enough of this war. Rellik was captured. What were the rest fighting for? Then he remembered. Rellik was not dead, they did not know he was captured. The bonds to the dragons were still there. He had to do something about it.

Melvin called on all his talents. His aura shone multicolored, sparkling around him. There was a humming in the air, like the humming of electricity. Then he screamed with all the emotion he had. He let out all his power against his enemies. Some got caught up in whirlwinds, some got entangled by branches, and some just got air punched many mega spans away. The same as his love was doing, wave after wave of fire engulfed his enemies. Lightning struck, whirlwinds blew, and gaps opened up in the earth and swallowing them. When all were dispatched or held captive. He elevated his voice so everyone could hear. He spoke to every ear and every mind.

"Listen to me now, Rellik is defeated. Your master is held captive. There is no escape for him. He is bound by light and magic. If you keep on fighting, you all will perish. So I am giving you a choice. Cease and desist and go back to your homes and do not come to battle again, or if you do continue to fight, you will die. I will give you 5 minutes to make your decision."

He released them and straight away, most of them, ran away. The other lesser humanoids stood there dazed and confused. They thought, *Why were they fighting again?* Their master was captured. Should they go try to save him? Who was their master again? Then, finally, one by one, they just dropped their weapons and wandered aimlessly about as if in a stupor of thought. Rellik's power over them was gone.

As for the dragons, they were magically bound to Rellik. As long as he was alive, they had to do his bidding, and since his last command was for them to defeat Melvin and Adara and their army, they would continue to do so until either Rellik or they themselves were dead, then the bond would be broken.

The dragons had to free their master. The funny thing is, most of them didn't want to. But as they were bound to him, they were obligated to do so. And so they did.

Melvin sent a message through his dragons to all of his troops to stop fighting anyone who was left and stand down. He told them to gather at a place not too far from the castle and watch. So they did.

Through the link, Rellik's dragons knew exactly where he was. So they went for the domed room in the center of the castle. They tried to scorch it with their fire, but since it was stone and a metal roof, that did nothing. They clawed off the roof, thinking that they could get in that way, but they were met with disappointment when they found Rellik was bound inside the magic shields. They tried to claw and bite and breathe fire, ice, acid, and whatever they used at the shield, but were repelled at every attempt. At the same time, other powerful warlocks managed to enter the castle and tried to free him. They cast every spell they could think of at the shield. However, just like the dragons, nothing worked. It held strong, for it was crafted from the ancient magic of the Na' Van—magic they did not understand. After about an hour of relentless attempts, their power was drained, exhaustion overtook them, and they finally gave up.

Finally, Melvin had enough amusement because he knew the Dragons, warlocks, or anyone else would never be able to get to him. He didn't want any more war, he didn't want any more bloodshed. To look at the scene of bloodshed before him was enough to haunt anyone for the rest of their lives. So he did the most humane thing he could think of, not that the enemy deserved it, he just didn't want any more deaths. He looked into one of his soldiers' body to find a certain artery in the neck. He mentally squeezed it, and the soldier went limp and fell over. He checked some other vitals in the body, smiled, then did the same thing to one of his dragons. Which in turn went limp and fell crashing to the ground. One by one in rapid succession, he did the same thing to Rellik's remaining dragons. They all came crashing to the ground. Then he sent his consciousness around the grounds and then into the castle, and looked for life there. Whatever human or humanoid life, even animal life, he found that was on Rellik's side, he did the same thing. Then he checked and made sure that all of the enemies were dealt with. They were not dead, but he pinched a nerve that went to the brain, which caused them to pass out. They would awaken in about 12 hours.

Adara and the others were astonished at what they had seen. Melvin had defeated the mighty dragons. Dozens of them by himself. Then, not only that, but all the warlocks and everything else around. In mere seconds.

"How did you do that?" Adara asked. "What did you do??"

"Nothing much," Melvin said.

"That's not nothing." Adara said, still amazed, "They were dropping like, well, Dragons. How did you do that?"

"I just put them to sleep." He said humbly, "There is a nerve in the neck that once pinched sends a signal to the brain, and it causes you to lose consciousness, and you go to sleep."

"Where did you learn that?" Adara asked.

"Aria did it to me one time when we were sparring. She knocked me out cold. I had no defense for it." He explained, "Then she showed me how to do it. I had to do a bit of anatomy research to find out which exact artery it was and how to do it with magic, but the effect is the same."

"Why didn't you do this before?" Adara asked, "Especially with Rellik?"

"It has to be a small group." He said, "And since Rellik is shadow most of the time, it would not have worked on him. You have to be solid."

"And why didn't you magic punch all of the enemy earlier? The war would have been over a long time ago." Adara asked, rather annoyed.

"I'm sorry. But I was dealing with Rellik. He nearly beat me. But thanks to our training, I was able to overcome that and ended up capturing him."

"I knew you could do it, sweetheart," Adara said. Then smiled and winked.

"I have to deal with Rellik, but I want you to come with me," Melvin said, very tired.

"I would have it no other way. I want to see up close and personal who this is that we have been dealing with all these annums." Adara said. Then she turned to some of the troops who were standing near. "Get the word out to the rest of the troops from here to the staging area, and wherever else fighting was, that Rellik has been captured. This war is over. Have any surviving, able-bodied men search through the fallen for those still alive. Sct up triage stations and assign healers to tend to the wounded. Instruct the leapers to bring in healers from Lilenhamür, Wazervĭl, and the elves and get them started on treating the troops. Begin with the less severe injuries first, then move on to the critical cases—but ensure the most severely wounded are stabilized so they can receive proper care.

"Yes, Commander," they said and got to work.

At the news, cheers erupted from the Empress's army—the war was finally over. Melvin had done it! He had defeated Rellik. The dragons swiftly carried the news across the empire, and celebrations broke out in every city and town.

Chapter 69
Healing

Night had fallen by the time the battle ended. Melvin returned to the ruined, domed chamber in the black obsidian castle, accompanied by Adara and a few remaining soldiers and wizards. The once-mighty room lay in shambles from the dragons' futile attempts to free Rellik—walls reduced to rubble, wood scorched, and stones scattered throughout the castle. Yet, at the center of the devastation, Rellik remained exactly as Melvin had left him—trapped in the glowing light of the orbs, encased within the impenetrable shields. They shone like a beacon in the darkness.

Melvin, his strength spent, didn't know if he could do any more right then. He felt something soft brush his hand and smiled. Gently, a soft hand that he knew all too well slipped into his, and the ring on his finger flamed up.

"I don't have enough strength to do it," Melvin said softly. "You want me to kill him for you?" Adara asked tenderly.

"If I wanted him dead, I would have done it already," Melvin responded. Notice all the light and reinforced shields around him. This is so he wouldn't escape. They slowly walked up to Rellik through all the shields. Then Melvin nodded to Rellik. "Look at him."

Adara looked at the man standing in the shields before her. "Are you sure it's him?" she asked, startled. "Yes, I am sure. It's him, but at the same time it's not." Melvin said tenderly. "Look into his eyes, Adara,

tell me what you see."

Adara looked into the bright blue eyes of the man standing before them. She gasped. "I see tears, I see." She paused, looking for the right word. "pain." It came out almost as a whisper.

Melvin replied softly. "I need to heal him. He has a lot of brain damage, I can't tell you the whole story right now, but something happened to him, an accident, and I think if I heal the damage to his brain, he will be able to return, at least most of the way, back to normal."

"Then let me give you my strength, my magic," Adara said tenderly.

"No. I can't ask that of you. You are so exhausted already. If I take any of your strength, you will have none left."

Heal me first, then I will lend you back what you gave me." Then, from the edges of the room, he heard, "So will I," coming from all over the room as the soldiers and wizards who were still alive and could walk or limp came towards Melvin and Adara. They were battling Rellik's forces around the castle. When the enemy stopped or dropped, they simply sat down to rest. It wasn't long before they saw Melvin and Commander Adara enter the round room, and they followed, ready to assist if needed.

One spoke for the group and said, "You have done much for us, you have saved countless lives countless times without ever asking anything for yourself, except to let you rest and regain strength. Now it is our turn to lend you ours. We see who he is now, and heard you as you told Commander Adara that he suffered a great injury that made him what he is now. We know you can heal him, so use our strength, just a little from each of us, then that should give you enough strength to do what you need to do."

Then, in his mind, he heard his dragon speaking to him. *I will lend you my power and energy. I have enough for you all and to spare. You gave me my freedom when I had just hatched, you are my greatest friend, I will do this for you that you may return him to his former state. So will I,* he heard from another dragon. *So will I,* several more added. Then another came into his head. *If I could, I would.* Watcher said, *But unfortunately, I am still bound to Rellik. If you can unbind us, I will serve you gladly for the rest of my life.* Many more dragons affirmed this.

"Thank you all, but I cannot do it here, I feel residual power from Rellik here and the dragons he enslaved, we need to move him to a secure place that he cannot use his or his remaining dragon's power. Penelope, can you move him to the Lilenhamür?"

"I will leap you to Lilenhamür," Amira expressed.

"Thank you Amira for your offer, but this will take more than you have power to do. We need to take not only Rellik, but also the shields, the orbs, the mirrors. The whole thing. Though you have great ability, I am afraid this is beyond what either of us can do right now, we are all so weary we do not have the strength to do it. He needs to be physically carried back."

Amira nodded in understanding. "Could you do me one more act of service?" Melvin asked.

"Of Course," she replied.

And he communicated this to the Dragons as well. "Can you please find all those of our army that are left alive and transport them to Lilenhamür? Bring them to the lakeside in the center of the fortress. We have wizards and dragons who can tell if someone is alive, even if just barely. Not just the men, but dragons and other animals as well. From the mightiest dragon to the tiniest mouse. Also, transport the healers so they can begin healing the injured. Not only from our army, but any human, dragon, or animal from the other side as well. Have wizards erect barriers so they cannot escape or cause any more problems. I know most of them do not want to serve Rellik. And his influence over them has stopped."

"Of course we will do that." They all said in unison.

Melvin and Penelope wove another shield between Penelope, Rellik, the orbs, and the shields to ensure they all remained intact. Then, Penelope, Percilla, her mother, Melvin, and Adara flew through the night across the mountains, landing in the heart of Lilenhamür, by the lake where the magic was strongest.

He then cast a spell on himself to soak in as much of the magic as he could. But it would take him a while to gain back the strength he needed to perform this feat.

Melvin took Penelope's offer and they weaved a spell between them. Soon other dragons who were left in Lilenhamür joined in and gave of their sustaining power as well. Other dragons and the troops were lept in.

Wrapped in a warm enveloping love and the magic from the dragons, Melvin set upon the task. *"I don't know how long this will take, maybe hours, maybe revs"* He thought to her in images. *"Don't worry little one"* Penelope said. *"We will be here, take as long as you need."*

"I have never done quite this much healing. A broken leg is one thing, but this, this is much more than I have ever done."

"We are linked, we have way more power than you need, for as long as you need. Heal him."

"I will." With this, Melvin sat down in a cushioned chair that was brought to him, for they knew he couldn't stand the whole time. He opened up a string of magic, just as he had done before, and with it looked inside Rellik's body. He saw many things wrong, organs that didn't function right, strains, and sprains. Melvin fixed all first because they were easy to fix. Then, somehow, one of his seldom-used talents came into play. He saw something in Rellik he hadn't before. There was not only one soul in his body, but two. How can this be? He probed even more. He could now see that the two were in conflict, actually battling each other inside this one body, but the darker one was more powerful and had taken over the body. So instead of just healing Rellik, he needed to somehow vanquish this other soul first. He also noticed something else.

Melvin asked the dragons and Adara if they had any ideas. No one has had to deal with this before, so they could give no advice. Melvin thought. Somehow, the dark wizard came into this body and overpowered it. He remembered the memory he saw when he was lying on the altar. The soul of the other wizard must have entered this body; he himself was more powerful because he defeated him. Melvin then again probed the brain, this time searching for memories. He wanted to find out how this happened so he could reverse it.

Melvin went back to the area of the brain where memories were stored. In horror, he watched the scene again, paused it, rewound it, and slowed it down. He understood what had happened now. At one point in the ritual, just as the egg hatched and the lightning flashed, he saw the soul of the Dark Wizard, who must have been Zôltan, go into the body of the wizard on the stone slab. He saw the magic of the hatching dragon enter him as well. Not only the soul of the Wizard but also his magic. Then it all went black. Now gaining more understanding about what caused this, he saw other magic particles as well. Dark particles, particles shifting from solid to smoke to a shadow. He also saw lightning particles.

When he witnessed the baby dragon hatch, he absorbed a tremendous amount of shadow particles, and the magic from Zôltan must have transferred as well. That's why Rellik had been able to perform so many feats. He also noticed the light particles that had originally been within the body, though somehow, they had been locked away by thc shadow particles. If Rellik had used light magic, it would have caused him excruciating pain. Melvin knew what he had to do now—he must enter the body and force the other wizard out. *"This won't be easy,"* he thought.

He asked Penelope if he could borrow more of her power. *"We will give you all you need."*

Melvin opened himself up to the magic in that place to absorb as much as he could. He then opened himself up to the magic the dragons were sending to him. With this, he wove a spell that would sustain him and give him more magical power than anyone has ever had in the history of Estry.

Then he opened his heart up to Deo. Melvin asked for His guidance and his approval for what he was about to do, since he knew Deo gave him all his power and the ability to use it. Especially in healing. He got the answer that this was what he was meant to do. This is why he had this power. To use it as he needed. Melvin smiled and set to work.

He locked his consciousness in his own body, then he flowed his magic into Rellik, sending his tendrils of consciousness in full force into the body. Then he put the rest of his soul into the body. With the power of the dragons, he fought with the weakened soul of the other Zôltan. Zôltan, though weakened, was still strong enough to put up a good fight. Then an idea came to him. If light bound Rellik, then possible light will cast out this other soul. Melvin created a blazing light inside the body of Rellik and pushed the second soul out of the body and out of the first shield binding Rellik. Into the second shield. The onlookers saw the body of Rellik glowing. Melvin quickly created another shield to hold the dark soul of the Zôltan. Now Rellik was free of Zôltan. Melvin grasped onto the lock in his body and slid back into his own body. Everyone was shocked when they saw this other dark soul caught in the shield, thrashing about trying to get free, but nothing it did would get him free of his shield prison. Melvin explained to the crowd all that had happened and what he saw in the memories of Rellik. Now Melvin could concentrate on the task at hand. Healing Rellik.

Now that the other soul was out of the body and trapped within the new shield, Melvin could proceed with the healing. Melvin dug deep within the brain to the very smallest of the neurons and axons, each connecting fiber, blood vessels, and every other part of the brain. He looked at his brain to see the proper way to put it back together and then proceeded back to Rellik's brain. From the smallest atom to DNA structure, to the cells, he built from the bottom up. He saw where all the parts fit together from his brain, but using the DNA structure of Rellik to piece it all together in the proper order, from one side of Rellik's brain to the other side. He called upon the power of the dragons and built a web of cells, connected the cells, created pathways, moved the damaged areas to where they were supposed to go, all the while making sure that it all matched up to how it should have been before. He continuously looked at his brain for the pattern, but the other side of Rellik's brain to match it up right, so it would function properly. Melvin worked through the long night through the entire next rev, then into the next long night and the next rev, restoring the brain and the rest of the body, then he was finally finished with Rellik. He went through the body again, making sure that everything was healed and in working order. Some areas were even better than when he had started. Melvin was exhausted, but there was still one more thing to do.

While his consciousness was still in Rellik's body, he looked for the links. Looked for that string that connected Rellik to the dragons. He searched and searched. He could not find them. They were gone. He asked the dragons to ask those who were bound to Rellik if they still had the bond. The reply came. They were all free. Within the time Melvin was healing Rellik's brain, the connection vanished. Somehow what ever he had done while healing Rellik, he must have changed something, and the link had been severed. And now they were rejoicing. Those who wished to be free, and now were, pledged to bind themselves to Melvin. He said that there was no need, but to promise the same thing that Penelope promised. That if there was a need, they would be there for him. As long as it was a righteous desire. That, they all agreed on. Though some dragons were truly evil and would continue to be that way, whether or not they were bound to Rellik or not. To them, Melvin said if they ever caused any problems in this land, or Dragonia, or any other place on this planet, that they would have Melvin to deal with. They agreed that they would go in peace and not trouble this land or the world again. Most kept that promise. Some did not. But that is another story.

But he wasn't done yet, since he had this great use of the dragon's power, then healed all of the soldiers who were flown or leaped back that were not healed by the healers. He moved on to all the other wounded who were still alive, even just barely—elves, dwarves, unicorns, the other humanoids, animals, and creatures who had helped in the war and were in the vicinity of the lake.

It didn't matter what side of the war they had been on; he healed them all. Finally, drawing the greatest strength from the dragons, he healed them as well. Though some of the wounds were grievous and could have been life-threatening to lesser animals, these wounds were more easily healed than Rellik's had been.

"Finally," Melvin said with a sigh, "It is finished." And collapsed. Then Adara gave him more of her power to give him energy. Melvin finally let the shield down, except for the one holding the dark soul. Then said, "Everyone be ready in case this didn't work." However, no one doubted that it did. One by one, Melvin put out the orbs. When the last one went out, the man didn't flee; he just stood there. Finally, Melvin unbound the enchanted rope that Rellik was tied with, and finally, Rellik started to weep. Then he put out his arms wide. Melvin stepped forward cautiously, and Rellik took him into an embrace. As they held each other, the man sobbed and sobbed, "Thank you," he said over and over. "I'm Sorry, I couldn't help it, I tried and tried, but he was too strong."

"I know" Melvin said tenderly, "I know." "I love you my boy."

"I love you, too, Master."

"Now, you are the master." The man said tenderly, "You have achieved more than I ever could have. You have grown so strong physically and with your magic. I am so proud of you."

They called the Empress down to the side of the lake, along with all the wizards and soldiers who had returned to Lilenhamür from the war.

The empress was in shock when she saw the face of the one who had caused this war. She ordered he guards to kill him on the spot.

Melvin stopped them.

"Melvin," she said in her anger. "How dare you defy me and stop my guards?"

"Your Excellency," Melvin said humbly, bowing a little before the Empress, "I could have killed him myself, but I did not. Let me explain why."

"Very well." The Empress gave in, "If you did not, I know you have a very good reason. Besides, you have more power in your pinky finger than we all have combined."

"Yes, you keep telling me that." Melvin retorted. Then he recounted to them all about how he had to heal Reicuas' brain injuries. About how, as he was doing that he found another soul inside the body. He told them of the memories he found of the night of the transference. He told them that if they looked at the one shield that was still up, they would find the soul that he forced out of the body. They all looked, and there was a united gasp as the new people who came hadn't noticed it before.

"Who did that soul belong to?" the Empress asked.

"Zôltan." Melvin and Reicuas said in unison.

"He was the cause of all this. From the very beginning." Reicuas continued. With most of his memory restored, Reicuas told them the story of when he went to battle Zôltan and got captured, and what he could remember of the transference ritual. "Then I can't remember much of anything after that. This body was being controlled by Zôltan, and there was not much I could do about it."

"What will we do with the Soul??" The Empress asked.

"If it's not too much trouble," Reicuas said. "I would like to secure it in a secure place. I would like to let him know a few things that maybe had he known them, this war would have never happened."

"Very well, Take him to the special dungeon. He should be secure enough there." The Empress said "Melvin, Wrap some more shields around him wont you?"

"Of Course, Empress." Melvin said with a salute. Then he did so.

The guards, along with some wizards, took him far beneath Lilenhamür to the dungeon. Not just any dungeon, but one constructed for the most vile of creatures.

One, far beneath the lake they were at, was wrapped in webs of spells and enchantments—one where there was no escape. As for the Soul of Zôltan, it had been first encased in layers of shields and light orbs, then placed in this dungeon, which was also layered with enchantments—many of them by Reicuas himself. Escape was impossible.

Back at the lake, Reicuas stood up straight and took on an air of formality and beckoned all to come closer. "I Reicuas, As Master Wizard, and High Wizard by the order of the great wizard Wazzer. Do now here by bestow upon you, Melvin the Magnificent, the highest honor I can. The title of High Wizard of the order of Wazzer. I grant you all rights, privileges of the office thereof." With this, the parchment Melvin got when he was made Master Wizard appeared and magically changed to this new title. The Empress herself cheered at the advancement.

Adara grabbed Melvin and gave him a big kiss, and everyone who was there cheered. News traveled fast throughout the Empire, and all of the cities and towns celebrated the victory.

CHAPTER 70
CELEBRATION

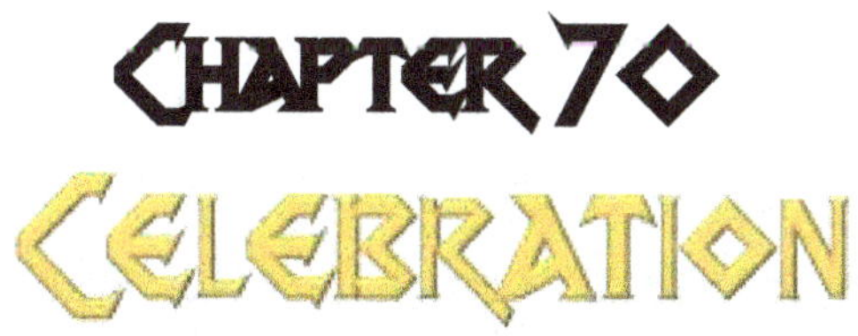

The Empress made an announcement: "After you have all rested and healed, I will honor Melvin the Magnificent, Commander Adara, and all those who helped us win this war in an official ceremony. Then, we will celebrate with a feast and a party that will exceed all other celebrations. It will last many revs."

About a week later, when everyone was healed and rested, the rev of the ceremony came. Melvin was all dressed up in the clothes he wore for his and Adara's wedding. Adara was wearing a very nice set of red lether armor, and the rest were dressed in their finest uniforms. In the Empresses throne room everyone was seated, Penelope and Percilla the dragons, were on their perches and Penelope Melvin's mother was of course in attendance in the front row, as well as NöGard and his wife, Est'iän Arnatuilë, and even the animals. All those who helped with the war effort.

The Empress stood up and the grand doors opened as a fan fare started playing. Melvin and Adara, walked down a gold carpet lined with purple, to the throne.

"Ladies First" The Empress said "Princess Adara, General of the forces of Bilbylund and Commander of the armies of the Arion Empire, I present you with this medal of Arion. For the valiant service to the Empire during this war and in defeating Rellik's armies." Then she slipped the medallion in the shape of fire around Adara's neck.

She then motioned to Melvin to come forward. "Melvin The Magnificent." She said for all to hear "For service to the Empire of Arion, and achieving a feat no one else could, in defeating Rellik. By the authority my station as Empress of the Arion Empire, I give you something that has not been given in many Millennia. I bestow upon you the title of *First High Wizard* of the Empire of Arion and even the planet Estry. You shall be above all other wizards in the Empire. This comes with all the rights and privileges of this title. Everyone shall know the name Melvin the Magnificent." The crowd erupted into applause. A new parchment appeared in the air bearing the new title, though Melvin didn't need it, as everyone in Arion, Dragonia, and possibly even on the planet Estry already knew who he was. News of this new First High Wizard spread across Estry quickly.

Then Empress Kayla called up other leaders in the war, including the dragons and animals and those who supported those who were fighting and gave out medals to them as well.

"Finally," The Empress said in a somber tone, with tears forming in her eyes, "I would like to honor Aria of Bilbylund, and also Wizard Brennon who has served in this war with Diligence. Also the King and Queen of Bilbylund, who were unfortunate casualties in this war as were many others. To them, and all of the fallen soldiers I would like to leave a rev of remembrance for their bravery and sacrifice for the Empire. May they be remembered now and forever." Then, banners with their pictures were hung in the great hall. They all took a moment of silence to honor their fallen friends and family.

After a few moments The Empress spoke up again. "Now on a happier note, let us celebrate this victory along with our fallen friends." She paused "On this rev each annum, a celebration will be held to honor those who helped win this war or were victims of it. May we remember this rev, so this may never happen again. Let the festivities begin." Empress commanded, then they started the celebration.

At the celebration everyone was eating and drinking and dancing, and some made fools of themselves. Men of valor were telling stories of their heroics, and the heroics of their fallen friends and soldiers. The Empress went up to Melvin and Adara and said to them in a soft tone so others could not hear "I would like to speak to you two privately."

They walked outside to the garden area. They walked along the stone path, until they reached the footbridge over the stream. "Melvin, Adara. I would like to ask you something."

"Yes, What is it?" they said in unison.

Kayla chuckled. "I have been putting a lot of thought into this. I know what your answer will be, but I will ask you anyway. I would like you both to come live here in Lilenhamür. Melvin, I would like you to be my personal Wizard of the Empire. Adara, you would still be the commander of the armies. If you so choose. You could have the pick of anywhere in the city to live. You did, after all, defeat Rellik, and for that we cannot thank you enough. We all know, you are the only ones that could have defeated him. So for that, you may have anything you want."

Melvin thought for a while and whispered to Adara, then answered. "Thank you for your offer your highness, but I have all I need right here." He said as he put his arm around Adara. "We would just like to go back home and just live life again, raise our daughter. We don't need a fancy house, or a palace. We just need a plot of land and a home to call our own. Of course if you ever need us, we will be ready and willing to serve. We are just a Dragon thought away."

"I knew that would be your answer" The Empress said. "And you deserve that life. Wait, What? You said a Daughter? Congratulations." And she smiled her genuine, brilliant, amazing smile "Anywhere in the Empire you want to have your land and however much of it you would like, you only have to ask. You may even have your own kingdom if you wish, But I know the answer to that as well."

"Thank you Empress. We would like to go back to Bilbylund. Maybe not back to Riecuas's house, but back home." Adara said.

"That is understandable. I knew that would be your answer. I will then go with my second pick for my Wizard. Reicuas. I have been trying to get him to come back for a long time. Though from this experience he has changed a bit, but that may be for the better. And you know with me, there will be no surprises."

"That would be a good choice." Adara said. "I will miss him greatly."

"So will I," Melvin said looking up at the bright violate sky. "But if he is willing, then he will be the best choice. He does not have to look after me or Adara anymore." He said with a chuckle. "However, You may want to ask my mother to come with him."

"Why is that" She asked, although she already knew.

"Just a hunch," Melvin said with a mischievous look.

Empress Kayla gave them both a hug and they all went back to the celebration.

Reicuas agreed to stay at Lilenhamür to be the Wizard for the Empire, as did Melvin's mother. As always, she became a schoolteacher, and all the children loved her. Melvin and Adara's hunch was right—they ended up getting married. And what a grand event that was.

Melvin and Adara returned to Bilbylund, built a modest but expandable home on 1000 square megaspans of land (That would be about 23 acres in your reckoning.) on the outskirts of the town Melvin grew up in, with workshops for tinkering and potions, stables, vegetable gardens, an orchard and even a small lake. They continued to help others with their needs. And when they were called upon by the empress, they were there to help.

With the King and Queen and Aria deceased, Bilbylund needed a new ruler. Adara had her own life with Melvin, so it fell to Amira to take up the mantle. She grew into a much-loved and wise Queen. Again, Melvin and Adara were there to help as needed. Melvin continued to be the Wizard for Bilbylund.

Melvin and Adara visited the castle often and anticipated their next adventure. Children.

There were more adventures to come.

The End

Appendix

– Note - Some of this work has been translated from the Estrian native tongue to English. I am attempting to translate as closely as possible. Some things will not translate and will be kept in their tongue with a definition. Times, seasons and measurements will be translated as closely to what you understand as I can.

CHARACTERS

Melvin- Main protagonist.

Eventual Master wizard. Aura all colors, all magical abilities, some potions; some spells some hexes, etc. Melvin does best magic by singing. Recruited by Empress to help destroy Rellik and his army. Goes on quest with Adara, Aria, and army to get rid of Rellik. Falls in love with and marries **Adara**. Direct descendant of Elfin, on both sides which gives him all the magical abilities, bright purple eyes. Denotes direct lineage of Elfin. Only elves and shield trees know this.

Age: umpteen - 270 Gender: Male

Job: Wizard

Appearance: Melvin is a tall and strong man with a humble demeanor. He has short, light brown hair and bright blue shining eyes until he sees a dragon egg hatch. Then his hair and eyes turn multi colored and gives off a sparkling rainbow aura. He typically wears brown trousers and a tan tunic, which adds to his mysterious and magical aura.

Personality: Melvin is a kind and gentle soul, always ready to lend a helping hand. He is humble despite his impressive abilities and has a strong sense of justice. Melvin is a deep thinker and often ponders the mysteries of life and magic.

Strengths: Melvin's physical strength and magical abilities make him a formidable force. His humble nature allows him to connect with others and gain their trust easily. He is also an excellent problem solver and has a sharp intellect.

Abilities: Melvin possesses all abilities related to magic, with a special affinity for manipulating the elements. He can control light, fire, water, earth, and air with ease, He can also create shields, and use his consciousness to look into anything, making him a versatile and powerful wizard.

Backstory: Melvin grew up knowing only his mother, who was an outcast from society due to her getting pregnant at a young age. He never knew who his father was, which has always been a mystery to him. Despite his difficult upbringing, Melvin's mother taught him everything she knew about magic, nurturing his powers and guiding him to become the skilled wizard he is this rev. He also has a master wizard Reicuas, who is his teacher and like a father to him.

Tone of Voice: Melvin speaks with a masculine tone, carrying an air of wisdom and authority. His voice is calm yet commanding, reflecting his deep connection to magic and his role as a powerful wizard.

THE 4 PRINCESSES

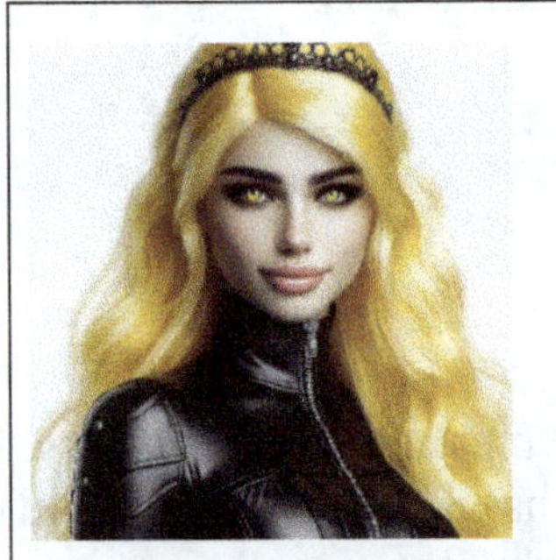	**Aria**- eldest daughter of King Bilby. Special ops of army.
	Adara- means Fire in Hebrew. 2nd oldest of Bilby's daughters. Leader of the army. Fiery red hair, can control fire. Shoot fire from hands, can light things on fire with mind. Love interest of Melvin. How Adara gets bright purple eye's . Can also talk to animals. Wizardess. Not at first, but ends up being one thanks to Melvin and elves' training. Eventually, one of the most powerful wizardesses in the land.

Appearance when using her magic: Adara has long flowing hair that seems to be made entirely of flickering flames, constantly dancing and crackling. Her eyes are a mesmerizing shade of glowing red, giving off an intense and powerful aura. She possesses a stunning figure, including a generously endowed chest, which she wears with confidence. Standing atop a hill, she gazes out over a picturesque green valley, with a river meandering through the middle and a magnificent golden castle visible on the horizon. Her attire consists of flowing.

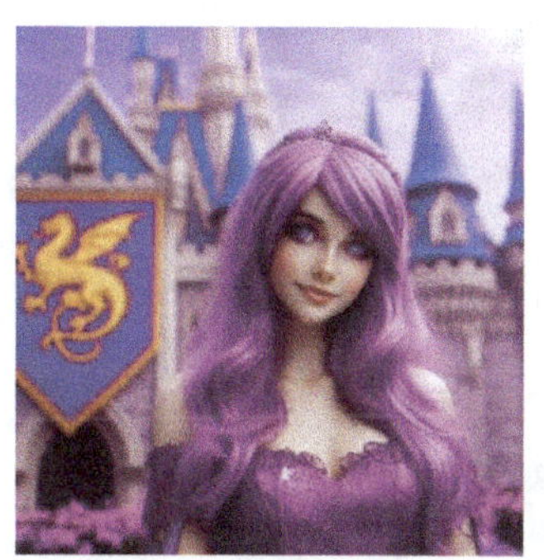

Amira - 3rd   daughter of Bilby - her quest was knowledge, if you asked her a question, she would know the answer, or find the answer. Though most of the time, she did all the asking. She was also always willing to help. Princess or not, if something needed to be done, she would do it. Nothing was too big a job or too small. If some grand ball needed to be organized, she did it. If someone needed a roof thatched or clothes mended, she would help. She was not afraid to get her hands, or the rest of herself for that matter, dirty to get a job done. The messier the job, the better for her. Everyone loved her for the service she was always giving, rich or poor, it didn't matter. You could tell by her yellow aura that she was helpful and giving. Leaper

Anna

The most beautiful of them all. She was world-famous for her beauty. Her infectious smile brightened everyone's rev, her gorgeous pink eyes inspired awe in all those who saw them. She had an aura about her that emanated love to all those who were near her. You couldn't see it, but you could feel it and knew it was there. Her touch was like being touched by an angel. People would come from far and wide just to get a glimpse of her. That was her gift, and sometimes her curse.

King and Queen Bilby

Obviously, theThe 4 princesses parents.

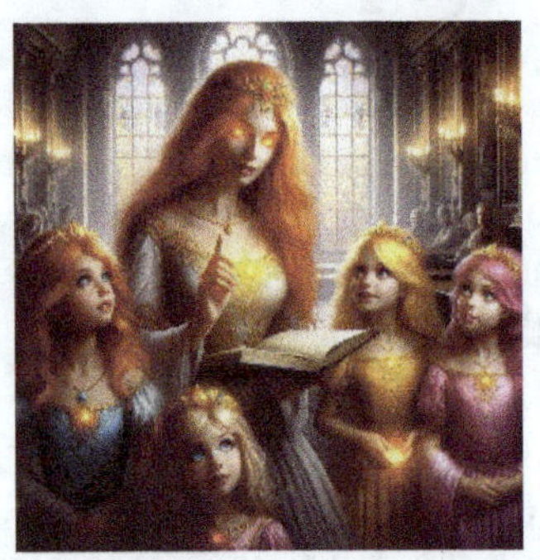

Penelope human

Melvin's mother. History is a mystery, but it will be revealed in the back story or another book. Previously a wizardess. Went to wizard school in Wazzerville. Friends to Reicuas and Zôltan. Talent – knowledge, teaching, and understanding children. Teacher of the 4 princesses and the kids in town.

Penelope —

Gold dragon, also Melvin's dragon. Helps Melvin and is his dearest friend. Melvin watcher her egg hatch.

Reicuas

Melvin's teacher, Master Light Wizard, taught and advised Empress Kayla, who taught Adara to use and control her power. Friends with Penelope (Melvin's mom) and Zôltan.

Personal wizard to the king Bilby. (He is a lot more famous and powerful than he lets on.) Keeps it on the down low.

– went to Wazzerville academy.

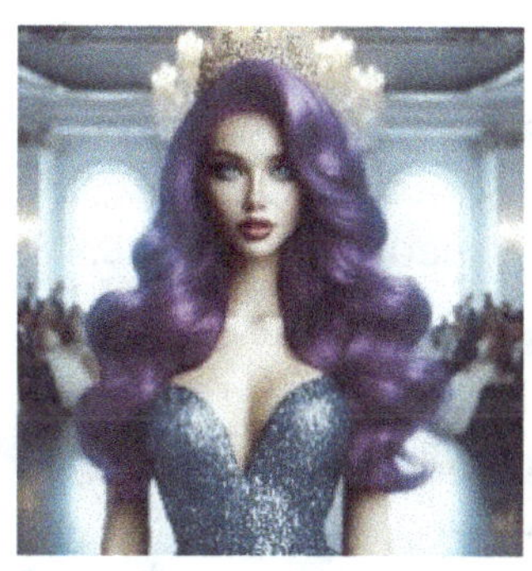

Empress Kayla

She is the Empress of Arion. The continent on which this story takes place. She lives in a ginormous citadel. Lilenhamür: an impenetrable fortress. Empress Kayla is ageless with a spell put on her by the elves. She appears to be about 200 annums old, 20 in human years, but is more than 5000 annums old. She knows the hearts of everyone. Sometimes has visions,

Zôltan

– Friends in Wazervïl with Reicuas and Penelope. After graduating, started trying to take over places. Growing more powerful. Descendant of Elfin. Eventually captured Reicuas and then tried to get his power.

Wizard Brennan Bailey

He is a nature wizard. Personal wizard to the Empress, for the past 200 annums, was a teacher of Reicuas, Penelpoe, etc. In Wazervïl Academy for Extraordinarily Talented Youngsters. (wizard school). A very old elder in the wizard's council has lots of wisdom and counsel. Goes to battle with Melvin against Rellik's army. Because he can't sit idly by and let others do all the work. Plus, he wanted some action. In a battle, one of the bad magic users reflects a spell and turns him into a sunflower. In the future, people come from far and wide to gain wisdom from the wise sunflower.

The Shadow Lord Rellik

He amasses a great army. He tries to take over Arion. Can control smoke and lightning. His body is no longer completely solid, but his matter was loose and not totally defined. More like a shadow, or smoke.

He was as a shadow, but a living shadow though he could appear in a solid form, he was not entirely, like a ghost but more solid. He can not stand bright light. He has to stay in the shadows. Torches are ok. Sunslight would kill him. Or at least reduce him to nothing.

Shadow dragon - Skügge, Means Shadow in Norse or Norwegian Shadow dragon

Rellik's dragon. can be solid at times, but usually a shadow. Spews dark shadow mist stuff, makes it so dark you can't see. And like choking on smoke. Or lightning

Rellik saw him hatch, so has control of the dragon.

Other Characters

Elfin – ancient scientist from another race, discovered magic particle. Ancestor of the elves. Was able to talk to the trees and give them magic

Elfes – first son of Elfin, Ancestor of Melvin

Galdür – Second son of Elfin means magic in Icelandic Ancestor of Melvin

BloodLust – A giant red dragon that works for Rellik

TIME

Time is different on this planet.

Time is an interesting thing. You only know time as it is on Earth. So, I will try to use terms you are familiar with. However, I will have to use their "terms" for some units of time, as Earthlings are not familiar with such concepts yet. On the Planet Estry, time is very different. Estry is larger than Earth, about 10 times the size. Therefore, it has an extremely slow axial rotation, but it has a similar gravitational pull to Earth. Since Estry is larger, the revs are longer. One revolution equals one revolution of the planet, which you would call a *day*. Their *day*, which is called a *rev,* consists of 34 of their hours. That would equal approximately 1 week on Earth.

Human Estrians age, grow, and develop more slowly. One decade for them is like a year for Earthlings. Everything is longer. Revs, Weeks, Moons, Annums, etc.

1 year for them is like century for Earthlings. Everything is longer. Revs, Annums, Moons (same idea as a month), weeks, etc.

Example. A 20 year old on Earth would be the same as 200 annum old on Estry. They would both be young adults. Just as people can live approximately 100 years on Earth, they can live to about 1000 annums on Estry. However 1000 annums on Estry would equivalent 10,000 years on Earth.

 Now there is a time during the lifecycle of the humans on Estry known as Umpteen. These are the annums between 120 and 130 Annums - after that of a child and before becoming what you call a teenager. It is a range of years that is critical in the development of the peoples of Estry. Usually, this is when they find out if they have a talent, and if so, what it is and how strong it is. This is the time when young Estrians, if they have a strong talent, would be taken for extra training at the local academy or to Wazervīl Academy for Extraordinarily Talented Youngsters.

There are other creatures on Estry with longer life spans. Peoples such as Dwarves, and Elves can live up to 5 Milleannums. Dragons on the other hand can live up to hundreds of thousands of annums.

Here is a breakdown of the times.

1 Rev = one revolution , called a "rev", of the planet (same as a day on Earth) of their 34 hours. That would equal approximately 1 week on Earth.

1 week = 11 revs

1 Moon = 5 weeks or 55 "revs" The time it takes for a cycle of the larger of the 2 moons to revolve around around Estry. (Same as a lunar month)

1 Annum = 1 revolution of the planet around the binary star system. 1 annum =16 moons or 880 of their revs (day). (same idea as an earth year)

Other Time Measurements

Light time = This is their term for day time. The time there is light on the surface of the planet from the dual suns.

These I will leave in Earth English terms

1 second = ok well a second

1 minute = 75 seconds

1 hour = 125 minutes

Estrian times frames

Umpteen – between 120 and 130 Annums

Decannum = 10 Annums equivalent to what Earthlings call a decade.

Cenannum = 100 annums or 10 decannums equivalent to a century.

Milleannum = 1000 annums, or 100 cenannums, equivalent to a millennium.

ESTRIAN TERMS FOR DAYS

Today = This Rev

Yesterday= Last Rev

Tomorrow = Next Rev

 Seasons

There are 6 seasons per Annum on Estry.

The seasons are determined by it's eliptical orbit around it's binary star system. The closer the planet is to the larger star Arōs, the warmer it is. The further away the colder. However, in the grand scheme of things, the orbital wobble is barely noticeable, but for the seasons of the planet it is very important.

Sowing – meaning sowing seeds in the ground same as **Spring**

Liten- The time of the annum with the longest revs of suns. Up to 30 hours of the rev in places. But not necessarily the hottest. Best time for crops to grow. Between Sowing and Heli - Like late spring or beginning of summer.

Heli – Named after Helios, the star, being the hottest time of the annum, closest to the 2 suns. Especially Arōs, Similar to Late **Summer**

Harvest –when they harvest the crops – Similar to **Fall, Autumn**

Frostfall - Time between **Harvest** and **Darken.** Time to get the harvest preserved, animals grow coats, and things ready for the long dark hours of Darken. This is when it starts getting colder. Some animals start to hibernate. Like late fall.

Darken – this time of annum is colder and darker, the elliptical part of the orbit is further away from the two suns. Similar to Winter. it is dark most of the rev, and very cold.

Measurements

Measurements are based on a Great King in ancient history, after the Great War. The king proclaimed the measurements was based on his, so all measurements would be the same throughout the world.

He was about 10 feet tall by Earth standards, which was a little taller than most of Estry's inhabitants.

<u>Digit</u> = the length from the knuckle to the tip of the finger — about 2 of earth's inches.

<u>Hand</u> =about the length of the Kings' hand from wrist to top of the middle finger tip. About 10 of earth's inches.

After that everything is based on a **<u>Span</u>**.

<u>Span</u> = the distance between the Kings fingertip to fingertip arms spread out about 10 Earth feet.

<u>Mid span</u> = which is half of a span. Approximately 5 Earth feet. If you want to go long distances you multiply spans.

<u>Deca Spans</u> = 10 spans or 100 Earth feet

<u>Mega spans</u> = 100 spans or 1000 Earth feet

<u>Giga span</u> = 1000 spans or 10,000 of Earth feet or approximately 2 Earth miles. For longer distance travel, this is the most widely used. The majority of the people do not travel far enough to use the next measurement.

<u>Tera span</u> = 1000 Giga spans or 10 million Earth feet or approximately 2000 miles.

People and Creatures

Deo – Their word for **God**

Estrians (Humans) live usually roughly 1000 Annums or more. Wizards live longer. As do other creatures, like Dwarves and Gnomes, Unicorns. Melvin, if he chooses, could live indefinitely.

Elves

Wood Elves- live for Apx 10,000 Annums, live in ancient forest, have magic, pretty much like any other elves in story. Use nature. At one with trees and stuff. More than 1 set of elves? Don't know.

Leprechauns- foul wood elves. These were a group of wood elves who turned bad. Started harassing other elves, then people, very mischeivious. Were always playing jokes and stuff on people. Elves rounded them up and had a council. Decided to punish them by cursing them- making them small- and banishing them from the elves land. Leprechauns were exiled to the north country, made to watch over treasure. Then when Rellik came to power they moved to the shadow land.

Jigabuji – Tribe of People that live on the plains other side of mountains from the Empress's fortress. Very primitive

Shield trees- trees in the ancient Forrest that can sense evil and or danger, they generate a shield around the branches, trunk and roots, to protect themselves and those within their borders.. These trees have been there since the world was created. No magic, or weapon can penetrate them.

Places

Continents –

Arion- the continent where Melvin lives and the war takes place.

Dragonia Large island or small continent west of main continent **Arion** ruled and populated mostly by dragons. Other magical beings live there as well. Dragons want to get away from humans and wizards and their affairs, wars, and all that. Want to be left alone. There is every climate on this island continent. Mountains, deserts, swamps, forests, grasslands ,jungles, everything in between.

Places in Arion

Land of Bilby- (Bilbylund)   Home of The Great Bilby, his queen, and the 4 princesses. Home of Melvin. Situated in a valley near a great mountain range near the east coast. Lush and with orange and purple vegetation. Mostly farm and grassland. Forrest here and there. Also beaches run along the east side. Lots of farming and fishing. Trade with other sea ports.

Wazervïl Academy for Extraordinarily Talented Youngsters.

A school for the teaching up of young Wizards. However, wizards here have 1 to 3 talents (abilities,) rarely have 4. So they learn to use those talents. Most people have talents of some sort, but wizards have an extraordinary amount of magic ability with a talent. Most wizards are really good at 1 talent so they focus on that. Be it nature, weather, fire, water , and so on.

Lilenhamür-

Empress's Fortress –, stronghold, fortress, city that is the seat of power for the Empress's Empire Arion. Hexagon shaped. The size of a very large city. Infact, it IS a large city. Holds apartments, shops, work shops, giant lake and orchards gardens in the middle. Was the original farm, then a stronghold, then city rose up around it, walls were built around that city, then a city rose up around that, another wall, and kept going. it's the largest metropolis area in the country. Farms rose up around that.

Illëngard- the elven city in the forest. Melvin, Adara, Aria, and troops go there to be trained by the elves.

The Land Of Shadows

West of land of great mountains. This land was one of darkness, with evil creatures all about. It was ruled over by a man who wanted to turn the world to darkness, The Shadow Lord Rellik. You would think it would be a desolate wasteland, but exactly the opposite was true. It was a lush green, rain forest due to the rain and many thunderstorms. Plants grow very big to capture what small amount of light there is. Tall trees made an impenetrable canopy where the suns rarely broke through. Always dark and cloudy, dark thick clouds rains a lot, at night pitch black. (Think Seattle forest areas) Many types of trees and animals lived there, as well as many different types of people and creatures. Everything from swamp hags who brewed their potions in crudely built huts, to orcs and goblins, who dwelt in vast caverns. Shriekers, ogres, imps. Leprechauns who lived in the woods. There were also humans, malcontent evil thieves and liars who lived in magnificent estates and some even in castles. As well sorcerers, bad witches, sorceresses, thugs, mostly the non-congenial sort.

Rellik's Castle – though Rellik is evil, he still appreciates beauty. He lives in a beautiful castle, well maintained grounds, art, lush carpets, draperies, etc. It's in the middle of an area where is always cloudy and rainy, like Seattle so therefore lots of trees, castle is usually in the shade of trees. Forrest all around the castle.

Also the costal cities of Pyne in the north west and **Heisenvad** in the South west. He razed the **Banaldür**

City on the River. <u>**Ündarhaven , Schiffenheim**</u> and many others. Ēstlund

Types of Dragons

Dragons – are the key to the war. Are very magical creatures. When hatched brings a large amount of magic into the world that wizards, witches, sorcerers, sorceresses, etc, can use. wizard who sees hatching gets part of the magical power. They try to avoid having humans or other magical creatures see hatchings. Some help the humans though, some forced into slavery by Rellik.

NöGard - King of Dragons. Very large, larger than other dragons Gold Dragon, King of Dragons in Dragonia, Shape shifter

Gold – good, wise, helpful breathes light. Can take human shape if so desires, Red- bad tempered, but neutral- breathes fire, mostly lives in Dragonia, will rather be bad than good. Rellik has lots of red dragons.

Purple – jolly, good natured, likes to laugh – breathes? Lives in the forests.

Green – indifferent. Will help whoever gives them treasure. Breathes acid. Most live in Dragonia, others live in jungles and swamps. Swamp near Rellik's Castle. Rellik has quite a few as well. That he stole.

Blue – lives in colder climates breathes water. Usually good. Unless you make them mad.

White – lives in Dragonia or polar regions, tops of mountains where there is ice capped all annum round.

Where humans don't go. Avoids humans. Breathes ice.

Black, usually evil, but not always. Lives in Dragonia. Used to make shadow dragons. Breathes a choking mixture of black smoke and volcano smoke. Makes so you can't see anything and can't breathe.

Shadow- made by dark wizards or sorcerers. Very bad tempered. Evil. Stay as shadows most of the time, but can solidify when need to. Breathes a choking mixture of black smoke and volcano smoke. Makes so you can't see anything and can't breathe.

Grey – lives in grassy plains on Dragonia. Neutral

Copper – Dragonia in rocky desert area. Very smart. Breathes lightning. neutral, but will rather help the good over the bad

Yellow – tiny dragons. Can't breathe anything, some used as pets. Neutral. Like a dog or cat. No preference.

Brown – Neutral, breathes fire. Lives where ever they want to.

RED – Large dragons, breathe fire, mostly bad, but some are good or indifferent. They try to stay to themselves, but will side with whoever think that will be most to their advantage.

Fire Dragon – This is a special dragon. This is Adara's dragon. This is a red fire breathing Dragon that volunteered his services to Adara and the Army of the Arion Empire. Adara and Melvin cast an enchantment on it so when Adara was in Fire mode the dragon also turns to flame. Red fire breathing are naturally resistant to fire.

CREATURES

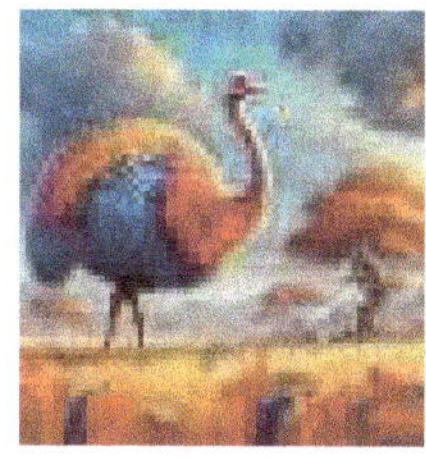

Blasmoth – Huge egg-laying bird like creature. Like a big colorful OstrichLives in the plains and lays big eggs. People often ride them. Such as the Jigabuji

Borlog – . Imagine an animal the size of three African elephants, put a rhino horn on its snout, and bull horns on its head, three rows of razor sharp teeth in it's maw and wrap it in a hide so thick that nothing can penetrate it. Oh yeah, they breathe fire, just like dragons.

Shriekers,-- Basically a wingless dragon can't fly and no magic More like a dinosaur. However, their primary weapon was their high pitched shrieks. Sends out a sound wave that pierces the ears, can even make them bleed. Gives you a tremendous headache, knocks you out and other stuff.

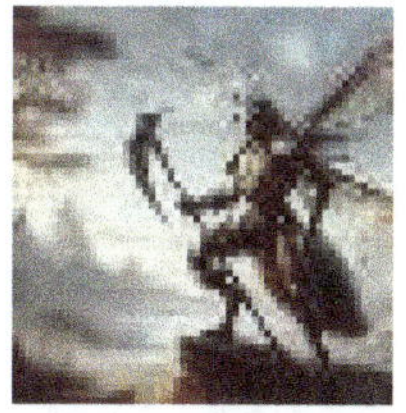

Hornswollop – a flying creature, with horns on their heads. Don't know the size   as of yet. Maybe the size of a pixie or a fairy. Or somewhere in between human and fairy. Giant sentient insect.

Qilin - A ridable animal equivalent to a horse.

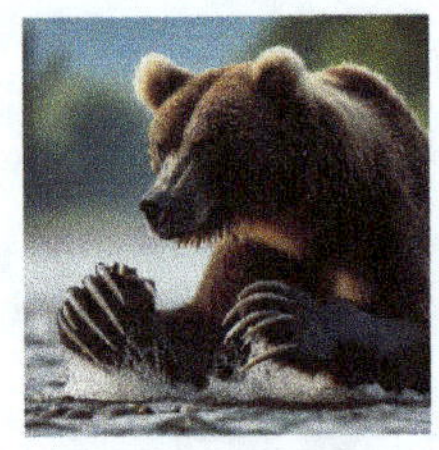

Mandra – An animal similar to a bear, but MUCH larger.

Gormlin – A cross between a Gremlin and a goblin

morcëgo Giant bat like creature